It Takes 2 to Tango

Also by Elise Darcy

Living Apart Together Series

Living Apart Together (Book 1)

Dear John (Book 3)

Love on the Rooftop (Book 4)

Standalone Books

Lola & The Man

A Mallorcan Affair

We'll Meet Again

The Villa in Sicily

AUTHOR'S NOTE

Living Apart Together is a series.
It Takes 2 to Tango is the second book.

It Takes 2 to *Tango*

Living Apart Together

Book II

ELISE DARCY

Penny Lane Press

For Mum, with my love.

1

John was making himself a cup of tea when he heard the doorbell. He wasn't expecting anybody to call this early in the morning. Either his neighbour in the apartment downstairs had visitors, or it was the postman. John checked the time and concluded it was the postman; you could set your watch by him. He ignored it hoping his neighbour would answer the front door. As he reached inside the fridge for a pint of milk, the doorbell chimed for the second time.

He slammed the fridge door shut in frustration. She wasn't answering the door which meant he had to make a special trip downstairs. He left the pint of milk on the kitchen counter and walked through his apartment and out the door. Taking the stairs two at a time, he reached the communal hall and glared at the entrance to the garden apartment as he passed by. He wouldn't be surprised if she was still in bed. He knew she was a night owl because her television was on late at night. Shaking his head in annoyance, John made his way across the hall and saw a familiar outline in red through the frosted glass. The postman who had delivered their mail for almost two decades was standing on the doorstep whistling a tune.

John opened the door.

'Good morning, Mr Baxter. What a fine day it is today.'

John didn't think so. It was cold and wet outside. However, he was used to the postman's cheerful disposition no matter what the British weather threw at them. It didn't mean John had to be cheerful too. 'Well, what is it?' he asked gruffly.

'I have a letter for you – recorded delivery.'

'Okay fine.' He was surprised he had to sign for the letter but did it anyway just to get shot of the postman. 'Is there anything else?'

He handed John a postcard.

John pointed at the other letters.

'Ah, these are addressed to your wife.' He held them out to John, expecting him to take them.

John glanced over his shoulder at the door to the garden apartment. He'd made a special trip downstairs all because she couldn't be bothered to answer the front door. He shook his head. He had no intention of taking in Sylvie's mail. 'You can put hers in the post box.'

'This one?' The postman indicated the black post box fixed on the outside wall that belonged to the garden apartment.

'Yes – that one,' John said brusquely, pointing at the identical post box next to his own.

The postman slipped the letters into the box. 'I take it that Mrs Baxter is still living in the apartment downstairs then?'

John nodded as he studied the envelope in his hand, wondering what was so important that he had to sign for it.

'I thought that when you converted the house into two apartments, you were going to rent one of them out?'

John looked up.

'Changed your mind about getting tenants? That wouldn't surprise me. I've heard some horror stories, I can tell you.'

John stared at the postman. He'd witnessed some horror stories himself, and that was just with his wife living downstairs. Sylvie liked to stay up late watching old black and white movies on the television. Sometimes the volume was so loud that he could hear it in his bedroom two floors up.

That wasn't the only thing that disturbed his sleep. There was that one time she hosted a seventies-themed housewarming party soon after she moved in. When John finally got to sleep that night, he woke up the next morning to discover the party had spilled out into the garden. There were empty beer cans and wine bottles littering his expensive newly turfed lawn, the lawn he thoughtfully laid for tenants who thus far hadn't materialized. She even got a pet – and a dog at that.

John never liked pets. In all the years they had been married – almost four decades – John assumed his wife didn't like them either. But that wasn't the worst of it. She had taken it upon herself to redecorate and furnish the flat downstairs without his knowledge. In the process, she turned the two-bedroomed rental apartment into a one bed.

John didn't tell the postman any of this, although the look on the postman's face said he really wanted to know how it came about that Mrs Baxter ended up moving downstairs.

On reflection, John wished he hadn't been so eager to tell everyone his plans. When he first had the idea to convert their house into two apartments, he intended to rent out the garden apartment downstairs to subsidise their retirement income. Little did he know that things wouldn't go according to plan. John sighed. If he hadn't been so blasé about telling all and sundry, perhaps he wouldn't be standing on the doorstep listening to the postman prying into his personal life, trying to find out what went wrong with his brilliant idea. The postman would have found out about the conversion eventually because of the two post boxes he'd fixed up on the wall outside. However, it didn't mean he had to find out that Mr and Mrs Baxter were now living apart under the same roof. Unless someone told him. John knew who that someone was.

As soon as Sylvie moved downstairs, she informed the postman she was living in the garden apartment. Sylvie wanted any personal mail put in her post box, presumably so her husband wouldn't have an excuse to knock on her door each day – on the pretext of delivering her mail – to persuade her to move back in with him.

'Just so I know what to do with Mrs Baxter's mail in future, do you have any idea when she might be moving back upstairs?'

John scowled at the postman. 'Your guess is as good as mine,' he said miserably. What the postman also didn't know was that it was John's idea for Sylvie to move downstairs in the first place – albeit temporarily. When the conversion was underway, he had the bright idea that one of them should live in the garden apartment to iron out any wrinkles before the first tenants arrived. What he didn't foresee was that his wife would move downstairs and stay there.

In hindsight, he should have seen it coming. It began with Sylvie's mother passing away which proved the catalyst for her to make some long overdue changes in her life; she started with her dead-end job. No sooner had she set the wheels in motion to leave her secretarial job – taking early retirement to spend some time figuring herself out – when out of the blue John lost his job

4

too. After a lifetime of work, he remembered following Sylvie around like a lost puppy. When she needed some time to herself, she had a depressed and irritable husband under her feet all day at a complete loss as to what to do with himself and looking to his wife for the answers. In order to get away from his constant whining about the unfairness of it all, she'd moved into the spare bedroom.

When John came up with the plan to convert the house into two apartments, he had a suspicion that Sylvie went along with the idea to get him out of her hair. It worked. He finally had something to do and Sylvie had a hiatus from her husband. Unfortunately, that didn't last long. Once the conversion was complete, a new challenge reared its head. With the family home now divided into two flats, their living accommodation had shrunk from a five-bedroomed four-storey townhouse to a small two-bedroomed duplex apartment. What neither of them anticipated was the fallout of living in such close quarters together: they were getting on each other's nerves.

Small wonder Sylvie moved downstairs, John thought at the time. A period of adjustment was to be expected after living together in a spacious townhouse for most of their married lives. Surely, she would come round and move back upstairs so he could rent out the garden apartment as planned? He was still waiting for that to happen.

'Any luck on the job front?' asked the postman.

John didn't want to talk about that either. Since he was forced to retire from work, he had applied for numerous positions with no luck. Losing his job came as a shock. He still had five years until he officially retired at the age of sixty-five.

It wasn't the money that was the issue – at least not to begin with. They could get by well enough on his pension and live quite comfortably. However, John wasn't ready to be thrown on the scrapheap. He couldn't face retirement. It was just a reminder he was moving one step closer to The Big Sleep. Besides, he wasn't the retiring type. He needed something productive to do. What he did was convert the house. On paper it was the perfect solution to fit their new circumstances. Their daughters were no longer living at home. That left the two of them rattling around a large property. On top of which, retiring five years ahead of plan meant a reduced income.

John knew he could never bring himself to sell the family home to fund their retirement plans. Not that he'd discussed those plans with Sylvie, but he had dreams of what they could do together. And dreams cost money. Even with a reasonably decent pension after a career as an accountant, John found the cost of running and maintaining their substantial home in London left little in the way of spare cash for all the things they had gone without over the years whilst raising a family and doing up the house.

They weren't exactly poor, but John wanted to go on those foreign holidays they never seemed to get around to and take his wife out for a restaurant meal once in a while. Sylvie's small pension from her secretarial job wasn't going to afford them any luxuries; all it amounted to was pin money.

John had looked into equity-release schemes, but he wasn't interested in getting hold of some extra cash this way. So, he came up with his own plan to generate an additional income. The idea was simple: divide the house into two apartments. This would provide a small two-bed flat, with substantially reduced overheads, for them to live in. There would be a nice sizeable rental income from the garden apartment of a similar size and layout on the basement and ground floor of the house. It would also provide him with a new job as a landlord, as well as the money for all those luxuries they couldn't otherwise afford.

Unlike some of their peers, John was aware there would be no financial windfall, like an inheritance, from either of their parents when they passed away. He didn't want the same for his children. He wanted to leave them a legacy; this house in Holland Park was it. That's why he could never bring himself to sell the family home and spend their inheritance. However, he didn't mind converting the house and using the rental income.

Unfortunately, the postman was quite correct: things had not worked out as John envisaged. If everything had gone according to plan, he would have a tenant by now and the rent money rolling in. Instead, he was separated from his wife, and she was living downstairs in the rental apartment. However, that was the least of his concerns. He was confident she would move back upstairs – eventually. Right now, John was focused on a bigger problem. He was strapped for cash, to put it mildly.

'Well, best be off,' said the postman cheerfully, sensing the conversation had run its course.

John frowned at the postman's jolly disposition. He felt down in the dumps. Cheerful people like the postie only made him feel worse.

'Chin up, Mr Baxter. Who knows, it might be your lucky day. The letter might be a job interview.'

John turned the official-looking letter over in his hands and hoped the postman was right. He had recently renewed his job search and sent off dozens of application forms. Perhaps today he would get a lucky break.

John bid the postman farewell and closed the front door. He glanced at the entrance to Sylvie's apartment as he passed by and wondered if she had taken the dog out for an early morning walk. He thought about knocking to find out. He briefly paused outside her door and imagined what sort of reception he'd get if she answered. John swiftly changed his mind and made his way back upstairs.

After pouring his cold mug of tea down the sink, John made another and carried it through to the lounge and into the study. He settled himself down in the office chair and opened the letter, hoping it was an invitation to attend a job interview. He could do with some good news. He slipped the note out of the envelope. The first thing he noticed was ominous bold lettering in red; it was another final demand. He stuffed the letter back in the envelope and tossed it in the drawer of his desk. John sighed as he turned his attention to the pile of new job application forms stacked neatly to one side. He picked a form at random, placed it on the desk in front of him, and leaned back in his chair with the postcard that was delivered this morning.

John studied the picture on the front. Palm trees lined a deserted beach with sand so pale it was almost white. Footprints in the sand disappeared into an azure sea stretching to the horizon. John stared at the postcard for some minutes lost in a world far removed from unpaid bills, job application forms and a recalcitrant wife living downstairs.

A strong gust of wind and driving rain outside rattled the sash window and interrupted his reverie, zapping a daydream he was rather enjoying and snapping him back to reality. He turned in his chair and glanced out the window. He was facing another miserable day, and it had nothing to do with the weather.

John sat alone in his study contemplating another day just like yesterday and the day before that. He wanted something to happen; anything to relieve the tedium. John sighed heavily and reached for his mug of tea wondering what lucky git sent him the postcard from paradise. He turned the postcard over. It was from Dave and his wife Linda on holiday in the Caribbean. He read the few brief lines scrawled by his brother and then remembered they were on a cruise. It sounded as though they were having a good time. Lucky them, thought John enviously as he lifted the mug of tea to his lips.

He was about to take a sip of tea when he heard the doorbell downstairs. Tea suspended in mid-air; John rolled his eyes when it rang again. Sylvie wasn't answering it which meant she must be out. He had to make another trip downstairs. Wondering who it could possibly be this time, he reluctantly left his mug on the desk and walked out of his apartment for the second time that morning.

2

John answered the door to find his brother standing on the doorstep. He looked him up and down and resisted the urge to ridicule his outfit. Dave was wearing three-quarter length shorts, a tee-shirt and flip-flops, even though it was cold and drizzling with rain. He was not dressed for the British weather. But more to the point, what was he doing in Blighty?

John still had the postcard in his hand. He held it up. 'I thought you were on a cruise in the Caribbean?'

'I was. We arrived home this morning, so I thought I'd come straight over and see you.' Dave caught John's confused expression. 'Remember that discussion we had on the phone about the problem you needed help with?'

Of course, he remembered. How could he forget? John glanced at the postcard. Even so, he still couldn't believe his brother was standing on his doorstep. Dave's holiday wardrobe wasn't helping. He looked as though he'd just walked off the beach to get another margarita. On the other hand, one might be forgiven for thinking he was heading off on some military expedition in his camouflage combat shorts and green tee-shirt. Considering the nature of his visit, John went with the latter.

Dave approached every problem like a military exercise. Today would be no exception. He was here to help his brother with a small problem – his downstairs neighbour, Sylvie.

'Come here, you,' said Dave, lunging at him before he had a chance to side-step the big man with the warm heart and the not-so-gentle bear hug. Although John was the middle of three brothers, he had always been closest to his elder brother. He was his big brother not just in terms of age, but in weight and stature too. When Dave released him from their brotherly embrace, they both stood back and looked each other over.

'You've lost some weight,' observed Dave, patting John's stomach playfully.

'One of the perks of having to fend for myself,' John replied, none-too-happily, glancing at Sylvie's door as they passed by on their way up to his apartment. Talking of losing weight, he couldn't say the same for Dave. The food on the cruise had obviously been very agreeable and very plentiful. He didn't comment on his brother's expanding waistline as he followed him up the stairs. Instead, John said, 'Nice tan.'

His brother looked not only tanned but very well after two weeks in the Caribbean. And by the look of his outfit, he was still in holiday mode. Holidays always agreed with Dave. His job, on the other hand, did not. John wouldn't go so far as to call his brother workshy, but he knew Dave would much rather be sunning himself on the open deck of a ship than clocking into work.

They walked up the stairs and John listened as Dave told him all about his holiday, before bemoaning the fact that he had to return to work. Although John offered a sympathetic ear, all he could think about was that he wouldn't mind in the least if he had a job to go to on Monday morning. He even joked about swapping places with his brother whereby Dave could sit around at home all day bored and he could go out to work.

Dave didn't find it a joking matter. Unlike John, Dave was still waiting to retire. With the expense of two drawn-out divorces behind him, he could not afford to take early retirement. He never particularly liked his job. With two years to go until he officially retired, at the age of sixty-five, Dave had been counting down the days for the last five years. He even had a homemade chart on the wall at home ticking off the weeks like a prisoner in gaol waiting for his release.

Perhaps it would have been a different story if he'd pursued a career in the military. A member of the Territorial Army for years and years, always ready to do his bit for Queen and Country, he saw no action apart from weekend training camps in the UK. And just when things were kicking off in Iraq and Afghanistan, he had to hang up his army boots and retire from the reservists; he was too old.

Unfortunately, he couldn't retire from his day job. However, it wasn't all bad. He worked as a foreman on construction sites for a living and there were parts of his job that he genuinely enjoyed. Dave relished taking charge and barking orders at people, much like he used to do as a child growing up with two younger brothers who looked up to him and always followed his lead. When the three brothers played together, it was Dave who came up with the big ideas – or military campaigns as he used to call them – and made his little brothers carry them out.

He often got them into trouble, especially John because he was the second eldest. John smiled as a childhood memory resurfaced of happy, carefree hours spent playing with Dave.

"This means war!" was Dave's familiar battle cry when a plan was afoot.

Now a plan was definitely afoot because Dave had asked him to draw up some detailed floor plans of Sylvie's flat downstairs. John didn't have to do that because he still had the architect's drawings from the conversion.

Dave walked inside John's apartment, his flip-flops making a clacking sound on the wood laminate flooring.

John shut the door and followed Dave through the open-plan lounge and into the kitchenette where he hastily spread the floor plans out on the kitchen table.

'Very good,' said Dave, bending over the table to take a closer look.

John stood back and smiled at his brother. Dave had a plan and he couldn't wait to find out what it was.

While his brother studied the layout of Sylvie's flat, John made two mugs of strong black coffee.

Dave looked up briefly to take his mug.

John skirted the small circular table and stood on the other side drinking his coffee. He stared at Dave intently.

Dave glanced at his brother. 'The first thing we need to do is get some more intel.'

'Of course, of course,' John nodded enthusiastically and then furrowed his brow. 'Er… what exactly is *intel?*' He could never get his head around all that military jargon.

Dave sighed. 'It's *intelligence*, John. We need more info.'

'Yes, I see.'

'Good. Now that means we have to do some recon.'

John opened his mouth about to ask—

'That's *reconnaissance,* John.'

'I knew that,' John quickly countered, although he didn't. John was getting impatient. He wanted to know *the plan*.

Dave shifted his gaze from the architect's drawings and studied John. 'I know what you're thinking. You want to know the plan. First, we need to gather intel by doing some recon.'

John looked down at the mug of coffee in his hand and wished it was a stiff drink, which was very telling because he didn't drink, apart from the odd tipple on special occasions. All this military gobbledygook was giving him a headache. He wished Dave would cut to the chase.

'So, let me cut to the chase…'

John smiled and nodded enthusiastically.

'Our first course of action is to go behind enemy lines.'

'Pardon me?'

Dave explained, 'We need to take a look around Sylvie's apartment.'

John's smile vanished. He groaned loudly.

Dave raised an eyebrow. 'Problem?'

John stared at his brother. Yes, there was a problem. He had no intention of sneaking back into Sylvie's apartment while she was out, not after the last time. John recalled that previous episode in vivid detail and recoiled. Returning from a shopping trip, she'd nearly caught him in the apartment downstairs. Little did she know that he had a spare key. He'd managed to get out the kitchen door just in time, but what followed was an interminable thirty minutes waiting for Sylvie to unpack the shopping and go back upstairs. He wanted to make a dash for it down the garden to the back gate but knew he'd be spotted. John was stuck on the patio, within inches of the french doors, with his back up against the wall – quite literally.

John gazed at the architect's drawings on the kitchen table. He had no intention of a repeat performance. Dave could go behind enemy lines to do the *recon* and gather some *intel* on his own.

Once Dave recovered from a fit of laughter after hearing all about it, to John's relief he agreed that it wasn't necessary for both of them to pay another visit to Sylvie's apartment. In fact, it would be preferable if one of them stayed upstairs as the lookout.

John's hand shot up to volunteer for lookout duty.

'Right, that's settled then, you'll be the lookout and I'll go behind enemy lines.' Dave paused. 'But first I have a question.'

'Fire away.'

'Can you tell me when Sylvie might go out today?'

John grinned. He knew precisely what time she would be vacating her apartment for an hour or so. He discovered the advantage of his wife getting a mutt; it was called *walkies*. John had been making a note of her movements, as per Dave's instructions, in his little black book. In the process, he made an interesting discovery. Sylvie walked her puppy regular as clockwork.

'It's the only advantage I can see of having an animal in the house,' said John, speaking his mind.

Dave glared at his brother. Dave was an animal lover with two dogs of his own. He said dryly, 'We call them *pets*, John.'

John raised an eyebrow. It sounded like the remark Sylvie made when he discovered she had a dog in the apartment downstairs. John shrugged and went to fetch his little black book.

He soon returned from the study with his little black book and checked Sylvie's next scheduled walk with the mutt. He knew the dog's name was Alfie; he'd heard Sylvie shouting his name on several occasions when she was scolding her misbehaving pet. John turned to the last entry to double-check walkies yesterday corresponded in time and duration to the day before. It did. He looked at his watch and frowned.

'What's the matter?'

He showed Dave the entries in his little black book and sighed heavily. 'I think today, of all days, she's departed from her normal routine.' John thought of the postman calling at the house this morning, and then Dave arriving a short time later. Both times Sylvie failed to answer the door, leading him to conclude that she'd taken the dog out earlier than usual. Now he had no way of knowing when she'd be back.

John closed the little black book and turned to Dave. 'She's already gone out. Unfortunately, I have no idea how long—'

'Oh, really? I could have sworn I saw her standing by the window in her dressing gown, holding a mug in her hand, as I walked up to your house this morning. She even waved.'

John stared at his brother. He was about to tell him he must be mistaken when he heard Sylvie's television downstairs. They both turned in unison to look at the floor.

'There you see, I knew my eyes weren't deceiving me. She's definitely in downstairs.' Dave frowned. 'That's loud.'

'Tell me about it!' John threw back sarcastically.

'Hmm. Well, looking on the bright side, I guess we can count on the entries you've made in your little black book after all. So, back to my original question, when can we expect Sylvie to go out today?'

John opened his little black book once more and flicked through the pages until he found yesterday's entry. He checked the time by his wristwatch. 'She's due to take the dog out in a quarter of an hour.'

'Ace.' Dave walked over to the kitchen worktop and un-zipped a khaki canvas bag. 'I brought some things with me that I thought we might need.' He reached inside his bag and out came a black pair of combat trousers, a black sweatshirt, a black balaclava and a couple of walkie-talkies, also in black.

John picked up one of the walkie-talkies and switched it on. He looked at Dave. 'Where did you get these?'

'I pinched… er… borrowed those from my grandson, Theo.'

'Kids have real walkie-talkies these days?' John said in surprise. 'What happened to using your imagination?'

Dave shrugged.

John was fiddling with the walkie-talkie when Dave returned from the bathroom. He'd changed into the black combat trousers and the black sweatshirt. John looked him up and down and frowned. He didn't see Dave's reasoning behind the change in clothing unless he was feeling cold. It wasn't as though he was doing his recon at night in the pitch dark. It was broad daylight out there.

'Something wrong?' asked Dave, catching him staring.

John thought he looked like some sort of cat burglar, albeit a very overweight cat burglar, although he wasn't exactly breaking and entering because John had a key. In fact, as Dave was entering Sylvie's apartment through the back garden, if he was trying to be inconspicuous it made more sense if he'd stuck to wearing his camo shorts and green tee-shirt.

John decided not to voice that thought. After all, Dave was only trying to help him out. Besides, he still wanted to know the plan. So he kept his mouth shut and decided that his brother knew what he was doing, until Dave picked up the balaclava. 'What's that for?'

'It goes with the outfit,' replied Dave, matter-of-factly.

John slowly shook his head from side to side. 'I don't think that's a good idea.' What was he thinking? John suddenly had visions of Dave reaching into his bag for a length of rope and abseiling from his kitchen window down to the garden below like a Royal Marines Commando.

John knew that was absurd. More often than not, Dave's ample paunch caused him problems just getting up from his chair, let alone climbing out of the kitchen window and abseiling down the back of the house. Even so, John nervously glanced in Dave's canvas bag. He breathed a sigh of relief when he saw it was empty. He turned to Dave and gestured at the balaclava in his hands. 'I live in a neighbourhood watch area,' he pointed out. He would much prefer that his brother was not arrested and carted off to the local nick before he had a chance to explain the all-important plan. John said as much.

Dave reluctantly put the balaclava back in his bag and picked up a walkie-talkie. 'Right, let's synchronise our watches.'

They both synchronised their watches.

John walked into the lounge carrying a walkie-talkie and took up his post on sentry duty by the window.

'Right on time,' said John smugly on hearing the front door bang shut in the communal hall downstairs. He glanced out the window and saw Sylvie walking down the front steps with a black mop of fur in front of her pulling on the lead.

The walkie-talkie in John's hand crackled to life, and Dave's voice intoned, 'Are you receiving me? Over.'

John jumped in surprise. He pressed the button on the side

and tentatively spoke into the walkie-talkie, 'I'm receiving you.' He depressed the button and caught Dave frowning at him across the room.

'Oh sorry,' mumbled John. He hurriedly pressed the button again and spoke into the walkie-talkie, 'Over and out.'

'Good,' said Dave. 'They work just fine. I'm now going downstairs. If Sylvie comes back early, you know what to do.'

They rehearsed it so John wouldn't forget. He held up the walkie-talkie, pressed the button, and said, 'The eagle has landed,' which meant that Sylvie had returned home. He looked at Dave who nodded in approval.

Dave would let John know when, 'The fox is in the hole,' meaning he has completed his mission to gather some intel and he was on his way back.

Obviously, the idea was that the fox was in the hole before the eagle has landed. That was the point of a lookout and the walkie-talkies. Just in case things didn't go according to plan. John knew all about that little eventuality from his last expedition downstairs.

John had been standing at the window for the last fifteen minutes, watching for any sign of Sylvie, when he heard Dave's voice over the walkie-talkie, 'I'm in the bathroom. Over and out.'

John rolled his eyes. This had been going on since Dave entered Sylvie's apartment. *I'm in the kitchen. Over and out... I'm in the lounge. Over and out... I'm in the bedroom. Over and out.* He really didn't need a blow-by-blow account of his movements. And he wished Dave would stop saying, "Over and out." It was getting on his nerves.

The thought crossed his mind that perhaps his brother was not the ideal person to approach for marital advice. He knew that the Caribbean cruise had been a make-or-break holiday for Dave and his current wife. With two failed marriages behind him and another one potentially on the rocks, Dave was probably not in the best position to advise him on how to get his wife back. However, John needed a plan, and if anyone was going to help him with that, it was his brother Dave.

John's mind wandered for just a few moments when he heard a dog yapping outside in the street. He glanced out of the window to see Sylvie at the front gate struggling to contain an excitable cocker spaniel pulling on the lead.

'What the...?!' He looked at his watch. She wasn't due back for another thirty minutes. For the first time since he'd been keeping a tally, Sylvie had returned home from walkies early. He froze unable to remember what he was supposed to do if this happened.

The walkie-talkie in his hand suddenly crackled to life and startled him. 'I'm in the—'

John fumbled and dropped the walkie-talkie. 'Shit!' He picked it up in time to hear Dave sign off with, 'Over and out.'

John shouted into the walkie-talkie, 'Oh my god, Dave, the eagle is in the hole!'

'Repeat that message. Over.'

'I meant the fox has landed... no that's not it... the eagle... oh for pities sake! It's Sylvie. She's come home early. You've got to get out of the apartment. *Now*!'

There was what felt like an interminable pause. John was wondering if he had pressed the right button on the walkie-talkie, when he received a response...

'Copy that. Over and out.'

John felt like tossing the walkie-talkie across the room in frustration until he heard it crackle again with another response from Dave…

'The fox is in the hole. Over and out.'

'Jeeze!' John exhaled in relief. He turned from the window and sat down in the nearest armchair. He looked at the walkie-talkie in his hand and thought that Dave's plan better be good because he was beginning to wonder whether all this was worth it.

Sylvie managed to get through the gate and up the steps to the front door without getting herself entangled in Alfie's lead. Alfie was, quite literally, running rings around her, and that's when he wasn't running off and not coming back.

She had taken him to the park for his morning walk as usual, but today he was exceptionally naughty, refusing to do as he was told. As soon as she let him off the lead, he started chasing other dogs. Sylvie shouted after him, but he wouldn't come back. After twenty minutes Sylvie had had enough. When she finally caught up with him, she cut short his walk and brought him home. Something had to be done. Julia's cocker spaniel didn't behave like this, but then her best friend was an experienced dog-owner. Sylvie had never owned a dog in her life. She was beginning to wonder whether getting one now was such a good idea.

'Honestly, Julia, I don't have a clue how to get him to do as he's told.' Sylvie had picked up the phone the minute she got home from the park. She was standing in the basement kitchen on the phone to Julia, watching Alfie out of the corner of her eye. He was furiously sniffing at the floor until his nose led him to the french doors. He stopped abruptly, let out a puppy growl, and then started barking at something in the garden.

Sylvie shook her head in dismay. 'Just a minute, Julia, Alfie is being a nuisance.' Sylvie raised her voice a few decibels and shouted, 'Alfie! Stop that this instant, you naughty, naughty dog.' Sylvie resumed the phone conversation. 'Yes, I know he's not a little person, he's a dog.' Sylvie coloured in embarrassment. Julia overheard her shouting at Alfie and discovered first-hand why Alfie wasn't listening to her. 'I told you I'll never make a good dog-owner,' Sylvie said glumly.

'Nonsense,' replied Julia emphatically. 'You need to attend some puppy training classes – that's all. Don't worry, leave it to me. I've already got someone in mind. I'll make all the arrangements.'

Sylvie put the phone down feeling much better after speaking with Julia. She stared at her black cocker spaniel puppy pacing back and forth in front of the french doors. It wasn't Alfie who was the problem; she understood that now. Sylvie resolved to do the classes and learn all about being a good dog-owner. She had always wanted a dog ever since she was a child. She never had one when she was growing up because her parents couldn't afford to feed a pet with five children to support.

When her own children came along, she wanted to get her three girls their very own puppy when they were old enough. But it wasn't to be. To her surprise, it turned out that the man she'd married didn't like pets and couldn't abide living with an animal in the house. Sylvie glanced at her puppy and then raised her eyes to the ceiling. Now he didn't have a choice; Alfie was here to stay.

Sylvie didn't realise how attached she'd become to the little rascal until this morning in the park when he disappeared out of sight. Her heart leapt in her throat when she thought she'd lost him. She had no intention of giving up her dog, even if he was the naughtiest dog in the world and she was the worst dog-owner in the world. Sylvie resolved to attend those classes and change all that. She just wished he would stop being so naughty.

'Alfie!' Sylvie called. He still had his nose up against the french doors. 'Come here!' Of course, he didn't do as he was told.

Sylvie rolled her eyes in exasperation and walked over to fetch him. She glanced outside to see what had caught his attention and noticed the garden gate was ajar.

'That's odd.' She could have sworn she had shut that gate. Ever since her puppy arrived, Sylvie always checked it was secure before she let him out in the garden. They lived in an end of terrace house. The side-gate in the back opened on to the adjacent street. If he got out, he could end up in the path of a car.

'So that's what you were barking at. Well spotted.' She knelt and gave Alfie a fuss. He wasn't being naughty after all. 'Good dog.'

Alfie yapped excitedly and licked her face.

Sylvie left her dog in the kitchen and went outside to shut the gate.

3

'Just one question before we discuss the plan.'

Even though Dave had just managed to get out of Sylvie's apartment in the nick of time, the fact that he was ready to divulge the plan meant he had come up with something concrete. This sounded promising. 'I'll tell you anything you need to know,' John said enthusiastically.

'Okay.' Dave smiled at his brother approvingly. 'This may sound like a stupid question, but can I inquire whether you have actually asked Sylvie to move back in with you?'

John hesitated. 'Well... er... no.'

'And the reason for that is...?'

'Um... well... the thing is, Dave, she looks rather settled downstairs. You've seen the way she's decorated and furnished the apartment. It all seems a bit...well...permanent. What if she says no?'

'But you won't know for sure unless you ask her.'

'I know that. But I can't seem to find the right moment to broach the question.'

'And...?'

John glanced sheepishly at Dave.

Dave was staring at him intently. Ever since they were little boys, Dave knew when his little brother was hiding something. He always managed to wheedle it out of him, eventually.

Dave changed tack. 'As I recall, Sylvie was going through a tough time after her mother passed away. Correct me if I'm wrong, but I thought you suggested to her that when the conversion was complete, she could stay in the apartment downstairs to figure things out.'

John frowned. He'd only said that to get her to agree to the house conversion. He didn't expect her to move downstairs and stay there. 'I told her to take as much time as she needed,' admitted John. 'That was stupid of me.'

'That's as may be. But if you told her she could stay downstairs for as long as she wanted, then why don't you let her do just that? I don't understand the urgency to get her to move out?'

John finally gave in and confided in Dave the importance of the plan to extract Sylvie from the garden apartment. The truth was John had overextended himself financially to complete the house conversion. The final bill for the two flats came in way over budget. He'd sunk all their savings into the project and taken out an additional loan. Now he desperately needed the rental income to pay off his debts.

In hindsight, he wondered if the conversion had been a costly mistake. He didn't see it that way at the time because he had taken on loans in the past when they first renovated the house. But that was over thirty years ago when he had his whole career and years of a good annual salary ahead of him to weather any financial storms. All he had now was his pension, mounting debts, and a wife living downstairs who had no idea there was a financial tsunami on the horizon.

John decided at the outset not to tell Sylvie all this, partly because he didn't want to worry her, but mostly because of his pride. An accountant all his working life John had always been careful with money, but for the first time in their married lives he had made a mistake. Too proud to admit this to his wife. Afraid of what she might think of him if she found out. He was determined that she wouldn't discover the truth. He hoped to continue with his plan to rent out the flat and eventually balance the books so Sylvie would be none the wiser.

The problem with John's plan was that he had not factored in his wife stubbornly digging her heels in and refusing to leave the rental apartment. He knew his behaviour since losing his job had been less than admirable. He'd moaned and whined at Sylvie, refusing to accept what had happened and move on. In the wake of losing his job, he was miserable, bored and unhappy. And Sylvie was the one in the firing line. No wonder she wanted a break from us, meaning *me*, thought John.

John confided all this to Dave. 'I was sick of *me* for god's sake.' He only realised this when the conversion was underway and he finally had something to occupy his time. In truth, he had been a right idiot. It was little wonder his wife hadn't packed her bags and moved out of the house altogether.

John still felt it was a bit drastic, this trial separation as Sylvie called it. It was all a bit dramatic. However, he was not perturbed when she moved into the spare bedroom, or the apartment downstairs. Although he missed his wife, as far as he was concerned there was nothing wrong with their marriage. Sylvie simply needed some time to work through some personal issues over the loss of her mother. John was confident she would move back upstairs, eventually. He was happy to give her as much time and space as she needed and only wished he could. But there were mounting bills to be paid, and he desperately needed the rental income. Sylvie had to leave the garden apartment ASAP so he could find a tenant.

John did not want to ask her outright to move back in with him. Apart from anything else, he was worried that if he confronted Sylvie, the truth will out and he would end up telling her all about the financial mess he'd got them into. He still thought his best option was to play it cool and let Sylvie believe it was her decision to move back upstairs.

It wasn't just his pride that was keeping him from telling her the truth. What was also troubling him was that he wasn't sure how she'd react. In the past, he could guarantee that when it came to her family, Sylvie would always put her children and her husband first. Whatever the girls wanted, whatever he wanted, she always acquiesced. But now things had changed. She had changed. John frowned. There were times he wondered how well he really knew the woman residing in the apartment downstairs.

When he finally finished telling Dave all this, John stopped pacing the kitchen floor and sat down at the table.

'So, what are you saying, exactly?' Dave asked bluntly, trying to get a handle on the situation.

'I fucked up – pardon my French – and now I want Sylvie to move back in with me before she finds out.'

Dave looked at John, and said, 'Fair enough, mate. Now here's what we should do.'

John sat there watching Dave as he circled the kitchen table holding one of his wooden baking spoons aloft. He came to a halt in front of the floor plans spread out on the table.

'Our first line of attack should be here,' said Dave, tapping the floor plan with the tip of John's baking spoon. John leaned over the kitchen table to take a closer look. He glanced up at Dave. 'The hallway outside Sylvie's apartment?'

'The fuse box – to be precise.' Dave smiled knowingly. 'The first mission will be codenamed…' He tapped the wooden spoon against his temple, deep in thought, until his eyes lit up. He pointed the spoon at John and announced the codename of the first mission, 'Operation *Lights Out*.'

John had already told Dave that originally the idea was that while Sylvie was temporarily residing downstairs; it would give them an opportunity to iron out any wrinkles, so to speak. If something untoward cropped up in the rental apartment post-conversion, he could get the builder in to sort it out before the real tenants moved in.

John had not anticipated that the *something untoward* would turn out to be his wife moving downstairs and stubbornly refusing to move out.

'Well, let her do her job,' Dave had said on hearing this, 'with a little help from us, of course.'

John didn't understand what Dave was getting at until he finally explained the plan. It was simple but brilliant. The plan, in a nutshell, was to sabotage the garden apartment. If things started to go wrong, it would make Sylvie realise that living on your own wasn't all about having fun redecorating the place, shopping for new furniture and throwing house parties. There was a serious side too because things often did go wrong. When that happened, she would discover it wasn't much fun living on your own. That's when Sylvie would come running back to her husband for help. She'd appreciate how much she needed him around to sort things out.

'She's down there to do a job,' stated Dave, 'so let's see to it that she does. It will make her realise how much she misses you.'

John beamed at his brother wondering why he hadn't thought of it himself. It was so simple; it was genius. John's beaming smile suddenly evaporated. He already spotted a flaw in Dave's brilliant plan; it was genius as long as Sylvie didn't find out what they were up to. 'What if—'

'There is no way she's going to find out,' said Dave, second-guessing John's question. 'We will choose the missions carefully, making sure they appear like everyday household occurrences. There's no chance she will discover we were behind it. Sylvie will imagine she's having a run of bad luck – that's all. And fortunately for her, you will be on hand to help her out when things go wrong.' Dave put a reassuring arm around John's shoulders. 'Now, are you ready for your first mission?'

'Yes,' said John confidently.

'Good. Operation *Lights Out* is a go.'

Getting into the spirit of the plan, John had an idea of his own to set the wheels in motion before he proceeded with his first mission. He told Dave his idea.

Dave listened attentively until his brother had finished, and said, 'Your idea sounds splendid. And you know what else? I think the plan is going to work a treat.'

John glanced at the floor plans on the kitchen table. 'So do I.'

He followed Dave out of the apartment and down the stairs to the communal hall. 'When do you think I should carry out my idea?' John whispered as he opened the front door.

Dave stepped outside and turned around. He glanced at the door to the garden apartment. 'Now is as good a time as any – don't you think?'

John agreed.

As soon as Dave left, John walked across the hall and knocked on Sylvie's door. Alfie started barking. John rolled his eyes at the sound of her dog. He waited patiently for Sylvie to answer the door, mulling over what he intended to say to her. He'd start by apologising for his behaviour the morning after her housewarming party, which was incidentally the last time they had spoken to each other. He'd follow that up with the reason he was knocking on her door this morning.

John heard Sylvie telling Alfie off behind the door.

'No, come away this instant, you naughty dog. I can't get to the door with you in the way.'

John could hear Alfie behind the door, and then Sylvie's irritated voice demanding, 'What have you got in your mouth? That's my slipper! No, this isn't a game, Alfie... give me that. Where are you going? Come back this instant!'

John cupped a hand over his mouth to stifle a laugh. He wondered what she thought of her adorable puppy now. Not so cute when he wasn't doing as he was told. He didn't recall that Sylvie had ever owned a dog in the past. He knew she'd always wanted one. By the sound of things, perhaps she was finding out that having a pet wasn't all it was cracked up to be. John hoped she was having second thoughts about getting a dog.

He was about to set the wheels in motion as a prelude to the plan. He smiled knowingly. When Sylvie got sick and tired of things going wrong in the apartment and discovered how much she needed her husband to sort things out, he envisaged she'd be moving back upstairs in no time. There was just one problem: the dog. He wasn't coming too. However, standing outside her door listening to all this, he was beginning to think he didn't have to worry about the dog; it sounded as though Alfie would get his marching orders without any help from him, Dave or the plan.

John was glancing at his watch, wondering how much longer he would have to wait for Sylvie to answer the door, when it suddenly flew open.

Sylvie, looking flustered, said, 'What do *you* want?'

John couldn't see any sign of the dog, but he could hear him howling in the basement kitchen downstairs. The dog had put Sylvie in a bad mood which wiped the smile off John's face.

'Well?' snapped Sylvie, hands on hips, her posture confrontational. She tapped her foot impatiently.

John was trying to remember his rehearsed lines, hoping this went according to plan because a lot depended on it. He smiled nervously. 'I've come to apologise about the other day.' John had turned up in the aftermath of Sylvie's housewarming party to find her new friends sleeping it off inside her apartment. Sylvie, who was still drunk, had then introduced him to the moving-in present her best friend, Julia, had bought her – namely the mutt now howling in the basement kitchen. That's when John flipped and probably said some things he shouldn't have.

Now he was back, with his tail between his legs, hoping that he could get on a good footing with her before Dave's plan kicked off. The plan was pointless if Sylvie didn't feel inclined to run upstairs to him for help.

John took a deep breath and continued with his grovelling apology. 'I had no right to criticise your friends or complain about the noise. I'm sorry for being a bit…' John stalled searching for the right word.

'Let me help you out,' said Sylvie sarcastically. 'How about confrontational? Argumentative? Boorish? Shall I go on…?'

'That's not necessary,' said John in a small voice.

'Oh, and did I mention the word *insulting*?'

'I don't remember insulting you,' said John hastily, quite sure he didn't do that.

'You called me a drunk.'

'I did no such thing,' said John indignantly. 'I may well have asked you if you *were* drunk, but there is a subtle difference – is there not?' John realised this conversation was not going according to plan when Sylvie slammed the door in his face. He stood there staring dumbly at the door.

John knocked on her door again. 'Sylvie? Look, whatever I said, I'm a silly old fart and I'm genuinely sorry.' He sounded as though he meant it because, in fact, he did.

He was just turning to leave when Sylvie opened the door a crack, giving him a second chance to say his piece.

John proceeded quickly. 'If anything happens...' He frowned wishing he hadn't said that. 'What I meant to say was that if you need anything, anything at all, call on me anytime. You know where I am.' John pointed at the ceiling. 'I'm right upstairs,' he added unnecessarily.

Sylvie looked him over. 'All right,' she said slowly, giving him a wisp of a smile.

John turned away from Sylvie's door and smiled a knowing smile. He'd just set the stage for Operation *Lights Out*.

The plan was now afoot.

4

Sylvie shut her apartment door. She stood there staring into space. She wondered what John's sudden rush to apologise was all about. Sylvie took a deep breath, strode across the lounge, picked up her laptop and headed down the stairs to the basement kitchen. At the bottom of the stairs, she opened the door to an excitable cocker spaniel jumping up at her.

'Alfie don't do that.'

Just for a change, Alfie did as he was told. He followed Sylvie to the kitchen table and watched her pull out a chair. Alfie jumped up on the chair.

'That chair is not for you. Get down this instant.'

Alfie did not do as he was told. Sylvie put her laptop on the table and picked him up. She set Alfie down on the floor and quickly sat down in the chair. She decided Alfie could have her company but not her attention. She chose to ignore him.

He soon got the message and padded over to sit by the french doors with his back to Sylvie.

From time to time she heard a low growl or a little yap. She imagined Alfie was watching the birds in the garden or perhaps the neighbour's ginger cat, Jasper. The next time she glanced at her puppy, he was a mass of black fur curled up fast asleep. 'Thank heavens,' whispered Sylvie under her breath. She didn't realise how demanding a puppy could be.

Sylvie turned her attention to the laptop. She was railroaded into getting one by her youngest daughter. Chloe couldn't imagine life without being connected. Sylvie was aware of these social networking sites that Chloe and her generation were so fond of.

Chloe insisted that Sylvie needed to be connected too. Sylvie disagreed; she couldn't afford to buy a laptop of her own. She had already spent the small lump sum that she received when she retired from her secretarial position. She used the money to redecorate and furnish the apartment. Fortunately, when Chloe ordered the laptop, she paid for it herself and gave it to her mum as a present. Now, much to her surprise, Sylvie couldn't imagine life without being connected either. She enjoyed using John's old desktop computer in the past to send emails to her daughter Jess in Australia and made that her first task.

As well as resuming the emails to Jess keeping her up to date with news from home – neglecting to mention that Mum and Dad were now living apart – Sylvie had started writing again. It was nothing of much consequence, just things going on in her day-to-day life. For the first time in years, Sylvie was keeping a diary. However, instead of writing longhand in a notebook like she used to years ago, she was using her laptop to type her diary entries in a *word* document.

She hadn't started a blog. Although the idea crossed her mind every time she switched on the laptop and saw the icon on the desktop. Chloe set it up for her and called it *Sylvie's Blog*. Sylvie wasn't exactly sure how it worked but all she had to do was click on the icon, and it would magically take her to the blog; Chloe called it a shortcut.

Sylvie stared at the icon. She wondered what would happen if she clicked on it. Using the mouse, Sylvie moved the cursor over the icon. Chloe had gone to all the bother of setting it up for her, the least she could do was take a look. Sylvie clicked on the shortcut for *Sylvie's Blog*. She didn't know what she was expecting, but the page that appeared was much the same as her *word* document and really not all that exciting.

When Chloe first suggested she could write a blog, Sylvie was worried about her personal life being "out there". Chloe had reassured her that nobody was going to take much notice of her blog if she did decide to write one. She looked at the page in front of her. Sylvie understood what Chloe meant; it was just one nondescript blog out of millions all over the world.

Sylvie spent the next hour diligently copying and pasting into *Sylvie's Blog* everything she had written about the recent events that had happened in her life. She started with her mother passing and the last two words she had spoken to her before she died: *forgive me.*

Then there was the trip to the solicitors when she'd discovered that her mother had left her a handwritten note. It was a final request for Sylvie to scatter her ashes in Cornwall. Her mother hadn't mentioned Sylvie's four siblings in the handwritten note, making it abundantly clear that it was up to Sylvie to carry out her final request.

Sylvie wasn't in the least bit surprised. She knew why she was chosen to fulfil her mother's dying wish. When they were children, Sylvie was the only one who accompanied her mother on her annual trip to Cornwall. Sylvie didn't know why her mother never took any of her siblings to Cornwall. She never got the chance to find out before dementia robbed Sylvie of her mother several years before she died.

Her mum had stipulated that she wanted her ashes scattered in the garden of the cottage where they used to stay. Sylvie hadn't been back to Cornwall since she was a child. From what she could recollect, the trips to Cornwall stopped when she was ten or eleven years old. Sylvie was still trying to locate the cottage. Meanwhile, her mother's ashes sat in an urn on Sylvie's mantel shelf in the lounge.

Sylvie knew there was only so much she could do from a distance, scouring the internet reading up on the area where they used to spend the summer. She kept meaning to book a train ticket and make the journey back to Cornwall, but things kept cropping up and getting in the way of her plans.

It all started when her husband lost his job and made her life a living hell because he couldn't accept the inevitable; life was moving on, and he was reaching retirement age. That's when she couldn't stand it any longer and told him she wanted a trial separation; she promptly moved into the spare bedroom.

Sylvie copied and pasted the diary entry into her blog all about what happened the morning after she'd moved into the spare bedroom. That's when John announced his plan to convert the house into two apartments. What Sylvie expected was her husband to make some effort to save their marriage. Instead, he thought up another project to keep him occupied. Perhaps he should have married his precious house, thought Sylvie sarcastically. Over the years he seemed to devote more time and energy to their home than he did to his wife.

Despite raising her concerns over spending more money on

the house when they were no longer in work, John wouldn't listen. He went ahead with it anyway. By the time the conversion was complete, and Sylvie experienced living in a small two-bedroomed flat with her obsessively tidy husband, she'd had enough and decamped downstairs.

Sylvie relished redecorating and furnishing the garden apartment to her own tastes, ignoring the fact that it wouldn't be long before John came knocking on her door asking her to move back upstairs so he could complete the plan to rent it out. She'd put that thought to the back of her mind while she enjoyed her sojourn downstairs.

She was getting reacquainted with her younger self; the person she used to be before marriage. Sylvie remembered a time when she did whatever she pleased, whenever she felt like it, without somebody constantly looking over her shoulder. It was very liberating.

Sylvie continued updating her blog. There was the entry all about the seventies-themed housewarming party her best friend, Julia, had organised in the apartment soon after she moved in. It was stupendous. It was everything she imagined one of Julia's parties to be – and some. Julia often threw parties in the London flat where she lived before she retired to a houseboat in Little Venice. Sylvie had never been to one of Julia's infamous house parties in the past because John refused to go. And he always found excuses for not looking after the children on party nights, which meant Sylvie couldn't go either.

Sylvie was under no illusions why John frowned on her friendship with Julia. In all the years Julia and John had known each other, ever since Sylvie first introduced him to her best friend before they got married, they had never hit it off. In fact, it wouldn't be an exaggeration to say they couldn't stand each other. That's why he'd refused every party invitation they received from Julia. She imagined that he must have been livid when he discovered Julia held one of those parties right here, under his own roof. He certainly acted that way when he confronted her after the party. It made John's apology this morning all the more surprising.

Sylvie stopped typing into her blog and paused for a moment mulling this over. John's grovelling apology sounded suspiciously like he was up to something. It made her wonder whether he was finally gearing up to ask her to move back upstairs, hoping he could get into her good books before he popped the question. Sylvie narrowed her eyes. The more she thought about it, the more it rang true. She shook her head. That wasn't something she wanted to contemplate right now.

Instead, she returned to the task at hand. Sylvie made sure she included all the major highlights that had happened recently in the Baxter household – and everything in between. All of it went into *Sylvie's Blog*. By which time her stomach was rumbling. She'd forgotten to prepare herself some dinner. It had taken the best part of the day to fill in her blog. After a quick spot of lunch, and walking Alfie, the afternoon had flown by.

She glanced over at Alfie sleeping by the french doors and then shifted her gaze to look outside. It was almost dark, the garden barely visible in the gloom. Sylvie's eyes drifted down to her puppy once more. She saw his floppy ears twitch. He would be waking up soon for another puppy meal and a toilet break.

Sylvie closed her laptop and rose from the table to switch the lights on in the kitchen. On the kitchen worktop below the light switch was a women's magazine. She picked it up and smiled.

Although Sylvie was proud of all her daughters' achievements, it was Harriet's career choice that was closest to her heart. A writer and journalist, her eldest daughter had worked hard to secure her dream job, at the tender age of thirty-six. She was the editor of a well-known women's monthly magazine; the one Sylvie was holding in her hands. Sylvie always bought the latest issue and read it cover to cover. This month was no exception, but she hadn't got around to reading it.

Every time she sat down with the magazine in her hands, she was interrupted by the dog or phone or the doorbell – or something. This evening Sylvie decided to take the magazine to bed and read it where she most definitely would not be disturbed. However, something on the front cover caught her eye.

'Calling all aspiring writers,' Sylvie read out loud. She glanced at Alfie. He was still fast asleep, snoring softly. She listened for the inevitable interruption. All was eerily quiet.

Sylvie sat down at the kitchen table, opened the magazine and turned the page to find the article. It began with the words: *Have you ever dreamed of becoming a journalist? Here's your chance . . .*

A long time ago Sylvie harboured an ambition to be a writer. That's why she encouraged her daughter, Harriet, when she first announced she wanted to be a journalist.

Sylvie had been doing an evening course in journalism and working as a secretary by day when she first met John. The journalism course dropped off soon after they met. And then marriage, the house, three children and a lifetime later, Sylvie found the diaries she used to write when she was young. It had breathed life into an old ambition; she'd started writing again.

She continued reading the article. They were looking for first-time writers, people who had never had anything published and wanted to break into journalism. In order to find this new writing talent, the magazine Harriet worked for was running a competition. The winning article would be published in the magazine. It might lead to a weekly column with a regular income.

Money wasn't the prime motivation for Sylvie. She didn't need a job because she knew John was covering all the bills. When her mother passed away, it proved the catalyst to make some changes. She started by taking early retirement from the part-time secretarial position that she never much liked, deciding it was time to do something more meaningful with her life. Something like this. She stared wistfully at the magazine article. This wasn't about finding a job and earning an income. This was about something more. Sylvie smiled. It was about following a dream.

Sylvie continued reading the article. She was just getting to the important part that explained how to enter the competition when suddenly the lights went out.

'Oh no!' exclaimed Sylvie in surprise as the room was thrown into darkness. To make matters worse, she woke her sleeping puppy.

Alfie started barking.

Sylvie got up from the table and peered through the french doors. The garden was partly illuminated by the street-lights in the side road. She could see there were lights on in her neighbour's house whose garden backed on to theirs. So, it wasn't a power cut, thought Sylvie. Which meant... She didn't have a clue what it meant. She recalled John mentioning something about tripping a switch. He'd then disappear for a couple of minutes and the lights would miraculously come back on.

Sylvie never asked what he meant by tripping a switch, or how he got the electricity back on; she just left him to it. If a light bulb needed changing, John was her man. If a fuse blew, John was her man. Sylvie didn't bother getting involved simply because she didn't have to. She knew it was pure laziness on her part, but Sylvie did just what she imagined most wives do in these situations: she left it to her husband. It had never crossed her mind how she would cope if something went wrong and he wasn't on hand to sort things out.

'Silly woman,' mumbled Sylvie to herself as she felt her way around the kitchen in the dark. She was looking for the kitchen drawer where she hoped to find a torch. Fortunately, there was some light from the full moon casting the kitchen in a monochrome hue. This helped her avoid tripping over Alfie who was getting under her feet, as usual.

She found the torch and switched it on.

Alfie darted around the kitchen chasing the beam of light, yapping exuberantly.

Sylvie shone the light around the room until she focused it on the stairs. She then made her way across the room hoping that the light bulb in the kitchen simply needed replacing. She flicked the light switch at the bottom of the stairs. To her dismay, the lights upstairs weren't working either.

'Blast!' That meant the electricity was definitely out.

Shining the torch up the kitchen stairs, Sylvie walked up to the lounge and crossed the room aiming for the front door of her apartment. She stepped outside into the communal hall and flicked the light switch. Nothing happened. She glanced upstairs and saw a thin strip of light coming from under the door to John's apartment. She sighed in relief; thank heavens he's home.

Sylvie raced up the stairs, followed by Alfie giving chase, and banged on John's door.

John answered the door almost immediately.

'Thank heavens you're in!' exclaimed Sylvie, forgetting about the torch in her hand and accidentally shining the torchlight in his face.

John held up a hand to shield his eyes. 'What on earth is the matter?'

Sylvie took a moment to catch her breath after belting up the stairs. 'It's the electricity in the garden apartment. It's stopped working... the lights... everything! I think I tripped something.'

'Really?' John scratched his chin. 'Would you like me to go downstairs and take a look?'

Sylvie nodded her head vigorously. 'I'd really appreciate it. I feel so silly calling on you like this. I didn't know what else to do.'

John resisted the urge to smile. 'Now, don't you worry about a thing, Sylvie,' he reassured her. 'Why don't you come inside and make yourself a cup of tea?' He gestured inside his apartment.

Alfie scurried between John's legs and through the door.

John turned around and caught sight of Alfie's tail wagging furiously as he disappeared inside the apartment. John frowned. He remembered to fix a smile on his face before turning back to Sylvie. 'I'm sure I'll have the lights back on in no time.'

'Oh John, I don't know what I would have done without you.'

Sylvie didn't see him smiling from ear to ear as he walked down the stairs carrying her torch. He was aiming straight for the fuse box in the cupboard under the stairs. He knew exactly which switches in the fuse box needed switching back; the very same ones he had tripped on purpose.

It occurred to him that he could prolong things so Sylvie

would stay for dinner, but John hadn't factored in the dog stopping for dinner too. Was he even house-trained? What if he had an accident on the carpet or started chewing? John shook his head deciding against that idea. Besides, Sylvie expected him to be able to sort these things out pronto; he'd always done so in the past. That was precisely what he intended to do: stick to the plan and show his wife that she can't cope without him. John was confident that one day soon she would come running up the stairs not just asking for help but begging to move back in with him.

John closed the cupboard under the stairs and switched the torchlight off. The hall lights were back on. The door to Sylvie's apartment was ajar, so he made a quick detour inside to double check the electricity was back on in the garden apartment too. This wasn't really necessary, but he liked to be thorough. He walked through Sylvie's lounge and glanced down the stairs to the basement kitchen, flicking the light switch on and off several times. Everything was tickety-boo.

Back upstairs, John walked into his apartment to find Sylvie sitting in the lounge with a cup of tea, and Alfie – her black hairy mutt – sitting right beside her on his white sofa. John had to restrain himself from yelling at the dog and darting across the room to toss him unceremoniously off the sofa. He didn't want to spoil Operation *Lights Out* all because of the dog.

'Did you manage to fix it?' asked Sylvie, putting her cup down on John's coffee table. Not on the coaster, he noticed.

'Uh-huh.'

'Oh John, you're so clever.'

'It was nothing really,' he replied, puffing out his chest and thinking, the hero returns.

Sylvie turned to Alfie sitting beside her. 'Did you hear that, Alfie? John fixed it!' She gathered his little face in her hands, leant over and gave him a hug.

Alfie gave Sylvie a puppy dog kiss in return, smearing his pink tongue down the side of her face.

Ugh. John inwardly shuddered. He didn't get the pet thing; he couldn't understand why people would want to share their home with an animal, no matter how cute it was. John raised an eyebrow. He didn't know why the word *cute* popped into his head. Alfie wasn't cute. He was a mass of black fur sitting on a white sofa. John frowned. He was going to have a considerable job on his hands vacuuming up all those dog hairs when the mutt left.

As if Sylvie had read his mind she stood up.

Alfie jumped down from the sofa.

Although John wanted the dog to go, he didn't wish Sylvie to leave. It was nice having some company for a change. 'Would you like to stay for dinner?' blurted John.

Sylvie glanced at the door. 'I really ought to go. There was something I was in the middle of when—'

'Oh right. I'll see you out then.' He couldn't help but sound disappointed, and it didn't go unnoticed.

'Perhaps another time?' suggested Sylvie.

John smiled. 'Yes, I'd like that.'

As they walked to the door, Sylvie asked conversationally, 'What do you think caused the electric to go off like that?'

'Oh, I don't know,' said John casually, trying not to think about what he was up to earlier when he was in the cupboard under the stairs. After tripping the switches, he had raced back upstairs to his apartment before Sylvie banged on his door.

'Perhaps you plugged something in, in the kitchen, and it

tripped a switch?' That was a plausible explanation. 'These things happen,' he added, making it sound as though it was a common everyday occurrence. Which it might have been if your husband wasn't sabotaging your apartment.

'It is odd though,' continued Sylvie. 'I didn't put the kettle on, or any of the kitchen appliances. In fact, I hadn't even started preparing dinner.' Sylvie was too engrossed in reading that article in the magazine. She quite fancied the idea of staying for dinner, but she couldn't wait to get back to her apartment and finish it. She wanted to find out how to enter the writing competition.

'You haven't prepared yourself anything to eat?' asked John, trying to avoid being drawn into a discussion about what exactly may have caused Sylvie's power cut just in case he caught himself out and said something that might arouse her suspicions.

Sylvie shook her head, no. 'Before I had a chance to make some supper the lights went out.'

John had an idea. 'Wait here a moment, would you?'

Sylvie shrugged. 'All right, John.'

He left Sylvie standing on the landing outside his apartment. 'I'll just be two ticks,' he called out as he strode through the lounge into the kitchen. John opened the fridge and reached in for the dish on the top shelf. When he shut the fridge door, he discovered Sylvie's dog sitting on the floor beside the fridge looking up at him. John frowned. 'What are you doing here? Go back and wait with Sylvie.'

Alfie wagged his tail and stayed put.

John ignored Sylvie's naughty dog. He put the dish down on the kitchen worktop, peeled off the cellophane and took a sharp knife out of the cutlery drawer. He then proceeded to cut a generous slice of homemade chicken pie.

He glanced at the dog still sitting at his feet. Alfie was busy sniffing the air. He licked his chops and wagged his tail. John shook his head. 'It's not for you if that's what you're thinking.'

John returned to the door and handed Sylvie a plate.

A bemused Sylvie looked at her husband in surprise.

'That's homemade chicken pie,' explained John. 'All you have to do is pop it in the oven and heat it up.'

Sylvie's face was a picture. 'I don't know what to say.'

'Thank you, will do,' said John, feeling rather pleased that he'd surprised Sylvie, in a good way. This wasn't part of the plan, but he reckoned he'd scored brownie points for ingenuity. He'd baked the pie that morning. Not with the intention of inviting Sylvie to stay for dinner after he had completed Operation *Lights Out,* or even sending her home with a slice. It was just serendipity that he fancied chicken pie today.

'Thank you, John. I had no idea you baked.'

'Actually, I quite enjoy it,' he said truthfully. He hadn't at first. After Sylvie packed her bags and moved downstairs, he got tired of TV dinners straight out of a box from the supermarket and missed her home cooking. Without his wife around, John had no choice but to start learning to whip up some home-cooked meals of his own. *Needs must* as the old saying goes. Although he hadn't progressed from chicken pie yet, he had perfected his recipe.

He was especially proud of his golden shortcrust pastry. He hoped Sylvie enjoyed it. John didn't tell Sylvie any of this. He just stood by the door smiling and keeping his mouth shut because whenever he spoke to his wife of late, he always managed to put his foot in it. This time things were going well for a change. He didn't want to risk spoiling it by saying something out of turn that might lead to another stupid misunderstanding.

Sylvie turned to go, 'Well, thanks again for the chicken pie and for fixing my electric.'

'Everything's fine downstairs now,' John assured her. 'I even popped inside the apartment and double-checked your lights are back on.' John had barely finished that sentence when he realised his gaffe.

'You've been inside my apartment?' said Sylvie with a start.

John knew what she was thinking; he had used it as an excuse to get inside her apartment and look around.

'Now look,' said John quickly, not wanting this to turn into an argument, 'I know what you're thinking, but I only went in there to check—'

'You're not... angry?'

He looked at her in surprise. Then he remembered that Sylvie had no idea he had already been inside her apartment and seen the changes she'd made. Little wonder she was looking anxious and thought he was going to blow a gasket any minute.

'Why would I be angry?' he replied, acting all innocent.

'But you've seen what I've done to the apartment.'

'Yes, I have... So?' John was enjoying this immensely. Sylvie couldn't have looked more confused if she tried. What she expected was her husband to lift-off. However, unbeknown to Sylvie, he'd already got that episode out the way when he ventured downstairs the first time and received the shock of his life when he saw what had become of his neutral two-bed rental apartment. This time John had his temper-tantrum in check.

'But it looks so different...' she trailed off.

'You know what I think?' said John, trying his utmost not to let his expression give away what he was really thinking. With a tight smile he said, 'The apartment looks... marvellous.'

'You do?' asked Sylvie, still looking confused.

'Absolutely.' John was still smiling rigidly. 'Bloody marvellous,' he added, hoping Sylvie didn't detect the sarcasm in that last comment.

It took a moment for Sylvie to get over the shock, and reply. 'Well, I am surprised because our choice in décor isn't exactly—' She looked past him into his sparsely furnished, very neutral, very boring apartment, searching for the right word.

'—Compatible?'

'That's exactly right,' said Sylvie, staring at him avidly as she slowly repeated the word, *compatible*.

John did his level best to keep smiling. He looked down at the chicken pie in her hands and glanced at his watch. 'The pie takes about thirty minutes to warm up. If you turn your oven on as soon as you get in, it might be ready by seven-thirty.'

'Oh. Yes. Right.' Sylvie had forgotten all about the pie.

Alfie, sitting at Sylvie's feet begging, had not.

From his doorway, John watched Sylvie walk down the stairs carrying her pie aloft, with Alfie following in hot pursuit.

At the bottom of the stairs, Sylvie paused before she opened her door. She glanced up at her husband.

John gave her a little wave and walked back inside his apartment, grinning as he closed the door behind him.

5

Sylvie stepped inside her apartment and shut the door. She stood there for a moment with the plate in her hands staring at the slice of homemade chicken pie. Something was bothering her.

If her best friend was here right now, Sylvie knew what she would say to that: there's nothing to worry about. Julia always said Sylvie was one of life's worriers. She was inclined to agree. When good things happened in her life, she was left with the nagging feeling that, as with Yin and Yang, something negative would be waiting around the corner to balance the books. She had that feeling right now. She tried to shake it off as she made her way down to the kitchen.

Sylvie placed the pie in the oven and shut the oven door, keeping Alfie at arm's length. The next thing she did was feed her hungry dog.

She finally sat down at her kitchen table a full hour after the lights went out. At least she had an evening meal to compensate. Sylvie looked at the plate in front of her. John had given her a generous helping. All she had to do was add some vegetables and *voila*.

Sylvie opened the magazine and found the article she had

been reading about the competition to discover new writing talent. She then tucked into her evening meal, courtesy of John upstairs. The chicken pie not only smelled delicious but tasted delicious too. Sylvie was particularly impressed with John's homemade shortcrust pastry. She had no idea her husband was such a good cook.

If memory served, in all their married life together he'd never once cooked a meal. Sylvie recalled John's invitation to stay for dinner this evening which she gracefully declined. After this, she wouldn't refuse another dinner invitation from John. Her mouth watered at the prospect of what surprises he might cook up next time. Sylvie smiled. She was enjoying her meal immensely. All negative thoughts of Yin and Yang, and bad things happening had vanished.

Sylvie finished her meal and put her plate to one side to read the details of the competition. They wanted a thought-provoking article that would be of interest to women. She remembered her blog. There was plenty of material there all about women's issues, like trial separations, and bereavement, and husbands unexpectedly forced into early retirement. She wanted to write an article about what had been happening in her life of late. She thought it might strike a chord with other women of her generation. The only problem was which subject to choose? She hadn't decided yet. Sylvie read on to find out how much time she had before the competition closed.

'Oh no!' Sylvie discovered the closing date for the competition was tomorrow. She would have to get her skates on and start writing it tonight if she wanted to make the deadline.

At least she didn't have to worry about how she was going to get her submission into the right hands by nine o'clock in the morning. It would be too late to send the article by post, so she decided to visit the magazine's head office first thing in the morning and hand it to the editor, her daughter Harriet.

Sylvie wasn't expecting Harriet to show her any favouritism. On the contrary, she would have been quite happy to stick it in the post box. That way, it would arrive on someone else's desk who had no idea it was the editor's mum who submitted it. In fact, Sylvie would have preferred it that way. She didn't want to give anyone the excuse of accusing her daughter of nepotism if she won the competition. However, this late in the day she had no choice but to pay her daughter a visit at work to submit her competition entry in person.

Sylvie was so excited. She couldn't wait to see the look on Harriet's face when she handed in the competition entry and told her that her mother was a writer too.

The next morning Sylvie caught the bus to the magazine offices in Hanover Square. She squeezed in amongst the other passengers on the bus and was lucky to find a seat. She sat down and anxiously glanced at her watch. It was only half past seven in the morning, so she wasn't worried about missing the deadline, but was concerned about her puppy. It was the first time she had left Alfie home alone in the apartment.

Before leaving to catch the bus, Sylvie made an anxious phone call to Julia. It hadn't occurred to her that having a pet meant she couldn't just take off at a moment's notice without considering how long she would be gone, and what she would do with Alfie in the meantime. She wouldn't normally phone Julia so early in the morning but didn't know what else to do and hoped she wasn't going to suggest asking John to look after him. He didn't like pets. Sylvie would only do that as a last resort. She had phoned Julia looking for an alternative. Julia gave her one: the crate. Apparently, it was the safest way to leave her puppy for a short time so he didn't get into any mischief. Sylvie knew she wouldn't be gone long. Even so, she couldn't help feeling guilty, as though she had abandoned him.

The phone call to Julia wasn't the only thing that nearly held her up this morning. She'd spent far too long in front of the mirror in her bedroom deciding what to wear. It was as though she was going for a job interview, not just popping along to see her daughter at work and hand in an envelope with her competition entry inside.

Sylvie stifled a yawn. She'd been awake until the early hours writing and polishing her article. Once she'd printed off the final draft, she remembered to set the alarm clock — something she'd got out of the habit of doing since leaving her job. Sylvie did not sleep well. She was awake on and off throughout the night anxious that she might sleep through the alarm and miss the deadline after all that effort. But that was all behind her now because she was well on her way to submitting her article and finding out if she had what it takes to be a real writer.

Sylvie rose from her seat as the bus drew up outside the John Lewis department store in Oxford Street. She crossed the road and walked around the corner into Hanover Square, a large leafy square tucked in between Oxford Street and Bond Street in the heart of Mayfair. She walked past tall, elegant Georgian properties that were once private residences but now housed office workers. She was on her way to a large modern building on the far side of the square where Harriet worked.

She crossed the road and took a shortcut through Hanover Square Gardens. The public gardens in the centre of the square were enclosed by black iron railings and had park benches lining the pathway. Sylvie didn't have time to sit down and enjoy the oasis from the city hustle and bustle outside. She quickly made her way along the path and exited the gardens through the entrance opposite the magazine offices. Sylvie paused outside the glass-fronted office building. She wondered if this might be the start of her dream come true, to see her very own writing in print and become a published writer.

Sylvie admonished herself for imagining that she had won the competition when she hadn't even submitted her article. There were probably lots of aspiring writers and journalists out there who were much more talented than her. She had to keep reminding herself not to get her hopes up. There was bound to be some stiff competition. She didn't let that stop her. One can dream, thought Sylvie glancing at the envelope in her hand and then looking up at the sheer glass building in front of her, oblivious to the throng of office workers walking past her on their way into the building.

Sylvie hesitated before she took another step, letting self-doubt intrude and erode her confidence. She debated whether to turn around right now and head back to the bus stop, to avoid the disappointment of finding out she wasn't cut out to be a writer. Sylvie shook her head. That was a stupid thought. How would she know for sure if she didn't at least try?

She took a deep breath and forced herself to put one foot in front of the other. 'Here goes,' she said under her breath as she moved forward, falling in step with other people walking confidently into the office building. Sylvie lost some of her confidence and zeal when she walked into the huge building and promptly got lost trying to find Harriet's office.

Sylvie stepped into the elevator for the third time, after getting off on the wrong floor yet again, and found herself standing next to a young man in an otherwise empty lift. She looked at her watch. It was five minutes to nine. She shook her head in disbelief. 'I'm going to be late.'

'Me too,' said the young man, glancing at Sylvie anxiously. The young man was a trainee journalist who had recently started work at the magazine. He asked Sylvie, 'Are you new here, too?'

I wish, thought Sylvie enviously, avoiding his gaze. 'No, I don't work here. I'm just... visiting.' For some reason, Sylvie didn't want to mention that she was only here to hand in a competition entry, especially as she was in the presence of a *real* journalist even if he was a trainee.

She gave him a sideways glance as they rode up in the lift together. He looked awfully young. Self-doubt crept in again, making her question what she was doing, at her age, trying to forge a new career as a writer; and had half a mind to turn around and head home. Trouble was the lift doors had already closed. Sylvie watched the digital display above the lift doors count up the floors. She supposed having come this far, she might as well hand in her entry. Besides, what had she got to lose? Surely, she had as good a chance as any entrant as long as she found Harriet's office to hand it in.

Sylvie got out at the right floor this time thanks to the nice young man. He surprised Sylvie by shaking her hand when he found out she was the editor-in-chief's mum, no less.

Although late for work he didn't head straight for his desk as soon as the lift doors opened. Instead, he insisted on escorting her through the office maze as he called it, to Harriet's office. And he was honest enough to admit that he was already in trouble for being late for the second day in a row, but at least Sylvie gave him a valid excuse this time, making it appear that he had been delayed by doing a good deed. Perhaps he might even score points with the editor-in-chief by personally escorting her mum right up to her office door.

He didn't.

'Mum, what are you doing here?'

Harriet wasn't in her office when Sylvie arrived. She took a seat opposite her desk and waited. Sylvie turned around in her chair the moment she heard Harriet's voice and could tell by the look on her face that she wasn't pleased to find her mother sitting in her office at nine o'clock on a Monday morning. She wasted no time telling Sylvie that Monday mornings were always diabolically hectic, making it abundantly clear that she couldn't possibly make the time to see her this morning.

Harriet's irritability suddenly gave way to anxiety, causing worry lines to appear on her forehead as she said, 'Mum, is something wrong?'

'No, not at all,' Sylvie replied, wondering why her daughter would think that. She hardly ever visited Harriet at work. On the odd occasion she had, knowing how busy her daughter was, Sylvie always made an appointment. She would never dream of dropping in unannounced – until today.

'Everything is fine,' said Sylvie reassuringly. 'I know you're busy, my sweet.' Sylvie sat forward in her chair and slipped the envelope out of her bag. 'The reason I stopped by…'

She was about to hand over her competition entry when the door to Harriet's office flew open. Sylvie turned around in her chair to see a young woman standing in the doorway waving some papers.

'Are you busy?' she asked Harriet, glancing Sylvie's way.

Harriet ushered her inside the office with a royal wave.

Sylvie kept the envelope on her lap out of sight and watched with interest as Harriet took the paperwork from the young woman. She skimmed the pages, scribbling some notes in the margin, while the young lady stood nervously to one side biting a fingernail.

Sylvie thought Harriet looked very important sitting behind a large desk in her own office. She hadn't visited her daughter at work for ages. Sylvie smiled at her and then cast her gaze around the room. Harriet had been promoted and by the looks of things, moved to a larger office. On her desktop was a wooden name-plate with her name stencilled in gold lettering and her job title beneath. Sylvie also noticed a small photo frame on the table. Although she couldn't see the photograph from this side of the desk, she knew it would be a photograph of her grandchild, Gertie. Sylvie intended to look in on Gertie on her way out; she would be in the company crèche downstairs for the morning while Harriet was at work.

Sylvie offered to look after Gertie when Harriet returned to work after maternity leave. Harriet wouldn't hear of it and was determined to manage her career and motherhood on her own. She knew Harriet wasn't one to ask for help, even if she needed it. Sylvie told her daughter that she mustn't see it as a failure if she called the grandparents to step in at any time to help out. She knew from her own experience that juggling work with raising children wasn't easy, and she only worked as a part-time secretary. She couldn't imagine the pressures of having a professional job like Harriet's. At least Harriet's husband Dominic was supportive. Perhaps it helped that he was a journalist too. She glanced at the envelope in her hands and wished she hadn't given up on her personal dream when she met John. But she couldn't turn back the clock. All she could do was learn lessons from the past and move forward. And that, Sylvie realised, was exactly what she was doing right now, sitting here waiting to make her submission to the magazine. Whatever came of it, she had no doubt that she was doing the right thing.

Sylvie glanced at her watch. She wasn't going to worry that it was now gone nine o'clock, past the official deadline. She'd arrived on time. The nice young man who showed her to Harriet's empty office this morning was sure to vouch for her.

Sylvie sat waiting patiently. She was pleased that the deadline happened to coincide with one of Harriet's days in work. Harriet wasn't planning to return to her job full time until Gertie started school, even though Sylvie knew money was tight. Harriet did freelance writing from home to subsidise her income; money that Harriet and Dominic depended on to meet the hefty mortgage payments on their London home. Unlike her parents, Harriet and her husband didn't have the good fortune to buy a property in London at a price that, by today's standards, was a steal.

Sylvie believed good fortune had smiled on her generation, for those who had the opportunity to take advantage of it, so wasn't about to sit there and feel sorry for herself over past mistakes. *No regrets.* That was a piece of advice her mother once imparted to her. The trouble with that piece of advice, Sylvie discovered, was that it was almost impossible to go through life without some regrets. It was what you did about those regrets that really mattered. Do you let them fester or do you do something about it? That's why Sylvie was here today, doing something about hers. She glanced down at the envelope in her hands dying to surprise Harriet with her submission.

Harriet put her pen down and handed the paperwork back to her colleague. 'Not bad,' said Harriet, sending her on her way with what was obviously a huge compliment because the young woman left the room with a spring in her step and a smile on her face. Harriet turned to her mother. She didn't apologise for the interruption, and Sylvie didn't expect her to. 'Mum, what are you doing here?'

Before Sylvie had a chance to explain, Harriet added, 'I'm at work. Can't this wait until later?'

'Not really. You see, the reason I stopped by—'

The phone rang cutting Sylvie off.

Harriet answered the phone. Her voice sounded clipped and irritated, 'What is it now?' Harriet looked exasperated as she glanced over Sylvie's shoulder into the office beyond.

Sylvie turned around in her chair, following her gaze. It took her a few moments to locate the young lady on the phone in the busy office; she was looking in their direction.

'How many times do I have to tell you?' Harriet rolled her eyes in frustration before continuing, 'We are not interested in anything submitted from people who are after a second career or, heaven forbid, retired people looking for a way to earn some extra cash.' She added sarcastically, 'Perhaps they should consider working for Tesco?' Harriet put the phone down and turned to Sylvie just as her office door opened. Harriet looked up and sighed heavily. 'Didn't I make myself clear on the phone?'

'I'm sorry, Harriet,' said the young lady who was talking to her a moment ago. She was standing in the doorway holding a large pile of paperwork. 'I'm still sifting through the competition entries. I wanted to be absolutely sure what we are looking for.'

Harriet held out an impatient hand. 'Give them here.'

The young lady passed the stack of competition entries over to Harriet who quickly started to weed them out. 'I told you before that we are looking for bright young things. The next generation of journalists with something interesting and fresh to offer our readers who, I'm sure you don't need reminding, are in their twenties and thirties. Do I make myself clear?'

Sylvie found herself nodding along with the young lady.

By the time Harriet finished talking she had cast aside most of the submissions.

The young woman looked surprised. 'How did you—?'

'—Do that so fast?' Harriet smiled. 'Easy, just check their date of birth. We're looking for articles from women, for women, in their twenties, thirties and up to their mid-forties.'

Sylvie stared at Harriet. That explained why they had asked for all those personal details in the competition entry. They could quickly weed out every writer over the age of fifty without even bothering to read their submission.

Sylvie watched how many entries Harriet cast aside. If it was just the twenty-five to forty-five-year-old demographic that comprised most of their readership, then why were there so many entries from women over fifty? They must be reading the magazine, or they would not have known about the competition?

Looking at the number of entries from women over the age of fifty as a proportion of the entire pile on Harriet's desk, it made Sylvie wonder if they had misjudged the true composition of their readership. Perhaps they should take on board how their readership might have changed in recent years. After all, wasn't fifty the new forty, and sixty the new fifty – or something to that effect? Sylvie felt like pointing that out, but who was she to argue with her daughter, the editor-in-chief? Sylvie wasn't a journalist. What would she know about these matters? Harriet, on the other hand, had been in this line of work for years; she obviously knew what she was doing.

The young lady left Harriet's office with a fraction of the original competition entries she had come in with.

Harriet picked up the pile of entries she had discarded and dumped them in the wastepaper bin beside her desk. People's dreams dismissed as rubbish in under two minutes.

Sylvie looked at the bin and then glanced at the envelope in her hands containing the competition entry that she had spent hours working on. She felt like tossing it in the bin with all the others. But if she did that, then she'd have to tell Harriet what was inside the envelope. Instead, she surreptitiously edged hers out of Harriet's sight, under the table, and into her bag.

Harriet finished disposing of the competition entries and turned to her mother. 'Look, Mum, whatever it is, can't it wait? I'm really busy.'

Sylvie clutched her bag and got up. 'You know what?' She glanced at Harriet's wastepaper bin. 'You're so right. I've got no business being here.' How could I be so stupid, thought Sylvie? 'I ought to go.'

'Okay,' said Harriet.

Sylvie got up and walked to the door.

'Mum?'

Sylvie turned around. 'Yes, Harriet?'

Harriet picked up the phone to make a call. 'Close the door behind you, please.'

'Yes, of course.' Sylvie made sure the door was firmly shut behind her. She stood for a moment gazing into Harriet's office daydreaming about *if-only* and *what-might-have-been*. She wondered where she might be today if only she had pursued her dreams.

Sylvie turned away with a heavy heart. Over the years, she'd let opportunities slip through her fingers because she was too afraid to step outside her comfort zone and try something new. Perhaps time had caught up with her, and now she was too old for second chances. She walked back through the office and saw bright young journalists turning their gaze in her direction. Just the sort Sylvie imagined Harriet was looking for to write for her magazine.

She made a huge mistake coming here. She wasn't twenty-something or thirty-something anymore. Why would anybody be interested in reading an article from a sixty-year-old former secretary? It was clear sitting opposite her successful daughter. It wasn't Harriet's fault. Sylvie didn't begrudge her any of her success. She just assumed she might be in for a fighting chance of realising her dreams if she entered the competition.

She was wrong.

Was this it? Was her journey to fulfil her dream over? Sylvie didn't want to think about that right now. She didn't want to wallow in regrets. Instead, all she could think about was damage limitation; she was relieved that she hadn't made a monumental fool of herself in front of all these important journalists. In front of Harriet. Fortunately, she hadn't shown anybody what was inside the envelope. At least she'd saved herself and Harriet the embarrassment of adding one more competition entry to the rubbish bin.

Sylvie desperately wanted to get out of the building and go

home. She had the sudden urge to run through the office to the lifts, even though she felt embarrassed enough as it was without making a spectacle of herself in front of Harriet's work colleagues. However, she couldn't hot-foot it out of there if she wanted to because she'd lost her sense of direction.

She found herself wandering aimlessly through the large open-plan office unable to find her way back to the lifts. It felt like the walk of shame, as though everybody who looked up from their desks as she passed by knew why she was here today: to make a fool of herself or learn a lesson – or both.

At least the other people in that pile of competition entries hadn't put themselves through the humiliation of turning up at the magazine offices in person, to discover their dreams were only worthy of the rubbish bin beside the editor's desk.

She wandered around in a daze, still unable to find the lift that would take her down to the ground floor. Sylvie was thinking about her journal entries that she had copied into her blog. Chloe had been right all along: she had no reason to worry about her personal life being "out there." Nobody was interested in reading all about a sixty-year-old baby boomer.

Sylvie gazed around the office desperately searching for an escape route. She was walking around in circles. She would have to add one more humiliation to the list by asking somebody to point a silly old lady in the direction of the exit.

She stopped in front of a desk and looked down at a young woman who was busy typing. 'Excuse me, I'm so sorry to interrupt, but I seem to have lost my way. Can you direct me to the nearest lift to the ground floor?'

The young woman looked up at Sylvie and smiled. She was about to get up from her chair when a young man seated at another desk overhead that exchange and swivelled his chair around to face Sylvie. 'I'll show Mrs Baxter the way out.' He grinned at Sylvie.

She recognised him instantly; he was the nice young man who had escorted her from the lift right to Harriet's door. 'Charlie?' Sylvie was surprised they should meet again in such a sprawling office.

'What a coincidence, eh?' he said, as if reading her thoughts. 'It must be fate.' He leaned in close, and said, 'You know, we really should stop meeting like this; otherwise, people will talk.' He said it loud enough so the young lady overheard every word.

Sylvie looked at him in surprise.

He winked conspiratorially and held out the crook of his arm. 'Shall we?'

Sylvie got the joke immediately and played along, taking his arm as though they were a couple courting.

As they turned to go, Sylvie glanced at the young woman who was staring at them both wide-eyed in the belief that her colleague was dating a much older woman. She thinks I've got a toy boy. Sylvie stifled a laugh. Thanks to Charlie, Sylvie's otherwise rubbish morning had improved considerably.

They strolled through the office arm in arm towards the lift.

People looked up from their work to stare at the odd couple walking by.

Sylvie didn't mind having an escort and was grateful for the company. She no longer felt like running out of the office, ashamed of herself. In fact, she was rather enjoying all the unexpected attention as she walked through the office with a toy boy on her arm.

Sylvie came here with her competition entry hoping that the

article she spent hours writing and perfecting would make her stand out from the crowd. That obviously hadn't happened. But thanks to Charlie, at least she had the satisfaction of creating some office buzz, even if it wasn't quite what she intended. She glanced at Charlie walking beside her who was also clearly enjoying the attention.

'Well, that's one way to get noticed,' he said, arriving at the lifts and grinning at Sylvie.

Sylvie smiled knowingly. She understood the double-meaning behind that remark. Journalism wasn't the easiest career to break into and make your mark. The trials and tribulations of Harriet's career, over the years, had proved that. It was not easy making it to the top. Charlie probably knew that.

'Did you manage to put in a good word for me with the boss?' he asked, meaning Harriet.

Sylvie hesitated. She barely had a chance to get a word in about the reason she'd stopped by, let alone mention how she'd found Harriet's new office, and what a good samaritan Charlie had been. What a shame he had gone to all the trouble on her behalf for nothing. Sylvie didn't know what to say.

'Mrs Baxter, please don't concern yourself. It's just one of those things.'

'I know what I'll do,' said Sylvie, determined to put this right. 'I'll go back and tell— '

'No!' Charlie caught her arm. 'Please don't do that. It really doesn't matter.'

Sylvie didn't believe him; he was just saying that to make her feel better. 'Of course, it matters.' Sylvie didn't want to return to Harriet's office, but she couldn't let him down. One good turn deserved another.

Charlie still had hold of her arm. He mumbled, 'Sorry,' and let go.

Sylvie didn't move from her spot. She studied him thoughtfully, taking in his glum expression. There was a haunting sadness in those chocolate brown eyes, a sadness Sylvie recognised. Was that regret already in one so young?

Charlie sighed heavily.

'What is it, Charlie?' Sylvie asked gently.

He glanced over his shoulder at the office beyond.

She followed his gaze to the mass of desks and people, heads down busy researching and writing their next articles.

Charlie fixed his gaze on Sylvie. 'Can I tell you a secret?'

Sylvie nodded.

He lowered his voice. 'All this…' Charlie waved his hand indicating the sea of journalists, 'it isn't me, you know. I'm just pretending this is what I want to do.'

Sylvie looked at him in surprise. 'I don't understand.'

'My father is a well-respected journalist working for the BBC. He encouraged me to take this job because he wanted me to follow in his footsteps. I'm only doing this for him.'

'Oh Charlie, you mustn't do something just to please other people.' Sylvie shook her head in dismay. 'You must follow your own path because let me tell you that hindsight is a terrible thing. Don't end up at my age with regrets that will haunt you.'

Charlie nodded. 'I wish I had the heart to tell him this is not what I want to do with my life.'

'What *do* you want to do?' asked Sylvie, interested to know what life's path Charlie would choose. He was a lovely young man with a heart of gold, and it was sad to see someone so young deeply unhappy.

He stared at her, afraid to voice his dreams. Afraid they would be criticised, shot down as they had been in the past.

'You can tell me,' Sylvie said earnestly, hoping he understood that she would listen without prejudice.

He smiled as he told her what he really wanted to do with his life. It turned out that ever since Charlie could remember he wanted to be a fireman. His parents had indulged him when he was a little boy with toys and a fireman's costume, imagining it was just child's play and he would grow out of it. He didn't. Charlie had found his calling early in life, but his parents didn't believe in his dream. So, he went along with their vision for his future and started a career in journalism; his dream eroded by the good intentions of others, as they so often are.

'I always dreamt of being a fireman, but journalism is like the family business. My father is a journalist. My grandfather is a journalist. My great-grandfather was a writer and founded a newspaper.' Charlie sighed. 'When I told them what I really wanted to do, my parents said I was immature. It was as though, by choosing a career based on what I loved as a child, I wasn't growing up and being responsible.'

Sylvie looked at him askance. From her own experience, she believed that *not* choosing a career based on what you loved was irresponsible and could lead to a lifetime of regrets. She thought back to her own childhood and the times she loved sitting alone writing. That was her calling. Pity she'd left it so late to start acting on it.

Sylvie thought about her three daughters. Although they each chose completely different careers, they had one thing in common: all three girls looked to their interests to discover their life's work. Harriet always loved writing. She started writing for teen magazines when she was still at school. Harriet was a journalist-in-the-making before she even realised that's what she wanted to do for a living. Jessica, their middle daughter, couldn't have been more different. She couldn't sit still for long and struggled at school, but from an early age she too had a passion. Ever since word dot Jessica loved the animal kingdom. It was apparent to anybody who knew her that she would work in some capacity with animals when she grew up.

As for their youngest daughter, Chloe, when her peers were dressing up dolls and stealing their older sister's makeup, Chloe was obsessed with John's computer. She taught herself computer programming as a hobby when she was still a teenager.

'My parents considered a job as a firefighter was beneath me,' continued Charlie, cutting across Sylvie's thoughts. 'They made no bones about the fact that they thought my dream was... well... stupid.'

Sylvie shook her head in disbelief. Since when did anybody have the right to call someone else's dreams stupid? 'What you want to do with your life is your own business, Charlie. No-one's dreams are stupid and don't you forget it. They're only stupid when you don't act on them,' said Sylvie, sounding like the voice of experience. 'And besides, since when was saving lives stupid?'

Charlie broke into a wide grin at that last comment. 'You're absolutely right. I never thought of it that way before.'

The lift doors opened behind Sylvie. Before she turned to go, Charlie stepped forward and enveloped her in a hug. He didn't say anything when he released her, just stood there watching her as she stepped into the lift.

Charlie was still standing there smiling as the lift doors closed.

Sylvie suspected Harriet was about to lose one of her trainee journalists.

Sylvie smiled to herself as the lift counted down to the ground floor. She had a feeling that something worthwhile had come out of her visit here today after all. Charlie was right: fate had transpired to throw them together. Maybe for good reason. If she saved Charlie from a lifetime of regrets, then that would make her day.

When the lift doors opened, and Sylvie was heading out of the building in the direction of the bus stop, she felt much better about her trip here this morning. Thinking back to that brief conversation with a young man she barely knew, it occurred to her that perhaps she should take her own advice: dreams were only stupid if you don't act on them. Sylvie believed there was a wasteland, somewhere she couldn't quite quantify, where once-cherished dreams lay broken and discarded along with a part of ourselves unable to walk a life's path that was meant for us.

Sylvie didn't want to consign her dream to that wasteland just yet. She hadn't won the competition. She hadn't even submitted her article. But that didn't mean this marked the end of her dream to be a writer. It was just a setback. At least that was how Sylvie chose to look at things. There would be other magazines, other competitions. Perhaps there were even better opportunities lying around the next corner. She just had to wait for the right one to come along. In the meantime, it wouldn't stop her from doing what she loved, which was to write. And it wouldn't stop her writing her blog.

As Sylvie took a seat on the bus for the journey home, her overriding thought was that after the disastrous visit to see Harriet this morning, at least her day couldn't get any worse.

6

John was sitting in his lounge reading the newspaper when he heard a woman scream. He paused for a moment, turned to the next page, and resumed reading. A short time later, he heard it again. John lowered his paper, folded it neatly in two, and placed it in the magazine rack on the floor by his chair. He looked at his watch. It was already mid-morning and Sylvie had just returned home. By the sound of things, his next mission was already moving along nicely.

He recalled the conversation on the phone with Dave last night. After the success of the first mission, they both agreed that he should strike while the iron was hot. John had already made preparations for the next wave of the plan, setting the wheels in motion for his next mission.

It was the day after Operation *Lights Out*. Conveniently, Sylvie had gone out for the morning, leaving John free to make preparations downstairs. He had not counted on finding her dog home alone. That could have posed a problem. Fortunately, he was out of harm's way locked inside a metal crate. He seemed happy enough with his doggy blanket and a chew toy.

However, the fact that Sylvie had left her dog home alone

suggested that wherever she'd gone first thing in the morning, she wouldn't be long. John didn't hang around. He quickly set to work. When he was done, he scooted back upstairs to wait for her return and the drama to unfold.

Sylvie screamed for the third time.

Alfie joined in furiously barking.

John rose from his chair and listened to the cacophony downstairs. He crossed the lounge, walked out of his apartment and down the stairs, not in any great hurry.

On the fourth scream, John banged on Sylvie's apartment door and shouted out, 'Sylvie, what is going on in there?' He knew full well what was going on in there, but what he couldn't understand was why she wasn't racing up to his apartment to fetch him like the last time when the lights went out.

He put his ear to the door and heard her yell back, 'John! Thank heavens it's you. You've got to come quick.'

John furrowed his brow wondering why Sylvie wasn't answering her door. This was not part of the plan. Then again, as Dave quite rightly pointed out, there were times he might have to improvise. He thought back to the last mission when he offered Sylvie a slice of chicken pie, which was rather a nice note on which to end the first mission. Perhaps there would be another opportunity to improvise for the good of the plan.

Sylvie was still calling from inside her apartment, so John tried the door. It was unlocked. He opened the door and stepped inside, starting to feel genuinely concerned. 'Sylvie?'

'I'm down here!' she shouted, her shrill voice coming from the basement kitchen.

He raced down the stairs. On entering the kitchen, John skidded to a halt. He was confronted by the peculiar sight of

Sylvie and her dog standing on the kitchen table. Sylvie had a closed umbrella in her hand which she was using to stab the air, as though she was attempting to ward off something. Alfie was hiding behind her legs yapping. John stared at them. This was not at all what he was expecting.

He suddenly felt the urge to run back upstairs and bury his head in one of Sylvie's colourful cushions to stifle a laugh that was building up into epic proportions. He clamped a hand over his mouth trying to contain himself from roaring with laughter.

'There it is!' exclaimed Sylvie, stabbing the air with the tip of her umbrella.

John lowered his hand and swallowed hard trying to think of the seriousness of the plan and all the reasons why he couldn't screw this up. Think debts, think bills, think about anything other than the sight of Sylvie and her dog standing on the kitchen table making him want to keel over in a fit of laughter.

'Oh god!' cried John. He darted out of the room and up the stairs, throwing himself on to Sylvie's sofa and burying his face in a cushion. He shook his head from side-to-side realising it was futile. He couldn't follow through on the mission now. It was impossible. What would he tell Dave? That he failed in his mission, cut down by a fit of giggles? It was ridiculous. But he saw no way out; the mission had to be aborted.

'You saw it too, didn't you?' Sylvie shouted out from the kitchen downstairs.

John looked up at the sound of her voice. He raised an eyebrow. Perhaps the mission could be salvaged after all. He tossed the cushion to one side. John had an idea. 'Yes, I saw it,' he shouted back. She hadn't heard his muffled, hysterical laughter which meant the game wasn't up. The mission was still a go. 'Just

71

stay where you are. I will be back in two ticks.'

'You're not leaving me down here!' cried Sylvie.

John shouted back, 'I promise I will be back before you can count to twenty.'

Sylvie started counting, 'One... two...' as he raced out of her apartment. By the time he made it upstairs, the fit of giggles had subsided to a knowing smile. He grabbed the equipment he needed to complete the mission and carried the items down the stairs as quickly as he could.

This was one aspect of the mission over which John and Dave had had a heated debate. These items were not the sort of thing he would normally have lying around in his apartment. There was the distinct possibility that Sylvie might question why these items were already on hand. They both decided it would just have to be a case of crossing that bridge when he came to it. Right now, John doubted she would even notice, let alone care to question anything that he brought down to her apartment, as long as it got her off that table and out of the kitchen.

Sylvie was still counting, '...sixteen, seventeen... John! Eighteen, nineteen...'

John reappeared at the bottom of the kitchen stairs feeling a lot more composed. He walked into the kitchen, passing Sylvie and Alfie still standing on the table, and placed the items on the worktop. He proceeded to put down a row of small traps on the kitchen floor. Satisfied that the stage was set, John walked up to the table and held out his hand. 'You can come down now, Sylvie.'

Sylvie grimaced as she scanned the floor.

'It's okay. I've put cheese in the traps so when it reappears, it will head straight for the cheese and not for you.'

John saw his chance for a bit of improvisation for the good

of the plan. 'I'll even carry you across the floor to the stairs if you want me too.' He turned towards the door leading upstairs. 'You can wait in the lounge until I've got rid of the infestation.' When he turned back, Sylvie was holding out the dog.

'Alfie goes first.'

John looked at the dog and grimaced. 'You have got to be kidding me,' he muttered under his breath. He was not carrying that thing over to the stairs. John peered up at Sylvie. He thought about the good of the plan and took the dog, carrying it across the floor to the bottom of the stairs.

Alfie seemed to be enjoying the ride. He licked John's face.

John put the dog down on the bottom stair and wiped the side of his cheek with the back of his hand, trying not to think about where that tongue might have been. He returned for Sylvie. John held her hand as she climbed down on to a chair. He then scooped her up in his arms and felt a sudden twinge in his lower back reminding him that he wasn't twenty-odd anymore. It didn't help that his wife was a good few extra pounds heavier than when they first married.

Carrying his wife across the kitchen brought back a memory of happier times. When they first bought this house together, John had borne his young bride over the threshold of their new home unaware of what lay ahead. He wondered what his younger self would have thought if he could look into the future and see where they were now: still living in the same house but living apart.

John banished that thought immediately; it wouldn't be long now and things would be back to normal. In fact, finding Sylvie standing on the table had an unexpected benefit – laughing fits notwithstanding. What could be more heroic than a man making a daring rescue to carry a lady in distress to safety. He concentrated on making it to the stairs before his back gave out. It would not make a good impression if he dropped her.

John made it to the stairs and deposited his wife beside the dog. He noticed that she kept her hands around his neck for a moment longer than was really necessary.

'Thank you, John. That was very gallant of you.'

'Not at all,' John replied, confident he now had the makings of another successful mission on his hands. He watched Sylvie walk up the stairs to the lounge.

Alfie remained sitting on the bottom stair looking up at him and wagging his tail.

John shook his head. 'If you think I'm carrying you up those stairs, you can think again.' He shut the door on the dog and heard Sylvie calling Alfie from upstairs.

Alone in the kitchen, John set to work. He picked up all the traps and put them in a plastic bag. He then took the cardboard box he had left on the kitchen worktop and lifted out the other item he brought with him. It was a small metal hamster cage. He put it down in the middle of the kitchen floor, opened the little door and placed some small pieces of cheese just inside the cage. Apparently, this worked every time.

John sat down at Sylvie's kitchen table and waited. Operation *Danger Mouse* was nearly complete.

It was an inspired idea of Dave's to borrow his grandson Theo's pet mouse. It turned out that Danger Mouse had an immense fondness for cheese. Theo often let him out of his cage, but he always found his own way back, encouraged by a nice dollop of Cheddar.

John turned in his chair at the sound of Sylvie's dog whining behind the kitchen door, despite Sylvie calling him numerous times. Operation *Danger Mouse* would have been impossible if Sylvie's pet was a cat. John smiled. Fortunately for him, Julia had bought her a stupid dog.

'*Alfie!*' Sylvie yelled from upstairs.

John heard the sound of four paws scampering up the stairs.

All went quiet.

John sat drumming his fingers on the table. The mission was almost finished. Now all he had to do was sit and wait for Danger Mouse to be lured out of his hiding place by the smell of cheese. He scanned the kitchen floor, looking for any sign of Theo's mouse. There was still no sign of him. He lifted his chin and gazed around the kitchen. His expression turned sour. He still couldn't get over what Sylvie had done to the new kitchen he had installed during the conversion. John's white kitchen units had been painted a vintage green. Ugh.

He'd seen Julia in and out of the garden apartment soon after Sylvie moved downstairs. There was no doubt in his mind that it was her doing, along with repainting the magnolia walls a vibrant yellow. And installing that Welsh dresser which he discovered Sylvie had bought for the kitchen. She'd always wanted one. John didn't. They were large and bulky, and took up too much space, on top of which it meant Sylvie would have somewhere to display her awful chintzy crockery.

He turned around in his chair to face the table so he wouldn't have to look at the chintzy crockery and spotted her laptop sitting on the kitchen table. He had an identical one of his own upstairs. That wasn't a coincidence. Not to be left behind, when he found out Sylvie had a new laptop, he ditched his ancient computer and bought himself one too.

John stood up, circled the table, and took a seat in front of her laptop. The screensaver was dancing around the screen which meant the computer was still switched on. He guessed that she must have been using it when Danger Mouse made an appearance.

John furtively glanced in the direction of the stairs and then back at the screen. He reached out and randomly pressed any key. The screen lit up. At first glance it appeared that Sylvie had more icons on her desktop than he did. John counted to make sure and discovered he was right. She had precisely one more. His eyes settled on that extra icon – *Sylvie's blog*.

'So, that's what you've been using your new laptop for,' John commented under his breath as he moved the cursor over the icon. Intrigued to find out what his wife had been writing in her blog, he was just about to click on it when Sylvie's voice startled him. 'John! What's happening down there? Is it all clear?'

John bounced out of his chair. 'Oh... er... nearly done.' He looked at the floor and spotted Danger Mouse – a small sandy coloured harmless field mouse – scurrying across the tiled floor. The mouse paused briefly, twitching his whiskers, and then continued on his journey back into the hamster cage. John darted across the kitchen and knelt to close the cage door.

Danger Mouse was busy demolishing a mound of cheese held in his tiny paws, oblivious to all the drama he caused.

John smiled at Theo's pet mouse as he picked up the cage. He deposited it carefully back in the cardboard box, ready to carry back upstairs for Dave to collect in the morning.

John opened the kitchen door, and shouted out, 'All clear!' He closed the cardboard flaps to the box as he made his way up the stairs.

John walked into the lounge and found Sylvie standing by the window. He held up the box. 'It's all taken care of.' He was counting on the fact that Sylvie would not want to look inside the box. If she did, she would not see a dead rodent but a field mouse, very much alive, happily polishing off the last of his Cheddar cheese.

Sylvie did not move from her spot by the window. 'Where do you think it came from?'

John looked down at the box he was holding and thought of Theo's bedroom. He said, 'I suppose it must have appeared as a result of the building work...er...disturbing things when we converted the house.' He frowned hoping his bullshit explanation sufficed.

Sylvie glanced nervously in the direction of the kitchen. 'Do you think there's any more?'

John shook his head. 'I can confidently say there aren't any more where that came from.' Theo only had one pet mouse.

There was an awkward silence.

John glanced down at the box. 'I better dispose of this.'

'Oh yes, of course,' said Sylvie, keeping her distance from the box and its contents.

He crossed the room.

'John.'

He stopped in the doorway and turned around, 'Yes, dear?'

'Your chicken pie was delicious.'

John smiled. 'I hope that means I can tempt you to stop by for dinner sometime?'

Sylvie nodded enthusiastically. 'We'll have to set a date.'

John looked at her in surprise. 'That we will.' He lingered a moment longer, staring at Sylvie across the room. John had the sudden urge to rush over and kiss his wife. He didn't want to push his luck and spoil the moment by being presumptuous. In any case, that might prove a bit awkward with the bulky cardboard box in his arms. He certainly couldn't put the box down and risk Alfie poking his nose inside, scaring his sidekick to death. John was under strict orders to bring Danger Mouse back from the mission in one piece. Reluctantly, he turned to go.

'John?'

He did an about-turn. 'Yes, dear?'

'I can't thank you enough for, you know, just being there.'

'You don't have to thank me.' John curbed a smile as he revelled in the moment. 'That's what husbands are for.' He walked out of Sylvie's apartment and up the stairs, delighted that Dave's plan was working. Once again, the mission had been a complete success.

He glanced downstairs before stepping inside his apartment and spotted Sylvie hovering outside her door. John guessed that she was still worried about rodents in her kitchen.

He was on the verge of offering Sylvie to stay the night at his place but thought the better of it. Firstly, there was the dog to consider. He didn't want another animal in his apartment. One was quite enough. Danger Mouse had to stay the night because Dave couldn't collect him until tomorrow. John didn't mind; the mouse had been useful. Unfortunately, the same couldn't be said for Sylvie's dog. Alfie was a nuisance. He had already cost John two hours of his life vacuuming all those black dog hairs off his white sofa after the last visit. After that episode, he didn't want that dog anywhere near his apartment. The problem was, if he invited Sylvie upstairs, she couldn't leave her dog downstairs alone all night howling.

However, the dog was the least of John's concerns. Even though they were back on speaking terms, nothing had really changed. What was the point of inviting her to stay the night if she ended up moving back into the spare bedroom? Not that she could actually do that because the spare bedroom in John's apartment was now the centre of operations. Or *mission control* as Dave insisted on calling it, although as John pointed out that this wasn't NASA, and John wasn't going on space missions.

Regardless of Alfie, or the now defunct spare bedroom, or Dave's mission control misnomer, John knew this wasn't the right moment to ask his wife to move back in with him. He knew this with certainty for one simple but significant reason: he had *not* completed the plan. John and Dave had discussed plenty of ideas to sabotage Sylvie's apartment and encourage her to move back upstairs. They came up with three sure-fire missions. John had one more task to go.

Once the final mission was complete, and everything was in perfect working order after he'd popped in and out to "fix" things, giving him ample opportunity to "engage with the enemy," as Dave had put it. Then he would thank Sylvie for her patience with ironing out the wrinkles in the rental apartment and suggest she move back upstairs.

So far things were progressing nicely. In less than a week, John was back on speaking terms with his wife. They had even tentatively arranged a dinner date. Things were going so well that he considered contacting an estate agent to start looking for a tenant.

Anticipating the success of the final mission, John was already confidently looking forward to telling Dave that the fox was in the hole.

7

The following day John was sitting in bed with his morning cuppa after the best night's sleep he'd had since Sylvie moved downstairs. He couldn't believe it was only a few days ago that he was still writing in his little black book about the issues he was having with his troublesome neighbour and wondering where all this was leading. Now, two missions into the plan, everything had changed. The little black book was gathering dust in the desk drawer in his study and he was confident that things were going to work out after all.

John had nearly finished his tea. He was debating whether he fancied sitting in bed with another and reading a few pages of his novel before getting up, when a loud noise startled him. It took him a moment to identify what it might be. It sounded like his next-door neighbour's fire alarm had gone off. John relaxed. He imagined his neighbour frantically trying to silence the din.

He was still considering whether to make himself a second cup of tea when it occurred to him; what if it wasn't a false alarm? He started to have visions of the fire spreading from next door. John shot out of bed to investigate. He hastily pulled on his dressing gown and slippers and dashed out of his bedroom.

The fire alarm seemed to be getting louder. He hurried past the bathroom and down the stairs, his anxiety levels increasing with every step. As he rushed through the lounge and approached the door to his apartment, he heard Sylvie banging on his door above the din.

'John? John!'

He opened the door.

Alfie immediately darted between his legs and scampered inside the apartment before John could stop him, intent on finding a hiding place away from the noise. Sylvie was standing outside. It didn't surprise him that she'd heard it too. The continuous high-pitched alarm seemed to be getting louder and, oddly, changing direction. John tilted his head to listen. It no longer seemed to be coming from next door but... downstairs.

He looked at Sylvie in alarm. *Oh god, the house is on fire!*

He didn't need an explanation, but Sylvie gave him one anyway, 'The fire alarm went off, and I didn't know what to do!'

John raced down the stairs followed by Sylvie bringing up the rear, the shrill alarm getting louder with every step. 'Did you close all the windows and doors?' exclaimed John, trying not to panic as they both pounded down the stairs.

'No!' Sylvie cried out behind him sounding breathless.

'Did you call the fire brigade?' shouted John, panting as he reached the bottom of the stairs.

'No!'

'Bloody hell!' John swore, thinking oh god this is all I need. It might be one sure-fire way of getting her to move back in with him, but this was most definitely not part of the plan; how could he rent out the garden apartment if it had been gutted by fire? What about the hassle of an insurance claim and the time it would take to get the builders back? That could take weeks. John was reeling at the prospect of all the lost income from being unable to rent out the flat in the meantime. He was sure an insurance claim wouldn't cover the loss of earnings when he hadn't even got around to finding a tenant yet.

He reached the bottom of the stairs and stopped outside Sylvie's apartment. The door was ajar. He was just in the throes of deciding whether to shut the door and phone the fire brigade when he smelt something. John tentatively pushed the door open and sniffed the air. He raised an eyebrow. He smelt the distinct whiff of burnt toast emanating from the kitchen downstairs.

Sylvie was shouting above the din, 'I was preparing some breakfast when I burnt the toast. That's when the fire alarm went off.'

John turned around to face Sylvie, and shouted, 'You could have told me that in the first place!'

'Well, you didn't exactly give me a chance. You kept firing questions at me all the way down the stairs!'

Panic over, John sighed in relief. 'Just wait here will you, and I'll go and sort it out.'

John left Sylvie standing in the hall and spotted just what he needed on Sylvie's coffee table. He strode across the room and picked up a magazine. He glanced at the magazine on his way down to the kitchen. It was the one she bought every month because their daughter was the editor. He knew how proud Sylvie was of all their daughters' achievements. She was particularly proud of Harriet, although he never asked why.

He glanced at the cover. Something caught his eye. *Calling all aspiring writers and journalists.* John recalled when Harriet was a teenager and announced she wanted to be a journalist. It had taken him by surprise. He wondered where she'd come up with that idea from. It wasn't as though there were any writers in the family. Just one of life's mysteries he thought, as he made his way downstairs to the basement kitchen.

John momentarily covered his ears with his hands to block out the piercing sound of the fire alarm. The next thing he did was unlock the french doors and throw them wide open. A blast of damp, cold air circulated the room, dissipating the smell of burnt toast.

John turned around and dragged a kitchen chair from under the table. He climbed up on the chair and stood directly under the fire alarm. The alarm, this close, was almost deafening. He frantically waved the magazine under the fire alarm. Suddenly all went quiet. John heaved a sigh of relief as he stepped down from the chair.

Sylvie emerged from upstairs, poking her head around the kitchen door.

'You can come in now,' said John, leaving the magazine on the kitchen table.

Sylvie walked in and smiled sheepishly as she lifted the slice of charred toast out of the toaster. 'How stupid of me.'

John thought so too but decided not to voice that opinion.

'I put the bread in the toaster and only popped upstairs for a minute or two. That's when the fire alarm went off. I didn't know what to do. I'm sorry if I woke you up.'

'You didn't wake me,' said John as he walked over to the french doors and pulled them both shut. He was relieved it was a false alarm. He turned around and smiled at Sylvie. 'You know me, always an early bird. I had just finished a cup of tea when…' John pointed at the fire alarm.

'Have you had breakfast?'

'Not yet.' John pulled his dressing gown tightly around him and concentrated on tying up the chord in a loose bow at the front. The kitchen now felt rather fresh after that blast of cold air.

'Would you like to stay for breakfast?'

John looked up, surprised by the invitation. He hesitated. This wasn't part of the plan. None of this was. What should he do?

'I didn't mean to snap at you back there, John. It's just that lately it seems to be one thing after another, first the electric, then that rat infestation – now this.' She paused. 'Making you some breakfast is the least I can do after everything you've done for me. To be honest, with all these things that have cropped up in the apartment lately, I don't know what I would have done without you.'

That was music to his ears. John smiled. Under the circumstances, having breakfast together wasn't such a bad idea. John's empty stomach growled loudly. 'If you're quite sure I'm not imposing,' he ventured, avoiding eye contact. John was starting to feel guilty about sabotaging Sylvie's apartment, even though the fire alarm was nothing to do with him.

'Of course not. Please,' she indicated the kitchen table, 'take a seat and I'll rustle something up.'

'Well... if you insist.' John pulled out a chair. 'But I'll only stay on one condition.'

Sylvie threw him a questioning look.

'You don't burn the toast!' he joked, slipping into familiar banter with his wife, as though it was just another regular morning in the Baxter household and they were sitting down to breakfast together like they used to. John glanced at Sylvie. It was meant as a joke.

He was just wondering if he had overstepped the mark when Sylvie burst out laughing. 'I promise I will not burn the toast. 'Now sit and tell me what you want for breakfast.'

John relaxed and sat down at the kitchen table. He only asked for tea and toast because he didn't want Sylvie to go to too much trouble, but she insisted on cooking a full English breakfast for both of them. He didn't argue. In truth, after all the excitement first thing this morning, he was famished.

John had forgotten all about the dog hiding upstairs in his apartment until Sylvie put the bacon and sausages into the frying pan and Alfie made an appearance. John watched him scurrying across the kitchen floor, heading straight for the sizzling sausages. He came to a halt by the cooker and sat at Sylvie's feet sniffing the air and licking his chops.

Sylvie ignored him. John tried to do the same.

When Sylvie finished cooking, she walked over to the table with two plates. She set the plates down, one in front of John, and took a seat at the table opposite him.

'That looks delicious,' John complimented her, his mouth watering at the sight of sausages, fried tomatoes, mushrooms, crispy bacon, scrambled eggs, and fried bread. This was the first time they'd had breakfast together in weeks. It felt like old times. He tucked into his English breakfast and glanced across the table at Sylvie doing the same. He smiled.

She returned his smile.

He was enjoying this unexpected treat – not only the cooked breakfast but Sylvie's company – and trying awfully hard not to get irritated by Sylvie's annoying little dog sitting at his feet begging at the table. He opened his mouth to complain about Alfie but thought the better of it. He didn't want to ruin the moment by getting into an argument over the dog. Instead, John gazed out of the french doors into the garden.

He imagined, just for a moment, that he hadn't gone ahead and converted the house into two apartments. This was just another ordinary day sitting together having breakfast in the basement kitchen of their London home, with no worries about debts and unpaid bills, and no thoughts of tenants or missions or the plan. And no new addition to the household; he glanced at Alfie. For the first time since he converted the house, John wished he could turn back the clock. He looked across the table at Sylvie, who was also uncharacteristically quiet, and wondered if she was thinking the same thing.

'Sylvie?'

Sylvie looked up. 'Yes?'

'I wish…'

He was interrupted by the phone.

Alfie started barking.

Sylvie put down her knife and fork. 'I better answer that.'

John watched Sylvie get up from the table to answer the phone.

'Hello?'

John turned in his chair to look out the garden once more. He never seemed to find the right moment to tell Sylvie that he missed her. That he wished he could go back to the way things were. That he had made a real mess of things. That he was sorry.

'Yes Julia, I still want the puppy training classes…'

John rolled his eyes and looked down at the dog sitting at his feet. 'What are you looking at?' He was annoyed by the phone call interrupting their breakfast date.

Alfie wagged his tail.

'You have?' said Sylvie excitedly. 'Oh Julia, that's marvellous news. When...?'

John pushed his chair back and stood up. There was no use hanging around if that was Julia on the other end of the line; Sylvie would be on the phone for ages. He gathered up his plate and walked over to the dishwasher.

Sylvie was busy flicking through her diary.

John loaded the dishwasher with their dirty plates and turned to go.

'Yes, I'm free that day. What time? Oh, I see... yes... fine.'

He glanced at Sylvie and caught her attention. He mouthed *I'd better go,* pointing towards the door.

Sylvie nodded.

John walked over to the stairs. He turned around to wave goodbye when he noticed the dog had followed him. 'Oh no, you don't,' John admonished Alfie. 'You are not coming too.'

'Hang on a moment, Julia.' Sylvie held the phone away from her ear. 'Alfie! Come here this instant.'

Alfie sat down in front of John and wagged his tail.

Sylvie made several attempts at attracting his attention. All to no avail. John bent down and pushed Alfie towards her – still seated on his rear – along the smooth tiled floor.

Sylvie returned to her phone conversation. 'Hi Julia, sorry about that. Now, where were we?'

John left the dog sitting in the middle of the kitchen floor and made a hasty retreat towards the stairs. He glanced over his shoulder.

The dog was gone.

When he turned back, Alfie was sitting halfway up the kitchen stairs looking down at him and wagging his tail. Alfie had craftily scampered past John when he wasn't looking.

John glared at the dog. He wasn't keen on the thought of trying to exit Sylvie's apartment while wrestling with a wriggly cocker spaniel determined to follow him back upstairs. Little wonder Sylvie was organising puppy training classes. Behind all that cute spaniel playfulness was a wilful little monster intent on getting his own way. He had Sylvie wrapped around his little paw.

'I am not so easily taken in with those doleful eyes and that cute puppy dog expression,' John told the dog as he walked up the stairs. John picked Alfie up and returned to the kitchen. He put the dog down, and said in an authoritative tone of voice, 'Sit!'

Alfie immediately sat on command.

John looked at him in surprise.

He wasn't the only one staring at Alfie in surprise; across the room, Sylvie had noticed it too.

John scratched his head. Now, all he had to do was get the dog to stay where he was. John spoke in an authoritative voice once more, 'Stay!' he commanded, holding his hand up in a stop sign. He didn't have a clue what he was doing; it just felt like the right thing to do.

Alfie, still sitting on the floor, cocked his head to one side.

John slowly backed away watching the dog intently. He turned around and put one foot on the bottom stair. He glanced over his shoulder expecting the dog to come bounding after him, but Alfie hadn't moved from his spot.

John walked up the stairs resisting the urge to turn around, in case the dog took that as an invitation to follow. He reached the top of the stairs without any sign of Alfie.

Sylvie heard John walk out of her apartment into the communal hall, and the faint sound of his footsteps on the way up the next flight of stairs to his apartment.

Sylvie looked at Alfie in astonishment. Alfie was still sitting on the kitchen floor, wagging his tail, waiting for his next command. If that wasn't enough, Sylvie assumed that as soon as John was out of sight, Alfie would scamper up the stairs after him. But he didn't. Sylvie had a feeling that if John had called him, Alfie would have come in an instant. That gave Sylvie an idea. 'Julia, can you hang on a minute, there's something I need to do?' Sylvie put the phone down and called out, 'Alfie?'

Alfie turned his head in her direction.

'Come here,' Sylvie patted her legs, willing her puppy to do as he was told. 'Come on, you can do it.'

Alfie stood up.

'Good boy,' said Sylvie encouragingly. 'What a good dog. That's right, come to Mummy.'

Alfie stretched, turned around and padded over to the french doors to look outside.

'Blast!' said Sylvie in annoyance, wondering why Alfie did as he was told for John and not for her? It wasn't fair. He didn't even like dogs. If he was so good with dogs, maybe she should ask him to show her how to train her puppy instead of going to all the bother of attending classes. Sylvie dismissed that idea. John didn't know the first thing about dogs either. Sylvie decided it must have been a fluke.

She picked up the phone. 'I'm still here, Julia. Now let me write the date and time of the puppy class in my diary so I won't forget.' Fluke or not, there was another reason Sylvie didn't want to ask John for help with her new puppy. She was embarrassed enough as it was over the number of times she had run upstairs for his help. It was making her wonder whether, after nearly four decades of marriage, she was so dependent on her husband that she was no longer capable of living on her own.

'I'm fine, Julia...Yes, I know I sound a bit low,' admitted Sylvie. 'It's just that things keep going wrong in the apartment.' Sylvie told her all about the nightmarish last few days. She listened as Julia reassured her that she was having a run of bad luck – that's all. In fact, Julia thought it was quite understandable, considering they had recently converted the house. With all that building work something was bound to crop up sooner or later.

'You're right,' said Sylvie, feeling better already.

Julia suggested she could pop in to see Sylvie and cheer her up. She wouldn't be able to make it for a couple of days because she had some unexpected repairs on her houseboat.

When Julia retired, she sold her London flat and bought a houseboat on Regent's Canal, in Little Venice. Evidently, it hadn't been all plain sailing. 'We can commiserate together,' said Sylvie. By the sound of it, she wasn't the only one having a run of bad luck at the moment.

Julia liked the sound of that.

Sylvie picked up her pen. 'It's a date then. I'll write it down in my diary.' She quickly scribbled Julia's name in her diary, then signed off with, 'In the meantime, fingers crossed, nothing else goes wrong in my apartment.'

John returned home to the apartment upstairs after a delicious home-cooked breakfast with his wife and decided to phone Dave straightaway to give him an update on how things were progressing. He confidently told Dave that Sylvie would be moving back in with him in no time. That's when Dave made a suggestion that took him completely by surprise.

'Abort the next mission?' John repeated, astounded at the suggestion. 'Are you saying we should stop the plan *before* it's completed?'

He heard Dave sigh down the phone before he responded. 'What I'm saying John, is that perhaps you should quit while you're ahead.'

Quit? Was he out of his mind? 'Are you out of your mind? What's the point of a plan if you don't follow it through?' John always completed a plan. Everybody knew that. Dave knew that. 'But I've still got one mission left,' complained John.

'Depends which way you look at it,' countered Dave. 'After the success of Operation *Lights Out* and Operation *Danger Mouse*...'

John was listening and nodding his head.

'Not to mention the fire alarm that went off in Sylvie's apartment this morning,' continued Dave, 'which was quite fortuitous, especially considering the added bonus that you were invited to stay for breakfast afterwards.'

John continued to listen and nod in agreement.

'Well, don't you think enough is enough? The fire alarm has saved you from the bother of carrying out the final mission.'

'Yes, but that was just dumb luck,' John protested. 'It wasn't *planned.*'

'I know, but maybe you shouldn't look a gift horse in the mouth.'

John remained silent on the other end of the line. Dave's suggestion was not at all what he had expected to hear when he gleefully picked up the phone to tell him about the latest news on the home front.

'Look, John, there's a reason why I think you should abort the final mission.'

'Which is?'

'There's something you haven't stopped to consider.'

'And what is that, exactly?' John was losing patience.

'What if something goes wrong?'

'Well, that's just ridiculous,' scoffed John. As far as he was concerned that wasn't even a remote possibility. Nothing had gone wrong so far. In fact, everything had not only gone according to plan but far exceeded their expectations. Surely, that was even more reason to crack on and finish what they started.

'John, are you listening to me?'

John wasn't listening. He didn't agree with Dave's sentiments at all. It was a stupid idea to stop now. He had no intention of aborting the final mission.

Operation *Noah's Ark* was a go.

8

Sylvie was on her hands and knees on the kitchen floor when the doorbell rang. 'Drat!' She was in the middle of trying to mop up a flood in her kitchen. She had bathroom towels, dishcloths and highly absorbent paper towels all over the floor. And Julia had arrived early.

She got off her hands and knees, wiped her wet hands down the front of her trousers, and walked up the stairs to answer the door.

It was Tuesday. For reasons Sylvie no longer remembered, she always did her washing on a Tuesday. Shortly before Julia was due to arrive, she'd loaded the washing machine with her dirty laundry. As soon as she switched it on Sylvie spotted a puddle of water seeping out over the floor, which quickly turned into a flood. She'd stopped the wash cycle immediately. But it was too late. Fortunately, she had a tiled floor so the water would cause no lasting damage. Something had gone wrong with her washing machine.

'What happened?' asked Julia when Sylvie answered the door.

Sylvie looked down at her clothes. The knees of her trousers were soaked through where she had been kneeling on the wet floor. She sighed heavily. 'It's that run of bad luck we were talking about the other day.'

Julia followed Sylvie downstairs into the kitchen and rolled up her sleeves. 'First of all, let's get this kitchen floor mopped up,' said Julia, taking charge of the situation. 'And then why don't I take a look and see if I can find out what's wrong with your washing machine?'

Sylvie readily agreed. Julia had lived on her own for years without a man about the house. She was used to dealing with household emergencies that cropped up from time to time.

Once the kitchen floor was mopped, and all the sopping wet towels and dishcloths were deposited in the sink, Julia knelt and opened the kitchen cupboard under the sink unit to see what the problem might be.

'I can't understand it,' Sylvie was saying as she picked up a wet dishcloth and rung out the excess water into the sink. 'The washing machine was working perfectly fine only last week.'

Julia reached into the cupboard. 'That's strange.'

'What is it?'

Julia looked up at Sylvie. 'The inflow pipe seems to have come loose so when you turned the washing machine on, instead of filling up with water, it flooded your kitchen floor.'

Sylvie shrugged. 'There's nothing strange about that. As you said before, Julia, these things happen. Can you fix it?'

Julia nodded. 'I think so.' She reached inside the cupboard and fitted the pipe back into place. 'These things don't come loose of their own accord, you know,' she remarked as she tightened it up. 'There, that just about does it.' Julia got up off her knees and reached over to switch on the washing machine. 'Let's check this works.'

They both watched as the washing machine started filling with water. Nothing seeped out over the floor.

'Thank goodness for that,' Sylvie breathed a sigh of relief, not keen on the thought of running upstairs for John's help – yet again. It wasn't that she didn't welcome his support. She did, very much so. However, she didn't appreciate being reminded how dependent she was on her husband. It hadn't always been like that. Once upon a time, before she married, she was just like Julia. She was independent. She could cope on her own. But somewhere down the line she had lost confidence in herself or become just plain lazy, or perhaps a little of both.

'Before you arrived, I was about to run upstairs for the umpteenth time and call on John for help.'

'Hmm.' Julia stood staring at Sylvie's washing going round in the machine.

Sylvie studied her best friend. 'What are you thinking?'

Julia turned to Sylvie. 'I want to hear all about your recent run of bad luck. Every last detail.'

Over lunch Sylvie told Julia all about the eventful past few days, ending her tale with, 'I've just been so lucky that John was on hand to help a lady in distress.' Sylvie smiled.

Julia did not return the smile.

Sylvie noted Julia's grim expression. 'What's wrong?'

'You're not going to like it,' warned Julia, before she went ahead and said exactly what she thought about Sylvie's apparent run of bad luck.

'*Sabotage!*' exclaimed Sylvie in astonishment. 'You think John has been sabotaging my apartment?'

'Oh yes.'

She stared at Julia in disbelief. 'Well, that's just ridiculous.'

'Is it?' Julia cast a hand around the kitchen. 'Do you honestly imagine John likes what you've done with the place?'

'But...but he said he liked it.'

Julia gave her one of those looks which said, *come off it, Sylvie.*

'From what you've told me, the original idea was that you could temporarily move into the garden apartment to have a bit of time to yourself. And while you're down here, you could see if anything untoward cropped up that might need sorting out before he found a tenant. Am I right so far?'

Sylvie slowly nodded her head. She was beginning to get an idea where Julia was going with this.

Julia narrowed her eyes. 'Bit of a coincidence, all these things suddenly cropping up, eh?' She looked around Sylvie's kitchen. 'I don't think he expected you to start redecorating the place. Maybe he thought it was time you moved out.'

'Why now?'

'Take a look around you, Sylvie. Does this still look like a temporary arrangement to you?'

Sylvie cast her eyes around the kitchen and thought about all the things she had done to the apartment since she moved in. It had started as a bit of harmless fun when she went shopping with Julia to get a rug and some cushions to brighten up John's bland rental apartment. In the beginning, all Sylvie wanted was to feel more comfortable while she was temporarily living down-stairs. The problem was that she didn't stop there. With Julia's help and encouragement, and Sylvie's pension lump-sum, together they had transformed John's rental apartment into Sylvie's new home.

'Personally, I think you've got him worried.'

'If he wanted me to move back upstairs, why didn't he just

ask me!' said Sylvie, throwing her arms in the air in frustration.

'Would you have said yes?'

Sylvie stared at Julia. 'Okay, that might explain the *why,* but it doesn't explain the *how.* If it was sabotage, like you said, it doesn't explain how he got inside the apartment without my knowledge. I'm the only one with the keys to the front door.'

As soon as those words slipped out of Sylvie's mouth, both Sylvie and Julia exchanged glances and turned their heads simultaneously in the direction of the french doors that opened on to the back garden. Sylvie didn't have the spare key.

Sylvie narrowed her eyes when she recalled returning from walkies with Alfie the other day to discover the garden gate was ajar. She always made sure it was shut in case Alfie got out. Which begged the question: why was the garden gate swinging open? Unless...

Sylvie turned to Julia. 'Okay, let's suppose for a moment that you're right, that John has been in and out of the apartment without my knowledge. How am I going to find out for sure?'

Julia considered that for a moment and then her face lit up. 'I've got a brilliant idea. Here's what you should do...'

9

It was Tuesday. For reasons John no longer remembered, Sylvie always did her washing on a Tuesday. That's why he had pencilled in his next mission, Operation *Noah's Ark,* on that particular day of the week. And that's why his last mission to complete the plan should have turned out the most straightforward. All he had to do was loosen the cold-water inflow pipe under the sink unit in Sylvie's kitchen some time before Tuesday. Then just sit back and wait for the drama to unfold. It should have been that easy, but to John's surprise nothing happened.

When Tuesday had been and gone with no sign of Sylvie banging on his door after The Great Flood, John had gone to bed that evening trying to fathom what might have gone wrong with the mission. He decided to sleep on it.

In the morning, he wrote down two possibilities in his little black book: he failed to loosen the pipe sufficiently, or Sylvie simply hadn't used the washing machine.

'But washday is a Tuesday,' said John, scratching his head and staring at the little black book open in front of him. The only way to find out what had happened for certain was to go back behind enemy lines and do some recon. It had crossed his mind that he ought to phone Dave and give him an update on his progress, or lack of, with Operation *Noah's Ark*. However, he wasn't too keen on telling Dave that there had been a slight setback. He didn't want to give Dave any excuse to say *I told you so*. As far as John was concerned nothing had gone wrong. There had just been a slight delay in completing the mission – that's all.

He closed the little black book and checked the time. Sylvie was due to take Alfie for his morning walk. John wandered out of his study into the lounge and stood by the bay window. He glanced down at the street below just in time to catch Sylvie opening the front gate. He watched her striding up the road in the direction of the park with Alfie pulling on his lead.

John gathered up his bag of tools and left his apartment. He paused at the front gate where he had seen Sylvie leaving with the dog five minutes ago. He glanced in both directions up and down the street. Sylvie was nowhere in sight.

John stepped on to the pavement, closed the gate behind him, and walked briskly around the corner alongside their end-terrace house. He was aiming straight for the side gate into the back garden. Crossing the lawn, he came to a halt on the patio outside the french doors. He was just putting the key in the lock when he thought he saw something reflected in the glass.

He turned around and stared into the garden. At the far end of the lawn, he spotted Sylvie's washing hanging out to dry on the rotary clothesline. So she *had* used the washing machine yesterday. John stood there frowning. She hadn't run upstairs banging on his door, which meant he couldn't have loosened the pipe sufficiently. Perhaps this time he would have to disconnect it altogether. It would mean a delay of another week to complete Operation *Noah's Ark* as washday had come and gone.

It did fleetingly cross his mind that maybe now was the time to take Dave's advice and forget about the last mission because it was beginning to feel like more trouble than it was worth. He had already snuck into Sylvie's apartment on three separate occasions. John didn't want to think about when his luck might run out. So, he didn't. What he thought about was the importance of completing the plan. He kept reminding himself that this was just a minor set-back – nothing more.

John unlocked the french doors and stepped inside the kitchen. He walked straight over to the sink unit, opened the cupboard door under the sink, and knelt to look at the inflow pipe. John unfastened his bag of tools and then reached into the cupboard to disconnect the hose. That's when he discovered it wasn't loose at all. In fact, he was having a bit of trouble loosening the pipe, as though someone had tightened it up.

John was absolutely one hundred percent positive he had loosened that hose. He was completely flummoxed. He scratched his head and leaned further into the cupboard to take a closer look. 'That doesn't make any sense,' said John out loud.

'What doesn't make any sense?'

Stunned at the sound of Sylvie's voice right behind him, John hit his head in his haste to get out from under the sink unit. '*Yeow!*' he yelped, rubbing his head as he turned around.

Shocked at the sight of his wife standing right there in the kitchen, John blurted, 'You were meant to be out walking the dog.'

'My kitchen floor flooded yesterday,' said Sylvie calmly. 'But then you knew that – didn't you.'

John gulped. He stood up and smiled nervously. 'Sylvie, I can explain—'

Sylvie cut him off. 'Don't give me excuses. I know exactly what you've been up to, John Baxter.' She stepped forward and held out her hand. 'Now give me that key!'

'It's not what you think, Sylvie. I thought I heard a burglar.' John was trying to think up a plausible excuse on the hoof that didn't sound like complete bullshit. 'So, I came downstairs to investigate.'

'Oh, really. You thought the burglar was hiding under the sink unit?'

John's face dropped.

Sylvie put her hands on her hips. 'What a fool I've been. And to think, I even made you breakfast!'

'Ah-ha!' said John, pointing at Sylvie. 'The fire alarm wasn't me!' he proclaimed, realising too late that that statement was tantamount to an admission of guilt.

'So it *was* you! My lights going out. The rat infestation. I bet you found that hilarious when you discovered me and Alfie standing on the kitchen table scared out of our wits.' Sylvie shook her head and demanded, 'Why did you do it, John?'

Although Sylvie believed Julia had been right about John's motives, she still wanted to hear it from the horse's mouth. She must have been out of her mind to think for one moment that he liked what she'd done to the apartment. She knew their taste in décor was entirely at odds.

Despite that, what she didn't understand was why the sudden urgency to get her to move back upstairs? She thought he was going to give her as much time as she needed. Something was up, and Sylvie wanted to get to the bottom of all these shenanigans. 'Well?'

John saw a very, very slim chance to redeem himself. He

thought carefully before he answered that question. 'I miss my wife,' he said in all honesty. 'I thought that if things started to go wrong in the apartment, it might make you realise how much you missed having your husband around and perhaps you'd want to move back in with me.'

Sylvie's hands dropped from her hips in surprise. She was expecting some cock-and-bull story and was taken aback by his candour. It sounded like a genuine heartfelt answer. 'Why on earth didn't you simply ask me to move back in with you?'

'Because I thought you'd say no,' whispered John, staring at the floor.

'How would know for sure unless you asked me?'

John looked up. That's exactly what Dave had said before they started the plan to sabotage Sylvie's apartment.

'Well?'

John looked at her agog. It couldn't possibly be that simple. If he had any inkling that all he had to do was ask, he would have dispensed with the missions and just asked her to move back upstairs.

Sylvie cocked her head to one side. 'Are you going to ask me – or not?'

John didn't want to get his hopes up. He still couldn't quite believe, after everything he'd done, she was willing to give him a second chance. John took a moment to recover realising the plan was nearly complete. Who would have thought that after all this he could still tell Dave the last mission was a success.

He took a deep breath. Feeling as though he was asking Sylvie for her hand in marriage, John said, 'Sylvie Baxter, will you move back in with me?' He smiled thinking the fox was in the hole.

'No!' said Sylvie emphatically.

'What...?'

'I can't believe you fell for that.' Sylvie smiled mischievously, clearly enjoying herself at John's expense, before her expression turned sour. She glared at him. 'Seriously, do you really think I'd move back upstairs now, after what you've put me through?'

The fox most definitely was not in the hole, thought John miserably. On top of that, the look on Sylvie's face said he was most definitely not in the fox's good books either.

Sylvie glanced at the cupboard under the sink unit before settling her gaze on her husband. 'Who put you up to this?' She didn't believe that he'd thought all this up by himself. She was convinced he had some help. Sylvie would not have been at all surprised to learn that John had been getting these ideas from his brother, Dave. In fact, now she thought about it, hadn't she seen Dave stop by after his holiday?

'It's Dave, isn't it?' Sylvie didn't wait for an answer. 'I knew it! Trust Dave to come up with some hair-brained scheme.'

John looked at his shoes.

'I bet he concocted a plan to get me out of the apartment, thinking up different ways to cause disruption until I caved and moved out. I bet he even called them *missions*.' Sylvie was no stranger to Dave's love affair with all things military.

The look on John's face told Sylvie she'd hit the nail on the head. She rolled her eyes. 'Honestly, when you two get together, you act like a pair of schoolchildren.'

John was looking anywhere but at Sylvie. He realised he was on a losing streak. It crossed his mind that perhaps he should tell her the other reason why he desperately wanted his wife back or, more to the point, his rental apartment. John stole a glance at

Sylvie. Her face looked like thunder. He couldn't tell her the truth now. Not after this fiasco. If she thought he had been acting irresponsible and immature by carrying out Dave's missions to sabotage her apartment, what would she think of him if she found out he had been irresponsible with their money too?

Sylvie said, 'You've had your fun with me, and I've had my fun with you.' Sylvie held out her hand. 'Now, give me that key!'

John gathered up his tools and threw them in his bag. With shoulders hunched he walked slowly to the french doors where Sylvie was standing.

'I mean it, John.'

John got the key out of his trouser pocket and stood there staring at her outstretched hand. He suddenly had a strong sensation of *déjà vu*; they'd been down this road before when Sylvie demanded the key to the garden apartment before she moved in. He shrugged the feeling off and reluctantly placed the key in her hand. He was still holding on to the key fob.

Sylvie gave him an exasperated look. He let go.

He looked at her expectantly, searching her face for any glimmer of hope that she might change her mind and put an end to this living apart nonsense. He tried offering her a disarming smile. When that didn't work, he racked his brain trying to think up something profound to say that would make her reconsider. He couldn't think of a damn thing, apart from the obvious. He opened his mouth to make a grovelling apology, but the look on her face said, *don't even bother John.*

John looked away and caught sight of Alfie sitting on the floor by Sylvie's feet. It gave him an idea. It was something he wouldn't consider under normal circumstances, but he was desperately grasping at straws.

'If you move back in with me,' began John, 'you won't need a puppy trainer.'

Sylvie looked at him quizzically.

'I can train your dog.' John thought that if had to put up with the dog in his apartment, he would have to teach him some house rules. No jumping up on his white sofa for a start. 'Look, I'll show you. Here, boy!'

Alfie slowly backed away.

'Aw, don't do that,' said John as the dog retreated. 'Come!'

Alfie turned around and darted behind Sylvie, poking his head out from behind her legs. Even the dog sensed John was out of favour and made his choice.

John had run out of options. He slunk out of the door and heard the key in the lock behind him.

Operation *Noah's Ark* had just sunk without a trace.

10

John dumped the bag of tools on his kitchen table, found the bottle of Drambuie at the back of a kitchen cupboard – he was intending to save it for a special occasion – and poured himself a drink. It was only ten o'clock in the morning, and he had absolutely nothing to celebrate, but what the heck.

He sat down at the desk in his study and swirled the golden liquid around in the glass before raising it to his lips. He smelt the distinctive aroma of malt whiskey, honey and spices before downing the sweet liqueur in three steady gulps, savouring the intense sensation of his favourite drink sliding down his throat.

John reached for the bottle and poured himself another drink, then opened a desk drawer to retrieve his little black book. He placed it on the desk in front of him and flicked through the pages. Stopping at the last entry that detailed his final mission, he thought about that phone conversation with Dave and his prophetic warning: what if something goes wrong?

'Isn't hindsight a wonderful thing,' said John sarcastically, shaking his head as he picked up the glass of Drambuie. If only he hadn't been so hell-bent on finishing the plan, he might have listened to his brother instead.

John raised his glass. 'To hindsight.' He swallowed the Drambuie and placed the empty glass down on a coaster, resisting the urge to pour a third one. Instead, he grasped the bottle and screwed the lid back on – tight.

John was only an occasional drinker, which amounted to a drink here and there on special occasions, or the odd glass of wine over dinner. Consequently, he could already feel the effects of two glasses of neat whiskey. If he didn't stop there, he could see himself getting very drunk, very quickly, and then who knows what might happen? John didn't know because he had never been drunk in his life. Perhaps he would totter downstairs, knock on Sylvie's door, and tell her the whole sorry financial mess he had got himself into. John shuddered at the thought.

He put the bottle of Drambuie to one side, out of harm's way, and reached for the phone on his desk. He wasn't looking forward to telling Dave that something had gone disastrously wrong on his last mission. He wanted to get the *I told you so* over with as soon as possible.

John knew he was back to square one with Sylvie. There was no question she was going to move out of the garden apartment now. He only had himself to blame. After the success of the last two missions, together with the added bonus of Sylvie's burnt toast setting off the fire alarm, John realised he was under the illusion that nothing could go wrong.

The fact was he had become too blasé; things were going so well that he had stopped being careful and tripped up on his last mission. If he had waited at the window for just a few more minutes before sneaking downstairs, he would have seen Sylvie double-back. She passed the house and darted around the corner dragging a reluctant Alfie behind her, the dog realising that walkies in the park had been abandoned and he was heading to the back garden.

Unbeknown to John, Sylvie had sneaked into the garden ahead of him. She was already sitting on the wooden bench under the old elm tree at the back of the garden when he made an appearance. Sylvie was conveniently hidden from view by the sheets billowing in the wind on her washing line.

Alfie was good enough not to yap and give them away when Sylvie heard the tell-tale click of the garden gate. A few seconds later, she'd risked a peek to check it really was John in her back garden, and not a burglar. She watched him unlock the french doors and step into her kitchen. Sylvie waited another five minutes to be sure she caught him in the act. By the time she ambled down the lawn towards the french doors, all she could see was John's ample derrière as he huffed and puffed under the sink unit, wondering aloud why the pipe he had loosened was loose no longer.

John winced as he recalled Sylvie telling him all this. He wished he hadn't phoned her up, as soon as he got home, and asked her to satisfy his curiosity as to how she had managed to double-back and catch him in the act.

When he found out what a fool he'd been, fortunately he already had the bottle of Drambuie on hand to drown his sorrows when he got off the phone. John stared forlornly at the bottle. He didn't have the first clue what to do now, apart from two stiff drinks at ten o'clock in the morning, and a phone call to his brother to get an earful of recriminations and one big *I told you so*.

Glancing at the clock on the wall, John picked up the phone and dialled Dave's mobile phone number. He knew Dave would be at work. His brother would be out and about on a construction site somewhere. He would be far too busy to have all but the briefest of conversations. That's exactly what John was counting on. He'd jotted everything down in his little black book so he could tick off the facts one by one, aiming to get the debrief out of the way ASAP.

John opened his little black book at the relevant page. While he waited for Dave to answer the phone, he read the latest entries. They made for a depressing read.

Fact: John had breached enemy lines not realising the enemy had changed position. In other words, he screwed up.

Fact: Dave was right, he should have quit while he was ahead.

Fact: Dave would tell him smugly *I told you so,* several times.

Fact: John would get off the phone feeling even lousier than he already did.

John picked up a pen. He was getting ready to tick off each entry during the brief phone call when Dave answered the phone.

Fact: Dave was *not* at work.

John rolled his eyes. Oh great, my day just gets better and better.

It turned out John's timing was completely off. Dave had all the time in the world to be entertained by John's embarrassing tale of the one that got away, because Dave was at home. And he wasn't drowning his sorrows in a bottle of Drambuie, like John, but lying on his sofa watching mind-numbing daytime television – bored. He sounded incredibly pleased that his brother had rung and relieved his boredom.

Dave had come down with a bout of seasonal flu before he had a chance to get his flu jab. That didn't stop him wanting to hear all about John's last mission. 'Every last detail,' Dave added eagerly. 'But let's do this debrief properly. I'll phone you back on my landline so, there's no chance that my mobile phone dies in the middle of hearing all about it.' Dave clicked off.

'Bugger it!' John stared at the phone. How long did Dave think this phone call would take? He reached for the bottle of Drambuie.

Within the short time it had taken Dave to phone back, John was downing his fourth glass of Drambuie and trying to prepare himself for what he imagined would turn out an extremely protracted debrief. Especially when Dave found out he'd screwed up. He wasn't looking forward to it. Dave may have come up with the plan and the missions, but it was up to him to follow them through.

It had all gone horribly wrong when he stopped listening to Dave – that much was obvious. Ever since John could remember, he had always looked up to his big brother and took his word as gospel; a fact that he had forgotten when he went ahead with the last mission, ignoring Dave's sage advice to quit while he was ahead.

After recounting the whole sorry episode that happened downstairs this morning, when Sylvie discovered him under the sink unit in her kitchen, Dave dropped a clanger.

'Let me get this straight,' said John down the phone. 'Are you suggesting your plan was wrong?'

'Not exactly.'

'Well, what are you suggesting – *exactly*?' John didn't want to hear that all these missions had turned out a complete waste of time because *the plan was wrong*.

Dave said, 'Let's both agree that your position has now been compromised.'

John rolled his eyes as Dave explained unnecessarily what he meant. 'Sylvie knows what you've has been up to, sabotaging her apartment.

'Yeah – so?'

Dave continued, 'As a result, new intel has come to light which casts doubt on the original plan. However, on the upside, that might mean the fox is in the hole after all.

John finished his fifth drink in a single gulp, surprised to discover that the more he drank, the more he understood Dave and all his talk of *intel* and *positions* and *foxes*. 'So, just to clarify, Dave, you're saying that as a result of making a *soup sandwich* of my last mission behind enemy lines, I've gathered some new *intel* that might strengthen my *position*. And if I play my cards right, the fox might actually be in the hole as we speak?'

'Um, yes that's exactly what I was saying,' agreed Dave.

'Bravo Zulu,' exclaimed John. 'I'm glad we've cleared that up.' John poured himself another drink.

'Bravo Zulu?' repeated Dave in confusion.

'That's military slang for well done or good. But of course, you knew that,' said John offhand.

'Of course, of course,' Dave lied. He didn't know that but made a mental note to add it to his repertoire.

John added, 'Sometimes Bravo Zulu is just shortened to BZ.' He had no idea how he suddenly knew all this. Perhaps it had something to do with the Drambuie. He tipped his glass at the bottle, '*Salut!*' and downed another drink.

'BZ, you say,' mused Dave.

John asked, 'Please enlighten me as to why you believe we have been working from the wrong plan all along, and why you think the fox might still be in the hole?'

'Roger that,' said Dave, returning to the issue at hand. 'First of all, can you repeat the conversation you had with Sylvie after she discovered you kneeling on the floor in her kitchen with your head under the sink?'

John sighed. Wasn't this just what he deserved; forced to regurgitate that embarrassing episode over and over like some form of mental torture? God, when was this excruciating phone call going to end? John was too drunk to remember that he could choose to put the phone down. Instead, for what felt like the umpteenth time, he repeated the whole cringeworthy conversation he'd had with Sylvie. How many times did Dave need to hear that, 'I asked her to move back upstairs,' John reached for the bottle, 'but she said no.'

'There you have it!'

'Have what?' John said flatly as he poured himself another drink.

'You've gone over the conversation and nowhere did I hear Sylvie say she wouldn't move back in with you.'

John was just lifting his glass to his lips when he stopped and looked quizzically at the phone. 'Dave, are you drunk? You're not making any sense. Of course, she doesn't want to move back in with me. She said so herself. I just told you that.'

'No. You said Sylvie refused to move back upstairs. That doesn't mean she doesn't want to move back in with you.'

John looked at his glass and shook his head, trying to shake off the mental fog that was enveloping his brain. If Dave's use of a double negative wasn't confusing enough, John thought he just heard Dave contradict himself.

'Hold up,' said John, trying to get a handle on what Dave was getting at. 'Let me get this straight—'

'Think about it for a moment,' interrupted Dave. 'Did the words "separated," as in "we're separated," or "I want a divorce," ever enter the conversation?'

'Well...no,' said John slowly, but he did wonder if he'd pushed her on the issue whether they might have. With that thought, John raised his glass and had another shot.

'So, there you have it!'

John refilled his glass wishing Dave would stop saying, there you have it. He was about to reply when he realised this conversation was going around in circles.

Dave continued, and John really wished he wouldn't. 'Sylvie has done up her apartment just the way she wants it. She's had the builders in and redecorated and bought new furniture—'

'Don't remind me,' said John miserably. He was thinking of that hideous Welsh dresser displaying Sylvie's ghastly crockery as he poured himself another drink.

'Well, there you have it!'

Oh, for pities sake! John shook his head in frustration as he raised the glass to his lips.

'John, don't you see? Is it little wonder she won't say yes to moving back in with you? It doesn't mean that she won't have you back. What it does mean is that she wants to stay in her apartment downstairs.'

John blinked and slowly lowered his glass. 'Run that by me one more time. Very. Slowly.' John's head hurt.

'We've been going about this all wrong. The plan was to get Sylvie to move back in with you. But it's obvious she doesn't want to leave her flat and move back upstairs. So, if you want any chance of renting out an apartment, I think you will have to move in with Sylvie.'

John put his glass down. 'Are you saying I have to rent out *my* apartment?'

'That's exactly what I'm saying.'

'But... but I don't want to,' said John sulkily, sounding like a spoilt child on the verge of a tantrum. Sylvie wasn't the only one who had organised her apartment just the way she liked it. John was settled and quite content living upstairs. He couldn't imagine renting out his flat to strangers, not to mention having to move downstairs and live with that godawful vintage-green kitchen, and those bright yellow walls, and that horrible wicker furniture, and that disobedient dog and... and everything. Was he insane? That was never part of the plan.

'I hear you, John. I really do.'

Did I just speak my mind, thought John wishing he hadn't had quite so much to drink?

'Don't you want Sylvie back?'

'Of course, I do!' John said indignantly.

'Then I don't see what your problem is.'

'Have you seen the apartment downstairs?'

'Yes, you know I have. I must admit that it is a little bit different to your— '

'A little bit different!' exclaimed John, his voice dripping with sarcasm. 'How am I going to live with... with...' The word on the tip of John's tongue was *Sylvie*.

He raised an eyebrow realising he had finally come to the crux of the matter; how could he possibly go back to living with his wife? John didn't even know where to begin. There was the clutter for one thing. Sylvie wasn't the tidiest person in the world. Since moving downstairs, it seemed to exacerbate all her bad habits.

'Sometimes,' began John, pointing his finger as though Dave was standing right there in the room, 'she leaves a whole day's worth of washing up stacked in the sink. I've seen it, Dave. I've seen it with my very own eyes!'

Dave sighed heavily down the phone. He knew his brother all too well – and Sylvie. To be honest, he thought they were both as bad as each other. They had got themselves in this predicament – living apart together – and now neither of them would back down and compromise. Both stubbornly digging their heels in and refusing to meet each other half-way. John didn't need his brother and the plan. All he had to do was sit down with his wife and talk things through. The fact that they couldn't even do that was reminiscent of Dave's own experience with three failed marriages behind him. It made him wonder how their marriage had lasted this long.

Dave would never voice that opinion. John had enough on his plate without finding out his brother really didn't believe in the plan to get her back. All he was trying to do was help his brother out of a financial fix in the short-term. Where things were leading with his wife was anybody's guess. Dave didn't know because he would be the first to admit he wasn't exactly an expert in the field of relationships. On the contrary, he seemed to have a gift for screwing things up. Dave only hoped his gift didn't extend to screwing up other people's relationships too. However, by the looks of things, he needn't worry about that. It sounded as though John was managing just fine all on his own.

'Well?' John said impatiently. 'Haven't you got anything to say?'

Dave had plenty to say; he just kept most of to himself. What he did say was, 'Desperate times call for desperate measures, brother. You need to rent out one of the apartments. Why does it have to be the garden apartment? If Sylvie won't move back in with you, why not suggest moving in with her? Show her you can live by her rules for a change.'

John picked up his drink and sat swirling the liquid around in the glass, silently contemplating this new plan. The annoying thing was, despite being blind drunk, Dave's new plan made perfect sense.

'You've got to take one for the team, John. You will have to compromise and let go of your apartment in order to move in with Sylvie. It's the only solution to your problem.'

John gulped down another shot and sat there staring into the bottom of his empty glass. Wasn't this poetic justice if it turned out that he was the one who was forced to give up his apartment? After all, it was his idea to convert the house into two flats. It was his idea to rent one out for an extra income. And it was his idea that had got them into this financial mess in the first place. Perhaps this was the price he had to pay to sort all this out once and for all.

The more John thought about it, the more he was coming around to the idea that Dave's plan might work. Another consideration was that if he rented out his place, it would save him the time and expense of getting a builder in to turn the garden apartment back to its original condition before Sylvie got her hands on it. Sylvie's one-bedroomed apartment in its current state, with its brightly coloured décor and clutter, would not be to everybody's taste. Consequently, it might not be easy to find a tenant. John would undoubtedly make more money from renting out his two-bed apartment. With its clean lines and contemporary feel, John reckoned he'd find a tenant in no time.

John grudgingly conceded it was a good plan. Excellent in fact, from a financial standpoint. He was still unhappy about the prospect of tenants living in his flat upstairs, but Dave was right: he had to take one for the team.

'John?'

'Roger that. I'll do it.'

'Bravo Zulu!' Dave replied, enjoying the banter, although he was wondering where John had suddenly picked up all this military slang. 'Well done,' Dave quickly translated just to be sure they both understood each other.

'Hooah!' John exclaimed gung-ho, punching the air with enthusiasm. He poured himself another drink to toast the new plan. After downing another shot, John suddenly needed the loo. 'I'll be back in a minute, Dave. I need to hit the head.'

'You need to what?'

John returned from the bathroom feeling light-headed and a little dizzy. He staggered to his chair and sat down. He picked up the phone, dropped it, picked it up again and got his arm entangled in the phone wire.

'John, are you there?'

John grunted in reply.

'Good. Now I suggest you strike while the iron is hot. Go downstairs right now and tell Sylvie the time has come to move back into together. Be sure she understands that you want to rent out *your* apartment and move in with her downstairs. If you don't mind me saying, it might be prudent to consider telling her the truth, so she understands the gravity of the situation. Whatever this dance is that's been going on between you two, it's got to stop. No more funny business. You need that rental income if you both want to keep the roof over your heads.'

John rubbed his face with his hand. It all sounded like a good plan. 'There's just one problem, Dave,' murmured John, staring at the half-empty bottle of Drambuie on his desk.

'What's that?'

'I think I'm drunk.'

'You're wasted?'

John nodded.

'But it's only ten thirty in the morning!'

John nodded again. He slowly lowered his head until the side of his face was resting on his desk. The phone receiver lay on the desk in front of his nose. He could still hear Dave talking.

'I'm sure we can still figure this out. You'll have to leave it until later in the day until you've sobered up, but I've got an idea. Weren't you guys planning to have dinner together?'

With his face still resting on the top of his desk, 'Uh,' was all John managed in response. He was too wasted to string a coherent sentence together and tell Dave that after this morning, when Sylvie discovered him sneaking into her kitchen, he had no illusions that the dinner date was now firmly off the menu.

'Why don't you go downstairs later today, when you've slept it off, and offer to cook Sylvie dinner in her apartment as an apology. Sort of like a peace offering.'

John yawned.

'Who knows, one thing might lead to another and... John?'

'One for the team,' mumbled John.

'Are you still there?'

John snored loudly down the phone.

'Roger that,' said Dave and hung up.

11

John woke up with a crick in his neck. He put the phone back in its cradle and dragged himself off to bed to sleep it off. He vaguely remembered Dave's suggestion about cooking dinner for Sylvie, before he drifted off in a drink-induced coma. He'd decided to carry out the plan when he didn't look or smell like the town drunk.

Later that afternoon John had a chicken pie baking in the oven and had showered, shaved and dressed for the second time that day. He was ready to start the new plan. He was convinced that moving into the apartment downstairs was the answer and that Dave's new plan would work. Sylvie did not want to shift out of her apartment, which was something they had not accounted for in the original plan, so the solution was obvious.

John repeated his new mantra, 'You've got to take one for the team,' as he contemplated the new plan to move in with her. It sounded simple enough. There was just one problem. After tripping up on his last mission, how was he going to persuade Sylvie to let him move in with her now? That's where the homemade chicken pie came in.

John knelt and checked the pie in the oven. She said she

really enjoyed the slice he had given her after the success of Operation *Lights Out*. John was hoping Sylvie would let him cook dinner for her – or rather heat up the chicken pie in the oven – while they sat and talked. That was the most important part of the plan, talking things through. John realised belatedly that's where things had started to go wrong when they stopped communicating.

Whether during that conversation he would tell Sylvie the reason he desperately needed the rental income, John was undecided. It depended on how things panned out this evening. The last thing he wanted to do was ruin a perfectly good chicken pie by spilling the beans and admitting he had put their comfortable retirement in jeopardy because he'd made a mistake; Sylvie had yet to find out that he had completely underestimated what the final bill came in at for the conversion. John wasn't looking forward to telling Sylvie the truth.

Perhaps it wouldn't come to that. He recalled something Dave had said before he dozed off in a drunken stupor. Something about having dinner with Sylvie and then one thing might lead to another. In his woozy, drunken state John had an idea. He had kept hold of that idea and was now in the process of carrying it out.

John left the chicken pie cooking in the oven and wandered upstairs to his bedroom where there was an overnight bag unzipped and open on his bed. He had already laid out a pair of neatly folded pyjamas, slippers, his toothbrush and a tube of toothpaste, his shaving kit, the novel he was currently reading, and a clean set of clothes for tomorrow. He then proceeded to carefully pack the bag, clearing the items from his bed as he did so. John zipped up the bag and carried it downstairs. He was just placing it in the lobby by the door when he heard the oven timer ping, signalling his chicken pie was ready.

'Perfect timing.' It was not quite four o'clock in the afternoon, so the chicken pie would need reheating for dinner. That would give him ample time to build bridges with Sylvie beforehand. If after dinner one thing led to another...

John glanced at his overnight bag. The plan was to move downstairs tonight.

He returned to the kitchen and got the chicken pie out of the oven, placing it on a wire rack to cool. Everything was nearly ready. John paced the kitchen floor and then decided to do one last sweep of his apartment before heading downstairs. He always liked to leave his flat clean and tidy before going out, even if he was only stepping out to nip downstairs.

When John was satisfied everything was switched off, the curtains were drawn, and the cushions straightened on the sofa in the lounge, he found himself back in his study. He stood by his desk staring at the half empty bottle of Drambuie. This was it. If all goes according to plan, he might well be leaving his apartment tonight. There was no doubt in his mind that if he could move downstairs, it would solve all his problems. So why wasn't he feeling particularly happy about it?

John's attention was drawn to the little black book on his desk. He picked it up and casually leafed through the pages. John had bought it with the intention of writing down anything that might crop up in the garden apartment that would need fixing by the builder, to avoid the hassle of sorting things out once a tenant moved in. What he hadn't envisaged was that his little black book would become a detailed account of all the irritating things about his nuisance neighbour downstairs – Sylvie.

The experience of having someone living downstairs made him realise the potential pitfalls of renting out one of the apartments. It's not that he thought all tenants were bad news. On the contrary, he imagined that most people at one time or another in their lives had lived in rented accommodation. What was really bothering him was what if he had another Sylvie? What if they had parties, and redecorated, and had pets, and left their televisions on until the early hours? And now, to make matters worse, he had no option but to rent out his flat and move in with Sylvie downstairs.

John was trying very hard not to think about the reality of having tenants living in his flat. Would they look after his home? Would they hoover his new carpet and keep his apartment in pristine condition? John tried not to dwell on the obvious; no tenant was going to treat a rental quite the same as if it were their own property. Instead, what he focused on was how much time and money it would cost to turn Sylvie's apartment back to his own version of normal, and what he considered a prospective tenant would pay good money for. John was trying to convince himself this was a good plan.

'You've got to take one for the team,' John reminded himself as he snapped the little black book shut. He opened a desk drawer and tossed it on top of the pile of unopened bills and red reminder letters that were stacking up. They might be out of sight, thought John shutting the drawer, but they were most definitely not out of mind.

He returned to the kitchen and checked the chicken pie had cooled sufficiently before he placed it on a plate. John took the pie with him and gathered up his overnight bag on his way out. He walked down the stairs and knocked politely on Sylvie's door.

John glanced at his overnight bag. He had put it down out of sight to one side of the door, afraid that coming prepared might back-fire if Sylvie spotted it. He knew it was rather presumptuous of him to pack the overnight bag. However, in the eventuality things went well, and Sylvie wanted him to stay tonight, he didn't want any chance she might change her mind when he whipped upstairs to get some things.

John stared at the door. Where was she? He was sure she was in, although he hadn't heard the sound of the dog barking which generally happened when he knocked on her door. He rang the doorbell in case she was downstairs in the kitchen and hadn't heard him knocking. He nervously shifted his weight from one foot to the other waiting for her to answer the door.

Anxious to get this right, John had rehearsed his lines. He was going to start by apologising about his behaviour, sabotaging her apartment like that. Although he was going to add that he wasn't entirely to blame. Dave had put him up to it. Then he was going to tell her how much he loved her – true. How much he loved what she had done to the garden apartment – untrue. And that he understood why she preferred to stay in her apartment rather than move back upstairs – complete bullshit. He couldn't figure out was wrong with his place.

John heard footsteps behind the door and the sound of the key in the lock. He glanced at his freshly baked chicken pie. John took a deep breath as he held out the pie in front of him. He was really looking forward to making her dinner and —

The door opened.

John took an involuntary step back in surprise. 'Who the hell are you?' John momentarily forgot about the plate in his hands and just caught the chicken pie in time before it slid off the plate.

When John had recovered the pie, he looked past the stranger standing in the doorway of Sylvie's apartment. 'Where's Sylvie?'

'Sylvie's out in the garden teaching Alfie the sit command as we speak. I think Sylvie is marvellous.' He hastily rephrased, 'Ah, what I meant to say was, she's doing very well with the lessons.'

'You're the dog-trainer?' John frowned. He assumed all dog-trainers were Barbara Woodhouse types, not bloody Nigel Havers types.

'My name's Nigel by the way.'

Was he joking?

'Nigel Tanner.'

John raised an eyebrow. 'I didn't know dog-trainers did house calls. I thought she was going to puppy training classes.' Not having one-to-one sessions in the privacy of her own home. Alone. Together. Just the two of them.

'Ah yes, well it turns out that Sylvie and I have a mutual friend called Julia. She contacted me and thought it would be a grand idea if I did the puppy training with Sylvie.'

John scowled. He might have guessed Julia would have a hand in this.

'Julia suggested that Sylvie might get on better having one-to-one sessions at home.'

'I bet she did,' scoffed John, looking him up and down. He knew exactly what Julia was up to. One-to-one sessions indeed. 'I want to speak to Sylvie,' demanded John.

'Sylvie sent me upstairs to answer the door. I'm afraid she asked me to tell you that she's busy. Shall I take that for you?' Nigel reached for the pie and took the plate off his hands before John could stop him.

'I say, that smells delicious. I'm sure Sylvie will be delighted.' Nigel started to close the door. 'I'll be sure to let Sylvie know it was her neighbour upstairs who called round with the pie.' And with that, he shut the door.

John glanced at his overnight bag sitting redundant on the floor outside her door. He threw his arms up in frustration. It had all been for nothing: the pie, the overnight bag, his plan to beg Sylvie to let him move in with her. He knew he was on a losing streak the minute Nigel opened the door.

John had little choice but to beat a hasty retreat and regroup; that would most certainly involve reacquainting himself with a half-finished bottle of Drambuie.

He bent down to pick up the bag and turned towards the stairs wondering what the dog-trainer had meant by that last remark, *her neighbour upstairs?*

Sylvie stared at the homemade chicken pie on the kitchen table. She knew what John was up to. That pie was an apology. She had to admit, it smelt delicious. But if he thought he was getting around her that easily, he could think again. Did he really believe she was such a pushover?

'I say, you've got such nice neighbours, Sylvie. 'I wish my neighbours cooked me chicken pies.' Nigel peered at Sylvie. 'Are you absolutely sure there's nothing going on between you two?'

Sylvie avoided his gaze, thinking *you only ought to know.* Julia had been very naughty and neglected to fully explain Sylvie's current living arrangements to Nigel before his visit, implying that the man living in the apartment upstairs was only her neighbour.

Sylvie stole a glance at Nigel and decided not to correct that misconception. Julia wasn't lying when she said Nigel was very charming. When Sylvie found out she was having one-to-one puppy training classes, she was worried about the cost. Julia insisted on paying for them herself. She said it was her treat. As soon as Sylvie answered the door to Nigel, she understood what Julia meant by that comment. Sylvie knew what she was up to. She was trying to fix Sylvie up with one of her single, available friends. Sylvie smiled. Sometimes Julia was incorrigible.

Sylvie stared at the chicken pie and wondered how she was going to eat all that by herself. On the spur of the moment, she looked at Nigel, and said, 'Would you like to stay for dinner?' Sylvie didn't see the harm in asking Nigel to join her for dinner. She couldn't let a perfectly good chicken pie go to waste, now could she?

John did not head straight for his study and the bottle of Drambuie, as was his intention. On the way upstairs he'd had a change of heart. Perhaps all was not lost? Maybe if he waited for Nigel to leave after the dog-training session, then he would have an opportunity to return downstairs when he knew the coast was clear. All was not lost he repeated to himself, until it started to get dark outside and, as far as John was aware, Nigel still hadn't left. John had been keeping watch at the front window. How long did it take to train a dog to come, sit, and stay for goodness' sake? He had attempted it in Sylvie's kitchen that one time and it worked. What was taking so long?

Perhaps Sylvie wasn't getting it, and she should accept that owning a dog really wasn't for her. It would certainly make his life easier. He didn't like animals in the house with their hairs and fleas and god-knows-what-else. He knew that Julia had bought the dog for Sylvie so she would have some company while she was living on her own downstairs. John reasoned that once he moved in, the mutt could go because Sylvie wouldn't be lonely anymore.

With thoughts of Sylvie not being lonely anymore, John's focus of attention returned to her visitor, Nigel. John checked the time and started to pace. Once again, he was back to wondering what was taking so long? This dog-training session was going on far longer than he anticipated. It was making him feel uncomfortable. What were they up to down there?

John opened his apartment door and listened.

Nothing.

He crept halfway down the stairs.

Still nothing.

John continued down the stairs until he was standing on the bottom stair. That's when he heard voices. Were Sylvie and Nigel talking in her lounge? John resisted the urge to step off the bottom stair and put his ear to her door. Instead, he leaned forward, held his breath and listened intently. Was that the chink of wine glasses? John's eyebrows shot up in consternation. Bloody hell, had this turned into a date?

The door to Sylvie's apartment suddenly opened, catching him unawares. Frozen like a rabbit in headlights, John saw Nigel step out of Sylvie's apartment. Fortunately, he had his back to the stairs as he stood in the doorway talking to Sylvie, which gave John a chance to scoot back upstairs before he was seen. Luckily, he was only wearing socks which softened his footfalls as he made a hasty retreat. Reaching the top of the stairs, John dived into his apartment and hid behind the door. He kept the door open a crack so he could spy on Nigel. To John's utter relief, Nigel wasn't staying the night.

'Thank you for dinner, Sylvie. Your neighbour's chicken pie was delicious.'

John scowled.

'We must do it again sometime.'

John strained to hear Sylvie's response. He opened his door a bit wider.

'Yes, I would like that, Nigel, but unfortunately I'm going on a trip. Perhaps we can arrange something when I get back?

A trip? John arched a questioning eyebrow.

'Sounds all a bit hush-hush,' said Nigel.

John thought so too.

'I'm sorry for sounding so vague,' Sylvie replied. 'I have some family business to attend to in Cornwall. My mother passed away, and I'm going there to—'

—Spread her ashes, thought John recalling that business. It sounded as though Sylvie had found the cottage.

'Forgive me, Sylvie, I didn't mean to pry,' said Nigel earnestly.

'No, not at all. You don't have to apologise. Look, as soon as I get back, I'll give you a call, and we'll make a date.'

A date? John shut his apartment door and retreated to his study.

John sat in his study with a glass of Drambuie in his hand, back on the phone to Dave. 'And that's what happened,' John said miserably. He had just finished giving Dave a blow-by-blow account of the whole sorry episode.

John had started by telling Dave all about Sylvie's one-to-one puppy training sessions with the dog-trainer, aptly named Nigel, who looked the spitting image of his namesake, that suave actor he'd seen on television. He ended the tale with how he lost his chicken pie when it fell into enemy hands. The chicken pie wasn't the only thing he'd lost in the course of his visit downstairs. After meeting Nigel, John had lost confidence in the plan to move in with Sylvie.

'Describe Sylvie's new friend.'

'I thought I did that already,' said John curtly. He didn't see why he had to repeat himself. And he didn't appreciate the way Dave emphasised the word *friend*.

'No, I mean in detail this time. His hairstyle. His physic. The clothes he was wearing. Every last detail.'

John rolled his eyes. Why did his brother have a knack of rubbing salt into the wound? John sighed and did as he was asked hoping there was a point to all this.

'I see.'

'You see what, exactly?' said John irritably.

'I see that we have a problem on our hands.'

'Oh, ya think?' John blurted sarcastically, sounding like his youngest daughter, Chloe. John felt depressed enough as it was. Dave was not helping matters by stating the bloody obvious. Meeting Nigel had cast doubt in John's mind about Dave's new plan. What if the issue wasn't simply that Sylvie didn't want to move out of her apartment and back upstairs? What if she didn't want to move back in with her husband?

He really didn't want to face that possibility, so he poured himself another drink and tried to push that thought to the back of his mind. But once again Dave wasn't helping matters.

'Perhaps it's not which apartment she wants to live in that's the issue here, John. Maybe she no longer wants to live with you.'

'Gee thanks, you really know how to cheer a guy up,' said John, even though he was thinking the self-same thing.

'Think about it for a moment. She has moved out. She has left you.'

'It's only temporary.'

'Are you sure about that?'

'Now, hang on one minute.' John was getting cross. 'This morning, you said all I had to do was show my willingness to move in with Sylvie downstairs and rent out my apartment.' John poured himself another drink. 'You said that plan would work.'

'Ah, but now we've got new intel. And that new intel is Nigel, Sylvie's friend.'

John wished he'd stop using that word, *friend*.

'John, I don't mean to sound harsh but have you looked in the mirror lately?'

'Huh?' John was already on to his fourth glass of Drambuie. He could feel the alcoholic haze settling in quite nicely like a dense fog enveloping his brain, making it difficult to grasp what Dave was getting at. He poured himself another drink.

'I said have you looked in the mirror lately?'

'Just a minute!' John quickly downed another shot and rose from his chair. He glided out of his study and did the slalom around his furniture in the lounge, heading for the mirror in the lobby. He took a good look at himself in the mirror. 'Hey, I look like a drunk,' John said to his reflection swaying from side to side.

John staggered back to the phone. 'Yeah,' he said to Dave, 'for your information, I *have* looked in the mirror lately. So there!'

'Er...that was a rhetorical question, John.'

'Oh.'

'But back to my point. Maybe you need to show Sylvie you can change.'

'Change – how?' John wasn't sure he was following Dave, until his brain fog receded for a few seconds, time enough to catch his drift. 'Ah-ha! I get it. You think I should change my appearance to look like Nigel.'

'Yes – why not,' agreed Dave. 'I think meeting Nigel like that, catching you unawares, has done you a favour.'

John believed his brain fog had returned with a vengeance because Dave wasn't making any sense. He didn't see how that unexpected meeting with Mr smooth, debonair, slim, attractive, blue jeans, pressed shirt, dyed hair, I've-got-your-wife-in-my-sights dog-trainer, had done him a favour.

'Think on it a minute, John. If that's what Sylvie is looking for, then you've got a chance to make yourself a more attractive, more appealing proposition, before you suggest moving in with her downstairs. Look, Sylvie's off to Cornwall, and presumably you won't be going with her...?'

'No – I'm not.' John said glumly. He couldn't exactly ask her if he could accompany her to Cornwall. Unless she volunteered that information, how would he explain that he knew about her imminent trip?

'Well, there's the opportunity John. While she's away, you can change your appearance. You could start by shopping for some new clothes. Hey, you could even dye your hair. People do that, you know – even men. When she returns from her trip, you can surprise her with the new John. And then she'll forget all about her friend, Nigel.'

John went quiet. He couldn't decide whether that was the

most stupid idea he'd ever heard or the makings of a bloody brilliant plan. John shrugged and picked up his glass. 'I'll sleep on it.' He put the phone down.

Before he took himself off to bed, John intended to finish his last glass of Drambuie. He always liked to finish what he started. The bottle of Drambuie wasn't going to prove the exception to the rule.

Once he had downed the last glass, he decided the time had come to make a complete ass of himself by going outside in the front garden to tell the whole world how much he loved his wife and wanted her back. And then he'd most likely get himself locked out of the house and have to ring the doorbell. Sylvie would answer the door and see him in a drunken stupor...

John vehemently shook his head. He knew that was a bad idea. The problem was that his alcoholic-induced brain fog had now settled in so thick and heavy that he didn't have the first clue what he might get up to next.

'Oops.' John giggled as he found himself opening the door to his apartment. He was about to step out when he caught sight of himself in the mirror. John paused in front of the mirror and tutted at his reflection. 'Turn around right now, John Baxter, and go to bed before you do something you'll regret.'

John stepped out of his apartment.

12

Sylvie was awoken by the sound of the doorbell on a continuous loop. It sounded as though some kids were playing around in the street and pressed the buzzer as a dare, ready to run off as soon as the occupant of the house came to the door. Sylvie was doubly annoyed by this because it had taken her so long to get off to sleep. She was tossing and turning unable to get the unexpectedly nice evening she'd spent with Nigel out of her mind. Sylvie kept going over the conversation she had with Julia who phoned her soon after Nigel left. Julia asked her how it went with Nigel and the puppy training class. She confessed that not only did it go well, but Nigel stayed for dinner. Julia was delighted by this revelation. Sylvie also told Julia she was worried she might have given him the wrong impression.

'Why, what happened?' Julia asked.

'Nothing happened,' Sylvie hastily replied. What she didn't tell Julia was that something might have. Sylvie never intended to start a relationship. It never even crossed her mind that she might meet somebody else.

Although Sylvie followed Julia's advice about letting go of old things to make way for new experiences in her life, she had only been applying that logic to work and hobbies, not to people. Not to John. Deep down this was just what Sylvie was afraid of. Once she started to make changes in her life, who knows where it might lead? Like, for instance, to a lovely evening with a rather nice man who did not talk about house conversions or tenants or money. They'd spent a pleasant evening together simply enjoying one another's company, which made a refreshing change from John.

Sylvie was lying in bed wondering how she was going to get back to sleep once the kids got fed up with their game. If they didn't pack it in soon, someone would have to answer the door and put a stop to it. Sylvie was lying under her warm duvet hoping John would hear the doorbell and answer the front door. She wanted him to give those kids a piece of his mind for disturbing them at this ungodly hour.

Sylvie could still hear the doorbell, and there was no sign of John thumping down the stairs to put a stop to it.

'Oh, for heaven's sake!' Sylvie climbed out of bed, put on her dressing gown, and stormed out of her apartment.

When Sylvie opened the front door, she couldn't believe her eyes. 'What on earth are you doing out here at this hour?' Her first thought was that she must be dreaming until she saw the taxi moving off from the kerb. All the same, Sylvie said, 'I'm not dreaming, am I?'

'No, Mum, you're not dreaming.'

Sylvie stared at her daughter in disbelief, completely taken aback that she was standing right here on her doorstep. She had no idea Jess was on her way home from Australia.

Jess stepped inside the hallway into Sylvie's warm embrace.

Sylvie hugged her close and kissed her daughter's tanned face.

She then stood back, holding her at arm's length, overjoyed to see her.

'Why didn't you tell me you were coming home?' Sylvie glanced upstairs. 'Hang on a minute, I must go upstairs and wake up your father to tell him—'

'No, Mum, don't do that,' Jess cut in, looking up the stairs and frowning.

'He'll be over the moon to see you.'

'I know. But it's three o'clock in the morning, and I'm exhausted after my long-haul flight. You know what Dad will be like with all the questions about my trip and how long I'm staying and—'

'How long *are* you staying?' asked Sylvie, watching Jess take the rucksack off her back and dump it on the floor in the hall.

'It's just a flying visit, I'm afraid. I can only stay a few days. My job allowed me some compassionate leave.'

'Oh Jess, you do realise you missed Grandma's—' Sylvie stopped abruptly. The funeral was weeks ago. Jess knew that. So why had she flown all this way?

'I didn't come for that. I came to see you,' Jess glanced up the stairs, 'and Dad.'

Sylvie looked at Jess in surprise. Unlike her little sister, Chloe, Jess never ran back to Mum and Dad if she had a problem. Sylvie regarded her anxiously. 'Jess, what's wrong? What's happened?'

'Why don't we go inside, Mum?' Jessica cast her eyes around the communal hall. 'You'll have to lead the way. It all looks so... different.'

'Oh yes, of course. This way,' said Sylvie, heading for her apartment. She'd forgotten that although Jess was aware the house had been converted into two apartments, she hadn't seen it until now. Sylvie opened her door and glanced back at Jess, searching her face trying to glean what was going on.

Their middle daughter had always been so independent. It was a rare thing for Jess to call on her parents for help, and unheard of for her to travel home all the way from Australia just to speak to them. This meant only one thing: it was serious. Had something happened between Jess and her long-term partner, Alex? Had they split up? Was he ill? Even worse, was Jessica ill? Jessica didn't appear unwell. In fact, she looked the picture of health. She was now in her mid-thirties, but you wouldn't believe it to look at her. Tanned and toned, she could still pass for a fun-loving, free-wheeling young backpacker in her twenties returning home from a gap year.

Sylvie glanced at her rucksack in the hall. It brought back memories of happier times, of children leaving the nest and returning, of a time when the house was still a home, and she and John weren't living apart.

Sylvie recalled the breakfast she shared with John a couple of days ago before she found out who was behind her apparent run of bad luck. Sitting opposite him at the kitchen table eating breakfast together felt like old times. Sylvie had sat there wishing she could turn back the clock. She wanted to go back to the way things were before all this wretched business started with John losing his job, forcing him into early retirement. That's when he'd come up with the idea to convert the house and they were plunged down a road involving builders and disruption and, when it was all over, the prospect of living with tenants, strangers in their house. It wasn't what Sylvie envisaged for their retirement.

Sylvie had savoured that moment together. For a brief spell, she could fantasise that the past few months had never happened; it was just another regular morning sitting having breakfast together in the basement kitchen of their London home. Unfortunately, as soon as Sylvie turned her head and glanced out the window into the garden, the spell was broken.

No amount of wishing was going to bring back her garden full of flowers and shrubs that had taken years to nurture. No amount of wishing could erase what John had done. Sylvie would never forget the godawful day she found out that John had given the go-ahead for the builder to bull-doze her garden without consulting her first. John replaced it with a bland lawn and dull borders so that it was low maintenance for tenants.

Sylvie had sat there over breakfast staring at John's bland lawn and boring borders and realised there was no going back. She missed her husband – their meal together proved that – but now, after everything that had happened, she couldn't go back to the way things were, living in the apartment upstairs with John.

Sylvie walked into her apartment. Jess followed her inside and closed the door. Sylvie was worried how she was going to tell Jess about their trial separation. She had kept in contact with Jess by sending her regular emails. However, she'd failed to mention what had happened after the house conversion, namely that she'd packed her bags and moved downstairs. That was until Julia bought her a puppy. Sylvie had sent Jess photographs of her new puppy exploring his new home, forgetting that Jess wasn't privy to their new living arrangements. Jess knew all about her father's plans for the garden apartment and was still under the impression the flat would be rented out.

Sylvie tried to cover her tracks by telling Jess that she was living downstairs to iron out the wrinkles before he found a tenant. But that was weeks ago. Sylvie was rather hoping that by the time Jess made a trip home, relations between them might have improved. Now she would have to explain why they were still living apart. Sylvie didn't want to think about that right now.

Sylvie perched on the arm of the sofa and watched Jess sit down on the wicker chair opposite her. Jess looked tired. She had just arrived home from a long journey. Sylvie was aware she hadn't even offered to make her a cup of tea but was desperate to know what was wrong. Sylvie nervously kneaded her hands in her lap. 'Jess, tell me what's wrong. What have you travelled all this way to tell us?'

Jess took off her coat and glanced around the apartment. She turned to her mum, studying her thoughtfully. Finally, Jess broached the subject she had flown all this way to discuss. 'Mum, we're all worried about you…'

'Pardon me?'

'We're worried about Dad too.'

Sylvie looked at Jess in confusion. 'I don't understand—'

'Harriet and Chloe have been on to me about what's been going on at home since the house was converted into two apartments.'

Oh, good heavens! Sylvie's mouth dropped open. *Jess knows.* 'I'm sorry, Jess. I don't know what you're talking about,' said Sylvie defensively, hoping she was just jumping to conclusions, and Harriet and Chloe hadn't really contacted Jess and got her worried. So worried, in fact, that she'd put in for compassionate leave and flown all the way home from Australia after they'd told her that Mum and Dad were living apart. If that was the case, Sylvie couldn't see what they were all so het up about.

Jess leaned forward in her seat and studied Sylvie closely. 'Are you and Dad getting divorced?'

Sylvie sighed. *So that's what all this is about.* She hadn't once stopped to consider what effect this trial separation might be having on her children. Harriet and Chloe must have been concerned over what was going on at home to contact their sister. Sylvie momentarily thought back to her three girls growing up. Harriet and Chloe always appeared to be closer. They were both into similar things growing up, like boys, shopping and clubbing, in contrast to their sporty middle sister.

Jessica loved the great outdoors and spent many weekends away at camp with the Girl Scouts. In her free time, she often volunteered at animal shelters like Battersea dogs' home. Despite this, it was always Jess they turned to if they were in trouble and needed someone to confide in. Nothing had changed. That's why Jess was sitting here now, representing all three of them, asking the question her two sisters were too afraid to ask.

'I can't answer that question, Jess,' said Sylvie truthfully. She knew what they wanted to hear, but she was unable to give them any assurances that this trial separation wouldn't lead to the divorce courts.

Jess sat silently regarding her.

Sylvie stole a glance at her daughter. 'Why don't I make a nice cup of tea?' Sylvie wanted to get out from under Jess's scrutiny and avoid any more uncomfortable questions. Sylvie didn't know what she wanted in the future, and whether there was a place in her future for John. All she knew for sure, at this moment, was that she was happy in her apartment and she had a train to catch in less than five hours. Sylvie was finally making that trip to Cornwall.

Sylvie glanced at the clock on the mantel shelf as she rose from the sofa. It was almost four o'clock in the morning. She had no idea how she would get back to sleep now after all the excitement of Jess arriving home unexpectedly. She tried not to think about the reason for her daughter's visit, to find out if Mum and Dad were getting divorced. Instead, she thought about catching up on some sleep during the long train journey down to Cornwall. Sylvie hoped it didn't turn out a wasted trip.

Her mother had left Sylvie a handwritten note in her will outlining her final request to have her ashes scattered in the garden of a cottage in Cornwall. It was where Sylvie and her mother spent the summer holidays when she was a child. However, Sylvie hadn't returned to that part of the world for years. She had absolutely no idea whether the cottage still existed. At least she knew the name of the village where they spent those summers. That was a start.

In the basement kitchen, Sylvie made two mugs of tea and carried them upstairs. She handed Jess a mug of tea, and said, 'Jess, I realise you've just arrived home, but I'm leaving in a few hours to catch a train to Cornwall.' Sylvie already had the ticket booked and the taxi arranged to pick her up and take her to the train station.

'Oh.' Her face dropped at the mention of Sylvie's impending trip.

Sylvie felt bitterly disappointed that Jess arrived on the day she was leaving for Cornwall. 'I'll only be gone a couple of days. Enough time to…' Sylvie's excitement at the thought of returning home from Cornwall to spend time with Jess gave way to sadness at the reason behind her trip.

'What is it, Mum?'

'To be honest with you, I'm not really looking forward to the trip. It's not exactly a holiday.' Sylvie told Jess all about her grandmother's final wish to have her ashes scattered in Cornwall.

'Why do you think she left it up to you to carry out her last request?'

Sylvie smiled at Jess. She recalled John asking the exact same question. Sylvie had four older siblings. John had asked, *why you?*

'Let me show you something.' Sylvie left Jess sitting on the sofa and went to her bedroom to fetch a cardboard box. Inside were some of her mother's personal effects collected by the staff at the alms-houses where her mother used to live. They kept hold of the items to pass them on to relatives. Sylvie was the only one who came.

Sylvie placed the box on the coffee table in front of Jess. There wasn't much inside, certainly nothing of monetary value. However, Sylvie was immensely grateful to the staff for not tossing it out because inside that box Sylvie discovered some old black and white photos that she had never seen before. One photograph caught her attention the moment she laid eyes on it. She smiled as she handed it to Jess.

Jess took the picture and studied it carefully. She didn't recognise the woman and child standing together outside a white-washed cottage. Sylvie didn't expect her to because the photograph was over fifty years old.

Jess turned the photograph over in her hand and read the writing on the back. 'Sylvie and Mama circa 1959.' Jess looked up. 'This is you and Grandma?'

'Yes. I was six years old according to the date on the back.' Sylvie proceeded to tell Jess all about the summers she spent with her mother in Cornwall many years ago. Now all she had were her memories, an urn containing her mother's ashes, and an old snapshot of herself and her mother standing outside a white-washed cottage.

Jess passed the photograph back to Sylvie.

She took the small print gently in her hands and gazed wistfully at the picture. It must have been taken on a beautiful summer's day because they were both squinting in the bright sunlight. There were seagulls flying overhead in the distance. Staring at the image brought back a vivid childhood memory of skipping along a cobbled path through a garden of sweet-scented flowers. Sylvie closed her eyes and could almost taste the salty sea breeze and hear the cry of seagulls overhead. She opened her eyes and smiled fondly at the memory. Sylvie treasured that photograph. It was all she had left of those happy, carefree summers in Cornwall.

With the discovery of that photograph, Sylvie began her search for the cottage in earnest. It was Chloe's idea to put the picture of the cottage on the internet to see if it jogged someone's memory. They had a lucky break; a local history buff living in Newquay recognised the cottage. She emailed to say it might be situated in a small town called St. Columb Major. Sylvie had been thrilled by this discovery, although Chloe warned her not to get her hopes up. Sylvie took that on board.

There were probably many similar looking cottages in that part of the world. The lady who posted a reply on the internet could have been mistaken, but at least it was something. The only way for Sylvie to know for sure was to travel to Cornwall and find out for herself whether it was the cottage in the photograph. She hoped there might still be somebody from thereabouts who remembered Sylvie and her mother from all those years ago.

Sylvie studied the cottage in the photograph. If, by some miracle, she did find the property, could she convince the present owners to let her scatter her mother's ashes in their garden? Sylvie decided to cross that bridge when she came to it. For now, she had a lead, and that's what motivated her to finally make the trip.

Jess glanced at the old photograph. 'Do you think that's why Grandma wanted you to carry out her final request, because of those summers you spent together in that cottage?'

'Yes, I believe so.'

'It's kind of strange that Grandma only ever took you to Cornwall...'

'I know.' Sylvie sighed as she glanced at the urn on the book-shelf beside the fireplace. *Forgive me*; they were the last words her mother had spoken. Before Sylvie had a chance to find out more, she was gone.

She turned back to look at her daughter. Jess was a mirror image of Sylvie as a young woman, with her jet-black wavy hair, smooth olive skin, and soft hazel-brown eyes. She was so unlike her two sisters, who took after John's side of the family with their blonde hair, green eyes, and pale complexions. People would never guess Jess was related to Chloe and Harriet, let alone their sister, and therefore assumed she wasn't part of their family.

Growing up, Sylvie knew what that felt like, always an out-sider in her own family, often left out by her siblings. Jess had a similar experience. She was often excluded by Chloe and Harriet simply because they had nothing in common. But unlike Sylvie, who had always been close to her mother, Sylvie was painfully aware that she had never achieved the same close relationship with Jess that she had with her other two girls. It was only when

John pointed out that they were so alike – not just in looks but in temperament too – that Sylvie finally understood why they clashed so terribly when Jess was growing up.

Sylvie had hoped their relationship would change as Jess got older. She was barely out of her teens when she emigrated to the other side of the world, robbing Sylvie of the opportunity to get to know her. It was on these rare trips home that Sylvie took every chance she could to spend time with her middle child.

Jess glanced at the photograph. 'I wish…' she trailed off.

'What is it, Jess?' Sylvie searched her face. Perhaps Jess wished that when she was growing up she had the opportunity to spend time with her mum, without her siblings around. Thinking back, Sylvie was aware how much the other two often monopolised her and John's time, leaving their quieter, more introspective middle daughter to fade into the background. They never experienced the same teenage angst and issues with Jess that they had with the other two, which meant she didn't receive the same attention as her sisters.

Sylvie would never forget that conversation she'd had with Jess when she was just nineteen and packing to leave for Australia. Jess said that it didn't matter if she suddenly disappeared to the other side of the world because she doubted they would miss her, or even notice she was gone.

How wrong she had been, thought Sylvie. They all missed her terribly. 'I wish,' began Sylvie, second-guessing what Jess was about to say, 'we had the chance to spend some time together, just the two of us, like I used to with Grandma.'

Jess looked down at the photograph in Sylvie's hand. 'That's exactly what I was thinking.'

Sylvie had an idea. 'Jess, I know you've just arrived home…'

She glanced at the photograph before asking her daughter, 'Would you like to take another trip?'

The cab arrived outside the house five hours later. It was nine o'clock in the morning. In the twilight hours, before the taxi came to take Sylvie to the train station, she'd tried to get some sleep. She had returned to bed and left Jess asleep on the sofa. However, Sylvie couldn't bring herself to close her eyes, let alone drift off to sleep. Afraid that if she did, she would wake up to discover that this unexpected turn of events was just a pleasant dream; it turned out that Jess was coming with her to Cornwall.

Jess was delighted that her mum asked her to travel down to Cornwall together to carry out Grandma's final request. She wanted to see the cottage where Sylvie used to spend her summers as a child. Sylvie hoped the local history buff, who thought they knew the whereabouts of the cottage in the photograph, was right and it was in a town called St. Columb Major, because that's where they were headed.

Sylvie sat in the back of the taxi waiting for Jess. The taxi driver had already taken Sylvie's travel bag and Jess's rucksack from the hall and deposited them in the boot of the car. He was sitting in the driver's seat with the engine idly turning over waiting to depart. Sylvie looked out of the window to see Jess skipping down the front steps of the house heading for the taxi. A memory resurfaced of a child with big brown eyes and jet-black pigtails skipping down those steps. It made Sylvie wonder where all the intervening years had gone.

Jess reached the taxi, opened the car door and climbed in to sit on the back seat beside Sylvie.

Sylvie noticed there was no sign of John waving them off. She turned to Jess. 'Where's your father?'

'I knocked on his door, but there was no answer. Dad must have gone out.'

'Never mind, you can surprise him when you get back.'

Jess nodded her head although Sylvie could tell her daughter was disappointed that she hadn't managed to see him before they left. Sylvie squeezed her arm affectionately. 'You know your father, always an early bird. Perhaps he nipped out to buy a newspaper.' Sylvie glanced down the street wondering if they might be lucky and catch him heading back with his newspaper.

All their married life John had had his newspaper delivered from the local newsagents. It formed part of Sylvie's daily ritual before her unexpected move downstairs; she always made the first cup of tea in the morning, and she always collected John's newspaper from the doorstep on her way upstairs with the tea tray.

John was a creature of habit. He liked to start each day by reading the headlines while drinking his morning cuppa in bed. In the early days, having the daily newspaper delivered was a luxury they could ill-afford. They had few luxuries back then, and Sylvie didn't begrudge her hard-working husband his one vice – if you could call it that. Predictably, he never departed from this daily ritual.

To her surprise, she'd noticed that just lately John had stopped having his newspaper delivered. Sylvie stared out of the taxi window and wondered what had changed. He didn't have a job or any hobbies, so perhaps it had simply given him a reason to get up and leave the house in the morning, even if it was only to visit the newsagents.

'Yes, I'm sure you're right, Mum. He must have gone out to get a newspaper because he wouldn't still be in bed at this hour.' Jess looked up at the house. 'Would he?'

'Don't be daft,' said Sylvie. 'John, in bed at this hour?'

Sylvie and Jess looked at each other for a moment and then shook their heads in a resounding *no* as the taxi driver pulled away from the kerb in the direction of Paddington train station.

13

John awoke with a start. He thought somebody was banging on his apartment door. But when he sat up in bed and rubbed the sleep out of his eyes, all he heard was a car going by outside. That's when he remembered the most peculiar dream.

Instead of going to bed, which is what he clearly did, in his dream he headed out of the house in his socks and declared his love for Sylvie in the front garden. The dream seemed so real that it would never have surprised him if he *had* woken up in the garden instead of tucked up in bed.

And then it got really weird...

In his dream, he made his way back upstairs and was just closing his apartment door when the doorbell downstairs started to ring and ring on a continuous loop. It sounded as though some school kids were pressing the buzzer as a dare, ready to run off as soon as the occupant of the house came to the door. When Sylvie answered the door, it turned out that it wasn't school kids fooling around but Jess. And then Jess came into the house and stood talking to Sylvie, right there, in the hall.

John had forced himself to shut his door and dream about something else because it made him unhappy. Jess was thousands of miles away in Australia, not standing on his bloody doorstep. That's why he knew for certain it was just a dream.

John licked his lips. He was parched and gasping for a cup of tea. His mouth felt like it had been gritted by the local council in the middle of the night. He threw back the covers and swung his legs out of bed wishing to goodness he'd not finished off that entire bottle of Drambuie.

'What the...?' John looked down to discover he wasn't wearing pyjamas but still dressed in the clothes he had on yesterday. Worse still, there were muddy footprints on his new carpet. He lifted his leg, took off a soggy sock and held it up to inspect it. 'What the hell...?!' His sock was covered in mud and grass. And was that a dead leaf stuck to the end?

'Ugh.' John stared at the sock.

He pulled off the other sock and got out of bed to follow the trail of muddy footprints down the stairs and through the lounge to his front door. John stood in the lobby by the door to his apartment for some considerable time, scratching his head, trying to think of a logical explanation for his wet socks and muddy footprints – until he remembered.

'Oh my god.'

He couldn't exactly recall what he got up to last night, but he did remember the vivid dream. John groaned with the dawning realisation that it wasn't a dream – at least the part where he went out into the front garden in his socks.

John walked into the kitchen and deposited his wet socks in the washing machine, praying that none of the neighbours or, heaven forbid, Sylvie had seen him make a complete prat of himself on the front lawn last night, obviously blind drunk. Thank god he did not lock himself out of the house. At least he had managed to get back inside and crawl into bed before he did any further damage to his ego, and Sylvie's already low opinion of him.

John put the kettle on and debated whether he should call on Sylvie this morning when he made himself more presentable. He wanted to satisfy himself that she was none the wiser about that embarrassing episode on the front lawn last night. He was just wondering whether Sylvie had already taken Alfie out for his early morning walk when he glanced at the clock on the wall and did a double-take – *eleven o'clock*! John shook his head in dismay. He never ever got up *that* late, even when he was having a lie-in.

He was determined to turn over a new leaf and clean up his act. He resolved to begin today by marching into his study and getting rid of that empty bottle of Drambuie which, it turned out, wasn't completely empty. He was about to toss it into the wastepaper bin, just to be on the safe side, when something caught his eye. The red light was flashing on his answerphone; someone had left him a message.

John leaned across his desk and pressed *play*.

Hello, John, it's Sylvie from downstairs...

Of course, you're downstairs, thought John rolling his eyes, where else would you be?

I'm on my way to Cornwall. We tried to call on you before we left, to let you know I won't be around for a couple of days, but you were out.

I was out all right. John glanced at the bottle in his wastepaper bin.

I'm ringing on my mobile phone from the train. Oh, there's a tunnel up ahead... better sign off... poor recep... hope... get this.

John sat down at his desk and replayed the message three times on a loop, each time stopping the message after he heard the words, *we tried to call...* John stared at the answerphone thinking, *who's we?*

Yesterday, before he reacquainted himself with the bottle, he overheard Sylvie arranging to see Nigel the dog-trainer when she got back from Cornwall. As soon as she returned, she said she would give him a call and "make a date". John had no idea her trip was so soon. He stared at the answerphone. Had she changed her mind and asked Nigel to go with her?

'Dammit,' John swore. Why of all the days did Nigel have to come round to do the dog training yesterday? Things might have worked out differently if Nigel wasn't there. They could have had dinner together, and perhaps Sylvie would have invited him to accompany her to Cornwall.

John recalled waking up this morning imagining he heard someone banging on his door. *Blast!* What if that wasn't his imagination? What if that was Sylvie? Although, she said all along that she was going to return to Cornwall on her own, what if on the morning of departure, she'd had a change of heart? And what if, because he wasn't answering his door – still comatose in bed in a drunken stupor – she called Nigel instead?

John deleted the message and looked at the Drambuie he had tossed in the bin. There was just enough left at the bottom of the bottle for half a glass. Suddenly all thoughts of a turning over a new leaf vanished. He was just reaching for the bottle when the phone rang. *Sylvie?* He grabbed the phone.

'Hi, Daddy. You're never going to guess what I'm about to tell you!' chimed Chloe on the end of the line, sounding her usual excitable thirty-going-on-thirteen-year-old self.

John really didn't feel in the mood for any more surprises. His day had already got off on the wrong foot – John winced at that unintentional pun – with the discovery that he'd made a complete fool of himself in the front garden in his socks last night. Now he had a muddy, stained carpet which he was not looking forward to cleaning. And then there was that blasted phone message suggesting Sylvie had gone gallivanting off to Cornwall with Nigel.

'Daddy, are you there?'

John grimaced. Now what? He really wasn't in the mood. 'I'm sorry, Chloe, but I'll have to call you back.' John slammed the phone down and instantly regretted it. She sounded so happy. He felt a wave of guilt for cutting her off like that.

He was about to pour himself that drink when he suddenly had a moment of clarity. What if Chloe was calling with some good news? John put the bottle down. He decided that whatever it was – good or bad – hitting the bottle was not the way to deal with the unexpected. He tossed the bottle in the bin for the second time and reached for the phone.

Chloe's number was engaged.

John put the phone down and looked at the time. Whatever it was, would have to wait. It was nearly midday. He hadn't even showered and changed into some clean clothes.

Thirty minutes later, after taking a long hot shower, John emerged from the bathroom in a clean set of clothes. He stood in front of the long mirror in the bedroom combing his wet hair. John recalled the phone conversation with Dave last night – what he could remember of it. Have you looked in the mirror lately, Dave asked him? He looked in the mirror, and in the cold light of day, he finally had an idea what Dave was getting at.

'I look old,' said John to his reflection. It was a fact of life that he wasn't getting any younger, but what he saw in the mirror wasn't helping him any; here was somebody who dressed old. Nigel wasn't getting any younger either, but he didn't look like this. John scrutinized himself in the mirror. He hadn't changed his clothes or hairstyle in decades. Not that he didn't go to the hairdressers or buy new clothes; the problem was he never changed his style. That's what Dave was getting at. Dave was right: he needed a new image.

John sighed. He might have been up for it before he listened to that message on the answerphone. Now it appeared that Sylvie had gone to Cornwall with Nigel, what was the point? John stared at his reflection. Then again, what if it doesn't work out? It's not as though their trip was a romantic getaway. She was scattering her mother's ashes for heaven's sake. That was enough to make anyone depressed. It could spell the end of that little dalliance before it had hardly begun. He smiled at himself in the mirror. That cheered him up, so much so that he decided Dave's new plan was a go. He would make some much-needed changes to his wardrobe.

John's smile faded. He could already foresee a problem with the plan. Sylvie had always taken him shopping for his clothes in the same dependable department store for decades. He didn't have a clue where else to go or what clothes to buy. He needed someone who was good at shopping and could show him the ropes. More importantly, he needed someone with him to offer a second opinion on his new outfits; goodness knows what he would end up looking like if he was let loose in a clothes shop on his own. 'Chloe, how would you like to go shopping?' John was sitting on the phone in his study once more.

'If this is your way of apologising for cutting me off earlier,' began Chloe.

John had definitely ruffled her feathers. 'Look, I'm sorry about—'

'Then it's working,' said Chloe cheerfully. 'Besides, it's just as well you put the phone down on me. I was about to get myself into big trouble by telling you something I promised to keep a secret. I'm terrible at keeping secrets.'

Chloe sounded in such good spirits that John doubted this so-called secret would be anything troubling. His thoughts returned to the new plan. He knew it was out of the ordinary to ask his daughter to go shopping with him. He had never been clothes shopping with any of the girls before, not even when they were small.

'You did say you wanted to take me shopping and buy me some clothes, didn't you?'

John furrowed his brow. He was pretty sure he didn't actually say that. Although it wasn't his intention to buy Chloe some clothes too, perhaps it didn't hurt to sweeten his request with a little parental bribery. 'Yes, I'll take you shopping.' John added, 'I have to admit that I do have an ulterior motive.'

'What's that?'

'If I buy some clothes for you, will you help me shop for some new outfits?'

'You want *me* to help you choose some new clothes?'

He could tell by the tone of her voice that she wasn't as keen to go with him now she found out what the trip would involve.

'But you always shop in the same department store, and you've never had any problems choosing your own clothes before.'

'That's just it, Chloe. I don't want to go to the same department store and buy the same clothes. I want a change. A new style. I'm bored with the old me.' And so is Sylvie, obviously. 'But I don't know where to go to get something different.' To get a new and improved John Baxter.

John waited so long for a response that he thought he'd been cut off. 'Chloe, are you still there?'

'Yes.' There was a pause. 'Are you going to start dating again?' asked Chloe, her voice distant.

John was stunned by such an unexpected question. 'Of course not. Whatever gave you that idea?'

'I guess with you and Mum living apart, I thought maybe you guys were getting... um... you know...' Chloe trailed off.

'No, I don't know,' John said impatiently.

'Divorced.'

John felt his stomach lurch. 'Is that what your mother said?'

'No, not in so many words... but she *is* living downstairs.'

'I know that! It's only temporary.' This was getting tiresome; he'd been down this road already with Dave on the phone last night. Why was everybody assuming the worst?

'Where is all this coming from, Chloe? Why would you think we're getting a—?' John couldn't bring himself to say that word.

'I guess it's just that when you said you wanted to buy some new clothes, my first thought was that you and Mum were splitting up and you wanted to, you know, look nice so you could meet somebody else.'

'Oh, Chloe, you daft brush,' John said with a smile. 'I'm not doing this for somebody else. I'm doing it for your mother.'

'You are? So that's what this shopping trip is all about?'

'Yes, of course. I looked in the mirror this morning and thought it was about time I made some changes. I want to make an effort with my appearance for your mother. I know it sounds like a stupid idea, Chloe. Who knows, perhaps I'll surprise her.' John hoped so.

'I don't think it's a stupid idea at all,' said Chloe in relief, sounding a lot more enthusiastic. 'Oh boy, this shopping trip is going to be such fun. Mum and Jess are in for a surprise when they get back from Cornwall.'

'Pardon me?' John raised an eyebrow. 'Did you just say... Jess, as in *my* Jessica?'

'Oh hell. I think I just slipped up,' Chloe groaned. 'I told you I'm no good at keeping secrets.'

'Run that by me again, Chloe. What secret?' John thought he must have misunderstood because he was sure he just heard Chloe say...

'Jess arrived home from Australia early this morning.'

'Really? You're not kidding around and this is a joke?'

'No joke, Daddy.'

John was totally thrown by the fact that Jessica was back in England. He wasn't even aware she was on her way home. It took him a full minute to digest this. 'Well, where is she? When can I see her?'

'I told you already, she went to Cornwall with Mum.'

'She did?' John grinned as he digested another piece of good news; it was Jess who was travelling down to Cornwall with Sylvie, and not Nigel. Hooray!

John was over the moon for all of two seconds until it dawned on him that Jess had left this morning without bothering to come and see him first. 'Why didn't she call upstairs?'

Chloe explained, 'I spoke to Jess when she was on the train and apparently, she tried knocking on your door before they left, but you must have been out.'

John rolled his eyes. That bottle of Drambuie had a lot to answer for. He stared at the bottle in the wastepaper bin beside his desk. He was bitterly disappointed that he had been in bed this morning when Jess knocked on his door. On the other hand, he was not at all disappointed to learn that Jess really was back in Blighty, and it was Jess, not Nigel, accompanying Sylvie to Cornwall. John was now looking forward to his shopping trip immensely.

'And it was meant to be a surprise!'

'Pardon?' John hadn't heard a word Chloe said. He was too preoccupied with thoughts of Jess coming home and Nigel out of the picture. John's day had just got a whole lot better.

Chloe's day had not. 'Jess was going to surprise you when she returned from their trip to Cornwall. Jess is *so* going to murder me.'

14

'I am *so* going to murder her.' Jess had just read the text message from her sister: *Dad knows.*

Sylvie turned from the window to look at her daughter. 'What's the matter?'

Jess looked up from her phone. 'It's Chloe. She never could keep a secret!'

'Well, you'd better put that away. I think we get off here.' Sylvie stood up as the train pulled into the station.

Sylvie and Jess departed the train at Newquay train station and headed straight for the line of taxi's parked outside. Their destination was the village of St. Columb Major. It was about six miles inland and a fifteen-minute cab ride away.

Although the train journey was expensive, and they could save money on the taxi fare by taking a local bus Sylvie didn't want to waste precious time. She was eager to find the cottage and carry out her mother's last request. If they located the property today, and do what she came here to do, then perhaps there would be an opportunity tomorrow to take the day at their leisure before returning home.

Sylvie intended to spend more time in Cornwall visiting the

Cornish coves and quaint fishing villages. However, she'd decided to cut the trip short. Jess was only home for a brief visit and was looking forward to seeing the rest of the family and catching up with old friends before she left for Australia.

She felt guilty that Jess had made a special trip home just because the girls had been on at her about Mum and Dad. If Harriet and Chloe thought Jess had come home to persuade her to move back in with Dad, they were in for a disappointment. After Jess had asked *that* question, she dropped the matter like a stone. Jess hadn't brought up the subject of their separate living arrangements apart from remarking on how different the garden apartment now looked compared to the photos Dad had sent her. It turned out that Jess liked the way her mum had redecorated and furnished her flat.

'It feels so warm and welcoming and homely. I love the bright colours, the rugs, and the cushions. And the abundance of stuff, if you don't mind me saying.'

Sylvie didn't mind that remark at all. If John had said that, she would have taken it as a criticism. He didn't like clutter. Everything had to be tidied away until there was nothing left in John's apartment of interest to look at but four blank walls and sheet-white furniture.

Jess added, 'It reminds me a lot of Julia's flat before she sold it and moved on.'

Sylvie didn't mind that remark either. She imagined that Jess had fond memories of Julia's bachelorette pad. Before she retired to a houseboat in Little Venice, Julia had lived in the flat almost as long as John and Sylvie had lived in their house. Sylvie's girls were in and out of Julia's flat so often growing up that it felt like their second home – Sylvie's too.

During the school holidays when John was at work, and Julia wasn't because she was a teacher, they would all troupe over to her flat. Sylvie could relax and chat with her best friend knowing that the girls could let their imaginations run wild without someone walking in on them after work and spoiling all the fun. They could make as much mess as they wanted playing dressing up – Julia's poor dog had to join in too – or cutting and sticking or making dens in her lounge.

There was that one time Sylvie remembered the girls wanted to bake a cake in Julia's kitchen. When Julia and Sylvie had looked in on them, they discovered the three girls were having a food fight. Sylvie had been mortified at the mess they had created. She never lost her temper and shouted at the girls, but that one time almost proved the exception.

Sylvie was about to tell them off when she was stopped in her tracks by a lump of gooey cake mixture hitting her cheek. The three girls were standing right in front of her and hadn't moved a muscle. Sylvie had turned her head in Julia's direction to find Julia grinning at her mischievously as she hurled another gooey ball at Sylvie.

Sylvie had ducked her head, reached for the bowl of cake mixture and got her own back. When Sylvie's three girls had got over the shock of seeing two grown-ups being so silly, they erupted in whoops of laughter. This never ever happened at home with Mum and Dad. Sylvie recalled Chloe complaining that nothing exciting or out of the ordinary ever happened at home. It was true. The home they grew up in was nothing like Julia's.

Perhaps, mused Sylvie, there was a valuable lesson to be learned about what is important in life and what isn't. And how happiness often comes from the unexpected, spontaneous things we do, rather than the things we plan. The spur-of-the-moment decision to decamp downstairs had borne that out. It had led to a spontaneous food fight with John, metaphorically speaking. They had started with all the ingredients to finish baking the cake – or in this case to complete John's plans for the conversion by renting out the garden apartment. But she picked a food fight instead, throwing the ingredients of her husband's carefully conceived plan right back at him. She dismantled his neutral two-bedroomed rental until it was no longer fit for its original purpose. Sylvie was enjoying herself immensely.

That she was making a bit of a mess of things was par for the course; she hadn't expected Jess to take some compassionate leave and fly home as a result. Sylvie wasn't sorry, even when John started to get his own back by sabotaging her apartment. At least Chloe could no longer accuse her parents of being boring.

'I much prefer your flat to Dad's place upstairs,' Jess concluded.

Sylvie didn't know what pleased her most, Jess's comments about her apartment or that Jess had not asked her once if she was moving back in with John. In fact, the way she talked about Dad's place and hers, as though it was of no consequence that they were living apart, made their living arrangements appear almost normal. The trip to Cornwall with her daughter was the icing on the cake.

Sylvie had intended to make the trip alone with only her memories and her mother's ashes for company. Then she had a change of heart. She didn't want to travel on her own. But who could she ask to go with her? Sylvie had narrowed down her list of possible travel companions. Chloe was busy with work. Harriet couldn't just drop everything at a moment's notice and come with her; she had her own family to consider. Julia was looking after Alfie while she was away. That left John. And John was still in her bad books.

That didn't stop Sylvie considering whether to ask him, until she had a pleasant evening with a very nice man called Nigel the day before she was due to leave for Cornwall. Sylvie had told Nigel she would contact him on her return. However, after Julia's visit later that evening to collect Alfie, and a little friendly persuasion on Julia's part, Sylvie had phoned Nigel and asked him if he would like to accompany her after all.

He said yes and didn't even hesitate. They were due to meet at Paddington station to catch the train to Newquay. It had all been arranged until Jess had turned up on her doorstep. In her excitement at seeing Jess, Sylvie had forgotten all about Nigel. Sylvie thought back to the phone call she'd quickly made when she was waiting in the back of the taxi for Jess to say hello to her father before they left for the station.

She felt awkward cancelling the trip with Nigel. He sounded disappointed when he heard. However, he understood that Jess was on a short visit home from Australia and this was the only way Sylvie could spend some time with her daughter without postponing the trip.

Sylvie had kept the call brief. She was anxious Jess might overhear her talking to another man. That didn't happen. The conversation was over when Jess skipped down the front steps and into the waiting cab. And here they were a few hours later in another taxi not fifteen minutes from their destination. Sylvie had butterflies in her stomach.

'St. Columb wasn't it?' asked the taxi driver as they pulled out of the station.

'Yes, that's right. I'm looking for this cottage.' Sylvie held up the photograph. 'You don't happen to recognise it, do you?'

Jess rolled her eyes. 'Mum, I know you're eager to find it, but can we at least get there in one piece? He can't drive and look at your photo at the same time.'

'Give it here,' said the taxi driver. 'Let me take a look.'

Sylvie smiled at Jess as she passed the print over the front seat into the waiting hand.

The taxi driver glanced at it as they drove along.

Jess raised her hands in an *I give up* gesture, whispering, 'Mum, I have flown halfway around the world and travelled to many exotic destinations without incident. I'd rather not cop it travelling in a taxi on a back road in Cornwall.'

'Shh! Don't be so melodramatic, Jess. I bet he knows these roads so well he could drive this route with his eyes shut.'

'That's what I'm afraid of,' mumbled Jess.

Sylvie turned to the taxi driver. 'Do you know it?' she asked eagerly.

'Can't say that I do.' He returned the photograph. 'But it looks familiar.'

'It does?'

'Oh yes, lots of them there cottages hereabouts, I'm afraid.'

'I see,' said Sylvie flatly, putting the photo back in her hand-bag.

'Mum, there's no need to sound disappointed, we're not even there yet.'

'No, of course not.' Sylvie had a feeling that this might not turn out as straightforward as she thought. She fell silent and stared out of the window at the passing scenery as they sped along the country roads on their way to the small market town of

St. Columb Major. This was the first time she had returned to Cornwall since she was a child. Nothing looked familiar.

'Do you recognise where we are?' asked Jess as the taxi pulled into the small square. They both alighted with their bags.

'Unfortunately, not,' replied Sylvie.

'It *was* a long time ago,' Jess reminded her. 'Things change so perhaps that is to be expected.'

'Perhaps.' Sylvie handed over the fare.

The driver took the money and said, 'I'll be here at four o'clock tomorrow afternoon to pick you up and take you back to the station. I hope you find what you're looking for.'

'So do I,' Sylvie remarked solemnly. She watched the cab reverse out of the parking space and head out of town. Sylvie glanced at her overnight bag hoping that when she returned here tomorrow, she would not be carrying home the box containing her mother's ashes.

Jess gathered up her rucksack and put it on her back. She turned full circle, taking in the pretty square, and stopped in front of her mother. 'Right – where now?'

Sylvie had directions to the small bed-and-breakfast. The taxi-driver offered to drop them outside, but the owners of the B&B had forewarned them that drivers unfamiliar with the town often got lost in the peculiar one-way traffic system. Sylvie didn't want to waste what precious time they had. It was only a short walk from where they were dropped off.

The owners were right: it was a doddle to find on foot. Leaving the small parking area in the square, they cut down a picturesque side street passing by a no entry sign. They found the bed-and-breakfast at the end of the road on the corner. The double-fronted terrace cottage had ivy creeping around the lead-paned windows and two hanging baskets in autumn bloom hanging either side of the front door.

'Hello. Hello. Welcome to Cosy Corner.' The owner opened the door with a beaming smile and a warm handshake. 'I'm Harold.' He wasted no time showing Sylvie and Jess to their small but comfortable twin room on the first floor.

'Tea and coffee making facilities are there.' He pointed to a kettle, teapot and two cups and saucers next to a jar of home-made cookies on the sideboard. 'We replenish the cookies daily so eat as many as you like.' He laughed jovially and handed Sylvie a room key. 'Breakfast is from seven o'clock onwards. Now, is there anything else you need?'

Sylvie exchanged glances with Jess and reached in her hand-bag for the photo. 'I don't suppose you recognise this cottage?'

It turned out that Harold and his wife were not from these parts. They had recently retired to Cornwall and started the B&B. Harold shook his head. 'I'm so sorry we can't be of help. There is a public library in the town where you can pick up some information about the local area. I think we've got a map of the town around here somewhere.'

His wife found a town street map and circlèd the library. 'The library staff are knowledgeable. They may be able to help.'

Harold looked at his wife and nodded. 'Failing that, there are three local pubs where you can make inquiries. We rather like The Coaching Inn, don't we dear.'

'Oh yes, it's got a lovely atmosphere, and they're a friendly crowd in there. I'm sure they won't mind sharing their knowledge of the local area.'

'They do rather nice food too, home-cooked local produce, if you decide to stay for a bite to eat.'

His wife rolled her eyes. 'Honestly, sometimes I think you've got food on the brain. You're always thinking about your next meal,' she chided him.

Sylvie smiled at them thinking how lovely that after all these years they still appeared to have a close relationship. I would surprise her to learn that they hadn't long married and were almost newly-weds.

Sylvie and Jess left their bags at the B&B and headed out to find the public library. The town centre was compact, and it wasn't long before they saw it a short distance along the main thoroughfare. They must have passed it in the taxi on the way here. The library was housed on the ground floor of an old Victorian building. Sylvie stepped inside. On first impression it was surprisingly large for a small market town. She noticed several bookshelves full of books on local history.

Sylvie walked up to the counter on the right-hand side and smiled at the librarian. She already had her photograph to hand hoping that they might recognise the cottage.

The librarian lived in St. Columb Major and hadn't seen a property like that in the town. 'The cottage in your photo looks detached,' she pointed out. 'I'm afraid there aren't many detached properties in St. Columb. They're mostly terraced, like the B&B where you are staying.'

Sylvie didn't want to give up within an hour of their arrival. Although it had crossed her mind that the history buff, who got in touch because she thought she recognised the cottage, might have been mistaken and sent them on a wild goose-chase. Perhaps it wasn't in this part of Cornwall at all. The history buff lived locally and had sent Sylvie her address, but there wasn't time to visit her in Newquay.

'Mum, why don't we grab a bite to eat in one of the pubs? We could ask around. Perhaps one of the locals might recognise the cottage, or at the very least tell us more about St. Columb.'

'I think that's an excellent idea. Shall we take a bracing walk in the fresh air first to work up an appetite?' Sylvie couldn't see the harm in taking a walk around the small town just to satisfy themselves that the cottage wasn't sitting right under their noses.

'Ah well, I suppose it was worth a try,' said Jess, forty-five minutes later. 'You were right about one thing though: that walk worked up an appetite. I'm starving.'

'Me too.' Sylvie picked up a menu from the table.

They were sitting in a pub near a roaring open fire. The pub was a double-fronted Georgian building with a small central hallway and a door on the right leading through to the bar area with seating. The bar was already full when they arrived. Sylvie and Jess had crossed the hall and walked through a door on the left into another cosy room with beams and plenty of pub ambience, and the all-important roaring fire.

'What do you fancy to eat?' asked Sylvie, hoping Jess was having better luck reading the menu. It was only three o'clock in the afternoon, but this late in the year – it was November – the natural light outside was diminishing, casting the heavily beamed room in shadow. Even with her glasses on, Sylvie strained to see the menu in the poor light. She didn't mind. It only added to the olde-worlde charm.

Jess picked up an identical menu listing traditional English pub food. All the dishes were homemade with ingredients sourced locally. 'I can't decide. It all sounds delicious. Why don't you surprise me?'

'All right,' said Sylvie, smiling at her affectionately. She rose from the table and walked through to the bar in the other room to order their meals. Sylvie took the photograph with her.

The husband and wife behind the bar were open and friendly. Although they had run the pub for years and knew the local area well, they didn't recognise the cottage.

Sylvie glanced at the row of people to her left sitting at the bar. Not one to strike up a conversation with perfect strangers, Sylvie turned to the nearest person seated on a stool who was sipping his pint. 'I'm sorry to trouble you,' said Sylvie. 'You don't happen to know where I can find this cottage?'

Sylvie's photograph ended up being passed along from one person to the next. They all shook their heads and looked apologetically at her when they couldn't be of any help.

Sylvie took the photo back, thanking them for taking the time to look. She was still standing there, with the picture in her hand, when an old gentleman walked into the pub and joined the queue at the bar. He glanced over Sylvie's shoulder, and commented, 'Isn't that the old Trevelyan place?'

Sylvie turned around. The gentleman was dressed in brown corduroy trousers, a white cotton shirt with a dickey bow tie, and a tweed jacket. He was leaning heavily on a walking stick.

'Excuse me, do you recognise this cottage?' Sylvie asked, trying not to get her hopes up.

'Here, let me take a closer look.'

Sylvie handed him the photograph and waited with bated breath.

'Henry, come over here and look at this,' he called to his friend, who was sitting at a table by the door with an empty pint glass in front of him.

Henry stood up and ambled over.

'Doesn't that look like the old Trevelyan place to you?'

Henry scratched his head. 'It could be, George, although it's hard to tell. This picture is quite old. When was it taken?'

'Nineteen fifty-nine,' said Sylvie, keen to give them any information she could that might shed some light on the whereabouts of the cottage.

Henry and George bowed their heads together and studied the old black-and-white photo. That they hadn't dismissed it out of hand, like everybody else, made Sylvie hopeful that they might know something.

'Have you both lived here long?' Sylvie asked. It occurred to her that if George and Henry were living here back in the fifties, perhaps they might remember a young woman who used to spend the summers here – her mother.

'We've both lived here all our lives,' explained George.

'St. Columb born and bred – and proud of it,' Henry added.

'Do you recognise the young woman?' Sylvie asked them eagerly.

George peered at the photograph. 'Can't say that I do. She's a pretty lass.' George glanced at Sylvie. 'You look just like her.'

'She was my mother.'

'Was? I'm so sorry.' He looked at the photo. 'I don't recognise her, although this was taken many years ago and I'm afraid my memory isn't what it once was. But saying that, I'm fairly sure this cottage is Trevelyan.'

Henry agreed. 'It certainly looks like it.'

'Can you tell me which street it's in?' asked Sylvie, reaching in her bag for the street map of the town that the owner of the B&B had provided.

The two old gentlemen exchanged glances. 'That won't help

you none,' said George, leaning heavily on his walking stick. 'This cottage, if it is the one you're looking for, is not in the town.'

'Oh.' Sylvie folded the map away.

'I can give you directions,' offered George. 'You must take the road out of town toward—'

Sylvie stopped him right there. 'I'm afraid we don't have a car. We came by train and taxi.'

'Ah, that might be a problem.'

'How so?'

'If this is the old Trevelyan place, I'm afraid it's a bit off the beaten track.'

Henry raised an eyebrow at George. 'Just a bit?'

'I see,' said Sylvie disappointed. It was already late afternoon. By the time they called a taxi from Newquay and had a bite to eat while they waited, it would be dark outside. It was too late to find the cottage today, if indeed Trevelyan was the cottage in the print.

'Well, thank you anyway,' said Sylvie, tucking the photograph in her purse. 'If you give me those directions, I'll call a taxi in the morning.'

'Right you are. Henry, have you got a pen and paper?'

Sylvie turned back to the bar to discover she had lost her place in the queue. Jess would wonder where her food was. Sylvie sighed and joined the back of the queue. Although disappointed that she could not visit the cottage, by the name of Trevelyan, today. At least she had a lead. Which was more than she had when she walked into the pub half an hour ago.

Sylvie had just re-joined the queue when someone tapped her on the shoulder. She turned around.

George, the old man with the walking stick, was standing

behind her again. 'Come with me. I'll take you to see the cottage.'

Sylvie shook her head. 'That's really kind of you, but I couldn't possibly impose…'

'It's no trouble. I just had a word with my wife over there,' he pointed with his walking stick to a large lady sitting in a booth by the window. 'Martha is happy to wait here until we get back. It's not far, so we won't be long.'

Martha smiled at them from across the room.

Sylvie looked from George to his wife and thought what a stroke of good luck to bump into such nice people. She went to fetch Jess in the room next door.

'Mum, you've been gone ages. I was just about to come and find you.' Jess frowned. 'Where's the food?'

'Jess, get your coat.'

'Are we leaving?' Jess looked at her mother in bewilderment. Sylvie nodded.

'But we haven't eaten yet!'

'We'll come back later,' promised Sylvie. 'First, let's go and see this cottage.' Sylvie held up the photograph.

'You're joking!' Jess jumped up from the table in surprise. 'Are you saying you've found it?'

'I hope so.' Sylvie put on her coat and glanced out of the window as a car drew up outside. George was sitting in the driving seat. He waved at Sylvie. In the short space of time it had taken Sylvie to gather up her coat, her bag, and her daughter, George had already returned to collect his car parked a little way down the street.

Sylvie thought about the urn containing her mother's ashes that were still in her overnight bag at the B&B. She wasn't about to go back and get it now. There wasn't time. It would be dark soon. If it was the cottage, and if the owners were home, and if they were happy for Sylvie to spread her mother's ashes in their garden, then Sylvie would come back tomorrow. Because that was a lot of *ifs*.

15

Sylvie and Jess exchanged a smile as they sat in the back of the nice gentleman's car. As they set off, Sylvie explained to George the reason she had travelled all the way from London to find the cottage. She fell silent as they left the town behind them, searching the passing scenery for familiar landmarks hoping that she recognised something.

George drove the car down one country road after another until the road narrowed to a single lane track with occasional passing places. 'It's difficult to find,' said George conversationally. 'Like I said, it's a bit off the beaten track.'

'I see what you mean,' commented Sylvie. The narrow winding road weaved its way between heathlands of striking yellow gorse either side. There wasn't a house in sight for miles.

'It's beautiful – the scenery,' remarked Jess.

Sylvie smiled. Jess had never been to Cornwall before, but Sylvie could tell by her wide-eyed expression that she had already fallen in love with the place. Sylvie glanced out the car window. She too had been enjoying the scenery, but now the light was fading. Dusk was drawing in. Sylvie hoped they arrived soon before it got dark.

The cry of a seagull overhead interrupted Sylvie's thoughts. She could see them in the distance. 'Are we driving towards the sea?'

'That we are,' said George as they arrived at a farm gate and took a sharp left on to an unmade road. 'Nearly there.'

Sylvie leaned towards Jess to look out of the front window as a white building came into view.

Jess saw it too. 'Mum,' she whispered, 'it looks nothing like the cottage in your photograph.'

'I know,' said Sylvie. 'It might be further on,' she added just as the car pulled to a stop outside the house.

George switched off the car engine and turned in his seat.

Sylvie was afraid he would say this was it.

'We walk from here.' George shook his head. 'Ah, what I meant to say was that *you* will have to walk from here.' He slapped his thigh. 'Bloody leg. I can't get about like I used to.'

George pointed at the white building. 'If you walk past the farmhouse, you will come to a lane. Head down the lane toward the beach, and you will find the cottage about two hundred yards down on your left. If you reach the cove, then you've walked straight past it and you must double back.' He glanced at his watch. 'You better hurry, it'll be dark soon.'

Jess and Sylvie exchanged glances and got out of the car. They hurried past the farmhouse and located the narrow footpath with high hedges and brambles either side that led down to the beach.

Sylvie halted at the entrance to the lane.

Jess nearly walked into her. 'Mum, there's no time to dawdle. We better hurry before it gets dark, otherwise we will have to wait until tomorrow.'

Sylvie wasn't listening. For the first time since arriving in Cornwall, a vivid childhood memory surfaced; she remembered running down a narrow lane, bordered by hedges, to reach a vast expanse of sand sheltered by rocks on both sides.

'A cove,' breathed Sylvie, standing at the head of the lane. Was this the lane she used to run down from the cottage, carrying a bucket and spade, all those years ago?

'Mum, we have to go,' insisted Jess.

Sylvie nodded and stepped forward in between the narrow hedgerows. They walked briskly. So briskly in fact, that before they knew it the grass underfoot had given way to sand, and they were standing on a beach.

Sylvie stared at the wide expanse of sand sheltered by rocks before turning full circle to look back up the lane. If this was the lane, it seemed much shorter than she remembered. Sylvie frowned. There were many footpaths, just like this one, that led down to hundreds of coves all over Cornwall. Sylvie was already preparing herself for the inevitable disappointment if they discovered that they weren't in the right place after all.

'Oh wow.' Jess gazed up and down the beach. 'This is amazing.' Crystal green waters lapped gently on to the soft yellow sand. There wasn't a soul on the beach apart from Sylvie and Jess.

'Heavenly, isn't it,' commented Sylvie. She felt like stopping to watch the sunset, but they didn't have a torch to light the way back to the car. Besides, they hadn't come across the cottage yet. If they were in the right place, then they must have walked straight past it.

'We've passed it,' observed Jess, echoing Sylvie's thoughts. 'Perhaps we can see it from the beach?'

They both turned to face inland. The lane was a gentle slope down to the beach, so they should have been able to see the cottage from here. A row of tall conifers obscured their view.

Jess spotted something. 'Look over there, is that a chimney? Do you think it's the cottage?'

Sylvie saw it too. 'Come on.' Sylvie led the way back up the lane. They meandered, taking their time, until Sylvie spied a gap in the hedge up ahead and what appeared to be a gate partially obscured by overgrown foliage. Her pace quickened.

She stopped in front of the gate and brushed some foliage aside to reveal a small rusty metal nameplate. 'Trevelyan.' Sylvie's pulse raced in excitement.

'Do you recognise anything, Mum?'

So far, Sylvie thought she recognised everything. But she was loath to admit it until she had seen the cottage with her own eyes.

Sylvie put her hand on the gate and pushed it open. It swung forward off its hinge and fell to the floor in a crumpled pile of black rotting timber.

Sylvie and Jess exchanged glances. Neither Sylvie nor Jess wanted to voice their concerns. What if the cottage was now an empty ruin, just a shell, abandoned, forlorn and forgotten?

Sylvie stared at the gate that was no more. If that were true, what about the garden? There used to be a beautiful Cornish garden full of wildflowers. That's where Sylvie's mother wanted her ashes scattered. If the garden was somewhere beyond that broken gate, it would be unrecognisable – overgrown or dead – abandoned long ago just like the cottage, just like this gate. Sylvie couldn't leave her mother here. She turned to go.

'Mum, where are you going?'

'I made a mistake coming here, Jess.' Sylvie walked back up the lane shaking her head. 'How stupid of me to imagine after fifty years, things would be as I remembered them.' This scenario hadn't occurred to her, and she realised it should have.

Sylvie wasn't prepared for this. She didn't want to see a ruin, a relic of happier times. She needed to remember it as it once was, fixed in time by her memories; a cottage with a sunny aspect, white-washed walls, and small cottage windows either side of a sea-blue front door. She imagined the garden with seagulls crying overhead, and a gentle sea breeze whispering through flowers that stood taller than her, the way it used to be when she was a child. She wanted to remember it just as it was in the photograph.

'Mum, come back!'

Jess stood watching her mum disappear up the lane. She glanced down at the broken gate. Jess knew why she'd stormed off. In their enthusiastic search for the cottage, it hadn't occurred to either of them that they might not like what they find.

'Well, I will look anyway,' shouted Jess.

'Suit yourself,' Sylvie called out, her pace slowing. She wouldn't leave Jess down here alone; it would be dark soon. Sylvie turned back, and shouted, 'Be quick about it because it's getting dark!' She strolled down the lane in Jess's direction. 'And be careful!'

'I will,' Jess called back. She stepped over the gate and picked her way along an overgrown path that looked as though it had not been used in decades. A short distance away she could see the side of a white-washed building.

Approaching the building, Jess walked out between thick brambles on to a narrow neat pathway of small decorative stones which ran along the side of the property. She looked up and down the pathway, debating which way to go. She turned to her left, toward the beach and walked along the path until she arrived at a large shingle parking area. Jess stopped in the parking area and gazed up at the house. Her first impression was that it was far from derelict. The detached, white-washed property was immaculately presented, with white wooden windows that looked almost new, and decorative shutters painted sea blue. Expensive Venetian blinds were hanging at the windows. It was obvious this was someone's home. There was even a vase of fresh flowers in the window.

A security light flicked on bathing Jess in a pool of light and illuminating a paved driveway beyond the parking area that led up to a single-track tarmacadam road.

Caught in the security's beam, Jess peered up at the house expecting somebody to open the front door and ask her what she was doing trespassing on their property. However, she couldn't see any lights on in the house, and there were no cars parked on the drive. Jess presumed nobody was home. She was just wondering when the owners might return when she thought she heard something. It sounded like footsteps crunching on the stone pathway in the direction from which she had come.

'Oh Mum, you startled me!' gasped Jess as her mother came into view.

'Sorry,' said Sylvie as she walked over and joined Jess on the gravel drive in front of the house.

A few minutes ago, Sylvie had been standing at the broken gate calling Jess. Growing impatient, Sylvie had stepped over it and caught up with her.

'It's not the cottage, is it,' said Jess, sounding disappointed.

'No,' Sylvie replied emphatically. She stared up at the house. Apart from the white-washed exterior, which was not uncommon in these parts, it looked nothing like the double-fronted cottage in the photograph with its four windows straddling a quaint cottage-style front door. This is just what she had feared: they had demolished it to make way for a large modern property. Sylvie cast her eyes about her, taking it all in. There were neat, raised borders either side of the driveway. Two hanging baskets full of autumn flowers hung either side of the front door. The house looked well-maintained and cared for. It looked like someone's home.

'Mum, was this where the cottage once stood?'

'I think so,' observed Sylvie. When Sylvie had stepped over the broken gate, and walked along the overgrown path, she doubted the new owners even knew of the path's existence. It was a shortcut down to the beach that looked as though it had been unused in years, decades even. But it was that shortcut which brought back vivid childhood memories and confirmed to Sylvie that they had found the place where the cottage once stood. Sylvie's journey to find it was over. The cottage in her photograph, like her mother, was gone.

'We should go.'

Jess agreed. 'I'm so sorry, Mum.'

Sylvie still had the photograph in her hand. She held it up and sighed. 'I suppose it was to be expected that things wouldn't stay the same after all these years.'

'Come on, Mum, let's return to the car and go back to the pub with George to have a meal.'

'Jess, before we leave, I must knock at the house to apologise for breaking their gate and offer to pay for a new one.'

'That's not necessary, Mum. The gate hasn't been used in years. Maybe they weren't aware there was a path or a gate. Besides, I don't think the owner is in.'

Sylvie glanced at the empty driveway and then looked back at the house. Although Sylvie agreed that there was nobody home, she turned to Jess. 'Let's knock on their door just in case. I'd feel guilty if I didn't at least try.'

Sylvie stepped into the large gabled porch and knocked on the front door. She glanced about her, while she waited, and noted a pile of small logs stacked neatly on one side of the porch for firewood. The property looked modern from the outside, but had a cosy open fire, or perhaps a wood burner inside. Sylvie smiled. Although she didn't feel happy that she hadn't found the cottage, she much preferred this, to walk away knowing that fifty years on someone had built a home on the spot where it once stood. That was much, much better than discovering it had fallen into a state of disrepair, and all that was left was an abandoned shell. Sylvie preferred to walk away with her memory of the pretty little cottage still intact.

Jess joined her mother in the porch and rang the doorbell. 'See – nobody's home.'

'I suppose we should go.' Sylvie stepped out of the porch and glanced up the drive that led to the road. Perhaps that road led straight back to the farmhouse. Sylvie felt it might be quicker heading that way. However, it was getting dark rapidly and she didn't want to get lost. 'We had better retrace our steps to the broken gate and walk back the way we came.'

Sylvie came to a halt when she realised Jess wasn't following. She turned around. Jess was still standing in the middle of the drive peering up at the house. Sylvie retraced her steps. She could tell there was something on her mind. 'Jess – what is it?'

'We've established that the cottage is gone – no surprise there. But have we established the garden went with it?'

Sylvie shook her head. 'I don't follow...' Sylvie was keen to leave. The cottage was gone; that was all there was to it. At least she had found the spot where it used to be and could take back some memories of sharing that discovery with Jess.

'Grandma's last wish was to have her ashes scattered in the garden.' Jess turned her gaze on Sylvie. 'What if—'

Sylvie caught her train of thought. 'What if the garden still exists?'

Jess nodded emphatically.

Sylvie knocked that on the head. 'Jess, under the circumstances I don't think that's possible. I expect they demolished the old cottage to make way for rebuilding. The garden couldn't have survived that, surely?'

'There's only one way to find out,' said Jess, striding past Sylvie.

'Where are you going?' Sylvie watched her daughter take the narrow path alongside the house, passing the almost hidden gap in the bramble bush through which they'd come. At the end of the path, Jess arrived at a gate leading into the back garden.

'Jess, I don't think you should do that,' warned Sylvie, as she watched her daughter open the garden gate.

Jess ignored her.

'Jess, this is private property, and we're trespassing. We should wait for the owners to return.'

Jess looked back at Sylvie with a familiar glint in her eye, one Sylvie recognised from childhood: defiance. Jess had no intention of doing as she was told. 'Mum, what if they are away on holiday or something?' Jess called out. 'This could be our only chance to find out for sure.'

Sylvie was still wavering. She didn't feel comfortable nosing around someone else's home. She wouldn't like someone to do it to her. Out of nowhere an image of John sneaking through her side gate into the back garden, came to mind. It made her wonder how many times he'd been in and out of her place without her knowledge, carrying out those dastardly missions to sabotage the apartment, until she caught him in the act. Sylvie knew what John was up to when he knocked on her door later that day. Fortunately, Nigel was on hand to answer the door. Sylvie wasn't interested in hearing any more lame excuses for his behaviour or another grovelling apology. If he thought a homemade chicken pie would—

'Mum! Come quick. You've got to see this!'

Sylvie snapped out of her reverie. The garden gate was swinging wide open, and Jess was nowhere to be seen.

16

Sylvie hurried through the garden gate looking for her daughter and came to an abrupt halt. In an instant she was catapulted back to the 1950s. She stared at the familiar garden; a place she thought only existed in her memories. Rooted to the spot, she was afraid that if she stepped forward on to the narrow, cobbled path that snaked through the garden, like a mirage it would all disappear.

Sylvie reached out to touch a flower. The petals came off in her hand. 'It's real,' gasped Sylvie in astonishment as she took her first tentative step on to the path, still unable to believe the garden had survived.

On closer inspection, it looked different somehow. Sylvie realised she had never seen the garden in the autumn before. She was only familiar with those summers spent here as a child. It had left her with the lasting impression that it was forever summer in the garden. As she walked along the path autumn flowers swayed either side in the sea-breeze, some almost as tall as Sylvie. And there at the end of the footpath she saw the familiar cast iron garden seat for two looking out over the sea.

Sylvie stopped at the garden seat and looked down at the

cove below. It was a view she had not forgotten in over fifty years. Sylvie shook her head in wonder. It was as though the garden was frozen in time. She imagined that at any moment she would hear her mother's voice calling out for her to come in from the garden at teatime. Often her gentle voice was barely audible to the young Sylvie, lost in her own imaginary world as she played in this enchanting place.

Sylvie needed to sit down. She was overcome with so many emotions. Relief that the garden was still here, sadness at the inevitable passage of time, melancholy at the thought she would never walk in this garden with her mother again.

'It looks just like your garden at home,' remarked Jess as soon as Sylvie had caught up with her. Jess had been waiting for her by the seat at the end of the garden.

Sylvie decided not to spoil the moment by correcting her. Jess had not been home long enough to find out what John had done to her beloved garden during the conversion.

She sighed as she tried to push all thoughts of John, and what was going on at home, to the back of her mind. Instead, Sylvie concentrated on the view. It was just as she remembered it – all of it – the seashore, the cove, the white picket fence separating the garden from the gentle slope down to the beach.

Sylvie smiled as she walked up to the fence. On closer inspection, she discovered something had changed. When she was a child, the slope was full of wild brambles. Although the beach was just a short distance away, the brambles prevented access down to the beach from the garden. That's why she used to take a shortcut from the cottage along a footpath to the now rotting gate, which opened on to the public lane leading down to the shore. Sylvie glanced along the fence and noticed a gate that never used to be there. Jess noticed it too. She stepped forward to look over the fence. 'Look, some wooden steps lead down to the beach.' She voiced what they were both thinking, 'That explains the rotting gate, and why the path leading up to the side of the house was so overgrown.'

Sylvie nodded. 'They don't need to use the shortcut to the lane. They can walk to the end of their garden and stroll straight down to the cove.' Sylvie stared at the short flight of wooden steps leading down the gentle slope to the beach. The brambles had been replaced by shrubs and conifers providing a natural screen, and some privacy, from the beach. Sylvie glanced to her left and right and noticed wooden steps snaking down the slope from a handful of other properties.

Jess turned to look at her mother. 'Perhaps if we had walked along the beach a little further, we might have seen the garden.'

Sylvie shook her head. 'I doubt I would have recognised it even if we had. I was looking for the cottage that no longer exists, remember.'

'That's true,' remarked Jess, turning from the sea view to look at the back of the house for the first time.

Sylvie was about to sit down on the garden seat, and take a moment to reflect on all this, when Jess grabbed her by the shoulders and startled her.

'What is it?' said Sylvie in alarm, staring into her daughter's dark brown eyes. Only Jess could have brought her this far to find what she was looking for. If she had come on her own, or if she had come with Nigel, the garden would have been just a few feet away, but Sylvie would never have found it.

'Mum.' Jess looked very serious. 'I want you to take a deep breath. Will you do that for me?'

Sylvie wondered what was going on. Was Jess about to tell her she had spotted the owners, who had returned home to find two strangers standing in their garden? Sylvie didn't like the thought of that. She did as she was told and took a deep breath.

'Good. Are you ready?'

'Ready for what?'

Jess turned Sylvie away from the sea to look at the back of the house.

Sylvie's breath caught in her throat. 'Oh, my goodness, Jess.' Sylvie stared wide-eyed at her daughter. She held up the photograph clutched in her hand.

They both looked at the picture and then at the back of the house with its four small cottage windows straddling a sea-blue door. 'It can't be!' gasped Sylvie in astonishment.

'It can,' said, Jess beaming at her mother. She pointed at the photograph in Sylvie's hand. 'That photo was taken outside the back door of the cottage, not the front. This is where you and grandma were standing when it was taken. Right here in this garden.'

Now Sylvie did need to sit down. But it was too late for that; they could hear footsteps on the gravel path coming toward them from the side of the house. Before they could see who it was, they heard a familiar voice.

'Ah, there you are!' said George, holding his walking stick aloft before making his way up the cobbled pathway towards them. He joined them by the garden seat. 'I see you've found what you were looking for,' he said, leaning on his walking stick as he looked up at the cottage.

He glanced down at the photo in Sylvie's hand. 'It hasn't changed a bit.' Adding, 'At least the back hasn't. I can't say the same about the front of the cottage.' He chuckled. 'Still, all's well that ends well.'

'Yes,' agreed Sylvie, 'very well indeed, thanks to you and Jess.' She smiled at them both thinking how fortunate she was that Jess and George had joined her on her quest.

'Now, all we have to do is contact the owners and ask their permission to...' Sylvie trailed off.

They all stood there staring at the garden. The only sound was the gentle whoosh of the surf lapping on the beach below, and the occasional cry of a seagull.

Jess said, 'It's getting dark. If there's no sign of the owners, I guess we better head back.'

Sylvie nodded in agreement, and all three headed back down the cobbled path towards the cottage.

'Just a minute.' Jess stopped by the garden gate and unzipped the small canvas rucksack she had brought with her. 'George, do you mind...?'

George smiled amiably, 'Not at all.'

Jess handed George her digital camera. 'Mum? Do you mind if George takes a photo of us together outside the cottage?'

'Do I mind?' repeated Sylvie, feeling quite overcome with emotion. 'Of course not. As long as you take it before I end up in floods of tears!'

Sylvie and Jess stood together outside the back door of the cottage in the same spot Sylvie had stood with her mother all those years ago. Sylvie still had the old black-and-white photograph in her hand; as far as she was aware, it was the only one ever taken of them on holiday together in Cornwall.

Sylvie was staring into the camera lens, waiting for George to take a picture, when it dawned on her she had no idea who had taken that photograph of her and her mother all those years ago. As far as Sylvie could recall, it was only the two of them who holidayed in the cottage. But on that summer's day, back in 1959, somebody else must have been there with them in the garden. Try as she might, Sylvie could not remember who was behind the camera taking that picture.

'Say cheese!'

'Cheese!'

As soon as they took the photo, Sylvie reached for a tissue.

George handed the camera back to Jess and looked up at the brooding dark sky. They were losing the light fast. 'This way,' said George, holding his walking stick aloft as though he was a tour guide leading the way.

Sylvie and Jess followed him along the side of the house, passing the almost indiscernible gap in the hedge and the overgrown path beyond from whence they came. George insisted they follow him back to the shingle drive in front of the house.

'I brought the car.' George pointed at it with his stick. He turned to Sylvie. 'I must apologise. I was waiting for you outside the farmhouse where I dropped you off, when the farmer and his wife returned. I explained that I'd sent you down the lane to find the cottage. That's when they told me that the present owners had built a massive extension on the front, together with a new driveway leading up to the road. So, I'm afraid I sent you down the lane for no reason when I could just as easily have driven you straight here.'

'No need to apologise, George,' said Sylvie, squeezing his arm affectionately. It was just as well they had not arrived by car, but he had dropped them off at the farmhouse to walk the rest of the way. Without the lane leading to the beach, or the rotting gate, or the forgotten pathway through the brambles to the side of the house, Sylvie would have dismissed the house instantly. She would have assumed that it wasn't the cottage in her photograph without even stepping foot out of the car. What a stroke of good luck that serendipity had played a part in Sylvie finding what she was looking for.

Now she had the final leg of her journey to complete which was to say goodbye to her mother in this special place. First, she wanted to speak to the owners and make an unusual request: to scatter her mother's ashes in their garden.

'Does the farmer know the owners of the cottage?' Sylvie inquired. 'Do they have any idea when they will return?'

'We were chatting about that,' said George as he opened the car door for Sylvie and Jess before he got in the driver's seat. George started the car engine and recounted what they had told him as he drove back to town. 'The farmer has only seen the owners on a handful of occasions. They bought the property as a holiday home had it renovated and built the extension. However, it sounds as though that was some years ago. Now they hardly ever visit.'

'Oh,' said Sylvie, sounding disappointed.

Jess leaned forward in her seat with a question, 'Are you sure about that because the cottage looks so lovingly taken care of?'

Sylvie agreed with Jess's sentiments. 'Yes, as though it's someone's home.'

'I can see why you would think that,' said George, as he made a right turn at the farm gate on to the long winding road bordered by heathland. 'Now, according to the farmer,' continued George, 'the property is managed in the owner's absence by a local estate agent in the village. They send in a cleaner, a gardener, and even a handyman to take care of things. I think he mentioned the name of the estate agents. Oh, darn it. I can't remember.'

'How many estate agents are there in the town?' asked Jess.

'Only the one.' George made a left turn on to the main road. 'Maybe they could give you more information or perhaps contact the owners for you.'

'Yes, that's worth a try,' said Sylvie, 'but first, we are all going back to the pub to have a well-earned meal.' Sylvie leaned forward and rested her hand on George's shoulder. 'I hope you and your wife can join us. It will be my treat. You've been such a great help, George. It's the least I can do.'

'Well now, how can I refuse an offer like that from such a pretty, young lady?' George winked at Sylvie in the rear-view mirror.

Jess saw that and frowned at her mother.

Sylvie shrugged at Jess and turned to look out the window, smiling to herself. Although sprightly for his age, Sylvie guessed George must be in his eighties. And he was married. That didn't stop Sylvie enjoying the compliment.

A pretty, young lady. Sylvie hadn't been called that in years. Suddenly what came to mind was a rather nice evening she'd spent in the company of Nigel. There was someone else who seemed to appreciate her. Sylvie made a mental note to call Nigel as soon as she returned home.

Sylvie was relieved that it had turned out straightforward to find the property thanks to George and a spot of good luck. Having established that it was the cottage in the photograph, a crowd of interested locals gathered around their table in the pub that evening offering as much information as they could. Some of that information Sylvie already knew, thanks to the farmer and his wife who lived in the farmhouse nearby. George mentioned that the farmer and his wife had seen few visitors to the cottage over the years. They didn't know the owners by name, but they believed they were American. This was echoed by local gossip suggesting an American of Italian descent had bought the property in the sixties. It remained in the same family ever since.

Although it had been easy to locate the cottage, finding the owner would prove far more difficult than Sylvie first thought. According to the locals gathered around their table, nobody of that description had been seen around these parts in years.

Sylvie took comfort from the fact that the property was not abandoned. It wasn't rundown or neglected – far from it. From what she'd seen, the cottage had been lovingly maintained. If the amount of money they had lavished on it over the years was anything to go by, the absent owner loved that place just as much as her mother used to all those years ago.

Sylvie learned that the farmer was correct when he said that a local letting agent had held a contract for managing and maintaining the property. Rumour had it that the American owner was one of their oldest clients. Sylvie intended to pay the agent a visit first thing in the morning.

'We could pop in and see the estate agent before we leave tomorrow,' suggested Jess. 'All they need to do is give us a name and contact number, so we can make a quick phone call. Once we've spoken to the owner, the taxi driver could take us back to the cottage before we leave for the train station, so you can show grandma the garden.'

'Show grandma the garden,' repeated Sylvie, appreciating the euphemism. She smiled at Jess. 'We'll show her together.'

'I'd like that very much,' said Jess, returning her smile.

Sylvie couldn't wait until the morning when she could get in touch with the American and explain what she wanted to do. She only hoped he or she was agreeable.

Sylvie felt like pinching herself to be sure she wasn't dreaming. She still couldn't believe how well this trip had turned out and had every confidence that she would be on her way home tomorrow with an empty urn and her mother's final request fulfilled.

'I'm sorry, but I can't divulge that information.'

Sylvie and Jess were sitting in the estate agent's office in the town square the following morning. A young employee was not being helpful. At least that's what Sylvie thought when she asked for the name and contact number of the American who owned Trevelyan.

She tried asking again.

'I'm sorry, but I still can't divulge that information.'

Sylvie frowned at the young man. 'Then I would like to speak to someone who can, like your manager for instance.'

Five minutes later Sylvie and Jess were standing outside at the kerb waiting for the taxi to take them back to the train station.

'That was a waste of time,' remarked Jess, fiddling with the straps on her rucksack as the taxi drew up to the kerb.

'Not completely,' Sylvie replied as she opened the car door.

The taxi driver set off for the train station. He remembered the photograph Sylvie had shown him yesterday and asked them whether they had found that cottage. Jess told him all about their eventful trip, and how a chance encounter with a kind gentleman called George led them to a forgotten, overgrown pathway, and the cottage in the photograph – Trevelyan.

Sylvie was thinking back to the conversation she'd had with the manager of the estate agents. She had shown him the photograph and told him some of the history of the cottage. Many years ago, her mother had inherited the property from an aunt. Her aunt had no children of her own, so she had left the cottage to her favourite niece – Sylvie's mother. Sylvie had holidayed there every summer as a child. Strapped for cash raising five children on a vicar's salary, her mum was forced to sell her little corner of paradise when Sylvie was eleven years old.

Sylvie didn't add that it marked the end of her childhood, with the rows, silences and tension between her parents. It also marked the beginning of Sylvie's journey into adolescence, and her escape from an unhappy home.

Sylvie believed her mother never got over being forced to let go of her beloved cottage. She had grown up in Cornwall and had fond memories of visiting her aunt nearby, spending time at the cottage by the sea. It was something she had passed down to Sylvie when she took her there on holiday. Perhaps it was something she wanted for her grandchildren, to spend time with their mother, Sylvie, in the cottage by the sea. But it wasn't to be.

Once, when Sylvie visited her in the care home towards the end, when her mind had succumbed to dementia, she told Sylvie that she wanted to leave the cottage to her when she was gone. She had forgotten that it was no longer hers to give; it hadn't been for years.

It occurred to Sylvie that perhaps her mother had written

that note, outlining her final request for her ashes to be scattered in the cottage garden, still believing it belonged to her. Whatever the case, Sylvie intended to honour her wishes. However, her mother hadn't made things easy. Locating the cottage should have been a walk in the park; she once owned it after all. But Sylvie could find no address, not even on the handwritten note she had left in her will expressing her wishes.

At first, Sylvie wasn't concerned. She assumed a quick phone call to Cornwall Council would clear that up. However, her mother's name didn't turn up on the electoral register in Cornwall because they registered her to vote in London where she lived. The Land Registry was her next port of call. Unfortunately, Sylvie found herself in a catch-22; without the address of the property, or even an idea of the location, searching the Land Registry was a pointless exercise. She'd hit a brick wall until she found that photograph.

Sylvie had sat in the estate agents unable to believe that she had come this far, only for her plans to be dashed at the last hurdle. She had been candid with the manager about the reason for her visit and the need to contact the owner. She knew it was an unusual request, but it meant so much to her mother to return to that cottage.

The manager had listened attentively. He explained that the American was one of their oldest clients. They had looked after the property in his absence since the 1960s. It was an old-fashioned arrangement, at least by today's standards. All correspondence came through his solicitor in America. They never dealt with the owner direct and didn't even know his private address. They sent all bills to his lawyer and payment was always received in full. The only correspondence address was the solicitor's office in New York; the manager couldn't even divulge that because of client confidentiality.

The only thing they could do for Sylvie was send a letter to the lawyer in New York on her behalf. He passed her some notepaper and a pen, asking if she would like to write a letter. Sylvie had agreed. To her surprise, he then told her the name of the American who owned the cottage. Sylvie had thanked him for making it possible to address her letter personally to the present owner, Paolo Morelli.

She'd written everything she had told the manager. How her mother had inherited the cottage, and how fortunate she had been to spend summers there as a child. She explained how those holidays ended when her mother sold her beloved cottage some years before Mr Morelli bought it as a holiday home. Sylvie ended the letter with the sad news of her mother's death and the reason she was sending him this letter, to seek his permission to have her ashes scattered in the garden of Trevelyan Cottage. Sylvie had sealed the letter and handed it to the manager.

Before taking the letter, he had offered to drive them out to the property instead and turn a blind eye while they went into the back garden and did what she came here to do.

Sylvie and Jess had thanked him for the offer but refused even though they both realised they were making the whole affair more drawn out and convoluted.

The manager had promised to send the letter that day.

Sylvie hoped that when Mr Morelli received her note explaining the circumstances of their visit, he might contact her. She had included all her contact details in the letter just in case.

Jess and Sylvie both agreed that although they had travelled a long way, and it was tempting to take the manager up on his offer to return to the cottage and scatter her mother's ashes, for reasons they couldn't explain, contacting the owner felt like the right thing to do under the circumstances.

The taxi dropped them off outside Newquay train station. They boarded the train and Sylvie settled into a window seat. In her hand, she had the next issue of the monthly magazine she always bought – the one Harriet worked for – and a paperback novel by Daphne du Maurier to keep her occupied during the five-and-a-half-hour train journey back to London.

Sylvie put the book and magazine on the table in front of her. Jess passed her a large disposable cup of coffee that she had bought at the station before they boarded the train. They exchanged a smile before settling down for the journey, Jess plugging earphones into her mobile phone to listen to music, and Sylvie opening the magazine. She took the plastic lid off her disposable coffee cup and glanced out the window as the train left the station.

Sylvie knew her decision to send the letter had delayed things, and it would mean a return trip to Cornwall soon, but this didn't bother her. In fact, she was rather looking forward to it. Although Jess wouldn't be around next time she returned to Cornwall, Sylvie already had somebody else in mind as her travelling companion – and maybe more besides. She'd received a voice message on her mobile phone from him this morning saying he hoped her trip had gone well, and he was looking forward to seeing her when she got back.

Sylvie smiled. She was looking forward to seeing Nigel too and inviting him to accompany her on the next trip.

17

'People actually do this for fun?' John naively assumed he would enjoy his shopping trip with Chloe. He imagined they would spend two hours leisurely wandering in and out of a few shops to buy some new clothes. Although John bought his clothes from one department store, he thought this would make a pleasant change. Not to mention an agreeable way to kill an afternoon before Sylvie and Jess arrived home from Cornwall later that day. He couldn't have been more wrong.

John was not anticipating an expedition worthy of Ernest Shackleton. That was a huge exaggeration. Nonetheless, he did not expect to spend an entire day shopping, and to find himself so exhausted by the end of it that he felt as though he'd trekked to the South Pole and back, rather than up and down Oxford Street.

And it wasn't over yet.

'I want to visit a few more shops Daddy, and then I have a surprise for you.'

John was dragging himself behind Chloe, with umpteen shopping bags in his hands, wondering why she was still looking so bright and cheerful after a full six hours shopping. But then she was three decades younger and buoyed up because all the shopping bags were hers.

'You know I don't like surprises,' said John glumly, not bothering to hide his irritability.

'You'll like this one. We're going to the salon for a makeover. I was thinking of a haircut, manicure and pedicure – the works. A little something to look forward to when we've finished shopping. It will be my treat.'

It better be, John thought. He wasn't sure what a manicure or a pedicure was, but Chloe would have to foot the bill. John had neglected to mention that he was strapped for cash, although it probably hadn't gone unnoticed how many store cards he had signed up for during their shopping expedition. He had never owned a credit card in his life. In the space of one day, he had accumulated six and counting. And that was just on Chloe's clothes. John didn't realise how expensive this shopping trip with his daughter would turn out to be.

If the cost and accumulation of credit – as they now called debt – wasn't bad enough, he'd had enough of the shopping trip after only fifteen minutes when he realised Chloe expected him to try on the clothes in the store; John had never done that before. He just picked his size off the rail and paid for it.

'That's because you buy the same clothes, year in and year out, from the same department store, Daddy. This time it's different. This time you *have* to try them on.' They were standing outside the changing rooms of yet another shop, six hours later, having the same argument they'd had at every shop they'd walked into.

Chloe held up the new shirt. 'Are you going to do as you're told?'

John grabbed the shirt and stormed into the changing room. He caught sight of a shop assistant staring at him. 'What are you looking at?' John said rudely, before stepping into a cubicle and pulling the curtain shut.

'Dad – are you in there?'

'Of course, I'm in here,' snapped John, opening the curtain two seconds later. 'I've just stepped inside for goodness' sake, where else would I be?'

Chloe ignored the sarcastic comment. 'I've got a few more things for you to try on.' She was holding a pair of jeans, another shirt, a jacket and some shoes.

'Do I have to?'

Chloe handed them to the shop assistant who hung them on the peg inside the changing cubicle. His every move watched by a very tired, very irritable customer called John.

'I am not wearing *that*,' whined John, trying to wrestle the cravat out of the shop assistant's hands.

'The lady says you are.'

John glanced over at Chloe. She was standing with her hands on her hips staring at him intently. Next time he offered to go shopping with his youngest daughter... John threw her a dirty look and shook his head; after this experience, there wouldn't be a next time.

John shut the curtain. Trying on the clothes wasn't the worst of it. Then he had to suffer the humiliation of walking outside the changing rooms to show Chloe, and the entire shop floor, what he looked like. He peered out from behind the curtain. This was the bit that always made him feel self-conscious, as though he was stepping out in the emperor's new clothes.

John sidled out of the changing cubicle in his new set of

clothes, including a new pair of shoes, a jacket and a brown trilby hat that had appeared in his changing cubicle when he wasn't looking. He was fiddling with the cravat when he spotted Chloe. She had her back to him. 'Psst!'

Chloe was busy rifling through a rack of brown suede jackets looking for John's size.

'Chloe!' John called out softly, not wanting to attract too much attention.

She didn't hear him.

He had no option but to leave the safe haven of the changing rooms and walk out into the glare of the shop to attract her attention. 'Chloe!'

She must have heard him calling her name because she turned around and looked about her. But she didn't see John.

John walked right up to her and tapped her on the shoulder. 'Chloe?'

'Oh, Dad! You surprised me.'

'I was standing right there,' John pointed an irritated finger at a spot close to where Chloe was standing. He glanced down at his new outfit. 'Well, what do you think?'

Chloe looked him over.

John wondered why she was so quiet. 'What is it?'

'You look... different.'

'You mean I look stupid.' John eyed his daughter, trying to second guess what she was thinking. 'I knew it!' He flung his arms in the air, taking her silence to mean that's exactly what she thought of his new outfit. 'This is turning out a complete waste of time.' John turned toward the changing rooms and caught a young lady looking him up and down.

She smiled mischievously at John.

John stopped and tentatively smiled back as she walked past.

Chloe walked over to her dad and linked her arm in his.

'To borrow an Americanism,' said John, staring at the young woman, 'did she just check me out?'

'You do know it's rude to stare.' Chloe rolled her eyes at him. 'Come on, Romeo,' she said, pulling him toward the changing rooms. 'For your information, Daddy, when I said you looked different, I meant it in a nice way. I've never seen you dressed in these sorts of clothes before. You surprised me – that's all.'

'I did?'

'Oh, yes. You look good in that outfit.'

'Really?' said John, checking himself out in the long mirror in the changing rooms before he shut the curtain. He was inclined to agree. Maybe Sylvie was in for a surprise after all.

John smiled at his reflection thinking goodbye Nigel, hello the new and improved John.

18

The new and improved John was standing between Harriet and Chloe on his front doorstep later that afternoon. All three were looking up and down the street for any sign of the taxi bringing Sylvie and Jess home from Paddington station.

John looked at his watch and glanced at Chloe. 'I thought you said they would be here by now?'

Chloe checked her phone. 'Jess sent the text message that they'd arrived at Paddington station fifteen minutes ago. It only takes ten minutes by taxi, but that depends on the traffic.'

John pursed his lips. He was nervous and glanced down at the new set of clothes he was wearing. A pair of jeans – the first he'd bought in decades – a grey flannel shirt, a brown tailored suede jacket with the collar turned up, and a tanned leather pair of shoes pointed at the toes. John kept looking down at his shoes, still undecided if he liked them or not. He left the brown trilby hat and cravat upstairs because that might be overdoing it.

John was shocked to discover that he could have clothed himself for an entire year on the cost of that one outfit alone. It was only after their shopping expedition together that Chloe explained the difference between the high street stores and the designer shops where she'd taken him, and where they spent most of their time – and his money. John would rather not have bought designer labels if he'd known he would run up credit to the tune of the national debt of a small country. He told Chloe as much.

Chloe found that comment hilarious. John wasn't surprised his financial concerns went right over her head. As the baby of the family, she would not remember the years of struggle. She grew up in relative comfort with parents who always afforded to put their hand in their pocket. It would shock Chloe to learn that her father could barely cover his grocery bill, let alone designer labels. John hoped this was all worth it. Especially after the small fortune Chloe forked out at the salon for his new hairstyle. At least he knew she could afford it.

His full head of hair had impressed the ladies at the salon. They said it made him appear younger than his years, even though his honey-coloured hair had faded to pepper-grey years ago. When the ladies at the salon suggested that he should dye his hair he adamantly refused, insisting that he did not want to resemble an ageing film star trying to turn back the clock.

They cajoled John into having highlights instead. The colour was subtle and blended well with his grey hair. It would take time to get used to. John ran his hand through his hair for the umpteenth time, and Chloe noticed.

'Dad, you look fine.'

'Do I?' He was unsure whether Chloe was being serious or taking the mickey; sometimes, with his youngest daughter, he could never quite tell.

John turned to Harriet instead, looking for some reassurance that he wasn't about to make a complete fool of himself.

Harriet said, 'I agree with Chloe, the highlights are great, and the outfit suits you, Dad. It makes a change to see you dressed in something different. You always used to wear the same old-fashioned clothes. It was so... boring.'

John raised an eyebrow.

'Sorry, Dad. I'm just being honest. It's nice to see you experiment and try something new. I'm sure Mum will like the new you.' Harriet glanced at Chloe. 'We like it.'

Chloe nodded.

Alfie yapped as if in agreement.

John glanced down at the dog. 'I didn't ask you, Muttley.' He thought he'd seen the back of the dog when Julia arrived after Sylvie's one-to-one puppy training class and took the dog away. John assumed things hadn't gone well and Sylvie had decided not to keep the dog. He didn't know Julia was only looking after him while Sylvie was away in Cornwall. Imagine his disappointment when Harriet turned up at the house today with Alfie. She'd collected him from Julia on her way over. John was expecting Harriet to bring along his grandchild, Gertie, instead. However, it was Gertie's teatime, and Harriet had left her daughter at home with her husband. John wished she'd left the dog there too.

John was scowling at the dog when his eyes drifted to his pointy shoes. Despite Chloe and Harriet's reassurances, he still didn't feel comfortable in his new clothes, and realised that this different style would take some getting used after decades of conservative, boring John. There was also the unexpected attention he was attracting in his new outfit. When he nipped out to the local grocery store in his new gear, to buy a bottle of bubbly for this evening, some women shoppers smiled at him. To his surprise, one even struck up a conversation as he waited in the queue at the checkout. That never happened before. Women were taking notice of him; that was new.

John inspected himself in the mirror when he returned home from the grocery store. He turned up his collar and made sure his shirt was not tucked in his trousers, just as Chloe instructed. But somehow, despite all the positive attention in the shop, he still didn't feel he pulled off the Nigel look, and had an idea why.

John was aware he needed to lose a few pounds that had crept on over the years. Not that he was enormously overweight, but he knew he no longer cut a youthful figure like Nigel. John's slim build had given way to middle-aged spread years ago. And it stayed for the duration, much to his annoyance. That wasn't any surprise considering Sylvie's fondness for Italian cooking, together with his lack-lustre approach to any form of exercise over the years. A quick phone call to Dave, updating him on the success of his shopping trip with Chloe, resulted in John sharing his weight issues.

Dave suggested a personal trainer. John didn't like the idea of running around his local park with some fitness fanatic ordering him around. Besides, he didn't have the money for a personal trainer. Much better the gym which was Dave's other suggestion. He'd searched the Yellow Pages and signed up for a gym membership over the phone. The next hurdle was to attend the gym and see if he could shed some weight. But first, he was about to find out if Sylvie liked his new outfit.

'Oh look, it's them!' shouted Chloe, waving as the taxi approached.

Alfie started barking and wagging his tail in excitement.

John glanced down at his outfit one final time.

Sylvie thought she heard Alfie barking and looked out of the car window as the taxi drew up outside their house. She was aware Jess sent Chloe a text to let her know when they would arrive home. However, she wasn't expecting a welcoming committee. Sylvie's attention was drawn to John standing in between Chloe and Harriet. Was that a new outfit he was wearing? She had never seen him dress in those sorts of clothes before.

He looked different.

'Mum, we're home.'

He looked handsome.

'Mum, what are you staring at?' Jess leaned across her to look out of the window and find out what had caught her attention.

'Oh nothing,' Sylvie replied, not realising she had been staring.

Chloe, Harriet, and John walked down the front steps of the house toward them as Sylvie and Jess climbed out of the taxi.

John was first in line to greet Jess with a fatherly hug and an annoying mutt around his ankles. Alfie was jumping up and down trying to worm his way between them. He succeeded.

'Ah, this must be Alfie,' said Jess, her attention diverted from her father to Sylvie's puppy. She knelt. 'Isn't he adorable?'

John looked down at the dog, with a sour expression. 'That's what your mother thinks.'

Jess scooped up the wriggly black cocker spaniel in her arms and gave him a hug.

Chloe and Harriet came over and hugged their sister. Alfie was still in her arms and got a hug too. He licked everyone's faces in excitement, clearly enjoying all the attention.

Sylvie stood on the pavement by the taxi watching all this. Seeing her family together brought a tear to her eye. She smiled at the girls. Despite their differing lifestyles and vocations, over the years her daughters had not drifted apart as one might expect. The sisters had grown closer. Perhaps there was some truth in the adage that distance makes the heart grow fonder, thought Sylvie. She stole a glance at John.

The three girls linked arms and walked up the front path to the house, leaving Sylvie to pay for the taxi.

After Sylvie handed over the taxi fare, she turned around to find John standing on the pavement next to her.

'Hello, John.'

'Hello, Sylvie.' He bent down to give her a tentative welcome home kiss. He felt like an awkward teenager on a first date unsure whether he would get a slap around the face for being so forward.

'Have you done something to your hair?' remarked Sylvie, noticing on closer inspection that his clothes weren't the only thing that had gone through a transformation while she was away.

'Oh this?' John pointed at his head. 'I fancied doing something different,' he said casually, trying to make out that it was no big deal while feeling absurdly elated that Sylvie had noticed. 'I went to a salon to have some highlights.' He left out the part about how he was cajoled into doing it.

'Do you like it?' John asked, anxious that after he had gone to so much trouble, she might not like it – the clothes, the hair, him. Or worse, that she could see right through him and knew what he was up to: trying to appear more attractive. Trying to be more like Nigel.

Sylvie gave him the once over. 'You look nice,' she said.

More than nice; but she kept that thought to herself.

John looked down at his outfit and smiled as he followed Sylvie through the gate, along the path and up the front steps to the house. He walked into the communal hall where the three girls had congregated. They were all talking at once.

John shut the front door on the chilly November day.

'Dad, did you hear the news?' said Harriet and Chloe, both talking at once.

John turned around. Seeing them all together took him back to when they were children. Jess, always the quiet one, was standing off to one side leaving her sisters vying with each other to get his attention.

'They found the cottage,' announced Harriet.

'Can you believe it!' exclaimed Chloe, raising her voice to drown out her sister.

'That's excellent news.' John was pleased to learn that Sylvie's mother – or what was left of her – would no longer be residing in his house. He glanced at Sylvie who was unlocking her apartment door. 'So, that business is all taken care of then?'

Sylvie swung around to look at him. 'That business,' repeated Sylvie, narrowing her eyes. John had always referred to her mother as *that business*. Sylvie had forgotten all about it until he'd just reminded her.

John thought Sylvie had asked him a question. 'You know... that business of scattering your mother's ashes.'

Sylvie knew very well what he was talking about. She glanced at Jess and replied, 'Not exactly.'

'What do you mean *not exactly*? The girls said you found the cottage.'

'We couldn't find the owner,' explained Jess.

'I don't see why...?' John paused. 'You mean you couldn't get into the garden to—'

'They went into the garden,' interrupted Chloe.

'Jess even took a photograph,' added Harriet. 'They both stood right on the spot where Mum and Grandma had their photo taken all those years ago.'

'Isn't it amazing,' added Chloe, who always had to have the last word.

John stared at each one of them in turn. Was he missing something? 'I don't understand. If you found the cottage and went into the garden, then why didn't you—'

'I told you,' said Sylvie, a note of irritation in her voice. 'The owner wasn't around to ask their permission. They don't live there. It's a holiday home. So, I wrote them a letter explaining what I want to do. Hopefully, I'll hear back soon.'

'A letter?' John's voice held a note of derision. 'Why did you bother doing that?'

'It felt like the right thing to do.'

John looked at her askance. He couldn't believe they had travelled all that way to Cornwall, found the cottage, stepped foot in the garden, and *still* come back with... John stared at Sylvie's hand luggage and thought of that urn back in his house. At this rate, when was that business ever going to be over and done with?

'I'll tell you what would have been the right thing to do,' blurted John, 'you should have just scattered her ashes and got it over and done with.'

'Over and done with?' Sylvie repeated crossly. 'That's my mother you're talking about!'

'Yes, that's Grandma you're talking about!' Jess, Harriet and Chloe added in unison.

John looked at the girls all nodding their heads in agreement and casting a black look in his direction. He realised he was woefully outnumbered and had made a huge gaffe. 'On the other hand…' he said sheepishly, attempting to backtrack.

Sylvie ignored him and walked into her apartment. She held the door open and the three girls followed her inside.

Alfie scampered after them.

John tried to come too.

Sylvie stopped him at the door. 'Oh no, you don't.'

He could hear the girls inside Sylvie's apartment speaking in hushed voices until Jess called out, 'We've decided to have a girls' night in.'

Sylvie looked at John. 'You heard her.'

'Oh, come on! Is it because of what I said? I take it back.'

'Too late,' said Sylvie, and shut the door.

19

Sylvie couldn't remember the last time they were all together enjoying one another's company. Chloe had brought a case of wine with her and Sylvie ordered a takeaway from the local Chinese restaurant.

While they were waiting for the food to be delivered Jess found the bottle opener. They intended to have a glass of wine or two before dinner.

Harriet followed Chloe downstairs to fetch some glasses. From the lounge, Sylvie heard Harriet and Chloe deep in conversation although she couldn't discern what they were saying. Sylvie glanced over at Jess. 'I wonder what's taking them so long.'

Jess bounced off the sofa. 'Let's find out.'

As they made their way down the stairs, Sylvie could still hear Harriet and Chloe in the kitchen. They appeared to be talking in hushed voices. She noticed they fell silent as soon as she walked into the room.

'We were just on our way up,' said Harriet.

Sylvie knew that wasn't true but let it pass. She realised what they were talking about. The last thing she wanted was to get drawn into a discussion about John and their separate living arrangements and certainly didn't want to be asked *that* question again: are you getting a divorce?

Jess followed Sylvie into the kitchen and spotted the dramatic change in the garden. She was about to say something when she caught Harriet and Chloe shaking their heads, warning her off bringing up the subject of the garden. Jess shut her mouth and took a glass of wine instead.

Harriet poured one for Sylvie. 'Mum, we want to hear all about your trip to Cornwall.'

They all trooped back upstairs, apart from Chloe. She glanced at the small glass of wine in her hand and rushed back to the kitchen table to grab the bottle.

It wasn't long before Chloe made another trip downstairs to the kitchen to fetch two more bottles of wine. Drinking and chatting were in free flow as the conversation alternated between their trip to Cornwall, what Jess had been up to on the other side of the world, and news closer to home.

Jess wanted to hear all about her niece, Gertie. She couldn't wait to see her. She was surprised when Harriet showed her a recent photograph of her baby – now a little girl of two and a half. She'd changed in the space of a year. It put into perspective how much time had elapsed since Jess had last seen her family.

They vowed to get together more often. Chloe said she'd always wanted to take a break from work and go travelling. She suggested that on her travels she could visit Jess down under. Harriet thought that if Jess ever fancied visiting New York with her partner, perhaps they might get together during one of Harriet's frequent trips across the pond to attend meetings at the magazine's New York office.

All three girls avoided the subject of their parents' new living arrangements, Sylvie noticed, apart from their keen interest in how she had decorated and furnished the apartment. It pleased her to discover that they all adored what she'd done with the place. So much so that she took them on a grand tour.

Starting downstairs in the basement kitchen, Sylvie told them how, with Julia's help, they painted John's new wooden kitchen cabinets vintage green. Then they hunted high and low to find the perfect Welsh dresser to complete her kitchen.

Sylvie continued the tour back upstairs in the lounge. She explained that John's idea was to have two modernised apartments. 'During the conversion he stripped out all its original features, including the original fireplace, would you believe.' Sylvie grimaced. 'He had an ugly wall-mounted electric fire put in its place.'

Harriet looked at her in surprise. 'Really?'

'Never!' exclaimed Jess, staring at the fireplace.

'It is such a lovely fireplace,' said Chloe, who always had to have the last word.

Sylvie nodded. 'I agree, Chloe, that's why I had your father's ugly modern fire taken away and the original fireplace restored, as you can see.' Sylvie finished the tour in the bedroom.

Jess looked at her mum. 'I thought Dad intended converting the house into *two* two-bedroomed apartments?'

'That's correct, Jess. He did.' Sylvie wanted a bedroom with more space and light. She sacrificed the second bedroom to achieve it. 'The builders simply removed the partition wall separating the two bedrooms – and *voila*!' Sylvie showed them a section of blank wall in the hall where there used to be a doorway to the second bedroom.

As they all trooped back into the lounge, Sylvie told the girls that she knew their father would throw a fit if he discovered what the builders were up to, turning his two-bedroomed rental apartment into a one-bed. Perhaps because she'd drunk too much wine, she mentioned the fun she'd had at his expense. To keep him out of her apartment on the day she had left the builders to do their job, she informed them of a few things about her neighbour upstairs.

Before she revealed her tale, she made it quite clear to the girls that she hadn't told a single fib. She had simply informed the builders that as soon as John upstairs heard them at work in the garden apartment, he would be down here like a shot – like a nosy neighbour – to find out what they were up to. And he would use any tactic to get inside the apartment, telling them that he was her husband, and that he owned this house.

'And true to form that is exactly what he did.' Sylvie smiled. 'The builders formed a human barricade in front of the door and wouldn't let him in. They said he was fuming.'

The girls fell about laughing when Sylvie told them this. They were all in such hysterical fits of giggles, jollied along by countless glasses of wine consumed on empty stomachs, that nobody heard the doorbell.

John heard the doorbell downstairs and expected Sylvie or one of the girls to answer the front door. He wouldn't be surprised if they hadn't picked up on it, with all that hysterical laughter. He could hear them from his lounge upstairs where he was trying to read the newspaper.

He folded the newspaper in two and put it in the wicker magazine rack beside his chair before making his way downstairs.

He could still hear them as he passed by Sylvie's door. He raised an eyebrow, wondering what was so funny.

He opened the front door. A young delivery driver was standing on the doorstep. He handed John several white plastic bags that gave off the distinctive aroma of Chinese food. John's mouth watered. He didn't know Sylvie had ordered takeaway. There was an awkward moment when he realised he didn't have the money to pay for it. To his relief, it turned out that Sylvie had already paid for it over the phone when she ordered the food.

John shut the front door and walked across the communal hall to call on Sylvie. He could still hear their laughter. He looked at the plastic bags and hoped their good humour extended to inviting him in to share their meal. He was hungry and was feeling lonely sitting upstairs by himself listening to the laughter and joviality just a few feet below him. He couldn't remember the last time there was so much laughter in this house.

He knocked on the door.

Chloe answered the door. She could tell that he was angling to come in and join them.

John opened his mouth to ask the question that Chloe had already anticipated. 'Sorry, Dad, no can do. It's a girls' night in, remember.'

John smelt alcohol on her breath as he handed over the Chinese takeaway.

Chloe shut the door.

John turned towards the stairs when, to his surprise, Chloe opened the door again. 'Dad?'

John stepped forward and smiled. 'Yes?'

'I think this is for you.' She handed him a plastic bag and shut the door.

John looked at the plastic bag and shrugged. 'Well, at least I won't go hungry.' He shuffled off up the stairs carrying his single bag of Chinese takeaway to eat alone.

Meanwhile, downstairs Sylvie and the girls wasted no time unpacking the plastic bags and putting out the assorted boxes of food on the coffee table in the lounge.

Everyone helped themselves.

Chloe sat cross-legged on the sofa with her laptop balanced precariously on her lap. She was eating her Chinese takeaway and doing some research online at the same time. Greasy fingers tapped on the computer keyboard. Something caught her eye. She turned to Harriet, who was sitting on the sofa beside her, and said, 'Look, this is interesting…'

Harriet smiled at her little sister thinking typical Chloe, a computer geek, who never left home without her laptop. Harriet shifted her attention to the laptop and started to read an interesting article her sister had found on the internet.

'That *is* interesting,' said Harriet, reaching for her handbag.

Chloe gave Harriet a sideways glance. She knew what her sister was looking for in her handbag; typical Harriet, the journalist, she never went anywhere without her notebook.

Smelling the scent of a good story, Harriet picked up a pen and started making notes.

Jess and Sylvie were sitting in the two wicker chairs either side of the fireplace, eating their takeaway and reminiscing about their trip to Cornwall.

Although Sylvie had sent the letter requesting permission to scatter her mother's ashes in the garden, she was curious about the American who owned the cottage. He had lavished money on the property over the years but, according to local gossip, he rarely visited his Cornish holiday home. It struck her as rather odd.

Several bottles of wine later, and with most of the Chinese takeaway boxes lying empty on the coffee table, Chloe looked up from her laptop and Harriet put down her pen. They were ready to tell Sylvie and Jess what their bit of research on the internet had uncovered.

Harriet tapped her notebook with the nib of her pen and looked across the room at her mum. 'The cottage is near a town called St. Columb Major in Cornwall, isn't it?'

Sylvie and Jess exchanged glances and nodded.

Harriet continued, 'It turns out that during the Second World War there was a prisoner-of-war camp near St. Columb, POW camp 115, which held Italian prisoners of war.'

So far so interesting, thought Sylvie, but what did that have to do with the cottage?

'You're wondering what that's got to do with the cottage,' said Chloe, as if reading her thoughts. 'Well, we dug a little deeper and discovered the names of some of the POWs.'

'Now this is where it gets interesting,' said Harriet. 'One of the POWs has the same name as the present owner of the cottage.' She looked at her mother pointedly. 'What do you think the chances are of that just being a happy coincidence?'

Chloe added, 'You said that according to local gossip the owner might be of Italian descent.'

'Yes, I did,' said Sylvie slowly.

'Go on,' said Jess. 'Don't keep us in suspense. What else did you find out?'

Harriet read from her notebook. 'It appears the POWs were treated very well by us Brits during their stay.' She looked up.

'Is that it?' said Jess, sounding disappointed.

'Well... yes. But what if, when he was a prisoner of war in Cornwall, he fell in love with the place? And what if, when the war was over, he immigrated to America but vowed to return?'

Chloe glanced at Harriet and nodded enthusiastically, picking up the story thread, 'What if he returned in the sixties and bought that cottage in St. Columb near where the POW camp used to be?'

Sylvie looked from Chloe to Harriet. She thought this sounded more like a plot from a novel, not real life. Despite her scepticism, Sylvie's interest was piqued. 'Do you know what happened to him after the war?'

'Right, let's have a look.' Chloe turned her attention back to the laptop. 'It says here that before the end of the war the Italians were moved to make way for German prisoners of war.' Chloe frowned. 'And that's where the trail went cold.'

Sylvie glanced at the clock on the mantel shelf. It was almost time for the old black and white movie they planned to watch. Sylvie didn't see the point of pressing the girls to investigate further. As far as she was concerned, it was all just a coincidence. They had discovered there was a man by the same name who was a prisoner of war in Cornwall; it didn't mean he was the same person who bought the cottage.

No matter how well the Italians were treated as prisoners of war in Cornwall, Sylvie couldn't imagine it was a chapter in their lives they would wish to revisit, let alone return to the area and buy a holiday home. Something didn't ring true. And besides, even if it were true, it was of no consequence to Sylvie as long as he agreed to her request. However, the girls were so excited by their find that she didn't want to rain on their parade by voicing her thoughts. She didn't want them to waste any more time researching a dead end either. Sylvie glanced at the television. She would not get into that right now because the late-night movie was about to start.

There was a frantic rush to change into their PJ's, then Jess, Chloe, and Harriet sat down together on Sylvie's sofa, under one of her throws. They tucked it around their legs, getting themselves comfy before they settled down to watch the late-night movie. It was Chloe's suggestion to have a slumber party like the girls used to have at their friends' houses when they were teenagers. This was the first time they'd had a slumber party at their parents' house. They snuggled under the throw together, staring at the screen as the credits rolled before the old black and white movie began.

Sylvie wasn't watching the television but staring at her girls. She wondered why they didn't do things like this at home when they were growing up. Why didn't they do fun things like inviting their friends over for slumber parties? She already knew the answer to that question as her eyes drifted to the empty wine bottles and boxes of Chinese takeaway littering the coffee table, before settling on Alfie who was busy hoovering up strands of rice on the rug. The killjoy was sitting upstairs – John.

Sylvie glanced up at the ceiling and imagined she had x-ray vision and could see him sitting in his kitchenette, his Chinese takeaway neatly arranged in assorted china dishes on the table, the boxes and cartons already binned.

No hastily scoffed takeaway in the lounge, on the sofa, in front of the television, the way takeout food should be eaten. John wouldn't dream of doing that. Which meant Sylvie and the girls couldn't do that either. Not until tonight, sitting downstairs in her own apartment, in her pyjamas, having her very own slumber party.

She smiled at the girls before turning her attention to the screen. The movie was about to start. She reached for the TV controls to adjust the volume. This was the first time Sylvie had used her new television set. It wasn't brand new. Sylvie called it a hand-me-down. When Chloe and Declan moved in together, they treated themselves to a new television. There was nothing wrong with their old one apart from the fact that it was a thirty-two-inch screen. Declan wanted a forty-two-inch screen. Consequently, Sylvie found herself with a nearly new-flat screen TV which she was delighted with.

It was much more suitable for her small lounge than the clunky old tube television that John had left downstairs for tenants. It was also not too dissimilar from the one he'd bought for his apartment upstairs. But there was a difference. Sylvie's TV set had something John's didn't have – a surround sound system. Chloe had not only given her mum their TV but also five speakers and a subwoofer. Sylvie didn't bother asking Declan to explain what a subwoofer was when he came around to set up the surround sound system.

She glanced around the room at the five speakers. Declan minimised the cables by running some under her wooden floorboards. Sylvie didn't like the speakers dotted about her lounge, but they were small and compact. The same couldn't be said for the subwoofer speakers. Sylvie eyed the big, black, bulky boxes which sat either side of the television. They weren't aesthetically pleasing to the eye.

She would have been happy with her new television without all the bells and whistles. However, Chloe twisted her arm, insisting the surround sound system was worth it. She also told her mum that she wouldn't appreciate the difference it made until she heard it for herself. It was tantamount to having cinema sound in the comfort of your own home.

This was the first time Sylvie had used her new television since Declan had connected it up to the speakers. She noticed that Chloe kept glancing her way, the look on her face suggesting she was in for a surprise. Sylvie still felt dubious about it. She kept the sound on mute while they waited for the adverts to run their course before the movie started. Sylvie had the television controls at the ready, her finger hovering over the volume control. She was about to find out what the fuss was all about.

John was washing up the dishes in the kitchen after eating his Chinese takeaway sitting at the kitchen table. The cartons had already been binned and the plastic bin liner tied securely before he sat down to eat. When he finished clearing up, John opened the kitchen window to let out the smell before retiring to the lounge.

In the lounge, the first thing he did was check the plug-in air freshener was switched on; he didn't want the odour of takeaway food to waft into the room. He sat down on the sofa and stared at the floor. John hadn't heard Sylvie and the girls shift from the lounge to go downstairs and eat in the basement kitchen. Which meant only one thing: they had eaten their takeaway on the sofa – *ugh*. He shook his head in disgust.

In hindsight, John was pleased they hadn't invited him to join them; at least he didn't have to witness the carnage that lay beneath first-hand. He had an idea what was going on down there from visiting Chloe's flat, in the past, and seeing the empty wine bottles and takeaway cartons littering her lounge. The mess appalled him. Just imagining it down there was enough to get him going. He was relieved they were all staying the night in Sylvie's apartment and not his.

John picked up the newspaper and flicked through the pages until he found the television listings. He perused the channels to see if there was anything on the box. There was an old black and white movie about to start on BBC2. Everything else comprised reality television shows or crime dramas.

Nothing took his fancy, so he reached for the novel he was reading which he'd left on the coffee table. As he did so, John glanced at the time by his wristwatch and sighed. He wouldn't normally stay up this late. He was about to retire early when the Chinese takeaway arrived. By the time he'd finished the meal, he was too wide-awake to go straight to bed. Instead, he made himself comfortable on the sofa, leaning forward to tuck a cushion behind his back.

He was about to settle down and start reading the novel when he thought he heard Sylvie's television downstairs. If they were watching that late-night black and white movie, he hoped she didn't turn the volume up too high and disturb his quiet night in upstairs. John had been down that road before. He recalled the day Sylvie moved in downstairs and left the television on full volume well into the early hours.

John listened intently, but he couldn't hear a thing. 'Must have been my imagination,' he said to the empty room. He knew Sylvie loved old black and white movies. There was one on the box this evening. He assumed she'd be down there watching it.

John opened the book. He paused for a moment and cocked

his head to one side, listening. All was quiet – too quiet. He raised an eyebrow. Perhaps they had retired early. He shrugged and turned his attention back to the novel. He was just turning the page when...

John sat up with such a start that the book flew right out of his hands, landing on the carpet across the room.

'What the hell...!?' John covered his ears and stared at the floor in astonishment. If he hadn't already seen Sylvie's refurbished apartment with his own eyes, he would be forgiven for thinking she'd had her own movie theatre installed downstairs. John uncovered his ears just to be sure he wasn't imagining things.

'*You have got to be kidding me!*' he yelled.

He could shout until he was blue in the face, but nobody sitting in the lounge downstairs enjoying Chloe's hand-me-down surround sound system, creating Sylvie's very own movie-going experience right there in her own apartment, would hear John blowing a gasket right above their heads.

20

Sylvie rose early the next morning and walked into the lounge to find all three girls fast asleep. Jess was on the sofa under a throw with Alfie curled up at her feet. Harriet and Chloe were cocooned in sleeping bags on the deep pile rug in front of the fireplace.

She crept past them down the stairs to the kitchen. She woke the girls a few minutes later, handing out mugs of strong black coffee. There wasn't time for a lie-in. Jess had a taxi arranged to pick her up early and take her to the airport.

Sylvie and the girls sat in their pyjamas drinking coffee and eating toast and Marmite. They chatted about last night and how much they enjoyed themselves. Sylvie only wished Jess wasn't leaving so soon, and they had more time together.

They'd barely changed out of their pyjamas when the taxi arrived.

John, looking tired, walked down the stairs as Sylvie, Harriet, Chloe, Jess and Alfie emerged from her apartment. John yawned. He hadn't stayed up late watching television, but he might as well have. He heard every single line of dialogue and every sound-effect as he lay awake in bed two floors up.

There was a quick round of hugs and kisses and goodbyes. And promises to write and phone and email, and not to cry. The last promise already broken as there wasn't a dry eye in the house.

Jess dried her eyes and made her mum promise to write the moment she found out anything more about the owner of the cottage. She made her sisters promise to keep in touch and, out of earshot of Sylvie and John, to keep an eye on their parents.

Everyone made Jess promise to return home soon.

Even Alfie joined in, whining and jumping up at Jess, as though he sensed she was leaving.

She scooped him up and gave him a hug, reminding him he had to be a good dog for Sylvie, before passing him to Harriet.

Sylvie and John walked with Jess down to the waiting taxi, leaving Chloe and Harriet waving at the door with an excitable puppy trying to escape.

John glanced at his car parked on the drive. 'Jess, why don't I drive you to the airport?'

Jess rolled her eyes. 'You know why, Dad. I'll never get on my flight. It makes saying goodbye so much harder. It's better this way.'

They all knew it was true.

While John loaded her rucksack in the boot of the taxi, Jess had some parting words for her mother. 'Whatever is going on between you two, will you promise me one thing?'

'I don't know what you're talking about,' Sylvie shot back defensively. She didn't want Jess raising the subject of their separate living arrangements and ending things on that note after they spent such a pleasant evening together.

'Promise me you'll do whatever makes you happy,' said Jess, her voice full of concern. 'We all hope that means getting back together with Dad,' Jess glanced at her father chatting to the taxi driver, 'but you often find happy endings where you least expect them.'

Sylvie stared at John as she listened to her daughter, the voice of experience. She'd travelled halfway around the world to find her happy ending. It made Sylvie wonder where she would find hers.

John caught Sylvie looking in his direction and ambled over to join her.

Jess hugged them both and promised she would stay longer on her next trip home. She paused before getting in the taxi and took a long look at her parents standing together on the pavement outside their house.

Sylvie had a good idea what she was thinking. Jess was wondering whether the next time she saw Mum and Dad, would they be back together or still living apart. Sylvie wondered that herself.

Jess got into the taxi and waved goodbye.

Sylvie and John stood together waving, long after the taxi turned the corner and disappeared from view. Both lost in their memories of the countless times, over the years, they stood together and watched her leave. This was the only occasion when she wished Jess had been more like her sisters; not one to have adventures in far-flung places. Not one to find a new life abroad. However, Sylvie knew that even though it might have made her family happy, it would not have made Jess happy.

Sylvie believed that if they loved her, they had to let her go so she could find her own path to happiness, wherever that might be. It made her realise why Jess, more than anybody else, could truly understand what she was going through.

Jess had made Sylvie promise to do whatever makes her

happy. Jess knew you couldn't please everybody. Sylvie realised she had been trying to do that for so many years, she'd forgotten where her family ended, and she began. She had forgotten what it felt like to please herself. To look to her own happiness without having to consider anybody else.

This was her chance to do just that. Life had moved on. Her children were all grown up with lives of their own. They could take care of themselves. Even John could take care of himself. In fact, he seemed to be doing surprisingly well without her. The transformation in his appearance, since she went away, was evidence of that. Sylvie kept throwing furtive glances his way while they were seeing Jess off, still surprised how much effort he'd made with his appearance.

Sylvie waved for the final time even though the taxi was long gone. Thinking of John, she turned to find he was no longer standing by her side but already marching up the path towards the house. She was not surprised. It had been like this each time Jess left home. John, not prone to depression, always spent the next few days after Jess's departure down in the dumps and uncommunicative. He would busy himself with work or some project on the house just to take his mind off the fact that she had gone.

Sylvie looked up at the house as he disappeared inside. She wondered what he would find to occupy his time now he was retired, and with nothing more to be done to the house. Sylvie didn't have that problem. She knew exactly how she would occupy herself for the next hour – cleaning her apartment. After last night, it was in a mess. As she walked back to the house, she imagined Alfie on top of her coffee table scavenging amongst the discarded boxes of left-over Chinese food.

Sylvie stepped into the hall and approached her apartment. The door was ajar. She could hear the chink of empty glass bottles suggesting that Harriet and Chloe had already started clearing up.

She was about to march inside and tell them they didn't have to stay behind to help, when she heard Chloe say, 'Why wasn't it like this when we were growing up?'

Surprised by Chloe's question, Sylvie came to an abrupt halt outside the door to her apartment.

'Like what?' Harriet responded.

'Why didn't we have this much fun at home like we used to when we went over to our friends' houses?'

'We had fun as a family,' Harriet corrected her sister.

'Yes, I know we did. But it was never like this. It was never—'

'Relaxed at home?' offered Harriet.

The girls fell silent until Alfie started whining.

Sylvie heard Harriet scolding the dog, 'No Alfie, you can't have the box. Dogs do not eat Chinese takeaway.'

Chloe laughed. 'Alfie would disagree with you, Sis.'

Sylvie was intending to walk in and tell the girls that she would finish clearing up, when Chloe abruptly changed the subject.

'Things aren't going very well with Declan.'

'Oh, Chloe – not again!' Harriet sounded exasperated. 'You said he was *the one*? You *have* bought a house together,' she reminded her sister.

'I know,' mumbled Chloe. 'I thought he was the one, too. It's just…'

Sylvie held her breath waiting to hear what Chloe would say next. Of all her daughters, Chloe was the one she often worried about. Not that she didn't worry about all three of them; she was a parent after all, and it came with the territory. But it was different with the other two. Her eldest daughter, Harriet, always knew what she wanted in life. And she had a plan, just like her father. Jess didn't have a clue what she wanted to do with her life. However, she was the adventurous go-getter, and Sylvie had no doubt in her mind that Jess would find what she was looking for – eventually.

Chloe was the enigma. Out of the three of them, it was Chloe who reminded Sylvie most of herself, still looking for something that she couldn't quite put her finger on. That worried Sylvie dreadfully. She knew what it was like to go through life unable to shake off the feeling that something was eluding her. Sylvie always sensed that there was something else she was meant to do, or somewhere else she was meant to be, or even someone else she was meant to be with.

Sylvie shook her head. She didn't want Chloe to end up like her, at her age, still searching for something elusive. Still looking for whatever would make her happy.

Alfie appeared in the doorway and spotted her.

Sylvie looked down at him. She was just raising a finger to her lips – *please keep quiet, Alfie* – when he yapped excitedly, exposing her hiding place behind the door.

She picked up her puppy and patted him affectionately on the head as she walked through the door into the apartment.

The minute Harriet saw her, she said, 'Mum, guess what? Chloe is splitting up with Declan.'

'Harriet,' Chloe snapped, 'I never said that!'

'Oh, come off it, Chloe,' Harriet threw back. 'This is just the way it started with all your other boyfriends and look where those relationships ended up! It's not like you're getting any younger. You are thirty this year. By the time I was your age...'

Chloe rolled her eyes. How many times had she heard her sister smugly rub it in that by the time she was thirty, she was married and had a mortgage? She had responsibilities like a *proper* grown-up.

Harriet was still talking, '... and what's more, you haven't even got a permanent job yet.'

Chloe glared at her sister. 'What's that got to do with anything?'

Sylvie stepped in. 'Harriet, that's enough!'

'But Mum – it's true,' whined Harriet.

'So what if I do contract work,' Chloe said defensively. 'I earn a darn sight more than you do.'

Harriet couldn't dispute that. When she and her husband were struggling to pay their mortgage, Harriet often wondered how much money her carefree little computer geek of a sister had squirrelled away for a rainy day. She was the last of them to leave home, and she dragged it out royally. Harriet added, 'Yes, but it's still not a *proper* job.'

'Girls!' Sylvie said sharply, realising this was about to get ugly.

Chloe had to get the last word in, making it personal, 'At least I don't think I'm all high and mighty working as a journalist at a posh magazine, like a stuck-up—'

'I said that's *enough*!' Sylvie stepped in between them and folded her arms across her chest. She looked from one to the other, warning them not to say another word.

Chloe backed off and glanced sheepishly at her sister. She didn't mean to get the claws out, but Harriet had struck a nerve. It was true, she was pushing thirty. As the year drew to a close on her twenties, it had become clear that as her friends were getting engaged, married, having their first child, or for some their second, Chloe was not moving on with her life. That's why she bought the house with Declan. She was determined for things to change by the time she turned thirty. It was a milestone.

She thought making a commitment to buy a place together would be the catalyst to make her change. It wasn't working. She knew that for a fact because as soon as they moved in together, it stirred up the same familiar feeling of being trapped and wanting out. Perhaps they should have waited to buy their first home together. If they had waited, Chloe doubted she would feel any different in six months, a year, or even five years' time.

Harriet had struck a nerve all right. Not only that, if her mum hadn't stepped in, Chloe imagined the next thing Harriet would have suggested was that her little sister needed to see a shrink about her commitment issues.

Since Chloe left home, she had been living with boyfriends on and off for the last six years, but none of her relationships worked out. She thought she knew the answer to that conundrum: she hadn't fallen head over heels in love yet. Now Chloe *had* fallen head over heels in love – with Declan. It worried her, knowing the way she felt about him, why she *still* couldn't commit to their relationship.

At first, she thought it was the house that was the problem. Soon after she moved in and gained some inspiration from the way her mother had redecorated and redesigned the garden apartment, Chloe asked Sylvie and Julia to help remodel her house, hoping it would make her feel more at home. It worked to a degree until she realised it wasn't the décor that was the problem. *She* was the problem. Despite living in an area of

London she loved – Walthamstow Village – with the man of her dreams, she still wasn't happy. And the worst part was she did not understand why.

Chloe glanced at her sister. Perhaps Harriet was right. She had better see someone to sort out her issues before she lost her chance of happiness. Before she lost the man she loved.

Sylvie studied her daughter and approached her to offer some words of advice and reassurance. 'Chloe, nobody said relationships were easy. Nobody said living together was easy. You just have to—'

'Seriously?' Interrupted Chloe, the sarcasm in her voice was unmistakable. She glared at her mother. 'I am not having this conversation – not with *you!*'

Sylvie put her hands on her hips. 'What is that supposed to mean, young lady?'

Chloe stole a glance at Harriet before she turned on her mother. 'It means that maybe you should get your own house in order before you dish out advice on *my* relationship!'

Sylvie watched in stunned silence as Chloe gathered up her things and stormed out.

She turned to look at Harriet who was uncharacteristically quiet. Sylvie narrowed her eyes recalling Chloe and Harriet talking in hushed voices in her kitchen soon after they arrived yesterday evening. They'd been talking about Mum and Dad. Sylvie folded her arms. 'Well? Is there something you want to say to me, Harriet?'

Harriet shrugged. She avoided Sylvie's gaze and finally replied, 'Sorry, Mum, but Chloe's got a point.'

Sylvie couldn't believe it. Since when did Chloe and Harriet ever agree on anything?

They finished clearing up the apartment, the heavy silence punctuated by John popping his head around the door and offering to help.

Both of them shouted at him to go away.

John promptly disappeared, smiling to himself. That's what comes from eating a takeaway in the lounge and getting up to a right mess to clean up the following morning; no wonder they were cheesed off. He was pleased they didn't want his help. He was only offering out of politeness because in fact, he was just on his way out.

After Jess left that morning, John didn't feel like company, although he needed to keep himself occupied. Just as well he signed up for a year's membership at the gym. He was off to his first workout this morning. It gave him somewhere to go, and something to do, to take his mind off Jess boarding her flight right about now.

Sylvie heard the front door bang shut and glanced out the bay window. She caught sight of her husband walking to the car dressed in a tracksuit and carrying a sports bag.

Sylvie did a double take. John had done no form of exercise in the past. She thought back to yesterday when she arrived home from Cornwall to discover him standing on the doorstep looking quite different, very suave in his new clothes. He'd even been to a salon while she was away; that was something he'd never done before either.

Sylvie eyed John as he walked to the back of the car and opened the boot. He'd been shopping for more than casual clothes; the tracksuit and sports bag were also new. Sylvie didn't think he had ever owned a tracksuit or a sports bag in his life and was not inclined to join a gym before.

'That's odd,' mused Sylvie as she stood at the window watching him put his sports bag in the boot of the car. She wondered what all this was in aid of.

Suddenly the penny dropped. Was he seeing someone? Is that what this was all about – the new clothes, the new hairstyle, the gym – creating a fresh image for the new woman in his life?

'What's odd?' asked Harriet as she finished wiping the coffee table clean.

'Oh nothing,' said Sylvie, turning away from the window. She wasn't about to bring up the subject of relationships again.

They both stood for a moment in silence looking around the lounge. It was now tidy, and like the atmosphere in the room, devoid of any evidence of the fun evening they shared last night.

Harriet turned to her mother, and asked, 'Do you want me to see if there is anything more I can find out about the Italian prisoner of war we were talking about last night?'

'No.'

'Well, if that's the way you're going to talk to me, then I won't ask again!' Harriet gathered her things and stormed out.

'Harriet!' Sylvie called after her, but it was too late. She glanced out the window and saw Harriet thundering down the path and through the gate, slamming it shut behind her.

Sylvie sighed. She hadn't meant to sound so abrupt. She was thinking about John setting off for the gym in his new tracksuit when Harriet's question caught her off-guard. Harriet didn't give her a chance to add that although it was an interesting discovery, she doubted it was any more than a coincidence. She didn't want Harriet to waste any more time on a dead end.

Even if it turned out that the owner of the cottage had been a POW in Cornwall during the Second World War and returned to England in the sixties to buy that cottage. Sylvie was still no closer to getting his permission to scatter her mother's ashes in the garden of his holiday home. Sylvie believed there was nothing more she could do her end. The letter she sent to the owner via the estate agents in Cornwall had probably arrived by now and, fingers crossed, she hoped he replied soon.

Right now, that was the least of her concerns. Sylvie was preoccupied with the thought of John buying new clothes and joining a gym to impress a woman. Perhaps he was even meeting her there to work out together. She didn't understand why that should bother her so much. After all, she was the one who wanted this trial separation. She was the one who moved out of the apartment upstairs.

Sylvie turned from the window and looked into the room. The house felt so empty without the girls around, or John pottering about in his apartment upstairs. Even Alfie had gone, scampering downstairs to hide in the basement kitchen away from the sound of Sylvie and Harriet's argumentative voices.

She called out, 'Alfie!' She wasn't surprised when her naughty dog didn't appear.

The sound of a car outside prompted her to turn around and glance out the window once more. She saw John reversing his car out of the driveway. He must have spotted her standing at the window because he waved. Sylvie raised her hand and offered a tentative wave back.

She thought about the irony of the situation. Not long ago, soon after he was forced into early retirement, all she wanted was her husband to take up a hobby to get him out of the house.

Now, by the looks of things, he'd done just that. It's what she wanted, wasn't it? Sylvie shook her head. What she hadn't expected was John would not only take up a new hobby but take up with another woman too. Perhaps the girls' fears that their parents were heading for a divorce were not unfounded.

She turned from the window and looked around her apartment. This was it. She'd got what she wanted. She had all the time she needed to figure herself out. In fact, Sylvie realised she'd got a lot more time and space than she bargained for – permanently.

'What have I done?' whispered Sylvie to the empty room. 'This was meant to be temporary – wasn't it?'

Sylvie thought about John's very changed appearance. John off to the gym. John moving on with his life – without her. Whoever he was trying to impress, she felt it would work. He had certainly impressed his wife on her return from Cornwall.

Sylvie recalled her intention to go back to Cornwall as soon as she heard from the American, and her travelling companion for the return trip – Nigel. Perhaps it was time to renew that acquaintance. Sylvie decided to take a leaf out of John's book. It was time to stop looking in the rear-view mirror and move on with her life.

21

'Stop that right now!' demanded John. From his vantage point sitting at the table in the kitchenette, he could see Dave was up to something in his lounge, although he couldn't tell what. All he knew was that Dave had brought over more than just grocery shopping on this occasion. John watched him carry a box into the lounge, unwilling to reveal its contents.

He craned his neck trying to see what he was up to. 'I mean it, Dave. Whatever you're doing in there I want you to stop—'

Dave poked his head in the kitchenette and looked at John. 'Make me,' he said with a mischievous grin.

'That is not funny,' John shot back. All the same, he was eager to discover what was inside the box. He planted both hands on the tabletop, hoisted himself up from the table, and reached for the crutches. Careful to keep his right foot off the floor, he made his way slowly into the lounge.

John sighed. This was not how he expected to walk out of his first experience using a gym – on crutches. John imagined he'd walk out of there fit and healthy, not ending up in A&E. On top of which, he had paid a year's subscription in advance to a gym he had no intention of returning to. And he'd taken on more debt to pay for it. He didn't even like exercise and was only doing it to lose some weight. He wanted to look more like Nigel in his new clothes, instead of the old John who had rather let himself go over the years. He thought shifting some weight would make him feel more confident wearing his new outfits. Now he felt like an idiot wearing a big plastic orthopaedic boot on his foot. This wasn't the image he had in mind when he went shopping with Chloe.

John scowled at Dave as he hobbled into the lounge. The gym idea had backfired spectacularly, and it was all Dave's fault. It was his suggestion to join the gym. John decided that he wasn't listening to any more of his brother's great ideas. Even though it wasn't Dave's fault that he had been so busy ogling a pretty young woman running alongside him on the treadmill that, keen to impress, he had walked over to lift a weight, wasn't watching what he was doing, and almost dropped it on his foot. John was lucky that a quick side-step meant it missed his foot, but he fell and wound up with a badly sprained ankle and severe bruising.

Fortunately, nothing was broken. However, for the time being he had to walk on crutches, making it difficult to get around, and almost impossible to get out and about. He was a prisoner in his own home. And he wasn't pleased to see Dave. But needs must; John needed to eat, and he needed someone to fetch him some groceries.

He wasn't about to ask anybody else for help. He didn't want word to get out what an idiot he'd been. His predicament was embarrassing enough without Harriet and Chloe or, heaven forbid, Sylvie finding out what had happened. John grudgingly acknowledged that he would have to hide in his apartment until the orthopaedic boot came off.

He was still wondering what Dave was up to. He better not have another plan up his sleeve thought John, as he made his way across the lounge on crutches. Moving around like this was time consuming, and his patience was wearing thin. He glared at his brother. 'I want to know what's inside the box!'

Dave was kneeling on the floor in front of the box. He glanced over his shoulder as John approached. 'Relax. It's just some odds and ends from one of the housing developments I've been working on. The show home recently sold, so I nabbed a few bits and pieces that they used to dress the place. I've got some ornaments, lamps, that sort of thing.'

As far as John was concerned, he didn't need anything for his flat. He paused to take a breather. 'Dave, my apartment is fine as it is.'

'Oh, really? Look around you.'

John looked about him. He still couldn't understand what Dave was getting at. There was nothing wrong with his apartment – far from it; everything was clean and functional. Why bother with ornaments and such like? They would only need dusting and create more work.

Dave continued, 'Your place is kind of neutral and bland. You haven't even got any pictures on the walls. There's nothing of a personal nature. It's as though nobody lives here.'

'So what?' John said dismissively. 'That's the way I like it.'

'Ah yes but wait until to you see what I've got in the box. It may surprise you.'

John doubted it, although he was interested to see what Dave had brought with him, especially when he mentioned that the stuff came from a former show home. John liked show homes. They were always decorated in muted tones, often bland,

and most definitely neutral. At Dave's behest, John turned around and headed back to the kitchen, leaving Dave in his lounge to unpack the box and put some knick-knacks around.

'I'll call you when I'm finished. It will be a surprise.'

John raised an eyebrow. If this was Dave's way of apologising for sending him on the last mission called Operation *Get Fit*, that turned into Operation *Casualty*, resulting in Operation *Expensive Waste of Time*, then he might as well leave him to it. Although he didn't want things cluttering up the apartment, he supposed the odd well-placed neutral ornament or lamp would not go amiss.

He had seen Sylvie's flat downstairs. Although it was the opposite of his own, with its sheer amount of colour and clutter, he saw Dave's point. John glanced around his rather bland, almost stark apartment. Downstairs, Sylvie's flat felt like a home. His apartment was devoid of any personal touches and lacked a woman's touch. It was devoid of Sylvie, thought John miserably. It didn't matter what Dave produced out of that box unless he could magically summon Sylvie like some genie out of a bottle.

'You can come back and now,' Dave called from the lounge.

John hoisted himself up from the table once again, gathered up his crutches, and made his way into the lounge. He was careful not to catch his crutches or ample plastic boot on a piece of furniture. He made a mental note to ask his brother to move his sofa and chairs back against the wall before he left, so he had more room to move around.

John stopped in front of the sofa and stood there leaning on his crutches. He took a long look around the room. His eyes settled on Dave who was standing off to one side looking extremely pleased with himself.

Dave grinned. 'Well, what do you think?'

'What do I think?' John was trying his best to remain calm. 'Just what sort of show home was it?' John lifted off. 'Were they re-creating the seventies home for god's sake? I mean... look at this stuff!' He didn't know where to begin until his eyes settled on a bright purple lava-lamp. He picked it up and had the urge to hurl it across the room at Dave.

'Great isn't it,' said Dave, admiring his handiwork.

John was fuming. He glared at his brother. 'It's not great. It's... it's...'

'It's what people want, John. At least that's what the interior designers who work on our show homes tell me.'

'You're having me on.'

'Nope. You know how things come back into fashion? Well, decades come back into fashion too. And people want warm colours – not magnolia.' Dave glanced around John's apartment. 'They like cosy – not stark.'

'You mean people actually want this sort of stuff in their houses?' said John incredulously, shaking his head at the hideous things that had come out of that box and were now cluttering up his lounge. Did lampshades used to be that big and orange? Did people still go in for lava lamps? Surely not.

John glanced down at his couch and recoiled in horror. 'What on earth is *that*?' It looked like Dave had left a dead animal on his sofa.

'It's a Mongolian wool long-haired cushion, John. It's made from goat fur. I have another one just like it.' He held it up. 'In fact, I'm sure I have several more in this box somewhere.' Dave started rummaging through the box.

John sighed. He'd seen enough. Dave would have to pack it

all up and take it home. It was a nice gesture but most definitely not to his taste. He couldn't give two hoots what was back in fashion. He stared at the lava lamp in his hand as an interesting thought occurred to him. Perhaps Dave bringing over all this crap wasn't a pointless waste of time after all.

It got him thinking about the garden apartment. All this stuff wasn't unlike some things Sylvie had bought for the flat downstairs. If Dave was right, and this was the sort of thing people went in for, then there shouldn't be a problem renting out the garden apartment just the way it is. That didn't change the fact that he had to get Sylvie to move out. However, looking at all this stuff Dave had left around his lounge, it made John more determined that he would not rent out his own apartment if he could help it. He still didn't want to take one for the team.

'So, I was thinking,' said Dave as he draped a garish throw over John's sofa, 'Sylvie will be pop in to see you later, so wouldn't it be a nice surprise to show her you like the same things she does.' Dave dumped several long-haired cushions on top of the throw.

John wasn't listening to Dave; he was preoccupied with those long-haired cushions that made him feel itchy just looking at them. He was also trying to think up a diplomatic way to tell Dave – without losing his temper – that he had been exceedingly kind to bring all this stuff over to cheer him up, but he shouldn't have gone to all that trouble.

John looked up from the itchy cushion, and said, 'Wait. Run that by me again. What did you just say?' He could have sworn his brother had just mentioned...

'Sylvie's coming up to see you later.' Dave was smiling from ear to ear. 'You see, I have a *plan*…'

'A plan? Oh, no!' John slapped the palm of his hand to his forehead in disbelief, forgot he needed that hand to balance on his crutch, and pitched forward on to the sofa into the pile of itchy long-haired cushions.

'There,' said Dave smugly, 'I knew you'd like them.'

John remained spread-eagled face down on the sofa, his face buried in a large, hairy cushion, one booted foot on the floor. 'But I don't want another plan,' John whined. 'I just want my old life back.'

'And you shall have it!' said Dave triumphantly.

'But how?' John thumped the sofa in frustration. His face buried in a cushion, mohair tickling his nostrils.

'That's the beauty of my plan. You see, I was shopping for your groceries when it hit me that your little accident at the gym has had an unexpected side-effect.'

'Wath thath?' The cushion muffled John's voice.

'It's called the pity ploy.'

John slowly turned his head and looked up at his brother who was smiling down at him.

'That's right,' said Dave, playfully kicking his large plastic orthopaedic boot. 'The wounded hero returns to the arms of his fair lady – that's Sylvie of course. You're hurt. You need help with things like grocery shopping. And with Sylvie in and out of your place, running around after you, one thing might lead to another and... well you get the picture.'

John stared at Dave for a long moment before holding out his hand.

Dave reached down and pulled him up to a seated position. 'Do I take it you are interested in my plan?'

John was still wary of getting involved in another one of his brother's "great" ideas. He was also cheesed off with Dave for not telling him the real reason he'd brought over the stuff in that box – to impress Sylvie. John answered his question with a non-committal, 'Maybe.'

That was all Dave needed to launch into a full briefing of the next mission he had planned. It turned out that he had already phoned Sylvie and told her all about John's accident, explaining that his brother was too proud to ask for her help. On top of which, Dave told John that he had to embellish it a bit.

'You mean you lied.'

'I couldn't very well tell Sylvie the truth now, could I? She would not be sympathetic if she found out you had been ogling the girls in the gym and carrying on as though you were half your age. So, I told Sylvie that you—'

John interrupted Dave, holding up his hand to stop him right there. 'Whatever it is, I don't want to know.'

'But I really think—'

John wagged his finger, *still a no.*

'What if she asks you something about the accident?'

John hadn't thought about that. He took a moment to consider. 'I'll just say I don't want to talk about it – which I don't.'

'Fair enough, if that's the way you want it.' Dave shrugged. 'Anyway, back to the plan. Once I told her what happened, before I could say another word, a genuinely concerned Sylvie was already arranging to pop up and cook your dinner this evening, without a hint of a suggestion from me. She even asked if you needed some shopping.'

'She did?' John said in surprise. Although he didn't want to admit it, this wasn't a bad plan. Not bad at all. 'What do I do next?' he asked, interested to hear the finer details.

'That's the beauty of the plan. This time Sylvie will do all the hard work. All you have to do is just sit back, relax, and play the wounded hero.' Dave smiled at his brother. 'Do you think you can do that?'

John thought about it for all of two seconds, and replied, 'I think so,' returning Dave's knowing smile.

22

It took John some time to hobble over to the door on crutches when Sylvie rang his doorbell. He'd been ready and waiting for her to call upstairs for the last hour. John had been sitting in his lounge mulling over Dave's visit. He concluded that this was the best plan his brother had come up with.

There was no risk that he would get caught out like the last time when Sylvie discovered him in her kitchen up to no good. His plight was genuine. And he hadn't even asked Sylvie to help him out. That was all her idea, along with cooking him dinner. John's mouth watered at the prospect of Sylvie's home cooking. Talk about every cloud has a silver lining. He decided he quite liked his big plastic orthopaedic boot after all.

John made it to the door and gave himself a final once over in the long mirror in the lobby. He was dressed in one of his new outfits, clean shaven, and smelling of some ridiculously expensive fragrance for men that Chloe persuaded him to buy during their shopping trip together. He trusted the cologne wasn't overdoing it.

He opened the door hoping he didn't smell like the inside of a perfume factory.

'Hello, John.' Sylvie stood on tiptoes and greeted him with a brief kiss on the cheek. 'Is that new aftershave?'

'No, actually it's Hugo Boss, a fragrance for men. Do you like it?'

Sylvie frowned. 'I thought you didn't buy that sort of thing.'

'Well, not usually. But do you like it?'

She bent down, picked up two shopping bags, and walked past him without comment.

John stood by the door and sniffed the air wondering if he used too much. Or perhaps he'd just made an expensive mistake, and she didn't like it but was too polite to say. John shrugged. He turned around and steadied himself on the crutches before he slowly made his way through the lounge.

In the kitchen he stopped and glanced at the shopping bags on the table. 'You shouldn't have gone to all this trouble.'

'Don't be silly,' said Sylvie, unpacking the shopping. 'It's no trouble at all. Go and sit down. I'll get on with the dinner. Dave told me all about what happened – poor you.'

John smiled nervously. In hindsight, he wished that Dave had told him what embellishments he added that made Sylvie so empathetic about his unfortunate "accident".

'At least let me help you unpack the shopping,' said John, forgetting about his foot and planting it a tad too hard on the tiled kitchen floor. '*Yeow!*'

Sylvie turned around and shook her head. 'John Baxter, while I'm looking after you, you will do as you're told.'

'Yes, dear,' John said meekly.

'I want you to go in the lounge and sit down.' Sylvie paused. Her voice softened. 'Do you need my help to get to a chair?'

John looked at her and thought about Dave's plan; it was

time to play the pity card for all it was worth. 'I think I might need your help,' he said in a small voice.

'Now, that's more like it. You always made the worst patient.'

'That's true.' He placed his arm around her shoulders and let her help him into the lounge, even though he could manage on his own. He took his time lowering himself on to the sofa, adding a few winces of pain for effect. Some of them genuine.

Sylvie picked up a cushion intending to place it behind his back. She paused instead and turned the cushion over in her hands. Sylvie cast her gaze around the room, aware something was different. She stood there taking in the new ornaments, lamps, cushions and throws. There were colourful prints brightening up John's bare walls. And was that a lava-lamp? She had no idea he liked this sort of thing. Sylvie wondered whether after he'd seen how she transformed the flat downstairs, it made John realise what his bland, neutral apartment was lacking, and encouraged him to make some changes. Even so, she couldn't quite believe what she was seeing; it was so *not* John.

Sylvie gestured at the room. 'John, this is all very... strange.'

It wasn't quite the reaction he was expecting. Although he could tell by her expression, she was looking at him anew. He had been wondering what she'd think when she saw all the stuff Dave left in his apartment. 'Do you like it?'

'It's so bright and colourful and... kitsch.' Sylvie gazed around the room amazed that John had bought such lovely things. He had transformed his lounge into a place that was much more interesting and homely.

'But do you like it?' John was trying to read her expression.

'Of course I like it,' said Sylvie, turning over the cushion in her hands. 'You've just surprised me – that's all.'

'Have I?' he said innocently. He leaned forward so Sylvie could place the cushion behind his back.

'Comfy?' asked Sylvie.

'Yes, thank you,' replied John, smiling up at her.

'Good.' Sylvie turned towards the kitchen.

'There's just one thing…'

She did an about-turn. 'Yes?'

'Would you mind passing me my newspaper?' He glanced at the magazine basket on the floor. 'I can't quite manage to …' John held out his hand in a lame attempt to reach for it from his position sitting on the sofa with his feet up.

'Don't move. Let me get that.' Sylvie knelt beside the wicker basket and found John's daily newspaper neatly folded inside. She got off her knees and passed it to him.

'Thank you, Sylvie. Now, I wonder what I did with my reading glasses.' John looked about him until his eyes settled on Sylvie standing there ready to cater for his every whim. 'I can't recall where I had them last.' He made a show of attempting to get up and look for them.

'No, don't get up. I'll find them.' Sylvie searched the lounge until she spotted them on the armchair by the bay window. She handed them to him. 'Have you got everything you need before I cook the dinner?'

'I think so.' John opened his newspaper and paused before reading. 'Ah, there is one more thing…' He looked at Sylvie over the top of his newspaper.

'What is it now?'

'I'm a little parched. Is there any chance you might rustle up a cup of tea while you're in the kitchen?'

A few minutes later John had his newspaper open in front of

him, his reading glasses on his nose, and a cup of tea on a small side-table Sylvie had placed within easy reach beside the sofa. She even put a coaster on the table for his cup.

He took a sip of sweet tea, placed his cup on the coaster, and opened his newspaper to read while Sylvie prepared the dinner. It felt like old times. He winked at his orthopaedic boot like an old friend. He would enjoy being laid up for the next few days. John knew he was on to a winner, especially as this plan involved no missions and no Dave. And he didn't even have to lift a finger. Sylvie was doing all the hard work. Dave was right: all he had to do was sit back and relax. John smiled. He could get used to this.

John's attention wandered from the newspaper. He decided to return to the original plan and get Sylvie to move back in with him upstairs so he could rent out the garden apartment. Since Dave told him that sixties and seventies retro kitsch was all the rage, John was convinced he would have no problem finding a tenant who would like what Sylvie had done to the place.

He glanced over his shoulder at Sylvie who was busy in the kitchenette cooking dinner. He recalled Dave's suggestion that he should use the pity ploy for all it was worth and ask her to move back in with him, on the pretext he needed her here to help him out. It was a reasonable request. John could see that. He wouldn't be surprised if Sylvie agreed. It would get his wife out of the garden apartment, which was the point of the plan. That didn't mean it was the right thing to do – at the moment.

John thought back to Dave's original plan. Although he'd carried out the missions to sabotage her apartment, it had ended in disaster. John stared at Sylvie. What was that saying – once bitten twice shy? He might go along with Dave's new plan, but this time he would proceed with extreme caution. So far, things were going well. His plight was genuine. Sylvie was not coerced into helping him out. John heard her humming a tune in the kitchen. She seemed to be enjoying herself cooking dinner for the two of them. He couldn't see how this would go awry unless he chose the wrong moment to ask her to move back in with him. He was mulling this over when Sylvie called him for dinner.

She hurried into the lounge apologising for forgetting he had been in the wars, an expression Sylvie often used when the girls were small and had suffered cuts and bruises from falling over.

John let Sylvie help him up from the sofa, even though he wasn't an invalid. When he sat down at the kitchen table – again with Sylvie's help – he had already decided that he would not be asking her to move back in with him just yet.

By the time he polished off his meal in quite a while that did not comprise of chicken pie, and enjoyed an amiable conversation over dinner with his wife, John had hatched a plan all of his own.

After dinner, he walked her, albeit awkwardly on crutches, to the door. 'I really appreciate you stopping by like this and cooking me a meal.'

'That's all right. I had a nice time.'

'So did I.' John was genuinely pleased with how the evening had turned out. Perhaps it had something to do with him not bringing up the subject of their separate living arrangements. It just felt like two neighbours getting together for a meal and having a very pleasant evening in each other's company.

Sylvie stood in the doorway. She looked puzzled as though she expected him to say something more. 'Goodnight, John.'

'Goodnight, Sylvie.' John forced himself not to linger and

shut the door. He leant against the door and exhaled in relief. He now knew, without any doubt, that his plan to get his wife back would work. It was built on one simple premise: regardless of his new clothes, his new hairstyle, or the crap Dave dispersed around his apartment to impress Sylvie, the fact was they still enjoyed each other's company. Without that, their marriage was doomed. No amount of plans or missions to encourage her to move back upstairs would matter a jot if their relationship was over.

This new intel made John's plan simple. His intention was to make sure they continued to spend time together until Sylvie made up her own mind that she wanted to move back in with him. After their pleasant evening together, John doubted it would take long.

It occurred to him they hadn't enjoyed each other's company for some considerable time. He couldn't put that down to the mess he'd made of things since the conversion; it had been going on far longer than that. So why now, when they were living apart, had they enjoyed spending time together? It made little sense. Unless...

John raised an eyebrow. Could it be that living apart had something to do with it? He nodded. It was possible. It gave them plenty to talk about when they got together. However, John believed it was more than that. This evening it was almost as though they were getting to know each other all over again.

'Getting to know each other... hmm.' John scratched his chin. His eyes lit up with an idea. He knew exactly how he would proceed with the plan.

Sylvie hurried down the stairs after saying goodnight to John.

She'd had an unexpectedly good time all because he did not ask her to move back upstairs. She thought he would use his injury as a ploy to get her to move back in with him. She waited all evening for him to bring it up; even lingering outside his door to say goodnight expecting he would pop the question. But he didn't.

He hadn't talked about the house conversion or finding a tenant, or even broached the subject of when she would move out of the garden apartment. This took Sylvie by surprise. That wasn't the only surprising thing about their evening together. She could tell they were both enjoying each other's company. Try as she might, she couldn't recall the last time they sat together over a meal and talked, really talked, like they used to years ago when her husband used to hang on her every word.

Sylvie enjoyed telling John all about her eventful trip down to Cornwall with Jess and how much she treasured their time together.

John shared his interesting shopping trip with Chloe, making Sylvie laugh out loud when she found out what their youngest daughter had been up to.

When Sylvie stopped laughing, she explained the difference between designer shops and the regular high street stores.

'I've been had,' was John's reaction when he realised how naive he'd been asking his youngest daughter to take him shopping and offering to buy her a little something too. Her *little something* had morphed into several bags of designer clothing.

Sylvie was still smiling as she thought about poor naive John and his shopping trip with Chloe. Sylvie shook her head. It must have cost him a small fortune. Lucky he could afford it.

Her smile faded as her thoughts returned to their lovely meal together. Why wasn't it like that before? She wasn't just thinking about the past few months when they were going through the house conversion. It was before then, way before then, when they stopped communicating with each other and their marriage felt like they were just going through the motions.

What had changed? Why now, when they were living apart, had they enjoyed spending the evening together? It made little sense. Unless...

Sylvie blinked in surprise. Unless it was something to do with their trial separation; had the last few weeks living apart put a new spark in their relationship? It certainly felt that way. This evening, over dinner, it was as though they were taking the first tentative steps to get to know each other all over again. Perhaps their marriage wasn't over yet.

Sylvie sat back and re-read her blog entry. For the first time since moving downstairs, Sylvie felt a cloud lifting. She knew this was in no small part down to the fact that she had just spent an enjoyable evening with her husband, without either of them bringing up the subject of their separate living arrangements. Sylvie was now looking forward to spending another evening in John's company. She was also looking forward to cooking him another meal. Since living on her own downstairs, she'd discovered it wasn't the same cooking for one.

If Sylvie was honest with herself, any further visits upstairs weren't strictly in the capacity of a concerned neighbour. Enjoying John's company had undoubtedly thrown the cat amongst the pigeons as far as Nigel was concerned. He was still leaving her phone messages and interested in going on that date she promised him when she returned from her trip to Cornwall.

Sylvie meant to contact him. She hadn't returned his calls yet but thought perhaps she should. Despite a very pleasant evening with John, after seeing the way he had changed his appearance and joined the gym, Sylvie was still unsure whether he was, in fact, seeing somebody. She sensed he was keeping something from her. Was this just a hiatus, relying on his wife downstairs to help him out because he was too embarrassed to tell his new lady friend he'd had an accident?

Sylvie frowned. She didn't want to think about that right now; what was at the forefront of her mind was what she fancied cooking for dinner on her next visit upstairs.

John was already looking forward to what delights Sylvie might cook up on her next visit. And he had a surprise of his own. The dinner that he and Sylvie shared gave him an idea; he would inject a little romance into their lives.

He knew he was on to something when he recalled what Dave once said. It was when he was going through his second bitter divorce. Dave remarked that he suspected what women really wanted was some romance in their lives. Perhaps this was true for Sylvie. John wondered if that's what she wanted all along. She was a woman after all. And women were complicated. Women said they wanted one thing when they meant something else entirely, expecting mere mortal men to read their minds.

John raised a questioning eyebrow. Sylvie said she wanted some space, but what if what she really wanted was the exact opposite, to be paid some attention, to be made to feel special? John had given this a great deal of thought. He knew how to get her back, and it had nothing to do with buying new clothes or getting highlights at a salon. Changing his appearance to look like

Nigel wasn't enough. He saw that now. What he needed to do was make some romantic gestures to win her over before he broached the subject of moving in together.

There was just one flaw in John's brilliant plan: he couldn't take her out to a fancy restaurant, not with this big plastic boot on his foot. However, he already had a contingency plan. He would find some candles for a romantic candle-lit dinner for two at his place. Purchase a CD off the internet to play some romantic music later in the evening and arrange for some flowers to be delivered to Sylvie downstairs.

If this worked – the fact that it got off to such a good start this evening gave him every sign that it might – then Sylvie should move back in with him in no time. As soon as she vacated downstairs, he could rent out the garden apartment and get his financial affairs in order. Sylvie would be none the wiser. It was a good plan. The more he thought about it, the more he was convinced it was a bloody excellent plan.

It had been two weeks since their first meal together in John's apartment. Since then, Sylvie had arrived every evening to cook dinner. That wasn't all. She popped in and out, at different times of the day, to see if there was anything he needed. Every morning she brought him up a cup of tea and his newspaper on a tea tray like she used to.

Although Sylvie rose later now she was living on her own, which meant John had to sit waiting for Sylvie's arrival, it was worth the wait. She always remembered to buy him a newspaper on her way back from walking Alfie. She didn't question why he no longer had it delivered in the morning. Which was just as well because John didn't fancy coming up with some lame excuse to cover the fact that he couldn't afford it.

Each day followed a familiar routine. John drank his morning cuppa, and leisurely read the newspaper in bed, while Sylvie was busy downstairs in his kitchenette whipping him up a hearty breakfast. After breakfast together, she often stayed to do some chores. She vacuumed and dusted the apartment; although it wasn't up to John's standard, he didn't complain. On Tuesdays she did his laundry, collecting his clothes and taking them down to her flat to wash and hang out on the clothesline in her garden to dry. She even insisted on ironing his clothes. John's dirty clothes disappeared on Tuesday morning and reappeared Tuesday afternoon freshly laundered.

John knew he could do all this himself. But what the heck. If she wanted to wait on him hand and foot, so be it. Besides, it meant she was spending far more time with him in his apartment upstairs than he could ever have anticipated. At the end of each relaxing day, after she had run around catering for his every whim, there was the evening to look forward to, enjoying each other's company and Sylvie's home-cooking. There was just one blot on the horizon: the boot was coming off.

Sylvie drove John to the doctor's surgery for his follow-up appointment to determine how things were progressing with the sprain. Unfortunately – or fortunately, depending on which way you looked at it – John's ankle had improved immeasurably thanks to Sylvie. She was doing everything for him, bar bathing and dressing, leaving John to rest up and keep off his foot. In retrospect, that turned out a mixed blessing because the boot was coming off sooner than expected. Things would go back to the way they were damn quick if he didn't do something about it.

Sylvie noticed John was silent in the car on the way home from the doctor's surgery. Concerned, she asked him how his appointment went. He was evasive and non-committal about the outcome. He needed to figure out, considering the news, what he would do next.

Dave suggested that he should keep the orthopaedic boot on until she moved back upstairs, and just take it off when she wasn't around. John disagreed. What if she walked in on him one day and discovered he was up and about, as right as rain, without the boot or the crutches? It wasn't worth the risk. Things were going so well between them he didn't want any chance of messing that up if he got found out like the last time.

John cringed as he recalled his last mission – Operation *Noah's Ark* – when Sylvie caught him in the act. He wondered why he ever listened to Dave and relied on his outlandish plans and ridiculous missions to get his wife back. On the other hand, if it weren't for Operation *Get Fit* resulting in his accident at the gym, he wouldn't have had this opportunity to spend time with her. And he wouldn't have made the discovery along the way. They were still fond of each other. *Very* fond of each other. The last fortnight proved that.

It was like old times. John wasn't thinking of before the conversion but way before then. The last two weeks together reminded him of the early years of their marriage, before the children, before this house. Before they drifted apart. How ironic that he didn't appreciate what was happening until it was too late, and Sylvie had upped and moved downstairs. Now they were back together – after a fashion – John knew that was ending unless he figured out what to do after the boot came off.

He realised perhaps the time had come to pop the question

and ask her outright to move back in with him. He knew he'd been avoiding it, happy to leave things as they were for the time being. However, he was aware the situation couldn't go on indefinitely. He had no money. And soon he would have no orthopaedic boot with which to garner her sympathy. He needed to get his hands on Sylvie's apartment to rent it out. Unless he came up with something that would encourage her to move back in with him of her own volition, the next time John saw Sylvie he would have to bite the bullet and just ask.

23

John was sitting in his lounge when he heard Sylvie call out, 'Hello there.' He turned in his chair and saw Sylvie making her way through his lounge to the kitchenette. She was carrying a shopping bag. He guessed what was in the bag; she always bought fresh ingredients to cook the evening meal.

John no longer heard Sylvie's familiar rat-a-tat-tat at his door. She was back and forward so often that he now left the door to his apartment propped open, so she didn't have to knock; she just walked straight in and made herself at home. John smiled. Yesterday, when he made his first trip downstairs in two weeks to attend his doctor's appointment, he noticed Sylvie had done the same; the door to her apartment was propped open too.

John hoisted himself up from the sofa on one crutch, picked up the other one, and made his way into the kitchen where Sylvie was busy unpacking the shopping.

She turned around as he approached. 'Darling, you didn't have to get up. I'm just preparing dinner.' There were fresh vegetables lined up on a cutting board and a pan filled with boiling water on the stove. She was peeling a carrot.

'Sylvie, I—'

'Please sit down, John, you look uncomfortable.'

He put his crutches to one side and took a seat at the kitchen table. No sooner had he sat down when he spotted Alfie scampering across the floor towards him. Perhaps Sylvie brought him with her on this occasion, or he escaped from the downstairs apartment; either way, he was in his kitchen, and John would much rather he wasn't.

Alfie jumped up at John.

'Get off me,' he said irritably.

Sylvie glanced over her shoulder. 'Oh sorry, I forgot to shut Alfie in my kitchen like I usually do,' said Sylvie off-hand as she chopped the carrot.

John looked down at the dog wagging his tail, clearly excited by the great escape.

'Oh look, his brought you a present,' added Sylvie.

By John's feet, on his clean kitchen floor, was something all chewed and misshapen and wet.

He recoiled from whatever had been in Alfie's mouth. 'What is it?'

'That's a chew bone. There are treats inside. And the best part is it keeps him occupied for ages when he's left on his own.' Sylvie started peeling another carrot. 'It was Julia's idea.'

John rolled his eyes and looked down at Alfie. At least that explained why the dog wasn't howling in the basement kitchen whenever Sylvie ventured upstairs without him.

John tried to push the dog away with his boot when Sylvie wasn't looking. When she was looking, he leaned over and scratched him behind the ears, whispering, 'Your days are numbered, chum. If things go according to plan—'

'What was that, dear?'

John looked up. 'I said that this evening I have other plans.'

Sylvie turned around with a half-peeled carrot in her hand. 'Oh, I had no idea…'

John shrugged. 'Sorry.'

Sylvie put the carrot down. She felt foolish for turning up every evening to cook him dinner; she'd assumed he wouldn't have other plans. 'There's no need to apologise. It's just that…' She thought he wanted to have dinner with her.

'Look, Sylvie, this has to stop, you cooking for me every night. I should have told you sooner but—'

'Oh no, not at all,' interrupted Sylvie, sounding flustered. She knew what this was about. His orthopaedic boot was coming off, and he didn't know how to tell her he was seeing someone else. She washed her hands in the sink and took off her apron. 'I'll be going then.'

'Before you go, can you do one last thing for me?'

'Yes, of course.'

John already had a pen to hand. 'Can I have your phone number?'

Sylvie looked at him in surprise. 'You already know my phone number downstairs.'

He held out the pen and paper. 'Please, just humour me.'

She sighed wondering what he was playing at. She didn't bother asking. Eager to get out of his apartment in case his lady friend showed up, Sylvie took the pen and scribbled down the phone number. 'There – satisfied?'

'Great.' John took the piece of paper and smiled.

'Come on, Alfie.' Sylvie picked up her dog and strode out of the apartment. She reached the bottom of the stairs when she heard her phone ringing. She put Alfie down in the lounge and shut her apartment door, so he didn't go scampering back upstairs to disturb John and his date.

Sylvie walked down the stairs to the basement kitchen and answered the phone. 'Hello?'

'Ah hello, I'm so glad you're in.'

Sylvie frowned. What on earth had got into him? Of course she was in; she had just left his apartment a moment ago and walked down the stairs.

'I know it was rather forward of me to ask for your number, but the reason I'm calling is that I want to ask you out on a date.'

'A date?' Sylvie shook her head. John was being silly.

'Yes. I want to take you out to dinner this evening.'

'You want to take me out to dinner?' Sylvie couldn't mask her surprise. 'In a restaurant?' She didn't think he was serious. 'This evening?' She thought he had other plans.

'Is that a *yes*?' John said hopefully.

'Yes,' Sylvie replied down the phone. As it turned out he *did* have other plans.

Sylvie had an idea what he was up to. The boot was coming off, and he was taking her out for a celebratory meal as a thank you for all she had done for him. Considering all the trouble she had gone to, to shop and cook the evening meals, it was a nice gesture on his part. Even so, she was still wondering what he was up to, asking for her phone number, and now taking her out on a date. It was all rather silly, but it wasn't getting on her nerves. Sylvie was finding all this pretty amusing.

'It's a date, then,' said John. 'Shall we meet at Fellinis at eight o'clock? Oh, hang on. I'm getting ahead of myself. Do you know the restaurant at all?'

Sylvie smiled. He was being silly again. Of course she knew

that restaurant. Although it was under different management, and changed its name in recent years, it was the same Italian restaurant where they had their first proper date when they were courting all those years ago.

'You want me to meet you there?'

'Yes, around eight, if that's okay with you.'

Sylvie shook her head. She didn't understand why they couldn't just go there together. She decided not to question the arrangement and just play along, especially as she was finding all this silliness such fun. 'All right, John.'

The moment Sylvie got off the phone she raced to the kitchen table, switched on her laptop, and sat drumming her fingers on the kitchen table. As soon as the icon appeared on her desktop, she clicked straight through to her blog and made another entry, speaking out loud as she typed, 'Today, I was asked out on a date by my husband, no less. A Surprise dinner date at eight o'clock this evening in a restaurant. I'm feeling nervous, like a teenager going on a first date.'

Sylvie re-read the blog entry. She hadn't been out on a date for years. It was understandable being nervous if she was going out with someone new like Nigel, not her husband of nigh on forty years. She was already fretting over what she would wear.

John arrived at the restaurant early. He'd ordered some house wine and sat at a table waiting for Sylvie. He was feeling nervous, as though he was out on a first date, rather than just having dinner with his wife of nigh on forty years.

John fiddled with his tie. It was tight, constricting and uncomfortable. He had grown accustomed to wearing casual clothes. This was the first time since he lost his job he'd put on a suit and tie. He hoped he was not overdressed for the occasion.

'Sylvie!' John waved as soon as he saw her arrive. He smiled as the maître d' led her to their table. Sylvie had made just as much effort with her appearance as he had. She was wearing a dress John thought he recognised as one of her favourites – she only wore it on special occasions – along with a matching necklace, brooch and earrings. And she was wearing make-up, subtle, but enough to make him sit up and take notice. He thought she looked nice, very nice indeed.

As she approached the table, John bounced out of his seat and came around to pull out a chair for his wife.

She didn't comment on the missing orthopaedic boot. She was relieved to see him sitting at the table without his crutches, pleased he was on the mend.

When they were both seated the maître d' gave them each a menu.

Sylvie studied the menu; the meals seemed expensive. 'This has become very upmarket,' whispered Sylvie, staring at John across the table.

John agreed. 'It's nice though, isn't it?'

'Oh yes.' Sylvie stole a glance at the other customers. She had been worried that she might appear overdressed and was relieved to discover that the other diners dressed similarly. John was treating it as a special occasion too because he had worn one of his best suits. Sylvie was sure she recognised it as the one that always bolstered his confidence. He called it his lucky suit. She remembered he used to wear it to important meetings at work when something big was at stake.

Sylvie smiled at him. He looked very suave. She had never

thought that about her husband before when he wore a suit to work. Perhaps it had something to do with his new hairstyle; the highlights made him appear younger-looking, more attractive. Or maybe it was that she was looking at the man across the table from her in a whole new light. For once in their marriage, he had surprised her. She still couldn't quite believe she was sitting down to a restaurant meal organised by her husband. It was unprecedented. He'd done nothing like this before. Sylvie couldn't remember the last time her husband had taken her out.

Sylvie was staring at John, wondering what other surprises he had tucked up his sleeve, when a waiter came over to take their order. A short time later the first course arrived.

The food didn't disappoint, and neither did the company. Sylvie couldn't remember the last time she'd had this much fun with John. It brought back memories of the good times they'd shared when they were courting, before marriage and careers and property and parenthood. It had been decades since they'd sat in this restaurant together, but during that dinner date with John, Sylvie felt all those years – and what had gone on in between – fall away to reveal the people they used to be.

It was almost as though they had turned back the clock. They were just two individuals talking and laughing together, aware this might be the start of something new. Finding out about each other through things said and unsaid, as with the start of all new relationships.

By the time the maître d' brought over the bill, Sylvie and John were almost the last to leave.

John opened his wallet. He handed over a card hoping Sylvie didn't notice he had to pay for the meal with a credit card.

'I'd like to order a taxi,' he told the maître d'.

'Will sir be requiring one taxi, or shall I also order one for the lady?' The maître d' looked from John to Sylvie.

'Sylvie, would you like to share a taxi? We're going in the same direction, I think.'

He was being silly again. She tried hard not to giggle. Sylvie looked up at the Maître d', and in the spirit of silliness said, 'Yes, I think we could share a taxi.' She glanced at John. 'If you're sure that I won't be taking you out of your way?'

John furrowed his brow. It took him a minute or two to comprehend that she was playing along. 'Oh, not at all.' John grinned. 'I'm sure it won't be too much of a detour to your place.'

'That's settled then,' said Sylvie smiling at the maître d'.

'Very good, madam,' he said, taking John's credit card.

They were on their way home in the taxi when John told the taxi driver to pull over.

Before Sylvie had a chance ask him what was going on, he'd jumped out of the taxi, darted across the road to a late-night convenience store, and returned carrying a bunch of flowers.

'For you' John presented the flowers to Sylvie as he climbed back in beside her.

Sylvie didn't know what to say.

He sneezed.

She gave him a sideways glance as he found a handkerchief. Flowers triggered his allergies. Sitting in a confined space next to his wife holding a big bunch of flowers wasn't one of John's brightest ideas, thought Sylvie. But he bought them anyway, proving she was worth more to him than a bit of temporary discomfort. Sylvie smiled.

The taxi drew up outside their house. 'May I walk you to your door?'

Sylvie giggled. 'That's very thoughtful of you, John.' She glanced out of the taxi window as he got out of the car. It was almost midnight and pitch dark.

John circled the taxi and opened the car door for Sylvie, holding out his hand to help her alight. He walked with her up the front path and stopped on the doorstep.

Sylvie got out her key and opened the front door. She stepped inside.

John didn't follow.

She turned around and looked at him askance. 'Aren't you coming in?'

'Oh,' said John, 'I couldn't possibly do that on a first date. Perhaps next time you might invite me in for coffee?'

Sylvie's face lit up. John was being silly again. She joined in the silliness. 'Was I going too fast?' she said playfully.

'A little,' he replied coyly, enjoying the banter. 'Goodnight, Sylvie.' He bent down and gave her a tentative kiss on the lips.

'Goodnight, John.' Sylvie shut the front door.

John headed back to the taxi.

'Where to now?' asked the taxi driver.

'Not far.' John settled himself in the back seat. 'Just follow my directions.'

They set off down the street, the taxi driver following John's directions. 'Make a left at the end of the street.' They turned the corner. 'And another left.' The taxi turned left again. 'And left again.'

'But—'

'Yes, that's right, keep going.'

As they made the last left turn, John got out his mobile phone and dialled Sylvie's number.

The taxi driver eyed him through the rear-view mirror. 'Are you sure this is the right way because it looks like we've already been down this road—'

'Yes, keep going, my place is just a little way up the street.' John frowned when Sylvie didn't answer the phone. He left her a brief message instead, pocketed his phone and got out his wallet. He leaned forward in his seat, and said to the taxi driver, 'I think we're almost there. If you wouldn't mind pulling the car over right about... here.'

The taxi driver pulled up right outside the same house, in the same spot where he dropped the lady off not less than five minutes ago. The taxi driver turned in his seat to look at his passenger in the back.

'I told you it wasn't far.' John handed over a twenty-pound note, including a large tip.

The taxi driver looked at John a long moment.

'What?'

'Nothing, mate.' He took the money.

John got out of the taxi for the second time.

The taxi driver sat and watched him walk through the same gate, up the same path, open the same front door and step inside the same house. He slowly shook his head from side to side. 'Crazy people,' he said, tapping his temple before speeding off.

When John walked Sylvie to the front door, and she realised he wasn't coming in, she unlocked the door to her apartment, dodged her excitable cocker spaniel who was pleased to see her, and made it to the front window in time to see him get back in the taxi and leave. This puzzled Sylvie. Where was he going at this hour? The phone started to ring, but she didn't make a move to answer it. Instead, she stood transfixed at the window wondering what on earth he was up to now.

It didn't take long to find out. Less than five minutes later the taxi drew up outside their house with John inside. She saw him pay the fare before he alighted. As he walked up the front path to the house, Sylvie spotted the taxi driver making a gesture with his finger to his head, as though he thought they were crazy, before he switched off the light inside the cab and sped off.

Sylvie laughed out loud. She was still grinning as she walked downstairs to the kitchen to see if someone had left a message on the answerphone.

'Hello, Sylvie. I'm just calling to say that I had a really nice time on our first date this evening, and I was rather hoping we might do it again sometime…'

Sylvie was listening to the phone message as she was typing up the next entry in her blog, making sure she had included all the details of her romantic candle-lit dinner and the amusing shenanigans on the taxi-ride home. This was a side of her husband she hadn't seen in a long, long time. Not to mention the unexpected romantic gestures, like stopping off on the way home to buy her flowers, and the kiss goodnight at the door. It made her feel young again, carefree and full of hope and expectation for the future. Above all, it made Sylvie feel special. Something she hadn't experienced in a very long time.

She signed off her blog, as she always did, with the words: don't forget to tune in for the next exciting episode of *Love on the Rooftop*. Sylvie smiled when she remembered Chloe asking her why she had changed the name of her blog to *Love on the Rooftop*. She couldn't answer that question, without it sounding completely daft. Sylvie told no one, but ever since she'd moved into the garden apartment, she had experienced the most bizarre recurring dream.

In her dream, she'd fallen in love with someone on a rooftop; just who that someone is, and where that rooftop was, she had no clue. It was a mystery. That didn't stop Sylvie using it as the name of her blog. It wasn't as though anybody else would ask her why she called it that. Nobody was reading her blog. Even Chloe, who was the only other person in the world who knew her blog existed, admitted she hadn't found the time to read *Love on the Rooftop*.

Sylvie closed her laptop, made herself a cup of coffee and sat down at the kitchen table wishing she'd invited John in for a nightcap. Before heading off to bed, she listened to the message John had left her on her answerphone one more time. She shook her head and smiled wondering what silliness he had in store when she saw him next.

24

Sylvie cut another flower stem and smiled to herself as she arranged the flower in the vase with the others John had bought her last night. She glanced at the time. She was just debating whether it was too early to ring Julia and tell her all about the romantic dinner date with John when the doorbell chimed upstairs. Sylvie hadn't finished arranging the flowers. She hoped he heard it and answered the front door.

On the third chime, Sylvie rolled her eyes, put the last flower down on the draining board along with the scissors and made her way upstairs. She closed the door to the kitchen behind her so Alfie didn't get out.

Sylvie walked out of her apartment into the communal hall and answered the front door. She found her husband standing on the doorstep. She looked at him in surprise. Her first thought was he'd popped out for the morning paper and forgotten his front-door key.

'Hello Sylvie.' John grinned. 'It's such a beautiful morning, and I was in the neighbourhood…'

I was in the neighbourhood. That comment elicited a smile from Sylvie. John was being silly again.

'So, I thought I'd call on you to ask if you would like to join me for a morning walk in the sunshine,' he paused. 'Unless you're busy…'

Sylvie forgot about the flower arranging in an instant. 'Just give me two ticks and I'll grab my coat.' She disappeared inside her apartment and slipped on a comfortable pair of shoes and a warm jacket. She picked up her handbag on the way out and closed the door.

She was about to step outside but thought she'd forgotten something. With a start, Sylvie remembered what that something was. She looked up at John. 'Do you mind if I nip back inside? I just need to get—'

'Be my guest,' he replied. He hadn't forgotten his wife's annoying little foibles. This was one of them. Before they left the house, it was always the same routine: at the last minute, she would remember something that she'd forgotten to bring with her, be it a comb, lipstick, or an umbrella.

John stood on the doorstep whistling a tune while he waited. His tuneful whistle caught in his throat as soon as he saw Sylvie emerge from her apartment.

She shut her door and joined him on the doorstep. Registering his surprise, she explained, 'It's around this time in the morning that I take Alfie for walkies.'

Alfie yapped on hearing the word *walkies*.

In her excitement at going on another date, Sylvie had nearly forgotten her dog.

She wasn't the only one. John had forgotten all about the dog too. *Damn.*

'As we're going for a walk, would you mind if I brought Alfie along?'

273

'Fine by me,' said John, lying through his teeth. His original plan was to stop at a café for lunch. That idea had just been scuppered. He frowned at the dog. He didn't fancy trying to have a relaxing lunch together with a mutt sitting outside the café howling because he was lonely and wanted to come inside too. John had heard him howling in Sylvie's kitchen downstairs and knew what he was capable of. It left him no choice but to postpone their lunch date for another time. John sighed. He was regretting the walk idea.

As they strolled down the front path together, Sylvie said, 'We don't have to go to the park just because I've brought Alfie along.' She stopped to open the front gate and glanced at her husband.

John shifted his gaze from Alfie, who was busy sniffing his shoe, and smiled at Sylvie. They'd known each other long enough to second guess what the other was thinking just by reading their expressions. Although he tried to hide it, John guessed by Sylvie's comment that she felt he wasn't keen on Alfie tagging along on their walk.

He kept his gaze focused on Sylvie as he shifted his foot. The wet nose exploring his trouser leg followed. He tried his best to ignore the annoying mutt, and continued to smile at Sylvie as he asked, 'If you want a change from walking in the park, did you have something else in mind?'

Sylvie stared off into space, deep in thought, until her face lit up. 'I've got an idea. How about a trip down memory lane?'

'Sounds interesting.'

It sounded interesting until they had walked a fair distance and John realised where they were heading. He furrowed his brow. 'Sylvie, this is Little Venice.'

'I know.'

John really hoped Sylvie's intention wasn't to call on her best friend. He'd heard that she'd sold her flat when she retired from teaching and bought a houseboat in Little Venice. Bumping into Julia would not make for a pleasant addition to his idea of a romantic stroll with his wife. Julia was not one of his favourite people. Ever since they were first introduced, soon after he met Sylvie, John got the impression that Julia wanted to see the back of him. Her hostility towards him developed into a mutual dislike that had lasted to this day.

John wanted to avoid a confrontation with Julia. He turned to Sylvie. 'If this is meant to be a trip down memory lane, I don't see why you've chosen to come here.' Unless this was a detour to see Julia, as he suspected.

'Remember years ago, when the girls were small, we used to walk along the towpath beside Regent's Canal? Once we walked all the way to the market at Camden Lock.'

John cast his mind back a good thirty plus years. He raised an eyebrow. 'Yes, of course. Sometimes we used to get to London Zoo and stop there to take the girls into Regent's Park.'

'That's right.' Sylvie smiled. 'We could walk along the towpath and see how far we get?'

'What a grand idea,' John replied, trying to ignore the possibility that they might bang into Julia sitting on the deck of her houseboat as they passed by.

It wasn't long before they reached Bloomfield Road. They walked down the street and soon found the gap in the railings where a flight of stone steps led down to the towpath. John could already see the row of brightly coloured barges crammed one beside the other lining the canal. He wondered which one belonged to Julia. It wasn't long before he found out. A short distance along the towpath, Sylvie came to a halt in front of a red and green barge called *Mandalay*. There was an old bicycle, with a basket attached to its handlebars, propped up on the deck beside a small circular bistro table and two chairs. An assortment of plant pots containing winter flowers lined the deck.

'This is where Julia lives. She bought a houseboat.'

'I know,' said John flatly, praying Sylvie didn't—

'Julia!' Sylvie called out. 'Julia! Are you home?'

John groaned. At least he knew that Sylvie wouldn't climb aboard and knock on her cabin door. She didn't have a fondness for boats.

'Julia!' Sylvie called again before turning to John. 'I don't think she can hear me.'

'Ah well, that's a shame,' John said, feeling relieved. He turned to go.

'We can't possibly leave without seeing if she's in. That would be rude of us if we just walked on by.'

John had no qualms walking on by. Besides, what did Sylvie expect him to do about it? Climb aboard and knock on her door?

'Be a dear, climb aboard and knock on her door, would you?'

No bloody way. He stared at Sylvie. On the other hand, he didn't want to spoil a pleasant walk because he had refused to do as he was asked. John's shoulders sagged in defeat. He was in a no-win situation. He rolled his eyes in the direction of the boat.

He stepped aboard on to the small open deck and found the barge surprisingly stable. He skirted the bistro table and knocked softly on the cabin door.

No answer.

'There's no answer!' John called out to Sylvie standing on the towpath. John grimaced when Alfie barked. So much for softly knocking on her door, hoping she didn't hear him. If Julia was in, she would certainly hear that racket.

'Be quiet, Alfie!' Sylvie scolded her dog.

For once Alfie did as he was told.

'Try knocking again.'

John sighed, turned to the door and knocked – louder this time. Still no answer. He glanced at Sylvie and shrugged his shoulders in a *what more can I do* gesture.

'You can walk along further and look in the windows.'

'They're called *portholes*,' John told her in an irritated tone of voice.

'Portholes, windows – what's the difference? Just see if she's in.'

'What if she's in bed!' He was sure the last thing Julia wanted was to wake up to his face peering in at her through a porthole.

Sylvie insisted, so he did it anyway and could unequivocally report back that, 'Julia is not in.' He breathed a sigh of relief as he re-joined Sylvie on the towpath.

They continued on their way leaving the houseboats behind. Large elegant Georgian houses came into view on the opposite side, their neat terrace gardens sloping down to the water's edge.

'John, do you remember Jess liked to ride her blue trike along the towpath?'

'Oh, yes,' said John, thinking back. 'As I recall, she'd ride it all the way to Regent's Park. Then she'd decide she didn't want to ride it anymore, and I'd have to carry it all the way home.'

'And carry her too,' Sylvie reminded him.

They both smiled at the memory. It seemed like it was only yesterday that the girls were small, but now it wouldn't be long before their grandchild, Gertie, would be riding a trike. John thought he might buy her one this year for her third birthday. Perhaps she would enjoy taking it out for a spin along the towpath, with her grandparents, and then insist on being carried all the way home just like auntie Jess used to.

John was enjoying reminiscing about raising the children in London; the places they used to go, some of their favourite haunts. There was no shortage of things to do in the city when the girls were growing up. The sad part was that he always seemed to have a lack of time to spend with them, and with Sylvie. John recalled the futile job search soon after he was forced into early retirement.

Why did it never occur to him that his time would be better spent with Sylvie, enjoying his retirement, instead of being so preoccupied with returning to work? John realised what a fool he'd been. Not just in the recent past. But all those years ago when he was always too busy with work or renovating the house to spend what free time he had with his family. At least now he had a chance to put things right; he couldn't turn back the clock to when the girls were small, but he could spend more time with his wife and granddaughter. That was his intention.

John smiled at Sylvie. She was walking beside him busy concentrating on keeping Alfie in check. The dog was still pulling on the lead. Despite the annoying creature that he hadn't factored into their next date, John was enjoying the walk down memory lane.

A little over an hour later, after a pleasant stroll along the quiet canal towpath, the scenery changed as they entered the leafy green perimeter of Regent's Park. John could see the wire enclosure of London Zoo's bird aviary up ahead which meant they were coming up to one of the towpath's exits near the entrance to the park. Although Camden Lock, with its bustling market selling all kinds of oddities, was only half a mile further along, John fancied exiting the towpath here.

Sylvie agreed. 'Alfie has been so good he deserves a run off the lead in the park.'

John glanced at the dog. He wouldn't go so far as to say he was good. In fact, Alfie had pulled on the lead for the entire walk, testing John's patience. And he wasn't even the one walking the mutt.

They both left the towpath and walked up a gentle incline to the street above, with Alfie leading the way panting and pulling on the lead. They turned left and walked the short distance along the road to the entrance to Regent's Park.

'We should take Gertie to the zoo sometime,' remarked John as they passed by families queuing to get into London Zoo.

'I agree. It will be just like old times when we used to take the girls.' She stole a glance at John. Were they making plans to do things together? Not that long ago he didn't appear interested in doing anything other than finding another job.

Sylvie remembered when he'd first retired, before he came up with the idea of the house conversion. All she wanted to do was make plans for their future and how they would spend their retirement together. They didn't have to do anything extravagant like foreign holidays, just simple things like taking their grandchild to the zoo. But John didn't want to make plans for their future. Retirement was a taboo subject in the Baxter household. She felt as though he'd rather be at work than spend time with his wife. Sylvie regarded him thoughtfully wondering what had changed.

As they entered the park and walked along the wide central boulevard, John glanced at Sylvie and smiled. This trip down memory lane reminded him of the times they visited Regent's Park in the past. They often came this way because there was a swing-park close by where they used to take the girls. Afterwards, the girls would have some squash and a teacake in a little café opposite 221B Baker Street, the home of the famous detective, Sherlock Holmes.

John used to enjoy sitting in the café telling his daughters all about the detective who lived in the house across the street. Until one day, unbeknown to John, Harriet had checked the facts and piped up that Sherlock Holmes wasn't a *real* person, and 221B Baker Street wasn't a house but The Sherlock Holmes Museum.

John smiled to himself. He hadn't thought about that in years. His eldest daughter was already a journalist-in-the-making at the tender age of seven.

As they neared the park gates, Sylvie turned to John. 'I need to spend a penny. Can you hold on to Alfie?'

'Oh, I suppose so,' he said reluctantly.

Sylvie handed John the lead and disappeared up the path to the ladies' toilets.

John was standing there waiting for Sylvie to return when a dog ventured up to Alfie to say hello.

Alfie started to bark and pull on the lead.

John had to keep a tight hold of Alfie's lead to stop him from chasing the other dog. He grimaced. The dog-trainer hadn't done his job properly, and John had an idea why. Nigel had spent far too much time paying attention to Sylvie instead of her dog.

'Right, you,' said John sternly, 'we'll have none of that funny business – do you hear?'

Alfie stopped yapping and looked up at John.

'Okay, now I've got your attention...'

By the time Sylvie returned, Alfie was sitting as good as gold behaving himself, which surprised Sylvie and John both. All he'd told Alfie to do, in a strong authoritative voice, was *sit*.

'Gosh,' exclaimed Sylvie as soon as she saw her dog. 'At this rate, I won't need any further lessons from Nigel.'

John smiled at Sylvie, pleased to hear it.

'Do you think if we went into the café in the park, to have a cup of coffee, Alfie would behave himself?' Sylvie asked.

'Why don't we find out?' John remarked, hoping that Alfie remained on his best behaviour because he felt in need of a sit-down. After spending the last couple of weeks sedentary because of the accident at the gym, he wasn't used to this much exercise. While Sylvie appeared to have lost some weight recently by walking the dog, John had piled on a few pounds. The waistline on his new jeans felt tight. John guessed it was a combination of lounging on the sofa all day letting Sylvie do everything for him – pure laziness on his part – and Sylvie's delicious home-cooked meals.

Outside the small café, John saw a bowl of water left on the ground next to a wooden post for the customers' canine friends. He tied the dog's lead to the post while Alfie slurped some water. John waited until he had the dog's full attention. 'Alfie – sit!'

Alfie looked up at John, wagged his tail and sat on command.

'Good dog.' John praised Alfie and thought, now comes the hard part. 'Alfie – stay!' John held up his hand in front of Alfie's nose.

Alfie licked his hand.

With his outstretched hand still held high like a policeman

directing traffic, John slowly backed away from the dog.

Alfie stayed where he was, watching John and wagging his tail furiously.

When Sylvie and John sat down at a table in the café with their cups of coffee and looked out the window, they could see Alfie still sitting in the same spot as quiet as a dormouse.

'Well, I never,' said Sylvie, staring at Alfie in astonishment. 'He never does that for me.' She turned and looked at John in surprise.

John shrugged his shoulders. 'It's nothing, really,' he said modestly, feeling chuffed with himself. In hindsight, he was pleased Sylvie had brought Alfie along for the walk. He had just proved that Nigel's dog-training services were surplus to requirements; Nigel had just been made redundant.

'John, can you teach me how to do that because, if it wasn't for you, he'd be sitting out there howling like he does when I leave him outside the shops?'

'Of course, there's nothing to it,' he replied, hoping he wasn't getting ahead of himself by promising a repeat performance.

It turned out that because Alfie was being so good, John and Sylvie's coffee break extended to a spot of lunch. It was a simple affair comprising finger sandwiches and one large slice of Victoria sponge cake, which they shared along with a fresh pot of tea.

After a long lunch, John stretched. 'I need some fresh air otherwise I might take an afternoon nap like Alfie over there.' He pointed out the window at her dog. As they left the café, John turned to Sylvie and asked, 'May I walk you home?'

Sylvie couldn't help but laugh; the silliness had resumed. 'I'd like that, John. I'd like that very much.'

John paid for lunch and went to fetch Alfie. 'Good dog,' he said as he approached the sleeping puppy.

Alfie opened his eyes at the sound of John's voice.

He crouched down and stroked Alfie. 'What a good dog.' John had not expected Alfie to behave himself all the way through lunch too. His idea of a romantic walk with his wife was turning out very well indeed, all things considered. He had not accounted for Sylvie bringing along the dog, or the unscheduled stop to see his least favourite person – Julia – who, thank heavens, wasn't home. If there was one thing that could put a complete dampener on his otherwise perfectly executed plan, it was running into Sylvie's best friend.

John looked down at Alfie, walking beside him, and decided Alfie did deserve to be let off the lead for being good. He hoped the dog didn't spoil his hitherto exemplary behaviour by running off. It was a chance John was willing to take. He bent down and unclipped the lead from his collar.

'Here,' said Sylvie, fishing in her handbag. 'Throw this.'

John took the ball and threw it across the park as they walked along. Alfie returned with the ball every time he threw it. To John's surprise he discovered he was enjoying the game of fetch almost as much as Alfie.

'Someone is waving at us.' Sylvie squinted in the sunlight. She turned to John. 'Who do you think that is?'

John threw the ball again and then stopped to look in the direction Sylvie was pointing. He shook his head. 'Hard to say from this distance. I don't recognise—'

'It's Julia!'

John flinched. 'Sylvie, please don't—'

'Julia!' she called out waving her hand in the air.

John rolled his eyes. Until that moment, things had been going so well. He sighed and looked at Sylvie eagerly waving at her best friend. 'Why don't you go and say hello.' He knew that's what she wanted to do. 'I'll um hang back here and carry on with the game of fetch.' Alfie had already returned with the ball and dropped it on the grass at John's feet.

'Are you sure?'

'Go right ahead. You can catch me up.' Thank god for the dog, thought John. It gave him an excuse to avoid Julia.

Sylvie left John and Alfie to their game of fetch and walked across the wide expanse of lawn towards the rose garden. She knew it was Julia because she was wearing her distinctive wide-brimmed straw hat with the bright red ribbon. Sylvie would recognise that hat anywhere. Julia was sitting at a small wooden painting easel.

She looked up as Sylvie approached. 'Sylvie, darling! It *is* you.' She pointed the nib of her paintbrush in John's direction. 'I thought I spotted you both walking in the park. If you hadn't waved back, I would have assumed it was a case of mistaken identity.'

'You weren't mistaken.' Sylvie smiled. She was delighted to see her because she had been dying to tell Julia all about the romantic dates with John. 'We've been out on a very pleasant walk together this morning. We passed by your houseboat on our way here, but you weren't in.'

'I left home early. It's such a lovely day that I wanted to make the most of the weather and headed to the park to paint.' Julia paused. 'I see things are working out between you two.'

'Do you think so?' Sylvie glanced at her husband in the distance.

Julia nodded as she dabbed her brush in the paint palette. 'I'm rather pleased, actually. I like Nigel, and you two make the perfect—'

'Nigel?' interrupted Sylvie. 'You think I'm with Nigel?'

'Well, of course,' said Julia off-hand as she made fine brush strokes on the canvas. She stopped and peered up at Sylvie. 'It is Nigel over there with Alfie, isn't it?'

Sylvie looked at Julia in surprise. 'No, it isn't Nigel.'

'Then who is it?'

'It's John.' Sylvie glanced across the park at her husband. 'Don't you recognise him?' Perhaps it was his new clothes and hairstyle that made him appear like Nigel from a distance. John's new clothes were like the outfit Nigel had worn at the puppy training class, something Sylvie hadn't noticed until now. However, despite the new look, and the highlights, Sylvie believed it was more than that. 'John has changed.'

'I can see that,' observed Julia, putting her paintbrush down on the easel. She stood up to take a good look.

'No, I don't mean his appearance…'

'Oh.' Julia returned to her seat and picked up her paintbrush. 'So, what *do* you mean?'

Sylvie told Julia all about their romantic meal last night in a restaurant, and the fun and games in the taxi on the way home when John pretended they lived at separate addresses. 'He even stopped the taxi to buy me flowers on the way home – can you believe it!'

Julia listened without comment.

'This morning, while I was arranging the flowers, he called on me to ask if I would like to join him on a walk. After our lovely evening together, how could I refuse?'

Julia remained silent.

'It has turned out a delightful morning. We walked along the canal reminiscing about old times. We've even started to make some plans for what other things we might like to do together.' Sylvie grinned. 'I haven't felt this happy in ages, Julia. I still can't believe the change in John. He's paying attention to me, the way he used to when we first met and started courting.'

Julia narrowed her eyes. 'I wonder what he's up to?'

'What's that supposed to mean?' snapped Sylvie. She thought Julia would be pleased for her.

'Look, Sylvie, we've known John for a long time. We both know this isn't him.'

Sylvie couldn't dispute that. Until recently, she would have agreed with Julia; the restaurant meal and the flowers and the romantic walk together were not the sort of thing Sylvie expected from her husband. 'I agree, Julia. I have been thinking about that too. And do you know what I suspect...?'

Julia shook her head. 'Why don't you enlighten me?'

'Living apart has made him stop and think about us and what he can do to mend our relationship. The funny thing is, after all these years, it's almost as though we're getting to know each other all over again.'

Julia looked at her sceptically.

Sylvie frowned when she saw Julia's cynical expression. She wasn't about to let Julia's pessimism spoil what might be the start of a new chapter in their lives together. Sylvie didn't want anybody, least of all her best friend who always had it in for John, to threaten these fragile beginnings.

'I'm sorry, Sylvie, but I still feel he's up to something.'

'I thought you'd be happy for me,' Sylvie said crossly. She

stared at her best friend. Julia had never married, on top of which she had several failed relationships behind her. It made Sylvie wonder if the reason she never liked John was jealousy; they met when very young and it had lasted all these years.

'You never liked him,' said Sylvie, feeling as though she was building up to say something she would later regret. 'You're only jealous because you're on your own and I'm not.' With that, Sylvie stormed off in the direction of her husband.

In between tossing Alfie the ball John had been watching Sylvie and Julia from a distance. He could imagine what Julia was saying about him. John sighed. She took every opportunity to put him down.

Alfie came bounding over with the ball again and dropped it at John's feet, but he wasn't paying attention. He was standing there staring in their direction wondering if he was being paranoid. Sylvie had probably told Julia all about their romantic meal together; he knew what she would say about that, that he was up to something.

In the beginning, John would be the first to admit that he had a hidden agenda. This had started out as just another plan to get Sylvie to move back in with him. But along the way, things had changed. Now he was having a good time with his wife. He'd forgotten the plan. He didn't care about the apartments anymore and who lived where. What did it matter?

For that reason, John had done something rather foolish one evening and bought his first lottery ticket. Not a foolish act in itself. Plenty of people bought lottery tickets. A little flutter didn't hurt now and again. But it was stupid to think he could solve all his problems by winning the lottery. It's not that he had any desire to be a millionaire. What he needed was for these good times with Sylvie to continue. He wanted to throw the cards up in the air and let them land where they will. He wanted Sylvie back; there was no doubt about it, but only if that's what she wanted too. Unfortunately, his financial problems were still there, looming large, the urgency to deal with the pile of out-standing bills sitting unopened in his desk drawer a constant headache. He tried to push all that to the back of his mind.

From a distance, John saw Sylvie gesticulating. He recog-nized her posture: she was lifting off over something Julia had said. John frowned. Trust Julia to ruin a perfectly nice morning.

He heaved a sigh and glanced down at Alfie. 'Well, I think we can assume that's the end of walkies,' John remarked miserably. He knelt, attached the lead to Alfie's collar, and then picked up the ball. When he stood up, he saw Sylvie storming back from the rose garden, her face like thunder.

'What's wrong?' John asked innocently, knowing full well what was wrong. He was bracing himself for an earful from his wife after Julia had sowed a seed of doubt in her mind over what he was up to.

'It's nothing,' said Sylvie, dismissing Julia with a flick of her hand. She smiled up at him and linked her arm in his.

John looked at her in surprise and tentatively inquired, 'Shall I walk you home?'

'That's not a good idea, John.'

'Oh, I see.' John went to hand over Alfie's lead.

Sylvie added, 'Unless you're sure it won't take you too far out of your way?'

John threw Sylvie a questioning look.

She grinned mischievously.

He smiled at the in-joke, and replied, 'I'm sure I won't be

going too far out of my way if I walk you home first.'

They both avoided the subject of Sylvie's conversation with Julia on the way home. By the time they arrived back at the house they had already arranged another dinner date, and Sylvie was looking forward to updating her blog.

At the door, John asked, 'May I call on you again?'

'You may call on me whenever you like,' said Sylvie, standing on tiptoes and giving him an unexpected kiss. She left John standing on the doorstep and walked inside the house, closing the front door behind her.

As soon as she stepped foot inside her apartment, Sylvie kicked off her shoes and headed straight down to the kitchen, followed by Alfie in hot pursuit.

Alfie made a beeline for his empty food bowl.

Sylvie made straight for her laptop. The first thing she intended to do — while it was still fresh in her mind — was to write in her blog all about her husband calling on her this morning and the most enjoyable romantic walk along the canal that followed; leaving out the unfortunate altercation with Julia, which she was still trying to put out of her mind.

Julia was wrong. John was not up to something. And if he was, then Sylvie had a good idea what that might be. Although he had not broached the subject of when she was moving out of the garden apartment, it had already crossed her mind that maybe, during their next dinner date this evening, he would pop the question: shall we move back in together?

That would have been amusing, and worthy of consideration coming from the new romantic John, if it wasn't for Julia planting a seed of doubt in her mind; were the dinner dates and the flowers and the romantic walk together all because he wanted to spend time with her or was Julia right, and there was more to it than that? Was John on another mission to get the apartment back, so he could rent it out?

Sylvie stopped typing up her blog entry while she mulled this over. The last thing she wanted was to be made a fool of. She didn't write any of this down in her blog because she still felt Julia was wrong and her fears were unfounded. As far as Sylvie, and anybody who might happen upon her blog, was concerned, they'd just had a nice romantic walk together in the autumn sunshine, followed by a very pleasant lunch and an enjoyable walk home – that was all.

Sylvie finished her entry with how much she was looking forward to their next dinner date. She was hoping John did not bring up the subject of moving back in together. When Sylvie felt the time was right, she wanted to be the one to make that decision. She hoped John would respect her enough to wait for her to make up her own mind.

As always, she signed off her blog with the words: don't forget to tune in for the next exciting episode of *Love on the Rooftop*.

25

John saw the taxi draw up outside the house. He turned from the window, gathered up his coat and left his apartment. Taking the stairs two at a time, he stepped into the communal hall downstairs and hurried past Sylvie's flat on his way out of the house, closing the front door behind him. He then proceeded down the path to the waiting taxi.

John used the same taxicab company. As he approached the car, he recognised the driver who dropped them home the other evening. He wouldn't be surprised if he insisted on taking this fare just to see what the strange couple from Penfold Street got up to next. He couldn't care less what the taxi driver thought, so long as he didn't mind playing along with whatever John had in mind – no questions asked.

The taxi driver spotted him leaving the house. He pressed a button on the dashboard to open the car window as John approached.

'Good evening,' John greeted him cordially through the open window. 'Please can you wait here while I call on my date?'

The taxi driver nodded. 'Whatever yanks your chain, mate.'

John walked back up to the house and rang the doorbell. To

his surprise, Sylvie didn't answer the door straightaway. He raised an eyebrow. She knew what time he was calling. He glanced at his watch wondering where she was.

Sylvie was standing in the hall, the other side of the front door, feeling self-conscious in her new black chiffon dress. The lady in the boutique said it suited her figure and she looked amazing. Sylvie thought it better look amazing with that price tag.

Sylvie had never bought a designer label before. She'd withdrawn the last of her small retirement lump sum, which she was keeping to one side in case of an emergency, to pay for the ridiculously expensive dress. It meant she was broke until she received her small pension next month. She would have to resort to asking John for some money, but that didn't concern her. He covered all the household bills for both apartments, so she only needed some pin money to tide her over.

Sylvie glanced in the mirror once more, and decided the dress was worth the extortionate price tag.

'You look... stunning,' said John as soon as Sylvie opened the door. He was taken aback at how much trouble she had gone to on their second date. But then he'd made quite an effort himself. John had been shopping all on his own and visited one of the designer shops Chloe took him to on their shopping expedition together. He bought a new suit, paying an obscene amount of money for a label that said, Ralph Lauren. All because the young lady in the shop convinced him he looked dashing, and it was the perfect buy for a special date.

He then visited Chloe's hairdresser to have his highlights touched up, almost missing his dinner date with Sylvie because he thought he was having a heart attack when he saw the bill. He shouldn't have let himself get talked into having an expensive manicure by a charming young lass, with a flirtatious manner, who kept saying, "Ooh get outta here", every time he tried to convince her he was sixty years old.

As they walked arm in arm to the waiting taxi, John glanced at his date. He hoped the evening went well since there was a reason he was making such an effort. It was time to pop the question and ask Sylvie to move back in with him.

'John, you were saying you want to ask me something?'

'I did?' John was stalling. He'd been stalling all evening. He was about to pop the question at the end of their enjoyable dinner date when the waiter interrupted him with the bill, and he lost his nerve.

'John – what is it?'

He drummed his fingers on his lap under the table, telling himself to ask her – ask her now! He looked up. 'Do you want to share a taxi home?' he blurted instead.

Sylvie smiled at him across the table. 'I thought you'd never ask.'

John offered a weak smile and helped Sylvie into her coat. As they left the restaurant, a taxi drew up outside. To John's surprise the same taxi driver turned up; he was feeling like an old friend.

'Where to first?' said the taxi driver in all seriousness as he turned to look at Sylvie and John sitting in the back of the cab.

They both eyed the taxi driver for a long moment.

John turned to Sylvie, and said, 'Your place or mine?'

'Let's go to my place first,' Sylvie decided.

The taxi driver offered them a crooked grin and turned around in his seat to set off.

They arrived home a short time later.

John walked Sylvie to the door, leaving the taxi waiting at the kerb.

Sylvie got out her key and opened the front door. Before stepping inside, she turned to John, and asked, 'Would you like to come in for coffee?'

'Yes, I'd like that.' He glanced over his shoulder. 'Just give me a moment.' He walked back to the waiting taxi and bent down to talk to the driver through the open window. 'You don't have to wait. I'm stopping for a cup of coffee.'

'Could be your lucky night, eh?' The taxi driver winked at him knowingly.

'Well, I don't know about that,' said John, opening his wallet and handing him a note including the usual generous tip.

'Are you sure you don't want me to wait?' asked the taxi driver, trying to keep a straight face. 'It's late, and you don't want to get caught out if you need a taxi home,' he added, enjoying the banter.

'No, no. I'm quite sure. Who knows, maybe it will be my lucky night and I won't need one after all.'

'Ha ha ha. Okay, but if it turns out you do need a cab, ask for Mario. I'll take you any place you want to go.'

John watched the taxi speed away down the street. He imagined Mario at the wheel laughing about the strange affair of two people who lived apart in the same house on Penfold Street. John shook his head. Mario was probably sharing the story of those amusing cab journeys with the rest of the taxi rank.

John shrugged and walked back up the garden path towards the house. He got out his door key on autopilot. He was about to open the front door when he remembered he was still on a date.

He put the key back in his pocket and rang the doorbell instead.

Sylvie answered the door. 'Please come in, John.'

He stepped into the communal hall.

'My apartment is through here.' Sylvie led the way.

'My, what a nice place you have,' John commented as he stepped inside her flat. 'Have you lived here long?'

Sylvie shut the door and looked at her husband. They both burst out laughing. They were still smiling at each other when they took a seat in the lounge.

Sylvie had already made a pot of coffee and placed it on the coffee table in front of them, together with a bowl of brown sugar cubes, a small jug of cream, and a plate of cookies that she'd baked earlier.

John helped himself to a homemade cookie. He looked at the American-style chocolate chip cookie – one of his favourites – and guessed that Sylvie had planned to invite him in for coffee after their dinner date this evening.

'Perhaps next time…' John ventured, as he picked up the jug and poured some cream into his coffee, 'you might like to stop by my place for coffee on your way home.'

'I think that's an excellent idea,' agreed Sylvie. She reached for her cup and glanced at John. 'Perhaps I won't need a taxi home afterwards,' she quipped playfully.

John stared at Sylvie his biscuit suspended in mid-air. Did she just broach the subject of moving back in together?

Sylvie lowered her coffee cup, unsure by the look on John's face whether she had said the right thing. 'Am I moving too fast?'

Not that long ago they would have fallen about laughing at the absurdity of that question. Not this time. When had all this stopped being a game and began to feel more like a real couple on the cusp of a new relationship? She felt as though they were in uncharted territory, trying to find their way back to each other with no map or compass or clue where they were headed. Perhaps John was thinking the same thing.

Sylvie didn't get a chance to find out what he was thinking because John gulped his coffee down in double-quick time and excused himself, saying there was something urgent he needed to do. He left a rather confused Sylvie sitting in her lounge with a freshly brewed pot of coffee and a plate of cookies untouched. She looked at the coffee and biscuits and shrugged. She wasn't concerned. Sylvie glanced up at the ceiling. She could hear him moving about in the apartment upstairs. Perhaps John had an idea and was in the throes of organising another trip out together.

Sylvie poured herself a second cup of coffee, picked up a cookie, and leant back on the sofa wondering what surprise he had in store for the next time they met up.

John raced up the stairs to his apartment thinking about the surprise he had in store for their next outing together. He had already planned something different; he'd bought two theatre tickets to a West End musical. Although not his thing, he knew his wife loved musicals and couldn't wait to see her reaction when he surprised her with the tickets. Perhaps she would look as dumbstruck as he did when she popped the question tonight, taking him unawares. John had not entertained the possibility that Sylvie might make the first move and suggest moving back in together.

Until Sylvie hinted at staying the night, John had been putting off asking her to move back in with him because he felt if he asked her outright, there was still a possibility she might say no. He even checked his lottery ticket before taking Sylvie to dinner, hoping if he had a winning ticket, he could solve all his financial problems. Then he wouldn't have to pop the question.

He hadn't won the lottery. What a silly fool he was to think he might be one of the lucky ones, as it was the first ticket he'd ever bought. So, he binned the ticket and had hit the jackpot anyway when Sylvie hinted that, if he invited her upstairs for a coffee on their next date, she might well stop for the night. At the rate things were going, it looked more than likely she would stay for good.

This was what he wanted, wasn't it? For Sylvie to move back upstairs. His plan was working. So why had he hesitated when she suggested spending the night together? He should have jumped at the chance. But he didn't. Instead, he just sat there staring dumbly at his wife. John shook his head in confusion; and could not, for the life of him, fathom why he was acting as though he wasn't sure that's what he wanted. It was sheer lunacy.

John walked into his study to remind himself why things couldn't go on the way they were, living apart together. He stared at the bills littering his desk, some opened, most not; this was the reason he excused himself and ran upstairs in a hurry. Just in case Sylvie followed him and discovered the evidence of their dire financial circumstances. He opened one of the desk drawers forgetting that he'd already filled it with unopened bills. He groaned. It was worse than he thought. He opened another drawer and slid the pile of bills along the desk and stuffed them in before slamming the drawer shut.

John shook his head. He had just given himself a not-so-gentle reminder of the urgency of the situation. On his desk were the theatre tickets. They cost a small fortune. John could only imagine what sort of credit card bill he was running up, with the restaurant meals and the cash he kept withdrawing for the taxi. The reason he could only imagine his credit card debt was because he hadn't opened the bill. That too was in the desk drawer.

He gazed at the theatre tickets. When he first came up with the idea to take Sylvie to a West End show, he had no clue how much it cost to go to the theatre these days. When he found out, he threw caution to the wind and bought them anyway because he knew this would be the grand finale. John had every intention of inviting Sylvie back for coffee after the show and asking her to move back in with him. After what she'd said this evening, he had every confidence she would say yes.

26

Sylvie sat in bed in her pyjamas with her laptop resting on top of the duvet. She glanced at Alfie who was already asleep at the end of her bed. It was late, but she was buzzing after spending another lovely evening with John. Sylvie couldn't wait to write all about it in the next instalment of her blog.

Once again, their date had gone well. She thought inviting John in for coffee afterwards was a nice touch. So far, he had not brought up the subject of their living arrangements, or even asked her to move back in with him, which she found perplexing. When she hinted at staying the night, his reaction surprised her; he seemed a little unsure, as though they were moving too fast. It was disconcerting but Sylvie found it rather sweet. It was almost as though they were that young couple again exploring the terrain of their relationship, making sure they had a firm footing with which to move forward together. He seemed startled when she took the initiative to move their relationship to the next level.

Sylvie smiled as she typed all this into her blog. She hadn't quite finished when the page froze. And then the whole thing crashed. Sylvie threw her arms up in the air in frustration. She was in the middle of typing up her thoughts about moving back in together. Sylvie tapped some computer keys at random, but nothing happened.

'For goodness' sake!' She'd never had this problem before.

Sylvie forgot the time, reached for the phone and dialled Chloe's number. She twiddled the phone wire around her little finger waiting for Chloe to answer the phone. Sylvie was aware she wasn't in her daughter's good books after that misguided attempt to give her some advice on relationships. She hoped they could put that little spat behind them and Chloe wouldn't mind sorting out her computer glitch. She would avoid bringing up the subject of relationships for the time being. However, she still wanted to tell her daughter that she thought it would be a big mistake if she split up with Declan.

'Mum?' Chloe's voice sounded muffled. 'What is it?'

Chloe sounded as though she was in bed. 'I'm sorry, did I wake you?'

'Well – yeah! Do you know what time it is?'

Sylvie didn't. She had been so engrossed in updating her blog she lost track of time. She sighed. 'It's all right, Chloe. It can wait.'

'I'm awake now,' said Chloe irritably. 'What's going on?'

'It's my—'

'Go back to sleep, Declan, it's just my mother on the phone. Mum – what's up?'

By the sound of it, Chloe hadn't split up from Declan – yet. Sylvie breathed a sigh of relief.

'Mum – are you still there?'

'Yes. It's my laptop, Chloe. There seems to be a problem.' Sylvie was still trying random keys, but nothing worked. 'I was writing my blog, and then everything froze.'

'Hold on while I switch on my laptop.'

Sylvie could hear Chloe's laptop booting up in the background.

Chloe said, 'Right, let's see what's going on. You said you were on your blog?'

'That's right.' Sylvie waited.

'Mum!' Chloe exclaimed a short time later.

'What is it?'

'Your blog!'

'Yes – but what is it?'

'Oh my god, I don't believe it! Your blog has gone viral.'

Sylvie didn't understand. 'Are you saying I've contracted a computer virus?'

Chloe burst out laughing. 'No, Mum, you haven't contracted a virus. I said your blog has just gone viral. It means... Oh shutup Declan, that's my mother you're laughing at... Yeah, I know I was laughing too but that's different, she's my mum and I can laugh at her if I want to. Sorry, Mum, Declan is being an ass.'

'Don't worry about it,' said Sylvie smiling. 'But I still don't understand what you meant when you said my blog has gone viral?'

'It means your website is getting so many hits—'

'Hits?'

'There are so many people logging on to read your blog that it couldn't cope with the demand and it has temporarily gone down.'

'Oh dear, that *is* bad.'

'No, Mum, that's good. It means your blog is really popular.'

It took Sylvie a moment to grasp her meaning. 'Chloe, are you saying there's someone out there reading my blog?'

'Hold on,' said Chloe. 'I'm coming over.'

Fifteen minutes later, Chloe drew up outside her parents' house in the dead of night and got out of her car wearing bright pink fluffy slippers and a coat over her blue cotton stripy pyjamas. She joined her mum sitting in bed under her duvet, with Sylvie's laptop between them.

'Mum, I don't know what you've been writing in your blog, but people are loving it, really loving it.' Chloe stared at her mother. 'Whatever you were writing caused a traffic spike.'

Sylvie looked at her blankly.

Chloe explained, 'The amount of traffic jumped because there were too many visitors all at once trying to access your blog.' Chloe pointed at the laptop screen. 'Look here at all these comments from your readers.' Chloe had enabled comments when she set up the blog but hadn't bothered to tell Sylvie about this feature. She didn't think anybody would read her mum's blog, let alone post a comment.

'I didn't realise people were leaving comments on my blog.' Sylvie stared at Chloe in astonishment. She had no idea people were reading her blog, let alone responding to it.

Chloe started scrolling through them. 'Bloody hell!'

'Language please!'

'Sorry, Mum. I couldn't help it.' She pointed at the laptop screen. 'There must be hundreds of comments here.' Chloe turned to look at her mum. 'What on earth have you been writing about?'

'Oh, this and that,' said Sylvie self-consciously, still surprised to learn there were people following *Love on the Rooftop*. 'I thought you said nobody would bother reading my blog?'

Chloe shrugged. 'Guess I was wrong.'

Sylvie stared at her daughter as the enormity of all this hit home. Her face flushed with embarrassment. Writing a blog was just meant to be a bit of fun. Chloe said from the outset that she needn't worry about her personal life being *out there*. "Nobody will read your blog." Those were her exact words. Now people were reading all about her private life. And not only that, but they were also interested enough to post a response in a comments link she didn't realise she had, until Chloe pointed it out. Sylvie could strangle her.

Chloe was busy reading the comments. She glanced at her mum and caught the expression on her face. 'What's the matter?'

'Never mind,' said Sylvie, realising her blog – along with her personal life – were well and truly *out there* and there was nothing she could do about it. The reason she was not lifting off right now, was that she had decided from the outset to keep the identity of the blogger who wrote *Love on the Rooftop* a secret. Nobody knew it was Sylvie's blog, apart from Chloe. Sylvie wanted to keep it that way.

Chloe was busy browsing through the comments. 'These are all from the last few days,' observed Chloe. 'I wonder what you've been writing that has elicited such a huge response.'

Sylvie had a good idea. That's when she started writing about how living apart together, or LAT living as Sylvie called it for short, had put a spark back in their relationship. She'd written in her blog all about the romantic things they had done together in the past week.

Sylvie was just wondering how many people were reading her blog when Chloe laughed out loud. 'This is *so* good. I can't believe Daddy pretended you both live at separate addresses and asked the taxi driver to drop you off at the house first. Then the taxi circled the block—'

'We *do* live at separate addresses,' Sylvie corrected her. 'I live at number 67a and he lives at 67b.'

Chloe rolled her eyes. 'I know that, Mum. But he made it sound as though you lived in separate *houses*, not under the same roof!'

'Oh, I see what you mean.'

'I had no idea Daddy could be so much fun.'

Neither did Sylvie.

'Mind you, that taxi driver must have thought you both had a screw loose.'

Sylvie reached for her laptop. 'Give me that!'

'Be my guest.' Chloe handed over the laptop. 'You do know that as soon as I get home, I can pick up where I left off and read it on my laptop.'

'This is our secret, Chloe,' warned Sylvie. 'I've chosen to be an anonymous blogger, and I want it to stay that way.'

'Your secret is safe with me, cross my heart,' Chloe assured her. 'I won't even tell Dad.'

Sylvie frowned at her daughter. As she recalled, the last time Chloe promised to keep a secret from her father, when Jess wanted to surprise him on their return from Cornwall, that didn't turn out well. Chloe couldn't keep her mouth shut for one day.

'I mean it, Chloe,' reiterated Sylvie. She knew her youngest had never been good at keeping secrets. It crossed her mind that perhaps she would have to close her blog.

Sylvie wondered how many people she would disappoint if she stopped writing *Love on the Rooftop*. She turned to her daughter with a question.

'Chloe, how many visitors does it take to cause – what did you call it – a *traffic spike?*'

'You're asking me how many people are reading your blog.'
Sylvie nodded.

'Easy.' A keystroke later and Sylvie had an answer she wasn't expecting. She sat in stunned silence. Finally, Sylvie said, 'You're having me on.' She expected Chloe to admit that she was only larking about and the figure wasn't really in the tens of thousands.

'I'm not having you on. It's true!' Chloe looked up from the laptop. 'Mum, I've got an idea. Do you want to make some money?'

'Pardon me?'

Chloe's fingers danced over the computer keys. 'I'm setting up *pay-per-click* so you can earn some money from advertising revenue. You don't have to do a thing, if you don't mind some ads on your web pages. This way, you might even earn money while you sleep.'

'Is that legal?' asked Sylvie looking worried.

Chloe giggled. 'Of course it's legal, Mum. It's how people make money on high-traffic sites.' Chloe added, 'That's assuming you continue in this vein and write what people want to read.' Chloe smiled as she read the entry about her mum and dad taking a romantic stroll along Regent's Canal. The shopping trip with Dad had paid off, thought Chloe.

'By the looks of things,' said Chloe, reading on about how the romantic stroll had extended to a lunch date, 'I don't think you will have any problems maintaining the popularity of your blog, if there is plenty more where that came from?' Chloe eyed her mother keenly.

Sylvie wasn't giving anything away although she smiled. She was thinking about John rushing upstairs after coffee this evening, probably in the throes of planning another surprise.

Chloe sighed and mumbled under her breath, 'I guess we really had nothing to worry about.'

Sylvie watched from the lounge window as Chloe returned to her car. She offered to make up the sofa bed in the lounge, but Chloe had to get up for work in the morning and declined the offer to stay over, along with sharing her real motive for leaving. She couldn't wait to tell Harriet and Jess the good news: Mum and Dad are okay.

Sylvie returned to bed and checked the time. It was almost two o'clock in the morning. She knew that she should switch the laptop off and try to get some sleep. The trouble was, after Chloe's visit, Sylvie was now more awake than ever. Before she switched off her table lamp, she couldn't resist browsing through some comments to see what people were saying about her blog. One comment caught her eye. It was from a women's magazine that Harriet often talked about because it was their main rival. Sylvie read with growing interest what they had to say about her blog.

'Oh my!' exclaimed Sylvie, re-reading the last sentence in case she was mistaken. She'd been asked to write an article for the magazine.

Sylvie's eyes went wide when she discovered they would pay her a generous commission for the article. And not only that, if their readers liked it, they were considering whether she could write a new weekly column for their magazine.

It turned out that the magazine Harriet worked for wasn't the only one on the look-out for new writing talent. However, unlike Harriet's magazine, they were not ageist. They were prepared to cast the net wider to find new writers. One of the magazine's researchers had done just that and caught a buzz on the internet about a blog with a catchy name, *Love on the Rooftop*. When it was brought to the attention of the magazine editor, it gave her a sleepless night because once she started reading it, she couldn't stop.

'Oh dear,' said Sylvie, smiling as she read that last comment.

The editor realised that LAT living would make an excellent article for their magazine. She wanted the anonymous blogger behind *Love on the Rooftop* to write it.

Sylvie would get paid for writing the article and her blog would gain more exposure with the magazine's readers. An article in their magazine would bring the writer and her experiences of LAT living, to the attention of a wider audience.

Sylvie read all this with interest. Although she wasn't concerned about having more people read her blog – until this moment she wasn't even sure she would continue writing *Love on the Rooftop* – the prospect of seeing her writing in print was exciting. Then she had an idea.

'I will write the article,' she told Alfie.

Alfie was still on the bed at Sylvie's feet. However, after all the excitement of a late-night visitor when Chloe came over, he was no longer asleep. He pricked up his ears at the sound of her voice and yapped once as if in agreement.

'Shh!' Sylvie put a finger to her lips and glanced up at the ceiling. 'This is our secret,' she told Alfie in a hushed voice.

Alfie wagged his tail and crept up the bed to sit beside her.

Sylvie set to work writing her article all about living apart together and the effect it had had on their relationship. Most notably, the part about how it had brought the romance back into her life. She worked well into the early hours. Alfie got tired of watching her write and returned to his spot at the end of the bed where he fell asleep.

It wasn't until she heard the birds outside start their dawn chorus that Sylvie nodded off to sleep herself, a notepad and pen still in her hand.

Sylvie's laptop on the bed beside her was switched on, the cursor blinking at the bottom of a page of writing. Her article was finished and ready to send out into the world. As for Sylvie, the writer, her journey was just beginning.

27

Sylvie woke up with a start. After rubbing the sleep out of her eyes, she glanced at the clock on her bedside table and then rolled over intending to have another hour in bed. As soon as she saw her laptop, Sylvie remembered she had something important to do this morning; now was not the time for a lie-in. She showered and dressed for her big day. Today, she was going to submit her article to the magazine.

She carried her laptop down to the kitchen and put the kettle on for a cup of tea, intending to savour the moment before she sent her article. The magazine had provided their email address so all it took was the click of a button and the task was complete. She sat down at the kitchen table with her morning cuppa and read through the article on her laptop one last time. Sylvie smiled as she moved the cursor over to the *send* button on her screen. She hesitated. Her smile faded. What if they didn't like the article? What if it wasn't good enough?

Sylvie tried to push those negative thoughts to the back of her mind. At least she could send it knowing that she'd done her best. There was nothing for it now but to find out whether her writing was good enough for publication.

Sylvie was about to click *send* when she was distracted by the sound of the doorbell upstairs. She looked at the time. It was the postman. She knew it was him because the postman who had delivered their mail for over twenty years was so efficient you could set your watch by him. She turned back to her laptop and stared at the cursor hovering over the *send* button. Sylvie still wanted to savour the moment. She decided to answer the door first.

'Good morning, Mrs Baxter. What a fine day it is today.'

It was raining, but as far as their cheerful postman was concerned, come rain or shine, it was always a lovely day. That comment elicited a smile from Sylvie. 'It's a very fine day,' Sylvie agreed. She was still feeling giddy with excitement at the prospect of sending that email and, all going well, seeing something she had written in print, published in a real magazine. She just hoped they liked it and didn't change their mind.

Sylvie stood on the doorstep waiting for the postman to hand her a package or a large letter that wouldn't fit through the letterbox. She guessed it must be for John because she wasn't expecting anything herself. Whatever it was, she didn't mind taking it in for him.

'Do you need me to sign for it?' offered Sylvie.

'No, there's nothing for you to sign,' said the postman, busy sorting through some letters in his hand.

Sylvie noticed he didn't appear to have any packages. She frowned. If he wasn't delivering a parcel, then why hadn't he put the letters in the post box as usual?

The postman finished sorting through the large bundle of letters. He looked up and handed Sylvie two letters.

Sylvie took the letters and stood there watching the postman.

The postman put an elastic band around all the others. 'These are addressed to your husband. Do you mind taking these too?'

Sylvie looked at the bundle of letters addressed to John. She didn't mind taking in his post, but she had a question first. 'It's kind of you to hand deliver our post. May I ask why you didn't just put the letters in the post box?'

'I'll show you why.'

Sylvie stepped outside and joined him on the front doorstep.

'There, you see.' The postman pointed at the two identical black post boxes hanging side by side on the exterior wall of the house; one for each apartment. 'I could have posted your letters, no problem, Mrs Baxter. But the other one is full to bursting. I can't fit any more letters inside.'

'I see.' Sylvie stared at John's post box. The boxes were small, it was true. However, the idea was that you collected your letters regularly unless you were going away. John had not gone away, but his post box was full of mail. Some were even poking out the slit at the top. Sylvie looked at the postman in surprise. Now she had a question for her husband: why on earth wasn't he collecting his mail?

'Do you mind taking these?' the postman asked again. He held out the wad of letters meant for John upstairs.

'All right,' said Sylvie. The postman knew Mr and Mrs Baxter were living in separate apartments now. Sylvie had changed her address to 67a The Garden Apartment, as soon as she moved downstairs, so that all her personal mail came to her. Otherwise, it gave John an excuse to pop in every day after the postman had been.

Now they were back on speaking terms Sylvie no longer

minded if he popped in with her post, or vice versa. Although John was bound to call on her later – hardly a day went by when they weren't doing something together – Sylvie didn't mind nipping upstairs to hand John his letters. However, she would not do that right now. She had something important to do first, namely press that *send* button and submit her article.

Sylvie closed the front door, walked back into her apartment and down the stairs to the basement kitchen. She left the wad of letters addressed to John on the kitchen table and opened the other two. One was the information she had requested about pet insurance. She put that to one side to read later. Sylvie had already opened the other one when she realised too late that the postman had made a mistake; it should have been in the bundle of letters for John.

She was slipping the letter back into the envelope when something caught her eye. Did she just see the word *reminder?* Sylvie retrieved the message and read it. It was an unpaid electricity bill. Perhaps John had overlooked paying it when he was laid up after the accident? Or maybe the original bill had gone missing in the post. Sylvie wasn't concerned. These things happen. She knew what it was like nowadays; everything was automated. One slip and you got a letter like this, making you feel like a criminal for not paying your bill, even if it was just an unfortunate oversight.

Sylvie didn't believe it was an oversight. John was always so organised and meticulous with their finances. She wouldn't be surprised if the bill had already been paid and the letter sent out in error. She reached for the phone to sort out what was clearly a mistake on their part. John had never missed paying a bill before. She did not appreciate them sending out a threatening red reminder letter to her husband. He didn't deserve that. For all his faults, Sylvie knew she could always rely on him when it came to their finances. Sylvie intended to ring up the sender and give them a piece of her mind after she informed them of their obvious error.

She picked up the phone and dialled the phone number printed on the letter.

'What do you mean you've been chasing Mr Baxter for the payment?'

'You've sent how many other reminders already?'

'What do you mean has he tried to make an arrangement?' Sylvie didn't understand what they meant by an *arrangement*.

She listened as the person on the end of the line explained, 'If you are experiencing financial difficulties, we might accept a reduced amount towards the debt to give you a chance to sort out—'

'I don't know what you're talking about,' Sylvie cut in. She was furious at them for implying they were having financial problems and didn't have the money to pay their bills. Sylvie stated categorically, 'This is just one big misunderstanding. As soon as my husband gets on the phone to you, he will straighten this out.'

'Can you tell us when that will be because we have been try-ing to contact—'

'Today!' shouted Sylvie and slammed the phone down. She shook her head. 'Honestly, the cheek of it over one unpaid bill!'

Her eyes drifted to the wad of letters, held together by a thick elastic band, which the postman couldn't fit inside John's post box this morning. Sylvie would never, ever intentionally open someone else's mail. Not even her husbands . . .

Ten minutes later, Sylvie was storming up the stairs – Alfie hot on her heels – leaving the kitchen table smothered in John's opened letters. Most of them were bill reminders. Some were final reminders. But most worrying of all, there was one threatening to send in the bailiffs.

28

John was fast asleep unaware that just as things seemed to be coming together, it was all about to fall apart – spectacularly. He was woken by the sound of Sylvie knocking loudly on his apartment door. He sat up in bed and realised that he'd locked the door last night out of habit, not expecting that Sylvie would be up early missing him already.

John rolled out of bed, yawned and stretched. He stood up feeling odd; he was still getting used to walking around without a big plastic orthopaedic boot on one foot. John reached for his dressing gown. His thoughts drifted back to last night. They had another fantastic night out together, and he was looking forward to surprising Sylvie today with the theatre tickets. However, he hadn't expected that she'd be calling so early and, by the sound of it, so insistently. It was fortunate that he'd cleared away all those letters from his desk last night just in case Sylvie made a surprise visit.

'I'm coming!' John called down the stairs in a sing-song voice.

He'd already decided that he would invite Sylvie upstairs this evening for dinner and attempt to bake something other than a chicken pie. Afterwards, over coffee, he would surprise her with the theatre tickets. Tonight, was the night he would pop the question and ask her to move back in with him.

John had it all planned but he couldn't get to sleep last night. He phoned Sylvie at an ungodly hour hoping she was still awake, so he could apologise for upping and leaving like that when she had gone to all the trouble of offering him in for coffee and even baking his favourite cookies. What was bothering him, was what she thought when he bolted after she hinted that next time, he might stay the night? He didn't want her to get the wrong impression that he wasn't interested in her suggestion.

Sylvie didn't answer the phone, so he left a message on her answerphone before returning to bed. In the message he assured her he was looking forward to moving their relationship to the next level. John grinned. With all this frantic banging on his door, he assumed Sylvie had listened to the message and decided she couldn't wait until tonight.

John threw on a clean pair of pyjamas and sprayed a little cologne. He put his dressing gown on, debated whether to wear it open or closed and then answered the door. He leaned casually on the door frame, smiling enticingly at his wife.

'What took you so long?' Sylvie said crossly, looking him up and down. 'And when were you going to tell me about this?' Sylvie thrust a letter into John's hand as she barged past him into his apartment.

'I don't know what—' began John as he opened the letter and read the County Court Summons threatening further legal action if he didn't pay his council tax arrears. *Bloody hell!* He had no idea things had gone this far.

'Where did you get this?' he asked nervously. He stared at the letter and raised an inquiring eyebrow wondering why she had opened his post. Sylvie had never done that before. When she didn't answer his question, John walked into the lounge to find her standing by the window with her back to him.

She turned from the window and looked across the room at her husband. 'I'm waiting for an explanation, and it better be good.'

He looked at the letter in his hand and thought up a plausible excuse – or two. He'd missed the payment because he was stuck at home after the accident with his foot in a plastic boot. Or how about he'd overlooked the payment because the original bill got lost in the post? He'd never missed paying a bill before. Would she believe him?

'I want the truth, John Baxter.' Sylvie paused. 'Are we in trouble?' The look on her face said he'd better think very carefully before he tried to pull the wool over her eyes.

John stared at the letter in his hand and recalled all the others stuffed in the drawers of his desk. Not to mention what was lurking in his post box he hadn't bothered to check for days on end. He put the letter back in the envelope. Sylvie wasn't stupid; she knew what a County Court Summons was. He realised there was no use trying to come up with excuses or sugar-coat it. He glanced over at the sofa and decided he needed to sit down for this. John avoided her gaze. 'We're in trouble, Sylvie.'

'Oh. My. God.' Sylvie felt as though her legs had turned to jelly. She reached for the nearest armchair and sat down. Until that moment, she was expecting her husband to reassure her it was all just a huge misunderstanding and he had a good explanation. In short, the bills were paid, and she had nothing to worry about – like always.

Sylvie stared at John dumbfounded. This was so unlike him

that she was having a hard time comprehending how things had got so out of hand. 'I want you to tell me what happened. Why haven't you been paying the bills?'

Because you wouldn't move out of the rental apartment, thought John as he shot her a sour look. He knew that was unfair. She wasn't the one who miscalculated the final cost of the conversion and got them in this predicament. And now the time had come to admit his mistake and tell Sylvie why they desperately needed the rental income to pay their mounting debts.

John stared at the envelope in his hands and heaved a sigh, 'I made a mistake Sylvie. I underestimated the cost of the conversion and I... I took out a loan.'

'You took out a loan when neither of us are in work? When we've only got our pensions to live on? Are you crazy?'

John took that as a rhetorical question because, in hindsight, he thought so too.

'How could you be so irresponsible?'

Too embarrassed to look Sylvie in the eye, he looked at the floor, the ceiling, the dog sitting beside Sylvie's chair.

Alfie let out a low throaty growl at John, his tone almost accusatory as though he understood every word Sylvie had just said. 'Shush, Alfie.' Sylvie leaned forward in her chair and stared at her husband. 'How bad is it?'

John spilled the beans. 'We're in over our heads, Sylvie. We're in debt. There are no savings left. To keep up the repayments on the new loan, I let all the other bills slide. I didn't know what else to do.'

He felt an enormous sense of relief that the whole charade was over, and Sylvie knew the truth. It was like a huge weight had been lifted off his shoulders. At least now they might work this thing out together. They could get straight down to the business of renting out one apartment, for that much needed cash injection, and get on top of all those bills he'd been avoiding.

'What do you mean: you didn't know what to do?' Sylvie was livid. She stood up, hands on hips, and glared down at John. 'You could have at least told me what was going on!'

'I know. You're right. But I couldn't,' he replied in a small voice. 'I didn't want to admit that after all these years of marriage, when you depended on me to make the right decisions, I let you down.'

'So, instead of telling me the truth,' Sylvie said angrily, 'you decide it's better to keep me in the dark. Didn't it ever cross your mind that eventually I would find out?'

Sylvie thought she was stating the obvious until something else blindingly obvious hit her for six. 'So that's what this was all about. You desperately needed money and the way to get hold of some extra cash was renting out my apartment.' She narrowed her eyes. 'But let's not forget you had a little problem called your downstairs neighbour.' She glared at John.

He squirmed in his seat.

'So, when your little stunt to sabotage my apartment and get me to move out backfired, you changed tack. I get it now. The restaurant meals. The flowers. The romantic walk along the canal. It was all to encourage me to move back in with you before I found out what was going on. If I moved back upstairs, then you could rent out the garden apartment and use the rental income to pay off the bills. I would be none the wiser. What a brilliant plan,' said Sylvie sarcastically.

'Now hang on just a minute,' said John, jumping to his own defence. 'It's not like that.'

Sylvie gave him one of her looks that said don't lie to me, John.

'Okay.' John held his hands up. 'Yes, in the beginning I suppose that's what I was thinking. But I—'

Sylvie didn't let him finish. 'What a fool you must think I am, John Baxter, to be so easily taken in by a few romantic gestures. I must have seemed such a pushover. I bet you were rubbing your hands with glee, yesterday evening, when I suggested that I would stay the night next time we went out on a date. Well, I can tell you this,' Sylvie stood up, 'there *won't* be a next time!'

'Oh Sylvie, don't say that. This isn't the way I wanted things to turn out.'

'I bet it isn't,' scoffed Sylvie, striding past him.

John rose from the sofa. 'Where are you going?'

'Home!'

'Downstairs?'

'No, to Jupiter,' Sylvie threw back sarcastically. 'Of course I'm bloody well going downstairs!'

'I'm coming too.' He followed her to the door. 'I've thought this over, Sylvie, and I'm prepared to compromise. I'll move in with you downstairs and rent out my apartment. Under the circumstances that would be—'

'No!'

'Did you just say *no*?' He caught up with Sylvie at the door. 'Don't you get it? One of us must compromise. I'm prepared to give up my apartment so we can find a tenant and sort out our financial mess.'

'Don't you mean *your* financial mess?' Sylvie poked him in the chest with her finger. 'You don't want to move in with me. All those romantic gestures have been a con, a ruse to get me to move back in with you so you could sort out *your* cash flow problem. God, how could I have been so stupid?'

'Oh, for pity's sake!' John rolled his eyes. 'We're not back to that again.' He thought this conversation was about money. Why did she have to complicate matters?

'Yes, we're back to that again. I imagined things had changed. I thought *you* had changed.'

'But I have changed,' argued John. 'Look at me. Look at my clothes, look at my hair. I did it all for you, Sylvie.'

Sylvie glared at him. 'That's all superficial. Anybody can change their appearance,' she said in exasperation. 'That's not what I'm talking about.'

'Well then, what are you talking about?' John wondered if she was referring to all his little foibles and routines. The way he liked to keep his apartment spotlessly clean and tidy, and his clothes precision folded in the wardrobe. How he enjoyed a home-cooked meal at seven o'clock sharp every evening, and a lot more besides. Is that what she wanted him to change? It never seemed to bother her before.

Sylvie paused in the doorway of his apartment and looked at him a long moment. She shook her head. 'There's no spontaneity, no surprises, no fun anymore,' Sylvie observed of her marriage.

John argued, 'Didn't we have fun together during our dinner dates? Wasn't I spontaneous? Didn't I surprise you?'

'Yes, but for all the wrong reasons.'

'That's not true,' John protested. 'Didn't I prove to you I wanted you back, with all the meals out and the flowers and—'

'No, you did it because you had to.' Sylvie pointed at the bill in his hand. 'You did it because of that.'

John shifted uncomfortably under her penetrating gaze.

Sylvie felt all this romance was the start of something new, of something fresh in their relationship. She thought it was heartfelt. Not just a ploy to get her out of her apartment. 'I thought it was all about saving our marriage. Now I realise it was just about saving the house,' Sylvie said bitterly.

John raised an eyebrow. 'I didn't think our marriage needed saving. I thought we were okay.'

'Really? Are you blind? We're not living like a husband and wife anymore. We've been living apart for weeks. How is that okay?' She looked at him in bewilderment. 'Where did you think this was leading?'

'I... I thought you were just going through a phase.'

'Going through a *phase*?' Sylvie was fuming. 'You make me sound like a two-year-old!'

'Oh Sylvie, you're upset.' He reached for her shoulder.

'Don't patronise me.' She slapped his hand away. 'I know what you're up to. It's all out in the open, this financial hole you're in, and now you're looking to me to bail us out. Well, I'm not, I repeat *not,* moving out of my apartment to pay for your mistake.' Sylvie stepped outside John's apartment, grabbed the door handle, and slammed the door shut, leaving him on the other side.

'But that's just it,' said John to the door, 'I'm not asking you to move out of your apartment.'

Sylvie was already heading down the stairs when she realised she hadn't finished. She turned around, raced back upstairs, and shouted, 'Are you even sure you want us to move back in together?'

Sylvie waited. She knew he was still standing the other side of the door because she could hear John breathing, but he didn't answer her question. She bit her bottom lip. It was just as she feared. He'd been so intent on his plan to get the apartment back that he hadn't stopped to consider what he really wanted after all these weeks living apart.

She'd seen the way he'd hesitated after their meal last night when she hinted at moving back in together. It was not the response she was expecting. And now she knew why; John was unsure whether he really wanted her back.

'Fine!' exclaimed Sylvie, her eyes boring into the door. 'Well, guess what? Newsflash! I don't want to move back in together either – so there!' And the peculiar thing was, now she said it, she didn't feel like she had uttered a single untrue word. As much as she'd enjoyed the time they'd spent together. As much as she genuinely missed her husband, deep down she couldn't imagine going back to the way things were. The truth was, she couldn't imagine moving back in with him – whether it was his apartment or hers.

Sylvie turned away from the door. This personal newsflash should have made her feel better about the whole romantic episode with John. It shouldn't bother her now that it looked as though they were heading for a divorce. But it did bother her. It bothered her a great deal. She felt so cheated and betrayed to discover that all his romantic gestures were built on a lie.

He didn't really want her anymore. He didn't really love her anymore. That was most apparent because Sylvie had been standing behind the door for some minutes, aware that John was just the other side, and he *still* hadn't answered her question.

John lingered the other side of the door. He heard the question

Sylvie shouted at him. Of course he wanted her back. So why couldn't he tell her that before she jumped to conclusions and assumed he didn't? Perhaps it was because for the first time since converting the house, he was having a moment of honest reflection.

John thought back to the recent episode when he was stuck in his apartment after the accident at the gym. Although he really appreciated Sylvie's help and looked forward to her visits. Sometimes, at the end of a long day stuck in the flat with his wife, he was glad to see the back of her.

At first, it was the little things that John noticed; bad habits picked up from being left to her own devices downstairs, no doubt. After dinner, she always deposited the dirty dishes in the sink, even though he had a dishwasher, leaving his kitchen in a general state of untidiness. John rolled his eyes at the number of times he'd sat and watched Sylvie place a glass of wine on his coffee table without using a coaster, or brushed cake crumbs off her lap without bothering to use the cordless handheld vacuum cleaner.

He remembered that one time they retired to the lounge after dinner and Sylvie brought in a plate of biscuits. That was when he introduced her to his nifty little handheld device. Her reaction was not quite what he expected. He didn't see what was so funny. Someone had to hoover up the biscuit crumbs. One evening she even brought her pudding into the lounge to eat. It got to the stage where he thought that one of these days, she would suggest they sit and eat their dinner in the lounge, on his sofa, in front of the television. TV dinners – John shuddered at the thought.

All these irritating little things, and more besides, got on his nerves. Sylvie hadn't really changed. It's just that when they were living together, John guessed his penchant for tidiness had curbed his wife's unruly, disorganised tendencies. Perhaps that's why they didn't use to irk him quite as much before the house conversion. It didn't help matters that he'd grown accustomed to living on his own. He wasn't used to sharing his apartment with anybody else. And if he was honest, he liked it that way.

Therein lay the problem. As much as John needed Sylvie to move back in with him from a financial standpoint, there were times when he was playing the wounded hero, with that big orthopaedic boot on his foot, that he wished she didn't come around so often, disturbing his equilibrium. He missed his wife and looked forward to resuming their intimate relationship. But as much as he wanted her to move back in with him, a part of him didn't. A part of him was quite happy to walk her to the door and see her out. John shook his head grim-faced. It made little sense.

That's why he was standing in his apartment, hiding behind the door, unable to answer her question. He wondered what Sylvie would make of all this if he answered her truthfully and told her he was confused. He wanted them to get back together. Then again, he didn't. How could she make sense of that when he could hardly make sense of it himself?

He wasn't lying when he told her that he thought their relationship was rock-solid and their marriage didn't need saving. Now he wasn't so sure. In fact, John was questioning whether they could save their marriage at all.

Whose fault was that, he thought miserably. It was his idea to convert the house into two apartments and rent one for an extra income in their retirement. He thought he had found the perfect

DIY equity release scheme that wouldn't involve moving or touching the capital they had worked so hard to build up over the years.

He wanted to pass a legacy on to his children, and his grand-child, something neither of their parents had been able to do for them. However, after years of hard work John didn't want to find himself in a position where they had to watch the pennies, when they retired, just to keep hold of the house. As far as he was concerned, they had sacrificed enough for this house over the years. It was about time the house paid them back for a change.

John had it all planned. By reducing their overheads through downsizing, and increasing their retirement income through a rental, he assumed the house conversion would provide the opportunity to have some new experiences. John recalled the things they'd been doing together. While they weren't extravagant, they were little luxuries they couldn't afford when they were raising a family and renovating the house. Like dining out and taxi-fares and West End shows.

But this – John stared grimly at the door – this wasn't the payback he had in mind when he converted the house: the end of their marriage. In hindsight, John realised he hadn't stopped to consider what impact their very changed living circumstances might have on Sylvie, on their marriage, and even on him.

John had learned a thing or two about his wife he hadn't bargained for. He stood there staring at the door thinking about her choice of décor for the apartment downstairs, so different to his own. Then there was her pet dog; he couldn't abide animals in the house. The outrageous seventies-themed house party she hosted soon after she moved downstairs; John didn't like parties with loud music. Then there were the times he'd heard the television on well into the early hours when Sylvie stayed up to watch a late-night movie. John was not a night owl. Then there was her general tardiness when it came to tidying up. This was a side of his wife he'd never seen before. A side of Sylvie he didn't much like.

If they could turn back the clock and meet each other for the first time, knowing then what they knew now, would they still want to live together, to marry? Or would they have walked away without so much as a backward glance? John sighed. Had it taken a house conversion to discover that, despite almost forty years of marriage, they were not compatible, and they should never have lived together? Or was it simply the case that they were different people back then and they had changed with the passage of time?

With all this at the forefront of his mind, John was still wrestling with Sylvie's question: did he really want to move back in together?

He scratched his chin. Maybe that was now a moot point. He'd heard the last thing she'd said from the other side of his door, making it clear she didn't want him moving in with her. John raised an eyebrow. She didn't really mean that, did she? Were they playing a new game now: tit-for-tat? Or was this really it? Had their temporary living arrangements become permanent, and they were heading for a divorce?

Despite everything, John didn't want it to come to that. He couldn't simply erase forty years of marriage to the only woman he'd ever loved, and he didn't want to lose the house either. He needed to complete the plan and get that rental income coming in.

John shook his head in frustration. Sylvie was still refusing to play ball with renting out one of the apartments. All because of a silly misunderstanding; she didn't believe his actions over the past fortnight had been genuine displays of love and affection for his wife, rather than a ploy to get her out of the apartment. If he couldn't convince her he had been sincere, then the harsh truth was he stood to lose everything he had ever worked for his entire life – his wife and this house.

John decided he wasn't giving up without a fight. He flung open the door, half-expecting to find Sylvie still standing the other side waiting for an answer to her question.

She wasn't.

He raced down the stairs and banged on her door.

Alfie started barking.

'Sylvie? I know you're in there!'

Alfie stopped barking at the sound of his voice.

'I'm not giving up on the house,' shouted John, 'and I'm not giving up on *us*. Do you hear me?' He paused to see if Sylvie opened her door.

She didn't.

He thought back to the conversation earlier when she accused him of only making superficial changes. 'If it's fun you want,' John said to the door, 'you'll see fun! If it's surprises you're after? You ain't seen nothing yet! You'll find out how much I can change – just you wait and see.'

John was all bravado until he walked back upstairs. He still had unpaid bills and the threat of losing the house looming over his head if he didn't sort something out pronto.

He'd assumed that once Sylvie found out what was going on, they would put aside their differences to sort out this financial mess, rather than risk jeopardising the roof over their head. John thought she would compromise to rent out one of the apartments. It was the only sensible solution. If Sylvie wouldn't vacate her flat, and she wouldn't let him move in with her, then he had no choice. It forced him to take matters into his own hands. John always knew he had Plan B; he just hoped it wouldn't come to that.

29

John grabbed his overnight bag, locked the apartment door behind him, and headed down the stairs. He stood for a moment outside Sylvie's door, debating whether to knock one more time in another attempt to make her see reason; he had to rent out one apartment to get their financial affairs in order otherwise they risked losing the house.

He stared at her door and shook his head in defeat. He was wasting his time. He walked out of the house, slamming the door behind him. Now he had no choice but to resort to Plan B.

He was storming down the front path when he stopped and did an about-turn, taking in his car parked in the driveway. Sylvie would not need the car; she took the bus most places apart from the weekly shop, and she'd have to figure that out for herself. If he was going to do this, he was at least going to keep the car.

John dumped his overnight bag on the ground and returned to the house to fetch the car keys. They were in a dish on the sideboard in the communal hall. It wasn't a shopping day, so the keys were still there. John grabbed the keys and returned to the car. After tossing his bag on the passenger seat, he glanced up at the house as he put the key in the ignition and thought he saw movement behind the net curtains at the front window. Perhaps Sylvie was watching him from her lounge window wondering what he was up to. They only ever used the car to do the weekly shop.

John took his time backing out of the driveway, in the vain hope that Sylvie might come rushing out of the house to tell him she had changed her mind and that he could move in with her after all.

No such luck.

He backed the car out of the drive and dawdled at the kerb, watching the house. He was looking for any sign of his wife, still hoping she might appear even if it was only to ask him where he was off to.

She didn't.

John finally set off.

A short drive later, and a full hour spent sitting in morning rush hour traffic, John arrived at his brother's house wishing he'd left the car and taken the tube.

Dave lived in a modest red brick two-bedroomed Edwardian terraced property in Ealing, West London. With the expense of two divorces behind him, he was lucky he could still afford a house of his own at all. He'd bought a property in need of complete renovation. That was five years ago, and in the intervening years, he had done most of the work on the house himself with the help of some builder mates.

John remembered Dave saying he had just finished converting the attic into a large spare bedroom. The work on the house was complete. During the time it took Dave to complete the renovations, he met and married his third wife, Linda.

Linda answered the door not looking pleased to see John standing on her doorstep.

'Hello Linda, is Dave in?' John was only being polite. He knew his brother was home because he was still off work sick with the flu. He had tried phoning before he set off, but the line was engaged. John didn't fancy hanging around in his apartment trying to get through on the phone. He was eager to get the ball rolling with the new plan.

John followed Linda into the house.

'He's in there,' said Linda brusquely, pointing at the lounge before storming off down the hall to the kitchen.

John stared after her. He got the distinct impression that Linda was not happy that Dave was still off work.

John walked into the lounge to find him lying on the sofa reading a book. There were a variety of snacks laid out in dishes on the coffee table in front of him, together with a plethora of magazines and newspapers. Daytime television was on in the background. John glanced at *The Jeremy Kyle Show* before turning his attention on Dave. He didn't appear that sick. In fact, he looked as though he was making the most of his time off work.

John said, 'Hi Dave,' and reached for a crisp out of a dish on the coffee table before taking a seat on the sofa opposite. He put his overnight bag on the carpet by his feet.

Dave's two chubby Labradors, one black and one yellow, made a beeline for John. They sat, one either side of him, nudging his hands for attention.

John gave them an affectionate pat on the head. 'At least you two don't jump on the sofa and lick my face like Alfie.'

That comment elicited a chuckle from Dave. 'It might have been a different story if you still had that crisp in your hand.'

After they said hello, both dogs returned to their spot on the rug in front of the fire.

'It's a dog's life, eh,' said Dave, gesturing at his two fat Labs sprawled in front of the fireplace.

John looked at Dave, sprawled on the sofa scoffing a handful of roasted peanuts, and reserved comment.

'So, have you come to cheer the patient up?' asked Dave, offering John some peanuts.

He stared at his brother. By the looks of things, the patient didn't need cheering up. John cast his mind back to the not-too-distant past when he was still in work. How ironic that he had rarely taken a day off work sick, whereas Dave took any and every opportunity to throw a sickie, dragging it out royally. And yet here he was still employed. No wonder his wife looked miserable; Linda was probably tired of running around after him all day when he should be back at work by now.

John brushed that thought aside and got down to the reason for his visit. 'I'm not here to see how you are,' he admitted, casting a furtive glance at his overnight bag. 'The reason I came over is that Sylvie and I... well things aren't working out between us,' he said grimly.

John told Dave all about his plan to win Sylvie over by wining and dining her. How he had bought her flowers for the first time in years. The romantic stroll they took together. And the theatre tickets he'd booked for a West End show which Sylvie still knew nothing about. John even mentioned that along the way he had rediscovered how much he enjoyed his wife's company.

Then John told him how it had all been going well until his plan backfired when the postman arrived this morning. Sylvie had opened one of his letters only to discover the truth about their dire financial circumstances.

Dave lay on the sofa listening to all this. He was staring at John. He was also munching on some popcorn from a large bowl he'd procured from the coffee table. The bowl of popcorn was now balanced on his ample stomach.

When John paused and took a breath, Dave said, 'Go on, go on,' as he reached for more popcorn.

'The reason I'm here,' said John, coming full circle to his next plan, Plan B, 'is that I need to stay with you while I rent out my apartment and find a job.'

As far as John was concerned it was the only solution. One apartment had to be rented. Sylvie wasn't about to leave the garden apartment anytime soon, and she would not entertain any thoughts of John moving in with her. This left him with no alternative but to move out of his flat and find somewhere temporary to live. He couldn't afford to stay in a hotel, and he didn't have any close friends to call on for help. His brother, Dave, was his closest friend and the only person he could turn to under the circumstances.

There was his younger brother, Roger, who might help him out. But Roger lived in Spain. While it would probably make for a nice holiday and a pleasant diversion from what was going on at home, John couldn't see how he would sort anything out from such a distance. Besides, he barely had the money to put petrol in the car for the drive across London to Dave's house, let alone the airfare to fly all the way to Spain.

John sighed. He had debated whether to make use of the spare bedroom in his apartment and get a lodger to bring in some immediate cash. However, that meant sharing his home with a total stranger. The mere thought of what they might get up to in his flat, right under his nose, made his hackles rise. Besides, John needed more money than he could recoup by renting out his spare bedroom. He needed a whole apartment kind of income to get on top of his debts.

John looked across at Dave, waiting for his brother to tell him Plan B was a go. He anticipated Dave would have something to say about how stupid he had been not telling Sylvie about their financial problems in the first place and was expecting some flack and Dave to tell him, *I told you so.* But when he asked Dave if he could stay with him, what he didn't expect was an outright no.

'What do you mean *no?*' said John in surprise. 'You've got a spare bedroom in the attic. I promise I won't be any trouble. You won't even know I'm there.' John thought Dave, of all people, would be sympathetic.

Dave put his bowl of popcorn on the coffee table and sat up. 'You'll thank me in the end, John.'

'For what?' He couldn't for the life of him fathom how Dave felt he was helping the situation by refusing to let him stay at their house.

'Look, don't you see this is what Sylvie expects you to do? You'll be playing right into her hands.'

'How so?'

'Because this is what you have always done. Take charge of the situation. She expects you to have a back-up plan.'

'Well, I do... I have.' John pointed at his brother. 'You're my back-up plan. I have got to move out and rent my apartment, to get some money rolling in while I look for a job.'

'No, you haven't.' Dave reached for the platter of finger sandwiches on the coffee table in front of him. He picked one up. Before taking a bite, he said, 'My advice to you is...'

John rolled his eyes. He had not come here for more advice.

'Do. Nothing.'

John looked at him askance. Was he out of his mind? Did he want to see his brother lose his house and be declared bankrupt because he couldn't pay his debts? Did he want to see him made homeless, a vagrant begging on a street corner? John knew that was an exaggeration; he still had his pension to fall back on so it wouldn't come to that. Even so, he couldn't just sit back and do nothing. Where would he be without *a plan*?

'We need another plan,' said Dave, taking a bite of his finger sandwich.

John was confused. 'You just said—'

'I meant do nothing as in, don't move out of your apartment, don't get a lodger, and *don't* get a job.'

'But I need money, Dave.' John rolled his eyes in exasperation. Why was he not getting it? Unless...

John peered at his brother. 'Are you offering me a loan?'

'No.'

John didn't think so. He was nuts to even contemplate he could borrow money from his brother. Dave was not a saver. Whatever he earned he spent – and some. He was hocked up to his eyeballs in debt with credit cards, store cards and bank loans. And now John knew how that felt. The difference was Dave had a well-paid job and a wife who was still working. He could afford the mortgage, the credit cards, the store cards and any additional loans he had taken out on the house. John could not.

'What on earth do you suggest I do for money?' John said impatiently, wondering if Dave had not grasped the gravity of his situation.

'It's simple, John.' Dave licked his fingers and picked up another finger sandwich. 'The way forward is for Sylvie to move back in with you and rent out her apartment.'

'Are you out of your frigging mind?' John jumped off the sofa and metaphorically hit the roof. 'After all this, do you honestly think I've got even the remotest chance of a reconciliation?'

That was a rhetorical question. As far as John was concerned it was over. Anybody could see that except Dave who seemed to be two steps behind. Perhaps he really was sick after all.

Dave stood up. Ignoring John's rant, he started to pace.

John watched him cross the room several times.

Dave stopped pacing and turned to face his brother. 'After finding out you haven't been honest with her, Sylvie will be watching to see how you attempt to redeem yourself and make amends. Am I right?'

'How do I know?' said John, feeling deflated.

Dave folded his arms.

'Okay yeah, maybe you're right. I said to her... well actually, I shouted at her from behind the door that I wasn't giving up on us. I was going to show her I can change.'

'Hmm,' said Dave thoughtfully. 'Unfortunately, now she knows the truth, she will not believe a damn word that comes out of your mouth.'

As if John needed reminding. He heaved a sigh.

'You, brother, have got yourself in a bind.'

'Tell me about it,' John mumbled sarcastically.

'But here's the thing,' said Dave, sounding as though he was on to something. 'She's still interested in getting back together with you.'

John looked at him dubiously. 'How do you reckon that? She said herself she doesn't want to move in with me, or vice versa.'

'Yes, I know, but think about it for a moment. After she opened your letters and discovered those unpaid bills, why do you suppose she was upset when she thought your romantic gestures had all been a sham just to save the house?'

Despite his best efforts, John was still listening.

Dave continued. 'I imagine Sylvie was upset because she wanted you back. Now she feels your motives weren't sincere she's on the defensive. She's protecting herself from more hurt, don't you see?'

John sat down on the sofa and stared at his brother.

Dave walked over and patted him on the shoulder. 'All is not lost,' he said reassuringly.

John looked up at his big brother. 'You think so?'

'I know so,' said Dave forthrightly.

'But if that's true,' said John, hoping it was. 'If Sylvie doesn't want to leave me, then what in god's name am I going to do to get her back this time?'

'Now that,' said Dave, picking up a handful of crisps, 'is the million-dollar question.' He looked at John a long moment. 'You know what? I might just have the answer.'

John sat forward on the sofa. 'You do? What is it?' He had to wait for Dave to stop munching on his crisps to get a coherent reply.

'First of all,' said Dave, pointing at John with his last crisp before popping it in his mouth, 'I don't want to be the one to tell you this, but you have already let the cat out of the bag, so to speak. No matter what you say or do now, Sylvie will think she's on to you.'

'Huh?'

'She will be on the lookout for the first sign that you are trying to win her back.'

John nodded.

'And she will expect you to do any and every little thing you can think of to gain her approval.'

John agreed with that. So that was the plan: do any and every little thing he could think of to gain her approval.

'So, don't.'

'Pardon me?'

'Play hard to get.' Dave grinned. 'Act disinterested. Turn the tables. Show her you can have fun but don't invite her to join the party, so to speak. Let her see what she's missing. Surprise her, by all means. Just don't play right into her hands. Are you following me?'

John wasn't, until he thought about it some more and realised that in a weird kind of way Dave was making sense. 'You mean like some sort of reverse psychology?'

Dave pointed at John. 'Exactly!'

'But how do I know it will work?' John was already sceptical about Dave's new plan. 'How do I know it won't backfire? What if she thinks I'm just being an ass and ignoring her because I didn't get my own way?'

Dave shrugged. 'Honestly, I don't know. But what have you got to lose?'

'My house, for one thing,' said John wearily. He was feeling a lot less confident about this reverse psychology business. John's shoulders sagged in defeat. 'I should start looking for another job.'

'Don't be stupid.' Dave reached for a finger sandwich. 'That's just what she's expecting you to do. So, *don't* move out of your apartment and *don't* look for a job. That will get her thinking.' Dave munched on his sandwich before adding, 'Perhaps it's about time she started taking some responsibility for her part in all this. If she hadn't moved downstairs in the first place, you wouldn't be in this mess.'

'That's true,' said John. He hadn't thought about it that way before. 'You're right.'

Dave smiled. 'When she realises the bills are still mounting up, and you're not doing a damn thing about it, I guarantee she'll come running back to you rather than lose the roof over her head.'

'She'll come running back to me,' repeated John. He offered a weak smile hoping this plan worked.

'Hey, I've got an idea. Maybe you could meet another woman.'

John baulked at that idea. Meeting someone else hadn't even crossed his mind. 'I don't want—'

'I meant to make Sylvie feel jealous and get her thinking about moving back in with you before it's too late.'

'Oh, I see,' John sighed in relief. Despite his hesitancy when Sylvie asked him outright if he wanted them to move back in together, the plain fact was John couldn't imagine life without her. On reflection, perhaps he could see why Dave thought he was doing him a favour. If he moved out of the house and into Dave's spare bedroom, then it would be tantamount to throwing in the towel and giving up on their marriage. He didn't want to do that. He didn't want to be the one who walked out that door.

Sylvie was right when she said he had to make up his mind whether he was saving the house or saving their marriage.

Whatever happened to the house, John decided he wasn't walking out on their marriage. He wasn't walking out on his wife. In that moment of clarity, he felt much better, albeit slightly nervous, about the new plan.

John stood up and declared, 'Let's do it!'

Dave rose from the sofa. 'Good man.' He walked over and slapped his brother affectionately on the back. 'You won't regret it.'

John hoped not. 'Do nothing,' repeated John, convincing himself he was doing the right thing as he reached down to pick up his overnight bag.

Dave walked John to the front door. 'Now remember, when things get dicey, she will cave in and then you'll get one apartment back to rent out.' He opened the front door. 'Frankly, she has little choice. She financially depends on you John, and don't you forget it.'

'I won't.'

'Don't tell me it hasn't crossed Sylvie's mind what will happen to her if you lose the house. She knows she can't stay living in the garden apartment indefinitely. She's not stupid.'

'That's true.'

'I reckon that now she knows about the financial situation, and she thinks you were playing her, she'll drag it out for a bit longer just to get her own back. Then she'll give in.'

'Okay, Dave.'

'So if I were you I'd sit back, relax, and have some fun. In the meantime, have some letting agents around to get a valuation in readiness for when she caves.'

John nodded his head and smiled at his brother. That was excellent advice. John left Dave standing on the doorstep and walked to his car parked at the kerb outside their house. He put his overnight bag in the boot and got in the car. John started the engine.

Linda had joined Dave at the front door, and they both waved as he departed.

John waved back. He hadn't thought to ask that if things didn't go according to plan whether he still had the option to move into Dave's spare bedroom. He glanced in his rear-view mirror. Dave and Linda were still standing on their step. He was sure that in the worst-case scenario, if he found himself back on Dave's doorstep with his overnight bag, moving into their spare bedroom would not be a problem.

'What did he want?' asked Linda, closing the front door.

'John and Sylvie are having some problems.'

Linda sighed. 'What is it with you Baxter's?' She turned to look at her husband. 'Do none of your marriages ever work out?' The sarcasm in her voice was unmistakable.

Dave ignored that comment. 'John wanted to crash here in the spare bedroom while he sorted things out.'

Linda snorted. 'I see you put him in the picture.'

Dave studied his toes avoiding eye contact.

Linda folded her arms. 'You didn't tell him – did you.'

'The thing is, Linda, I didn't think John wanted to hear all about our marital problems.'

'Oh, is that it?' She looked at him sceptically. 'Or is it the fact that you're trying to save face because you didn't want to tell your brother that your wife, your *third* wife, is sleeping in the spare bedroom?'

Linda looked him up and down, and added, 'When are you going back to work?' She eyed him keenly.

Dave was still studying his toes avoiding the question she'd been asking all week.

Linda gave him a dirty look. She knew she could stand there until hell freezes over waiting for Dave to answer *that* question. 'God, you're such an asshole!' She turned on her heel and walked into the lounge, slamming the door behind her.

Dave breathed a sigh of relief. He shifted his attention to the front door. Linda was right. He should have told John that things weren't hunky-dory in his neck of the woods either. In fact, Dave felt guilty that he had persuaded John to carry out that bullshit plan just to make him leave, rather than admitting the real reason he couldn't stay in the spare bedroom.

Linda shouted out, 'I hope to goodness John is not coming to you for any marital advice because if he is then god help him!'

30

Sylvie saw John leave in the car and decided that she too needed some time away from the house. She didn't want to be at home when he returned and came knocking on her door with something that passed for an apology. She could just imagine he had driven to the supermarket to get a bunch of flowers and a big box of chocolates to diffuse the situation. Sylvie wasn't interested.

She knew what he was up to. Flowers or boxes of chocolates would not change her mind. She still had no intention of moving back upstairs or letting John move in with her. He would have to find some other way to pay the bills and save the precious roof over his head. Sylvie was not worried. No doubt he'd come up with something. She knew her husband; he always had a Plan B.

As soon as Sylvie saw John's car fade into the distance down the street, she grabbed her coat, bag, shoes and her dog, and headed out. Talking of apologies, Sylvie knew where she would spend the rest of the day, making a grovelling apology to her best friend, Julia. She was right about him all along. In hindsight, she should have listened to Julia instead of insulting her in the park. Sylvie just prayed she hadn't gone too far and damaged her longest friendship all because of John.

Julia was sitting at her painting easel, putting the finishing touches to a small canvas watercolour, when she heard a dog yapping outside. She glanced at her cocker spaniel, Daisy, who was in her basket. Daisy heard it too. She sat up and cocked her head to one side, listening to the yapping dog.

Julia put her paintbrush down and looked through a porthole window. As soon as she saw Sylvie standing on the deck of her houseboat with Alfie, she knew why she was here – John.

Five minutes later, Julia handed Sylvie a cup of sweet tea.

'You were right all along. John had an ulterior motive.' Sylvie took the cup of tea and dissolved into tears at the cruel things she'd said in the park after Julia warned her he was up to something. Julia only had her best interests at heart. 'I'm so sorry for what I said, Julia.'

Alfie jumped up on the sofa and sat next to Sylvie. He placed a consoling paw on her lap as if to say, *don't cry.*

Sensing something was wrong Daisy padded over and sat on the floor at Sylvie's feet, her doleful eyes looking up at Sylvie in sympathy.

'All is forgiven,' said Julia, handing her a Kleenex tissue. 'When I saw you in the park, and you told me all about the romantic candle-lit dinner with John and the flowers he bought you. And your walk together this morning. It just seemed so out of character. You know me, suspicious by nature. I was concerned – that's all.'

'I know,' Sylvie said miserably. 'I should have listened to you.' Sylvie realised why she didn't listen. She was so enjoying this new romantic side of her husband that she wanted to believe it was genuine and not just another game he was playing to get her to move out of her apartment.

'It was never about me at all was it?' Sylvie blew her nose. She then told Julia all about that episode with the postman this morning and how she'd opened John's mail – all of it. 'When I confronted John over the unpaid bills, he dropped a bombshell.' Sylvie shook her head. She was so overwhelmed by what she discovered he'd been hiding from her.

Julia poured another cup of sweet tea and handed it to Sylvie. 'Why don't you tell me all about it, darling? You know what they say, a problem shared—'

'—is a problem halved,' said Sylvie, managing a smile. 'It turns out that John overstretched us financially to complete the conversion on the house. He's been ignoring the bills piling up. I don't even know if he has been paying the mortgage. To be honest, I was too afraid to ask. We could lose everything!'

'Come, come,' said Julia, putting a comforting arm around Sylvie's shoulders. 'It can't be as bad as all that.'

'It is!' Sylvie recalled the County Court Summons she thrust in his hand this morning. She guessed that was just the tip of the iceberg. 'John said that we stand to lose it all if we don't move back in together and rent out one of the apartments. He said it was the only way.'

'Did he now.' Julia paused. 'So, what are you going to do?'

Sylvie shifted in her seat. 'It's already done. I told him to get stuffed, in so many words. I am not moving out of my apartment, and he is not moving in with me.' Sylvie registered the look of surprise on Julia's face. 'Are you shocked?'

'Bloody hell,' exclaimed Julia, her eyes wide, 'I'll say. What did you do with my best friend who wouldn't say boo to a goose?'

Julia peered at her. 'Time was when you wouldn't stick up for yourself if your life depended on it. And you would never ever dream of putting yourself first above your kids, or John.'

'You think I'm selfish, don't you?'

'No, that's not it at all, Sylvie. I think you're very...' Julia paused searching for the right word, 'brave.'

'Oh god,' said Sylvie as soon as Julia uttered that word. 'You think I'm being stupid.'

Julia shook her head. 'It's not stupid to find something you want in life and to try to keep hold of it.'

'Yes, I suppose you're right.' Sylvie was thinking about the garden apartment. Since moving downstairs on her own, she'd had some really good fun for the first time in ages. It was all the things she hadn't planned on doing that turned out to be the most memorable. Like redecorating her apartment on the spur of the moment, and saying yes to a seventies-themed party, and getting her first puppy out of the blue when Julia surprised her with a moving-in present. It was all the things that didn't seem to happen with John and *the plan*.

With John, there was no spontaneity. Life had been dull, in monochrome, with no colour, no vividness, like she was living in a black and white movie. It was as though she was just going through the same routines until the credits rolled on her life. Sylvie didn't want that life anymore. She wanted new experiences. That's what moving into the garden apartment had given her. That's when the fun started and where her life had begun anew.

She felt her relationship with her husband had begun anew when he started surprising her with evenings out together. They were enjoying the simple pleasure of each other's company with no plans, and no agenda. At least that's what Sylvie thought. It was like a breath of fresh air. All this led Sylvie to believe that John had changed. Until she discovered the truth.

Sylvie sighed. It was all built on a lie. How foolish to imagine the romantic candle-lit dinners, and the shenanigans in the taxi on the way home, was the start of something new and exciting and spontaneous in their relationship. Julia was right: that wasn't John at all. That was the old John pretending to be something he wasn't. Pretending he wanted to have new experiences and spend time together. Pretending he still wanted her when he didn't. She said as much to Julia.

'I am sorry to hear that,' said Julia, staring at her best friend. She didn't want to make Sylvie any more depressed than she already was, but she had to tell Sylvie the news, 'Nigel is seeing someone.' She offered her an apologetic look that said she was sorry she had to bring it up.

'Oh, I see.' Sylvie wasn't all that surprised considering how good-looking and charming he was. And to be fair, he'd left several messages on her answering machine, none of which she responded to.

'Why don't I put the kettle on and make another pot of tea,' suggested Julia, affectionately patting Sylvie's hand.

Sylvie nodded her head and reached for another Kleenex tissue from the box Julia had left on the arm of the sofa.

'The funny thing is,' said Sylvie, wiping her eyes dry with the tissue as she watched Julia in the galley kitchen, 'it was John I wanted,' she confided. 'Not the old John, mind you, but this new, interesting person who was fun to be with, and paid attention to me, and made me feel—'

A sob caught in her throat. It had all been so unexpected; John was making such an effort in their relationship at a time in their lives when Sylvie thought all that was behind them. After almost forty years of marriage, she'd assumed that their relationship amounted to nothing more than just being comfortable in each other's company. Like old friends. She considered it was too late to change. To experience new things together. To see a side of him she hadn't seen in decades since they were newlyweds.

Sylvie reached for a tissue. She didn't realise how much she wanted someone to make her feel special until John's clever little ruse to romance her into moving back in with him. It almost worked. Sylvie wanted romance in her life, and flowers and romantic walks along the canal. But what she didn't want was for all that to stop as soon as he got what he wanted. And it would stop, of that she was certain.

She'd visited his apartment enough times, when he was laid up after his accident, to see first-hand how his life upstairs was just a microcosm of the life they'd shared together for so many years before the conversion. Perhaps that didn't surprise her. What surprised her, and worried her in equal measure, was how she slotted back into the same old routines with her husband. It wasn't long before she resumed bringing up his morning cuppa, along with his newspaper to read in bed, like she always used to. Except she had to fetch it from the paper shop first because he could no longer afford to have it delivered. John didn't object. It was obvious he wanted things to go back to the way they were, with the same old routines, the same old life, the same old John.

Sylvie couldn't go back to that life now. She desperately wanted things to change. John didn't understand that. He didn't understand her. She realised that now. That's what upset her when she found out what he was up to. She thought, by some miracle, they had turned back the clock and John's motivation was to spend time together; the way they used to before forty years had been swallowed up in the minutiae of married life. But it wasn't about that at all. It was about money and bills and the house. It was still the same old issues and the same old John. And Sylvie was sick of it.

Julia put the tea tray down on the coffee table in front of her. 'I hate to say this, Sylvie, but if it's romance you're after, you are looking in the wrong place. John will never change.' Julia poured them both another cup of tea and handed Sylvie a cup. 'I think you know that already, darling. That's why you're not moving out of your apartment.'

Sylvie sipped her tea and eyed her best friend. Julia was used to being on her own. Sylvie wasn't. After living with someone for so long, Sylvie was afraid she would she end up like Julia – alone.

Sylvie admonished herself for such a mean thought about her best friend. Many people were living alone at their age for a variety of reasons. It didn't mean they were lonely or weren't leading fulfilling lives. In fact, Julia was the poster child for living alone. She always seemed perfectly content. Sylvie knew Julia would like to meet somebody new. However, it didn't stop her living life to the full. It didn't stop her pursuing her dreams; the houseboat they were sitting in was proof of that.

That explained why hearing the news about Nigel didn't bother Sylvie as much as she thought it would. She had other things on her mind right now besides relationships. Just like Julia and her houseboat, Sylvie was pursuing her own personal dream. She needed a break from relationships – old or new – to concentrate on herself and her new career as a writer and columnist.

'Julia, I've got some more news,' said Sylvie brightening. 'It's good news this time.' At least it was until the post arrived this morning and put a big dampener on it. Sylvie tried to brush that thought aside.

'What is it?' Julia put her cup and saucer down and gave Sylvie her full attention.

Sylvie opened her mouth and discovered she didn't know where to begin. Things had happened so fast. One minute she was just another online blogger and then everything changed.

Sylvie smiled. 'It had all started with a blog.' She told Julia all about the blog she had been writing these past few weeks, just for a bit of fun, until the day it crashed. That's when she'd found out her blog was popular.

Julia was captivated. Sylvie told her that an editor from a women's magazine approached her to write an article to publish in their next issue. 'If the readers like it, I might be offered my very own weekly column.'

'Crumbs, that *is* exciting. So, did you write the article?'

'Of course I wrote it.'

'Well?' Julia leaned forward. 'What happened? Did they like it? Did they offer you a weekly column?'

When she didn't answer, Julia leaned back in her chair and studied Sylvie thoughtfully. 'You didn't send it.'

Sylvie shook her head, no.

'Why ever not?'

Sylvie confided in Julia that she had written the article *before* she found out about the unpaid bills and what John was up to. 'I wrote all about how spending some time apart had brought the romance back into our lives. I thought if I wrote about my own experiences of LAT living—'

'LAT living?'

'Living apart together.'

'I see – do continue, Sylvie.'

'Well, as I was saying, I thought if I wrote from personal experience how LAT living brought the romance back into our lives, the article might interest them enough to offer me a weekly column. But…' Sylvie trailed off.

'But…?'

'There's a problem.'

'Which is?' Julia prompted.

'Well, isn't it obvious? That was before I found out the truth about John's motives. Now everything I've written is one big lie.'

Julia shrugged. 'What does it matter? Give them what they want.'

'I can't do that!' Sylvie stared at Julia. 'Can I?' Sylvie was considering the money. She tried to convince herself that she needn't worry about the bills because John was bound to have something else up his sleeve to get them out of this financial fix. But it wasn't working. All she kept thinking was that she couldn't rely on him anymore.

For the first time in their married lives, John had been burying his head in the sand about their financial situation. He was an accountant for god's sake. Sylvie would never have expected him to behave this way. But that was the reality. Now she was in a quandary. It was no idle threat that they could lose everything if they didn't move back in together and rent out one of the apartments. However, there was an alternative: lie to her readers, lie to the magazine, submit her article – which was now all lies – and take the money.

She needed the money – that was a given – but more than that, Sylvie wanted this. The commission from one article would barely scratch the surface of all the outstanding debts. If they liked her work, it would mean writing more articles, more lies, in order to increase her income. But if she was honest, money wasn't her prime motivation, not by a long stretch. Sylvie felt on the cusp of achieving something she had only ever dreamed of. She would be taken seriously as a writer. And nothing, not even her husband, or a few little white lies, would stand in the way of that.

'What are you thinking?' asked Julia.

'I will submit the article,' Sylvie replied without hesitation, adding, 'because I need the money.'

'Of course you do. And wouldn't it be a nice little bonus to see your words in print?' Julia grinned.

Sylvie picked up a cushion and threw it across the room in Julia's direction.

The two cocker spaniels barked excitedly, and both dived for the cushion that landed at Julia's feet. A friendly doggy tug-of-war ensued, with each dog pulling one end of the cushion, until Alfie still only a puppy, lost to the older, wiser and larger spaniel.

Alfie wagged his tail as he watched Daisy, head held high with pride, take her prize and deposit it in her bed.

Daisy climbed into her basket and turned full circle three times before slumping on the cushion and falling fast asleep.

Alfie yapped at his playmate but got no response. He scampered over to Sylvie and yapped at her instead.

'You naughty, naughty dog.' Sylvie wagged her finger at Alfie and looked apologetically at Julia. 'Sorry about that, Julia. I'll buy you another cushion.'

'Don't be daft. There's plenty more where that came from.' Julia gestured at the assortment of cushions scattered along the window seats below the portholes. 'Besides, I don't think Daisy has had that much fun in ages. I wish you'd pop round more often.'

Sylvie was still thinking about her decision to stay downstairs in the garden apartment. 'What are my girls going to say when they find out I refused to compromise and move back in with their father?'

'That you're selfish and short-sighted, and you had better apologise and beg him to take you back.'

Sylvie glared at her best friend.

Julia keeled over with laughter. 'How do I know what they will say? Who knows, they might surprise you and support your decision?'

'And what if they don't?'

'Then you, my darling, must ignore them.'

That was easier said than done. Her best friend did not have children – and three daddy's girls at that. Even so, Sylvie decided to remain living in her apartment. She intended to submit her article to the magazine as soon as she got home.

Sylvie frowned. She was worried about what she would do for money if they didn't like her article and she lost the option to write a regular column.

Julia noticed that Sylvie looked preoccupied. 'What is it now?'

Sylvie turned to Julia. 'I'm worried what will happen if they don't accept my article and I can't earn any money.' Sylvie shook her head. 'I wasn't feeling worked up about it last night when I was writing the article.'

'That was before you found out John wasn't paying the bills.'

'Yes – you're right. It was different when I thought I could rely on him.'

'I bet it did. Somebody paying the bills while you go off and find yourself. How long did you think that would last?'

Sylvie fell silent. She didn't want to say it, but it had just dawned on her that John wasn't the only one burying his head in the sand regarding their finances. How long did she think she could remain living downstairs on her own expecting her husband to cover everything?

When Sylvie left her part time secretarial job five years short of retirement, with a small lump sum and a monthly pension worth peanuts, she was not worried about money. She knew how lucky she was to have a husband supporting her while she found herself. Unfortunately, Sylvie's luck had just run out.

'Welcome to the real world, darling,' said Julia, gazing at her best friend. 'If you want to stay in your own apartment, you better take every opportunity that comes your way to earn some money.'

'Sylvie sat there biting a fingernail.'

'I don't mean to sound harsh, Sylvie, but your article better be good and lead to a weekly column. Otherwise…'

Otherwise, I might have to compromise, thought Sylvie glumly.

Once again, Julia noticed that Sylvie looked preoccupied. To change the subject, Julia had some news of her own. 'I know this isn't the right time to bring it up, but I can't keep it to myself any longer.' Julia took a deep breath, and announced, 'I've met someone.'

Sylvie stared at her in stunned silence. She had been so wrapped up in her own life that she hadn't even asked Julia how she was, or how things were going since she moved to Little Venice. Sylvie's face broke into a wide grin at this piece of unexpected news. 'Well, don't keep me in suspense.' Sylvie wanted to know all about the new man in her life. 'What's his name? Where did you meet him? What does he do for a liv—?'

'Not so fast,' interrupted Julia. 'It's only early days, so I don't want to give too much away. However, what I will say is that I met him right here in Little Venice. We are neighbours.' Julia smiled. 'It was his retirement dream to live on a houseboat too – can you believe it?' Julia stared at Sylvie in wide-eyed amazement. 'We've only met twice, had coffee, some lunch – that sort of thing. But the strange part is it feels like the start of something, do you know what I mean?'

Unfortunately for Sylvie, she knew what Julia meant. That's how she felt about the dinner dates and the romantic walk along the canal with John, as though it was the start of a new chapter in their lives together. If only she'd known how that would turn out.

Sylvie kept that thought to herself, not wanting to throw a bucket of cold water on Julia's news. Julia had had her ups and downs with relationships over the years. She deserved to find that someone special and finally settle down.

'I shouldn't say this, Sylvie, because it is only early days, but I think he's *the one*.'

'Really?' Sylvie was intrigued. Julia had never said that about any of her relationships in the past.

'It got me thinking about your situation. Please take heart. I believe if you follow your dreams, it could lead you to the person you were meant to spend the rest of your life with.' Julia glanced around her houseboat and turned to Sylvie. 'You might find love where you least expect it.'

31

Sylvie travelled home on the bus. She was relieved that she had broken the ice with Julia. However, the visit left her anxious at the prospect of losing the commission if her article wasn't up to scratch. She imagined an electronic version of Harriet's slush pile and her article ending up in the recycle bin of the editor's computer.

Sylvie was trying hard to remain positive and upbeat. It wasn't easy. She hadn't even submitted her article yet, and she was already thinking of failure. Perhaps it was because she knew how much was riding on it. Welcome to the real world, thought Sylvie with butterflies in her stomach at the prospect of going it alone for the first time since before she was married.

Sylvie tried not to think about that. Instead, she focused on the last thing Julia said to her before she left. Something about finding love where you least expect it. Sylvie stared out of the bus window as she recalled her bizarre recurring dream about finding love on the rooftop; where that rooftop was, or who that person might be, was not revealed in her dream. She sighed. Unfortunately, her dream brought to mind her blog called *Love on the Rooftop*, and the article sitting on her laptop waiting to be sent.

All her anxieties about what might happen, or not, when she submitted it came flooding back.

Sylvie opened the door to her apartment and knelt to let Alfie off his lead, thanking him for being such a good boy sitting quietly on the bus on the way home. She then made her way down to the kitchen. Her laptop was still on the table where she'd left it this morning when the postman called. Sylvie sent her article.

It was now late in the afternoon. She didn't expect a reply until tomorrow. That didn't stop Sylvie checking her emails for the third time in as many minutes. She knew she wasn't going to get instant feedback from the magazine after submitting her article; and hadn't even given them a chance to read it, let alone post a reply.

Sylvie tried to busy herself with some housework to take her mind off the waiting game. Within minutes she found herself drawn back to her email inbox. It was still empty.

She now regretted not sending it first thing this morning before she answered the door to the postman. Maybe the magazine had already found another writer to fill their weekly column. Or perhaps they had lost interest and moved on. Many things were running through her mind, all negative, when the phone rang.

'Hello...?'

'Ah hello there, my name is Marcia Hunt. You sent us an article on living apart together.'

Sylvie's heart skipped a beat. She had been so preoccupied with checking her emails it didn't occur to her she might get a phone call from the magazine instead.

'My team and I thoroughly enjoyed your article, so I would

like to invite you to pop along and see us for an informal chat. Shall we say tomorrow morning at nine o'clock, if that's okay with you?'

Sylvie was so stunned the editor had phoned her she was lost for words. *Answer her, for goodness' sake,* 'Yes... yes that will be fine. I'll be there,' said Sylvie signing off.

Two minutes later she phoned Julia and told her the news. Sylvie was wondering what Marcia Hunt meant by an "informal chat."

'It's a job interview,' said Julia down the phone. 'You, my dear best friend, have just got yourself an interview with the magazine.'

'Oh no!' She hadn't had a job interview in years.

'Oh yes!' said Julia. 'I'm so excited for you.'

Sylvie could feel her heart thudding in her chest, and her anxiety levels rising, at the mere mention of the word *interview*. Let alone the thought of going through with it. And it wasn't helping that she was desperate for them to publish her article so she could get paid.

'Sylvie, just remember that they liked your article. In fact, they must have been impressed to ring you up straightaway and ask you to come in and see them. They're obviously keen to have you. Congratulations are in order.'

Sylvie thought nothing of the kind. She didn't want to get ahead of herself and presume they would offer her a job. All she wanted to do was get through tomorrow morning and walk out with that commission money for her article. Perhaps, if she was lucky, they would ask her to write a weekly column. She hoped so because Sylvie had a feeling she hadn't seen the last of the bill reminders, overdue notices, and official looking correspondence threatening court action. She was still trying to get to grips with their finances.

She'd arranged with the postman for all the letters, including John's, to be put in her post box. Sylvie promised the postman she would deliver his mail upstairs; she cringed at the outright lie she'd told him, but it was the only way he'd hand them over secure in the knowledge he wouldn't lose his job. Sylvie needed to see those letters. In the past, she had always relied on her husband to sort out all the bills. Now she could not trust him to open them, let alone pay the bills. It forced Sylvie to take matters into her own hands.

She began by looking at all their outstanding bills and debts to get some idea how much trouble they were in. Sylvie had started the task last night with the bundle of correspondence addressed to John that the postman couldn't fit inside his post box. She had already prioritised the bills so that, fingers crossed, when she walked out with that commission tomorrow, she could use the money to pay one or two of the most urgent bills. She hoped she wouldn't have to make an arrangement with the creditors, but that would depend on how much money Marcia Hunt would pay for her article. Sylvie had no idea how much magazines paid freelance writers. She hoped it was at least enough to pay the electricity bill tomorrow because they were threatening to cut them off.

When Sylvie got off the phone to Julia, she'd opened another letter addressed to John that the postman had delivered in the afternoon, added it to the pile of unpaid bills on the kitchen table, and then checked her emails. The magazine had sent her an email to confirm the informal chat arranged for first thing tomorrow morning. Sylvie glanced at the pile of bills. She had butterflies in her stomach at the prospect that they might change their mind. They knew nothing about her. What if they didn't like what they saw when they found out she was just a sixty-year-old former secretary trying to reinvent herself and fulfil a long-cherished dream to become a writer? She wasn't going to tell them how desperately she needed the money.

If things didn't work out with the magazine and John didn't come up with another plan to get them out of this hole, as a last resort Sylvie intended to move back in with him. At least that was the plan until she'd inspected their finances and discovered things were far worse than she'd imagined. The reality was they didn't have time to find a tenant and wait for the rent money to come in. That time had been and gone. They now had urgent bills to pay that had to be dealt with right now otherwise the bailiffs would come knocking on their door.

Sylvie shook her head. It was obvious John had been burying his head in the sand and didn't have the first clue how serious things were. He was still under the illusion that renting out one apartment would solve all his problems.

She glanced at the unpaid electricity bill. How did he think they'd get a tenant if the electricity company cut them off? What sort of impression would it give a prospective tenant if they turned up at the house to discover the landlords couldn't afford to pay their bills?

Sylvie didn't want to think about that. Instead, she quickly moved on to another anxiety: what on earth was she going to wear tomorrow morning? If they were calling it an informal chat; did that imply casual wear, or was that a misnomer and she should treat it as a formal job interview? The last thing she wanted to do was jeopardise her chances because she hadn't dressed appropriately. Whatever the case, she felt the occasion warranted a new outfit.

Sylvie reached for the phone and dialled Julia's number. 'Julia, how would you like to go clothes shopping this afternoon?' Sylvie didn't have two brass farthings to rub together, but she had a very nice best friend with a generous nature. She wouldn't dream of asking to borrow money under normal circumstances.

'It will be my treat,' said Julia down the phone before Sylvie asked. 'We'll find the perfect outfit so you look drop-dead gorgeous tomorrow.'

Sylvie rolled her eyes. 'Julia, for your information the editor is a woman, so I don't need to look drop-dead gorgeous for my interview. Even if the editor were a man, I would hope they take me on for my writing skills and not—'

'Of course. But it doesn't hurt to look your best. You never know who might be around the next corner, or in the next office – if you catch my drift.'

'Julia, I'm hoping to walk out of tomorrow with a job – not a date.'

'Yes, I know that. But you're also following your dream to be a writer. Remember what I said about following your dreams? It might lead somewhere you least expect.'

Sylvie nodded. 'Like to the person I'm meant to spend the rest of my life with?'

'Good girl. Now let's go shopping.'

32

John was in his apartment when he was startled by the sound of a continuous buzzing noise. It was so unexpected; it took him a full minute to realise what the noise was – his doorbell – and a further minute to compose himself before he answered the door, because the only person who would ring his doorbell was Sylvie.

He raised an eyebrow as he strode to the door. This *was* a surprise. John assumed that he was still in the doghouse. Sylvie hadn't spoken to him since she found out the truth about their finances yesterday morning. Since returning from Dave's house, he'd been keeping a low-profile hoping she would come around and realise there was only one way out of this predicament.

John smiled. That she was ringing his doorbell suggested she had come to her senses and was ready to compromise, so they could rent out one apartment. He wondered which apartment she had in mind – his place or hers.

Perhaps it wasn't surprising that she'd caved already. She only confronted him with one letter from his post box. He knew there were more. John saw them poking out of the vertical slit on the front of the box. He'd been ignoring them. Then he nipped out early for his morning newspaper and discovered his post box was empty. If Sylvie had opened all his letters, it made him wonder whether she had worked out the full extent of their financial problems; something even he hadn't dared to face up to. He thought of all the other bills and demands for payment stuffed in his desk drawer which his wife knew nothing about.

John made a quick detour into his study, intending to collect all those letters from his desk drawer to show Sylvie, but then thought the better of it. He didn't fancy another row. Not at this hour. He hadn't even had breakfast yet. He closed his study door and returned to the lobby empty handed. He gave himself a quick once over in the hallway mirror, winking at his reflection.

He took a deep breath and opened the door to his apartment. To his surprise, Sylvie was not standing outside his door as he expected. John heard the familiar sound of the front door click shut in the communal hall downstairs. He poked his head around the doorframe and glanced down the stairs. He must have just missed her. 'Damn!' John swore, wishing he hadn't dilly dallied in the study before answering the door.

He shook his head and shut the door. John thought he heard something. He opened his door again. 'What the…!'

There on the landing, with his lead tied to the banister, was Alfie. He wagged his tail as John approached.

'What are you doing here?'

Alfie yapped in excitement.

John noticed a rolled-up piece of paper slipped under the dog's collar. He bent down and retrieved it.

Alfie sniffed John's hand.

John left the dog where he was and raced down the stairs hoping that he could catch her up. He skidded to a halt at the front door and flung it open. He glimpsed Sylvie looking very smart in a grey trouser suit as she climbed into the back of a waiting taxi. He stared at the black London taxi as it drew away from the kerb and sped down the street. John stood there wondering where she was off to at eight o'clock on a weekday morning dressed like—

His train of thought came to an abrupt halt. Did Sylvie have a job interview? John had no idea she was still applying for work. He thought they had packed that in weeks ago.

He didn't like the other possibility. From what he'd just seen, Sylvie had made quite the effort with her attire. He hadn't seen that outfit before. It looked new. He doubted she'd bought it for a job interview. They'd both been down that road before when they tried to get back into work; John because he couldn't accept early retirement, Sylvie because she needed to get away from her husband moping around the house all day bored and depressed. Despite sending off dozens of applications between them, they'd both had no luck on the job front. He couldn't imagine what would have changed.

John unfurled the piece of notepaper that Sylvie left with the dog, keen to find out what she was doing, where she was going and, more worryingly, who she was meeting.

Was Nigel back in the picture? John glanced up the stairs. He could see Alfie sitting on the landing outside his apartment door. Sylvie hadn't taken her dog, which meant Nigel wasn't doing puppy-training classes, which meant... John didn't have a clue what that meant. He read the note. 'You have got to be kidding me!' He turned the piece of paper over to see if she'd scribbled anything else. Nothing. Just two words: *walk me*. He threw his arms in the air. 'Just great. Now I'm a dog-sitter.' John closed the front door and trudged back upstairs.

Alfie stood up as he approached, wagging his tail, pleased to see John return.

John walked past the dog and into his apartment.

Alfie attempted to follow, scampering after John until his lead – still attached to the banister – caught Alfie by surprise. He let out a yelp as his forward momentum was curtailed. Alfie sat down on his rear with a whimper; he'd only made it as far as the doorway. Alfie cocked his head to one side watching the door swing to, almost touching his nose as it clicked shut.

John was sitting in his kitchen, pouring himself a bowl of cornflakes, when an almighty howl gave him a start. It caused him to spill the entire contents of the cereal box all over the kitchen table. Alfie continued to howl while John cleared up the mess, poured himself another bowl of cereal and ate his breakfast before returning to the door.

He paused as he reached for the door handle and winced. He could not believe such a small puppy could make so much racket. However, he wasn't about to jump to attention the moment Alfie started howling. That's why John had sat and eaten his breakfast. He assumed that Alfie would get the message and shut up.

John couldn't stand it any longer. He threw open the door to find the dog sitting just the other side.

Alfie fell silent the moment he appeared.

John glared at the dog sitting at his feet. 'What in heaven's name am I meant to do with you?' He didn't want the dog inside his apartment. Then he remembered Sylvie's note. He turned around and slipped on a pair of shoes, grabbed his coat, and stepped into the hall once more, closing the door behind him. He stopped and looked at the dog. 'Walkies?'

Alfie started to bark.

John had an idea. He darted back inside his apartment. He still had the ball Sylvie gave him when he'd played a game of fetch with Alfie in Regent's Park. It was the day they'd walked along the canal together.

John tried not to think about how much he'd been enjoying Sylvie's company before the postman ruined everything. He knew it wasn't the postman's fault. He had no-one else to blame but himself for not telling her the truth from the outset. John sighed. If only he was more like his wife; she never told fibs or did anything dishonest.

John untied the lead from the banister and walked down the stairs with Alfie pulling on his lead, much to his annoyance. John frowned at the dog. He wasn't going to put up with that for much longer. Alfie would learn to walk on the lead. John didn't have a clue how to make him do that. He might pay a visit to the library and pick up a book on dog training.

Sylvie appeared to have given up on the puppy-training classes. John hadn't seen Nigel around, much to his relief. That didn't mean Nigel had given up on seeing Sylvie. John frowned at the thought of her climbing into the taxi dressed in a smart figure-hugging trouser suit.

Downstairs in the communal hall, he opened the door and almost fell down the front steps; Alfie darted outside, yanking John behind him. This continued along the street with Alfie pulling him all the way to their local park – Holland Park. It was a relief to let the dog off the lead.

John rubbed his hand, where the lead had wound around his fingers, as he glanced up at the sky. He didn't think walkies would last that long by the look of the weather. It was a grey, overcast morning and John felt spots of rain soon after they walked through the park gates. At least he had the foresight to bring an umbrella.

After Alfie had done his business, and John had gone through the unpleasantness of scooping it up in a plastic bag to deposit in the nearest bin, he was standing throwing Alfie the ball when another dog appeared out of nowhere. It started chasing Alfie's ball. John saw the small dog beat Alfie to it and run off toward a lady standing in the distance.

John heard her shout, 'Give me that, you naughty, naughty dog,' before picking up the small dog and extracting the ball from its unwilling jaws. She turned around and started walking in John's direction, carrying the naughty dog under one arm. There was another identical dog trotting at her heels.

He watched her approach. She appeared to be around his own age and dressed in a similar outfit to the one Sylvie was wearing this morning. The lady looked very smart; too smart to be out over the park walking the dogs. John wondered if she had somewhere to be and was just doing a quick circuit of the park before heading off to work.

He felt envious. He wished he had somewhere to be and something to do besides taking Alfie out this morning. He wondered what Sylvie was doing at this moment while he was traipsing around the park – bored.

An image of a sophisticated, slim Nigel floated to the surface. John banished that thought. Instead, he concentrated on the well-dressed woman heading in his direction.

As she came closer, John noted that she was wearing a brushed-cotton navy blue coat over her trouser-suit, blue leather gloves, and designer shoes. He still had an eye for that sort of thing after Chloe introduced him to designer labels. In fact, he was wearing designer labels himself. John had dressed in one of his new outfits this morning. He'd made an effort with his appearance on the off-chance Sylvie would call. The last thing he expected was to be traipsing over the park walking her dog.

The lady approached him with an outstretched hand. 'I'm so sorry,' she apologised, handing John the ball.

Alfie started jumping up John's legs for the ball.

'Down!' said John in an authoritative voice.

Alfie stopped jumping up and sat obediently at his feet.

John looked at him in surprise.

'You're good with dogs,' she observed.

'It's nothing, really,' he replied modestly, although he appreciated the compliment.

'Do you come to the park often? I don't recall seeing you here before.' She looked him up and down. 'I'm sure if I had, I would have remembered.'

John felt shy under her gaze. Was she chatting him up? He raised an eyebrow thinking, for goodness' sake get over yourself. Just because he was wearing one of his new outfits, and he was still going to the expense of having his highlights touched up, that didn't mean women were falling at his feet. Still, he couldn't help feeling flattered by the attention.

'I... um... just got the dog recently, so this is only my second walkies.' John didn't know why he intimated that Alfie was his dog. He didn't even like dogs.

'Your dog is adorable. And so well behaved. Unlike my bichon frise. She's always stealing other dog's toys.' She put the naughty dog down on the grass beside Alfie.

John looked at the ball in his hand, and said, 'Alfie's still only a puppy, but he has got to learn to stand on his own four paws and look after his toys. Otherwise, other dogs will walk all over him. This,' said John, holding up the ball that was nabbed by the lady's dog, 'is a case in point.' John cracked a smile.

She burst out laughing at John's joke.

They walked on as the dogs frolicked together on the grass. What followed was an amiable conversation about dog behaviour and dog training, which John found interesting and informative. It turned out that the lady had owned dogs all her life. She sounded quite the expert.

They stopped at a park bench and sat down. John listened to the lady called Barbara – Babs to her friends – as she told him a bit about herself. Barbara had recently lost her husband, leaving her a comfortable widow. Like John, she had children – two sons – and three grandchildren, a boy and two girls.

'I miss my grandchildren,' confided Barbara. 'I used to care for them all the time when they were small, so their parents could work. Now they're at school they have their friends and after-school clubs. They don't need their grandma anymore. The eldest is starting high school next year. I can't believe how the time has flown. One minute they were babies and the next...' she trailed off.

The conversation made John think about his only grandchild, Gertie. Over the last few months, he had been so preoccupied with his own situation – losing his job and then converting the house. Not to mention his relationship – or lack of – with Sylvie, that he hardly ever found the time to call on Harriet to see his granddaughter. It seemed like one minute she was a bonny baby and the next she was a toddler. John felt he barely knew her.

Barbara listened attentively as John told her all about his three daughters and his only grandchild. She studied him intently.

Barbara walked her dogs over the park hoping that one day she might meet someone special; someone not unlike John. A thought she does not share with the nice man sitting next to her on the park bench.

The minute she set eyes on him she liked what she saw. She liked the way he dressed and the way he took care of his appearance, going to all the trouble of visiting a salon to have highlights put in his hair. But more than that, she liked that he was a dog-lover. That came top of her list of must-have qualities for potential suitors.

Barbara wondered what else she might discover about him that was right up her street. This was the reason she dressed up to the nines whenever she went out, even if she was only taking the dogs to the park. You never know who you might bump into around the next corner. Or in this case, thought Barbara with a smile, whose ball her naughty dog might steal. What a stroke of luck that today she'd bumped into John.

And then it started to rain. Barbara jumped up from her seat. 'Oh dear, I've forgotten my umbrella.' In this downpour, it wouldn't take long, and her new coat would be sodden. She didn't care about the coat. What bothered her was the time she'd spent doing her hair and make-up would be for nothing if her new friend, John, saw her in such a bedraggled state.

'Allow me,' said John, unfurling his umbrella and holding it aloft. He gallantly offered to walk Barbara to her car.

'Thank you.' Barbara smiled at him, ticking off another important quality on her list – kindness. Barbara called to her two dogs, 'Tweedledum! Tweedledee!'

John gave Barbara a sideways glance and thanked his lucky stars that Sylvie hadn't called her dog something really stupid. He called out, 'Alfie!' When all three dogs were back on the lead, John held his umbrella aloft as they all walked to the park gates. Barbara had parked her car a short distance along the road.

As John watched Barbara get into the old estate car, he smiled. Barbara's car looked almost as ancient as his own parked in the driveway at home, and in just as good condition. He guessed she was another one who kept hold of it for sentimental reasons. It wasn't necessary to own a car in London.

Barbara caught the surprised look on John's face when he saw her vehicle after mentioning that she was a wealthy widow. 'I know it's old,' said Barbara, 'but I'm rather attached to it, and there's hardly any miles on the clock. It's almost as good as new. All I must do is take it out for a little spin here and there. This car has never let me down once.'

'I understand,' said John. 'I have one just like it at home.'

'You do?' Barbara smiled. That was another thing they had in common. This was turning out her lucky day.

'Yes, you must come over and see it sometime.' John had no idea why he said that.

'Well…' Barbara's eyes went wide. 'I might just do that.'

He was just waving goodbye when Barbara put the key in the ignition, and nothing happened. She wound her window down. 'Oh dear, my car won't start.'

John noticed she'd left her lights on. 'I think the battery is dead. Do you need to borrow my mobile phone to ring—?'

'No, I have one here somewhere,' said Barbara, fishing in her handbag. 'Ah, here it is. I will phone the AA. I'll be fine.'

John hung around just in case there was a problem.

'How long? An hour!' exclaimed Barbara on the phone. 'But it's raining, and my car already smells of wet dog.' She grimaced.

'What am I supposed to do in the meantime, just sit here in the cold and wait?'

John overheard her phone conversation. He bent down at the car window. 'Barbara?'

Barbara looked up. 'I live too far away to walk home,' she complained. 'I'm stuck here until they turn up to fix my car.'

John glanced over his shoulder toward his house and then looked back at Barbara. It wasn't his intention to meet a woman over the park and invite her back to his place, but Barbara looked cold and miserable, and he felt sorry for her.

'Look, how about a cup of tea while you wait?' suggested John. 'I live just around the corner.' He pointed down the street. 'I'm sure there would be time to pop in and warm yourself up with a brew before they arrive to fix your car.'

He didn't expect her to jump at an invitation from a stranger to come back to his flat. He'd offered out of politeness more than anything; he couldn't leave her stranded without at least asking if she wanted to come back to his place to wait for the AA, even if she declined.

Barbara was out of her car like a shot. She gathered up her bag and scooped up her dogs. She handed one to John.

He took the dog and held it at arm's length.

'Well, what are we waiting for?'

'Er… this way,' said John in surprise. He walked back to his place feeling bemused that he'd stepped out of his house with one dog and returned with two. If you counted the wet bichon frise, belonging to Barbara, tucked under his arm.

'What a lovely house,' remarked Barbara, looking up at the four-storey Georgian facade as he opened the front gate. She turned to John. 'Do you live here on your own?' She hadn't thought to ask what his personal circumstances were. He hadn't mentioned a wife or partner. Barbara was hoping, rather selfishly, that he'd found himself in similar circumstances to her own and was a widower, or perhaps divorced.

'I'm separated,' said John in answer to her question. 'We don't live together anymore.' The words caught in his throat making it sound even more real for saying it.

That was music to her ears. By the pained expression on his face, they were good as divorced, thought Barbara.

As they walked up the garden path to the front door, Barbara was surprised to learn that the property was divided into two apartments. Even more surprising, John's wife was still living under the same roof, albeit in a separate flat downstairs. It was an unusual arrangement. However, she was open-minded. It didn't bother her that John's ex was living in such close proximity.

Barbara could tell he didn't want to talk about their unusual living arrangements, although she had an idea how that might have come about. These houses weren't cheap. If they had to split the proceeds neither one of them could probably afford to stay living in such an upmarket area of London. They would have to compromise with location. Barbara glanced up at John's gorgeous home. She could see why this might be the solution. Although it made her wonder how it was working out for them.

If she had split up with her husband, Barbara wasn't sure whether she could continue living under the same roof if she saw him with another woman. Still, that was none of her concern because, all going well, she would be the other woman. Barbara walked into John's apartment and liked what she saw.

John followed her inside hoping she wasn't put off by the garish throws, mohair cushions, lava-lamps and all the other seventies retro paraphernalia Dave had dispersed around his apartment. All that stuff was intended to impress Sylvie. John hadn't bothered to pack it all away in boxes and give them back to Dave. Yesterday, he thought he was moving into Dave's spare bedroom and renting out his apartment. He'd left the stuff around his flat thinking a prospective tenant might like it.

John looked around his lounge, embarrassed that someone had visited him at home and seen all this crap. He glanced at Barbara, 'Sorry about the—'

'—Mess?' Barbara thought that's what he was about to say next. She assumed all bachelor pads were messy and lacking that vital ingredient – a woman's touch.

Casting her eye around his lounge, Barbara didn't know what he was apologising for. John's home was spotlessly clean and much to her taste.

'I adore your apartment,' gushed Barbara. 'The décor is bland and neutral, but I like what you've done with the place, brightening it up with throws and cushions, and such like. And would you look at this?' She picked up a purple lava lamp. 'I haven't seen one of these in years.'

She stared at John a little surprised by all this. When she met him over the park, her first impression was that he came across as uptight. So, when Barbara walked into his apartment, she was not surprised to find it clean and tidy. However, she was surprised by everything else.

She turned to John and held up the lava lamp. 'It's all very bohemian.'

That sounded like something Julia would say, thought John.

Barbara put the lava lamp down and cast her gaze around the room approvingly, under the misapprehension that all of this was really John. The dog. The bohemian apartment. His clothes. John's highlights. Barbara smiled at him. 'I just love it.'

'That's nice,' John replied with an empty smile. He couldn't stand the stuff cluttering up his apartment. He changed the subject. 'How about a cup of tea?'

She grimaced.

'Perhaps you would prefer coffee?'

Barbara shook her head.

'Cocoa?'

The look on her face was still a no, and John was running out of options. 'I might have some herbal infusions around here somewhere.'

'Actually,' said Barbara, 'I'm rather partial to dry white wine.'

John did a double take. It was only nine o'clock in the morning. He shrugged. 'Okay.' John picked out a glass from the sideboard in the lounge. 'A glass of wine it is then.'

Barbara watched John set the single glass down on the coffee table in front of her. She looked up at him. 'Won't you join me?'

'It's a bit early for me.'

John fetched the bottle of white wine from the kitchen. Sylvie bought it over on her last shopping trip. It was still unopened because that was the evening he sent her home and surprised her with a dinner date instead.

John sighed as he reached for the bottle. All that seemed like a distant memory now, even though it was only this time last week they were enjoying each other's company over dinner in a restaurant. He assumed that by now Sylvie would have moved back in with him and everything would be back to normal.

Who would have thought a week later he'd been sitting in his lounge with three dogs and a woman called Barbara?

He looked at the bottle and decided to join her for a drink after all. He fetched another glass wishing he had something stronger than wine, like another bottle of Drambuie.

They sat together on the sofa with a wine glass in hand and the bottle on the coffee table within easy reach.

John was thinking about Sylvie and those wasted theatre tickets when he turned to Barbara, and blurted, 'Are you doing anything tomorrow evening?' And before he knew it, those theatre tickets weren't going to waste after all. Barbara loved musicals and was eager to accompany him to the theatre tomorrow night.

John poured another glass of wine each and Barbara silently toasted her first proper date with the new man in her life.

They both had one too many glasses of wine. John was growing concerned that Barbara would be in no fit state to drive home even if the AA managed to fix her car.

'Now, don't you worry,' said Barbara. 'I'll be fine.'

To John's relief, she had no problems getting up from the sofa and walking down the stairs to the front door. The AA had rung her on her mobile and said they were ten minutes away, just enough time for her to walk back to her car.

John opened the front door.

Barbara stepped outside and turned around. 'Thank you for saving me from an hour of boredom stranded in my car.'

'It was nothing, really.'

'Oh, but it was,' said Barbara, thinking about her invitation to the theatre tomorrow evening. She clasped John by the shoulders, leaned in and kissed him on each cheek, taking him by surprise.

'Oh, er... thank you,' said John awkwardly.

'Don't mention it.' Barbara smiled at her new beau. She was

the one who should thank John for being just the man she was looking for. Barbara glanced down at Tweedledee and decided her naughty dog would get an extra treat this evening for bringing them together.

As Barbara turned to leave, she glanced over his shoulder into the hall catching sight of the door to the other apartment. She wondered what his wife would make of the fact that Barbara had her husband in her sights. Soon-to-be ex-husband, she reminded herself.

John stood in the doorway as she strode down the path with her two dogs trotting along at her heels.

'Nice car, by the way.' She nodded toward John's car parked in the driveway as she passed by. Barbara was opening the front gate when a black taxi drew up outside the house.

John didn't take much notice of the taxi; he was too busy keeping an eye on Barbara to make sure she was walking in a straight line. She seemed perfectly fine, although it concerned him whether she should drive home after consuming several glasses of wine.

Barbara stopped at the gate and waved at him before setting off down the street toward her car, holding an umbrella aloft. It was still drizzling, and John had lent her his umbrella.

Satisfied that she wouldn't need a lift home in his car, John shifted his attention to the black cab idling by the kerb. He spotted Sylvie sitting in the back. She handed the taxi driver her fare, opened the car door and stepped outside. John watched her pause at the front gate and glance down the street in Barbara's direction before heading up the front path towards him.

'Who was that?' asked Sylvie, pointing down the street as she approached John standing in the open doorway.

He was so surprised she'd spoken to him that he just stood there in stunned silence thinking, are you talking to me? They had not spoken since that row over the money. John noticed a slight inflection in her voice when she asked that question. Was that the first stirring of jealousy? Her interest in Barbara brought to mind Dave's plan to win Sylvie back. Perhaps this reverse psychology would work.

Sylvie came to a halt on the doorstep in front of John and folded her arms; she was waiting for an answer.

John decided to play it cool, and answered casually, 'Oh, she's just a friend,' knowing full well that since they married, he didn't have female friends unless they were joint acquaintances. Small wonder Sylvie looked taken aback. Perhaps she was wondering where this new friendship was leading. John hoped so because he was trusting it would lead to Sylvie changing her mind and moving back in with him, on the assumption that if she left it too late, this new friend might become something more. John had no intention of that happening, but Sylvie didn't know that.

Sylvie glanced down the street and turned back to him with a frown, her disapproval evident.

John shrugged acting as though there was nothing wrong with a married man inviting another woman over to his house. Which technically there wasn't if there was no hanky-panky. The idea never crossed his mind. But then Sylvie didn't know that either.

'Aren't you going to come in?' He stepped back and motioned for her to enter the house.

John closed the front door and passed Sylvie in the hall fumbling in her purse for her door key. Out of the corner of his eye, he saw Sylvie glance his way.

As John walked back upstairs, he sensed her lingering in the hall outside her door, watching him. He shut his apartment door without so much as a backward glance. By appearing to do his own thing and ignoring her, John thought he might just win her back. Along the way he would prove to his wife that he had a life too, he had friends, and he could be all the things she wanted him to be, like spontaneous and fun. That would make her think.

John had already decided that he would invite Barbara back to his place again. He wouldn't do it straight after their evening out at the theatre. He didn't want to give the wrong impression that they were out on a date. He wasn't looking for anything more than friendship. He just wanted to invite her round for Sylvie's benefit. The only way around that conundrum was safety in numbers. He wondered if Barbara had a few friends he could invite over too. John thought they could have a few drinks, some music, perhaps a small dinner party...

John smiled. For the first time since falling out with Sylvie over their dire financial situation, he was feeling a sense of optimism again because he had a plan.

33

Sylvie lingered outside her door watching John walk up the stairs and disappear inside his apartment, without so much as a backward glance. She shifted her attention to the front door. Seeing that woman leaving the house only confirmed her suspicions; it left no doubt in her mind that their romantic dinner dates, and the walk along the canal, was all about John trying to get her out of the garden apartment to save his precious house.

It was never about saving their marriage. She knew that for a fact because as soon as his plan backfired, he quickly moved on and found somebody else. Sylvie shook her head in dismay. She couldn't believe, after all these years together, how little she really knew the man upstairs.

Sylvie unlocked the door and stepped inside her apartment, closing the door behind her. She stood there alone and furrowed her brow. Something was missing. With a start, she remembered. 'Alfie!' She was so taken up with finding out about John's new friend that she'd forgotten all about her dog. She hoped John got her message and walked him this morning. However, she didn't want to call on John right now and find out.

She was just debating what to do when a horrible thought

occurred to her: what if something untoward had happened to her puppy? What if he'd run off and John had lost him, or Alfie had run in the road into the path of a car? Or John left him at the dog shelter, convincing the RSPCA she was an irresponsible dog owner for abandoning her pet because she'd left him tied up outside her neighbour's door. Many scenarios were running through her mind – all bad.

In hindsight, she should never have left him with John. He didn't know the first thing about dogs. He didn't even like dogs. She was aware he didn't approve of her having a pet in the house. In fact, she had just given him the perfect opportunity to get rid of her puppy. What if he'd sold Alfie; flogged him at a market for a few quid. After all, he needed the money. Sylvie's heart was racing at the thought of losing her beloved pet all because she'd left him with someone she couldn't trust.

'What have I done?' exclaimed Sylvie rushing to the door, intending to run upstairs and confront John over what had happened to Alfie.

Sylvie flung open her apartment door and stopped abruptly. There in the hall at the bottom of the stairs, with his lead tied to the banister, was Alfie.

'Alfie!' cried Sylvie in relief.

He barked and wagged his tail, jumping up at her as she knelt to give him a cuddle.

'What's this?' she said in surprise, finding a rolled-up piece of paper tucked in his collar.

Alfie sniffed the piece of paper in her hand.

Sylvie recognised the notepaper; it was the one she'd tucked into his dog collar this morning. She unfurled the piece of paper and read the brief message from John. Sylvie glanced upstairs and muttered, 'Very funny.' The original message, *walk me*, was crossed off and ticked, and underneath John had written *feed me*.

Sylvie silently berated herself for letting a wisp of a smile cross her lips as she untied Alfie's lead from the banister. She walked Alfie inside her apartment and closed the door.

Now she had got over the euphoria of discovering that Alfie had not been run over by a car, lost, sold, or otherwise disposed of by her not-so-animal-loving husband, Sylvie stopped to take a good look at her puppy. He had muddy paws, and there were some dead leaves and a small twig matted in his coat. By the looks of things, John hadn't just taken Alfie for a quick walk around the block this morning; Alfie had been to the park.

Sylvie recalled the woman with the dogs she saw leaving the house. She stared at her cute puppy. 'I bet you came in rather handy when John was making new friends.'

Alfie yapped.

'I thought so. Well, never mind that, Alfie. You and I have got some celebrating to do.'

Alfie wagged his tail in response.

'I am now a bona fide writer. Can you believe it?' Sylvie could hardly believe it herself. She waved her first pay-check in front of Alfie, careful that he didn't jump up and nab it. To Sylvie's relief, the informal chat had turned out just that. If it was a proper job interview, it didn't feel like one. The editor, Marcia Hunt, was around her daughter Harriet's age. Marcia was very approachable, very chatty. Sylvie could tell they hit it off as soon as she walked into her office.

During their informal chat, Marcia did most of the talking. She was impressed with Sylvie's article and pleased she chose to write for their magazine. Sylvie could have taken her article almost anywhere – apart from Harriet's magazine – and it would have been snapped up. That's why Marcia was offering more money than she paid the other more experienced freelance writers. It was also a sweetener to encourage her to write more articles for them. Marcia wanted Sylvie to write her own weekly column exclusively for their magazine.

Marcia then asked Sylvie if she wanted the job.

Sylvie had politely replied, 'How could I refuse?'

What they didn't realise was that Sylvie didn't need a sweetener to come on board. She would have accepted the job as a columnist whatever the salary. The money really wasn't the deciding factor; you couldn't put a price on a dream. However, they didn't know that. And under the circumstances, with the mounting bills, the more they were willing to pay the better.

Marcia Hunt seemed almost as anxious that Sylvie would accept the job, as Sylvie was over whether the magazine would offer her one. Marcia felt her column would prove popular with her readers if she continued to write about how her unconventional living arrangement – living apart together – was a recipe for marital bliss.

Marcia had no qualms telling her they were in stiff competition with a rival magazine which she wouldn't mention by name. Sylvie already guessed it was the magazine Harriet worked for. Marcia thought Sylvie's new weekly column might well turn their fortunes around.

Sylvie couldn't guarantee that. But when she discovered what they would pay her to write a weekly column, she felt confident that it would turn her own fortunes around. Sylvie was shocked to discover that for one article, they would pay her what she used to earn working in her secretarial job for an entire month. In the space of one day, her income had gone from zero to four times what she was earning in her old job. And she was getting paid to do something she loved. Sylvie couldn't believe her luck.

She still had the cheque in her hand. She had to curb the impulse to bank the money and treat herself to something special to celebrate. She couldn't do that because the money was earmarked for the electricity bill. It would take a few weeks of work, at least, to clear the outstanding bills and debt repayments. That was without the additional loan John had taken out and the re-mortgage he'd neglected to mention.

Sylvie found out about the re-mortgage when yet another reminder letter arrived, this time from the bank. When she opened it this morning, to Sylvie's horror, she discovered John hadn't been keeping up with the repayments on the house. It turned out that he wasn't exaggerating when he said they could lose the roof over their heads.

Sylvie didn't know how she kept it together and put her personal problems to one side during her meeting with Marcia this morning, but she did, and her professionalism paid off. She had a cheque in her hand and a monthly salary to look forward to, thanks to Marcia who had given an unknown writer an opportunity of a lifetime.

Sylvie looked at the cheque and sighed. She had visions of packing a suitcase, taking her laptop, and going off to rent a cottage somewhere by the sea to sit and write her weekly column; but that, like her article, was pure fantasy. After paying the bills, she was lucky if she had the taxi fare to work, let alone the money for a busman's holiday.

Sylvie tucked the cheque in her purse and walked down to the kitchen to put the kettle on and feed Alfie. As she gathered up his bowl and poured out some puppy food, her thoughts returned to the informal chat with Marcia.

After a brief discussion about what they felt was attracting people to her blog, Sylvie realised she had a responsibility to her editor, to the magazine, and to her readers to keep writing the fairy-tale romance that was no longer her life. Sylvie had crossed the line from fact to fiction, and there was no going back. Not if she wanted to keep her new job. She couldn't afford to get found out. So, when she was offered the weekly column, she had one stipulation before she accepted: she wanted to continue writing under a pseudonym.

Sylvie had a further reason to protect her anonymity. Harriet often said that when it came to journalism, it was a small world in which everyone seemed to know everyone else. The last thing she wanted was for anyone to find out that Harriet's mum was working for a rival magazine, especially Harriet. She didn't want her new writing career ruined before it had barely got off the ground.

What would Marcia think if she found out her new writing protégé was just a magazine editor's mum and former secretary, whose marriage was going down the pan, and who desperately needed money? This was not the impression or information she wanted to convey. She wanted to be taken seriously in her new career as a writer. Although Sylvie didn't really think Marcia would take that attitude, she didn't want to risk telling her the truth and finding out the hard way she'd been wrong about her new boss.

Marcia agreed to her stipulation when Sylvie asked for anonymity; as far as she was concerned, there were enough celebrity writers out there. She told Sylvie that it made a refreshing change to find somebody for whom writing wasn't an ego trip all about seeing their name in print.

Sylvie agreed with that statement knowing, in her case, that wasn't exactly true. Sylvie *did* want to see her name in print – what writer didn't? However, for the time being, Sylvie was content with her decision.

Marcia thought it would lend an air of mystery to the new column if they tied it in with her anonymous blog and called it *Love on the Rooftop*. Sylvie agreed it was an excellent idea until Marcia asked her where she'd found the inspiration for the name of her blog. That was the only part of their informal chat where Sylvie clammed up. She didn't take offence when Sylvie declined to answer that question. Marcia was already anticipating the day when she and her readers could look forward to Sylvie unravelling that little mystery.

Sylvie smiled nervously, praying it didn't all unravel before she got on top of their dire financial situation first.

The phone rang while Sylvie was making herself some lunch. She knew who it was before she answered the phone. 'Hello, Julia. Before you ask, yes I got the job.'

'You don't sound too happy about it,' remarked Julia.

Sylvie had doubts over the fact that her blog and her column were built on a lie. What if someone found out the truth and unmasked the writer of *Love on the Rooftop* as a fraud? Living apart together hadn't brought them marital bliss as she would have people believe – far from it. It had driven them further apart.

'I've got an idea, Sylvie. Why don't I fix you up on another date?' said Julia down the phone. 'That'll cheer you up.'

Sylvie doubted that. A new relationship was farthest from her mind now. If she were honest, she wouldn't say no to some romance in her life. She was enjoying herself with the new romantic John until she found out he had an ulterior motive. Sylvie felt it was too soon after John dumped her for another woman – somebody with expensive designer clothes and two little white dogs – to even contemplate getting involved with someone else. Besides, she had too much going on, what with the blog and her new job as a columnist.

Sylvie declined Julia's offer to play matchmaker. 'Didn't you say that if I followed my dreams, I might meet the person I was meant to spend the rest of my life with?'

'You're absolutely right. I did say that, didn't I,' mused Julia.

'Perhaps I'll find that special someone through my new career as a writer?' Sylvie was thinking about whom she might meet in her new job. Next week, Marcia would introduce her to the other writers who worked for the magazine. Although Sylvie would mostly work from home, they asked her to come into the office once a week in order to attend the editorial meetings.

If her column took off, Marcia warned her she might find she was spending more time in the office, as opposed to working from home, answering fan mail. Marcia hoped that wouldn't be a problem. Sylvie was more than happy to do that. She didn't have any responsibilities. She had all the time in the world to devote to her new career.

Although her first day in the office wasn't until next Tuesday, Sylvie wanted to make sure she was prepared. She didn't mean to cut the phone conversation short, but she knew Julia would understand.

'Of course I understand, darling. Now you're a hot-shot

journalist you haven't got time for your boring retired friends.'

'Oh Julia, I didn't mean—'

'Ha ha ha. That was a joke.'

Sylvie smiled. Before she put the phone down, she promised to keep in touch.

The first thing she did when she got off the phone was switch on her laptop. She wanted to do some research on the internet and find some topical issues to raise during the team meeting next week. She knew Marcia wasn't expecting her to participate; rather, it was an opportunity to listen to the team and get a feel for what their magazine was all about. Even so, Sylvie wanted to make a good first impression by attending the meeting prepared.

Sylvie was glad she'd started her research early because, before she knew it, the day of the editorial meeting had almost arrived. Sylvie ordered a taxi to pick her up outside the house at seven o'clock sharp the following day. She had already laid out what she intended to wear to work. During her first visit to the magazine's offices, she'd made a note of the dress code. All the staff writers dressed in office attire and were smart in appearance.

Sylvie spent the next few days sorting out her wardrobe. She filled four bin liners of the clothes she used to wear in her secretarial job. There were comfortable cardigans, knitted skirts, old polo necks she'd had for years, an assortment of blouses and several pairs of sensible shoes. It was all in excellent condition. Sylvie didn't feel guilty about getting rid of those clothes. They would have gone eventually because she discovered they no longer fitted.

Sylvie had lost weight, most notably around her thighs. It was the unexpected upside of owning a dog; for once in her life, she was doing some exercise, every day, come rain or shine. She was eating a lot less too. Sylvie was no longer cooking for two and sitting down to eat with John, matching his portion sizes. Her diet had changed considerably. She used to prepare large evening meals. Now she was content to sit down in the evenings with a salad or a bowl of soup, or even a small dish of pasta. She'd also discovered the health benefits of eating fish – John didn't like fish – and almost banished meat from her diet entirely. She was pleased that she had shed weight along with her old wardrobe.

Sylvie intended to deposit the four bin liners, full of clothes, in the wheelie bin outside their house. However, on her way out she caught sight of John's car keys on the sideboard in the communal hall. A quick trip in the car to the local charity shop, where she used to volunteer, got rid of her old clothes. On her way home, Sylvie made a detour. On the spur of the moment, she drove to the Bluewater shopping mall. It was a twenty-mile car ride away, and she didn't get home until late, but it was worth the trip. Sylvie came home with a new wardrobe to suit her new career, along with a new credit card.

Although Julia had bought her a new outfit for her interview, she could hardly expect Julia to buy her a whole new wardrobe. Besides, now she had a job, she could afford to pay off the card. When Sylvie was signing up for her first ever credit card, it made her wonder where John found the money to buy all those new designer clothes he'd purchased on his shopping trip with Chloe.

Sylvie didn't want to think about what other debts John was hiding from her. Instead, she took another look at the outfit she had chosen to wear to work tomorrow. She wanted to make sure she fitted in. She would be nervous enough as it was, meeting all her new colleagues, without dressing inappropriately and standing out like a sore thumb. Sylvie smiled. The shopping trip had paid off. At least that was one less thing to worry about.

Now all she had to worry about was the editorial meeting tomorrow. Sylvie reminded herself that she must try not to feel intimidated when she walked into a room full of writers. After all, she was one of them now. Her next weekly column was submitted and well-received. And Sylvie's research had paid off; she could confidently present some interesting topics if called upon during her first editorial meeting.

Still nervous about tomorrow, Sylvie glanced at the time. She had no intention of jeopardising her new career by walking into her first meeting tomorrow morning bleary-eyed because she stayed up late. She decided an early night was in order. It would give her ample time to toss and turn and fret over her first day, and who she was meeting, and what they would think of the newest member of the team.

Sylvie got in bed and switched on her reading lamp. She thought of John upstairs doing the same. Although Sylvie was a night-owl and had to force herself to get an early night, her husband was not. His bedtime routine never wavered. She glanced up at the ceiling.

He would be sitting in bed right about now, reading glasses perched on the bridge of his nose, book in hand having a quiet read before lights out. It was on this occasion, when Sylvie needed her beauty sleep, that she realised she had the perfect neighbour. Or so she thought.

Sylvie had just put her book down and switched off the light when she was startled by the sound of loud music. She sat up in bed in the dark. It took her a moment to comprehend that the music was coming from upstairs. Sylvie waited for John to turn it off. She assumed he must have switched on his Hi-Fi system by mistake. John enjoyed listening to Classic FM. It was early evening when Sylvie heard the radio faintly through the ceiling while he pottered about in his kitchen, preparing himself some dinner. She glanced at the time. It was well past his dinner time, besides which that didn't sound like Classic FM on the radio. Sylvie waited and waited, but he didn't switch it off.

'What is going on up there?' Sylvie clambered out of bed, grabbed her dressing gown, and stormed out of the bedroom. She hurried along the inner hallway into the lounge. She glanced up at the ceiling in surprise. The music was now directly above her, and it was deafening.

Sylvie reached the door to her apartment, intending to march upstairs and have words with John about the noise. But when she opened her door, she was met by several strangers milling around in the communal hall outside. She shut her door before anyone saw her standing in the doorway in nothing but her nightie and dressing gown. Who were those people? Did John have company? Sylvie glanced at the clock on the mantel shelf. It was almost nine o'clock. She furrowed her brow. Why was he having visitors at this time of night? And why was there loud music on upstairs?

'Oh no!' exclaimed Sylvie in dismay. Was he having a party? She shook her head. That made little sense. Since when did her husband like parties with loud music? And it wasn't even the weekend; since when did anybody have a party on a Monday night, for heaven's sake! What would the neighbours think? Sylvie recalled the party she'd hosted in her apartment a few weeks ago, soon after she moved downstairs. The party had been on a Saturday night, and she had the decency to invite her next-door neighbours. And inform John.

Sylvie put her hands over her ears to blot out the noise. It *was* a party! This was outrageous. 'I'm not putting up with this!' Sylvie shouted at the ceiling. She had an important day at work tomorrow; she needed a good night's sleep.

'Oh no,' exclaimed John in dismay. He couldn't believe how many people had arrived and how quickly the party had got out of hand. John didn't realise that Barbara had so many friends. Any thoughts of a dignified dinner party evaporated as soon as Barbara arrived with her entourage. She also brought along her own CD collection which she started playing at full volume on John's mini Hi-Fi system.

He put his hands over his ears to blot out the noise. This was outrageous. This was not what he planned. He assumed it would be a civilised affair not a full-blown rave with loud disco music. It reminded him of the housewarming party Julia had thrown in Sylvie's apartment downstairs soon after she moved in.

Several shots of Tequila did nothing to dispel his anxieties. John was worried about the noise and what the neighbours would think. He was worried about getting nibbles trodden into his carpet. He was worried about wine stains on his sofa as he hastily covered it up with a throw. In short, he was not enjoying himself one bit until he heard Sylvie knocking at the door.

John, wine glass in hand, tottered over to the door. He realised he'd had one too many when it seemed to take forever to grasp the door handle.

He got the door open eventually and was rewarded by his wife standing there, proving the plan was working like clockwork.

'What is going on?' asked Sylvie, peering into his apartment.

As if on cue, Barbara appeared. She draped an arm around John's shoulder.

John did his level best not to act surprised. He said to Sylvie, slurring his words, 'I'm having a party, do you mind not interfering?' John gulped down another shot of Tequila. He raised his empty glass and, in the spirit of Dave's plan, told Sylvie, 'You're not invited,' before slamming the door shut.

'Well, I never!' said Sylvie, stunned.

34

The taxi was late. Sylvie was standing on the front doorstep anxiously checking her watch. She yawned. It was Sylvie's first day in her new job, and she'd had a terrible night. The party upstairs finally wound down in the early hours, giving her the chance for a few precious hours of sleep before the alarm clock sounded. However, by then she couldn't get tomorrow out of her mind. She lay awake worrying about what else would go wrong on her first day. One scenario that hadn't occurred to her was that the taxi might not turn up.

Sylvie eyed John's car. She could drive to work. The problem was the car key wasn't in the dish on the sideboard in the hall. She'd have to call on John upstairs to get it. Sylvie didn't fancy the door slammed in her face again. Even if John handed over the car keys, Sylvie envisaged problems finding a parking space in central London. If she took the car, she would be late for her first day at work.

She glanced down the street. There was still no sign of the taxi. She looked at her watch and tried to remain calm. She nervously adjusted her jacket. Sylvie had taken care over her appearance this morning to look professional. She was wearing a simple brown trouser suit, cream shirt, and new shoes with four-inch heels to add height and a little gravitas to her five-foot-nothing frame. She was holding a new briefcase. Inside was a typed copy of her next column and a notepad with some ideas she had written for the editorial meeting.

Sylvie was not feeling as confident as she looked. At the forefront of her mind was the fact that a lot was riding on keeping this job. It didn't help that she had to take out her first credit card in order to buy some new outfits for work. After all this effort the last thing she wanted to do was make a bad first impression by turning up late to the meeting. She could not afford to lose this job.

And then to add to her growing list of woes, Sylvie's next-door neighbour opened his front door to collect a pint of milk from his doorstep, and spotted Sylvie. He forgot about the milk in an instant and came storming up the front path to confront her about the party last night.

Sylvie cast an angry glance up at John's apartment window as she apologised to her neighbour for her husband's behaviour last night, promising it would never happen again.

This was the same neighbour who told them that he didn't want their house converted into two apartments. He didn't like the idea of living next door to tenants. Now he was pressing Sylvie and John to move out of the house altogether and find tenants for both apartments. He made no bones about the fact that he'd changed his mind and thought tenants would make far better neighbours than them.

'To be frank,' said Sylvie's neighbour, 'since the house conversion, you two have turned into the neighbours from hell.'

Sylvie glared at him. She could do without this sort of

aggravation before she left for work. She held her tongue. He was confrontational enough as it was. She didn't want to say anything more that might stoke the fire. Instead, she glanced at her watch and looked down the street while her neighbour went on and on, listing all his grievances until the taxi arrived.

'Look, I'm sorry,' said Sylvie, when in fact the more he went on, the less apologetic she began to feel. She had invited him to her party, and he came along and enjoyed himself, drinking her booze and eating her party nibbles. He didn't have any complaints then. It wasn't her fault that John had held a party on Monday night without informing the neighbours.

'I'll have words with John,' said Sylvie, trying to brush him off. 'I have to go now. My taxi has arrived.'

Sylvie had no intention of confronting John again, not after last night. Besides, she had a feeling the party was just tit-for-tat; she had her party, so he was having his. He was just proving a point. She could guarantee there wouldn't be another one upstairs, especially when John woke up to the aftermath. She smiled at the thought. She would love to be a fly on the wall when he saw the state of his apartment. Sylvie's smile widened – served him right.

'Where to, luv?'

Sylvie sat down in the back of the black taxi and gave the cabbie the address.

'Off to work?' said the taxi driver, making conversation.

'Yes, I am,' replied Sylvie, a protective hand on the new leather briefcase sitting on her lap.

'What do you do for a living, if you don't mind me asking?'

Sylvie didn't mind him asking at all. 'I'm a columnist for a magazine.'

'You're a writer.' The taxi driver glanced at Sylvie in his rear-view mirror.

Sylvie smiled. It was special to hear someone say the words: *you're a writer,* if she wasn't late on her first day and didn't hear the words: *you're fired.* Sylvie's smile faded. She glanced at her watch. 'You wouldn't mind if I ask you to step on it? I have to be in a meeting in—'

'Don't you worry, Luv. I'll get you to the meeting on time.'

As the taxi sped off down the street, Sylvie sat back in her seat and yawned. She hoped she didn't do that in the team meeting. That would give the wrong impression. Her thoughts drifted back to that blasted party last night. At least there was one consolation; it was called the morning after the night before. Sylvie would never forget the state of the garden apartment after her party, with food trodden into her new rug and wine spilt on her new couch. Someone had even been sick in her bathroom. *Ugh.* Sylvie didn't want to think about it. But she did rather hope that John was in for the same experience. At least it would put a stop to any more parties upstairs.

With that thought, Sylvie put the events of last night to the back of her mind and turned her attention to the forthcoming meeting. She slipped on her glasses, opened the briefcase, found a pen and switched to a blank page in her notebook. She had just thought of another topic worthy of consideration: noisy neighbours. She had no shortage of topical issues to raise in the meeting, and she discovered she didn't even need to do any research to find a good proportion of her ideas. They were right on her doorstep – or specifically, upstairs.

By the time the taxi pulled up outside the office building, she had another page of topical issues to present in the meeting – all thanks to John. Sylvie smiled as she closed her notebook and thought how apt that she had this notebook, considering John was in her black books. The words *Little Black Book* were etched on the front.

Julia bought her the notebook as a gift to celebrate the start of her friend's new adventure as a writer. Sylvie knew what she was up to. It wasn't just any notebook. Everyone knew what a little black book was really for. Julia wanted Sylvie to find *the one*.

So far, she had not used the notebook as intended. It only had one name recorded in it: her nuisance neighbour upstairs. However, there were still plenty of pages left. As she put the little black book back in her briefcase, Sylvie was thinking about who she might meet in her new life as a writer.

Although she couldn't really afford it, she gave the taxi driver a generous tip for getting her to work on time. 'It's my first day,' she said as she handed him the cash.

'Looking like that, I'm sure you will knock 'em dead.'

Sylvie smiled at the compliment. 'Oh, I intend to.'

She walked into the office building wearing her designer suit, with her new briefcase in one hand and a large disposable cup of strong black coffee in the other. Sylvie felt as confident as she looked. She caught sight of her reflection in the glass door, as she stepped into the lift, and saw a woman who was going places. Sylvie had a lifetime of ambitions to fulfil, and this was just the beginning. In that moment, she knew there was no going back.

35

'Never again.' John was nursing a hangover the like of which he had never experienced before. However, it wasn't the hangover that put him off hosting another party in his apartment; it was the scenes of complete devastation that he'd discovered when he woke up. It was post-apocalypse at number 67b Penfold Street, and it reminded him of what he'd seen in Sylvie's apartment the morning after her party.

'We should do this again,' said one of Barbara's friends. 'The party was totally awesome, man.'

John stared at him. Did he realise how ridiculous that sounded coming from a man of sixty-odd? Had he forgotten what decade he was in? John shook his head and continued doing a circuit of his flat, taking in the mess, estimating how long the clean-up exercise would take. He seemed to step over inert bodies everywhere he went. Quite a few of Barbara's friends had stayed behind after the party finally wound down in the early hours. They'd slept on his couch, on the floor under his throws, and in his spare bedroom. He even found one sitting in the chair in the study, his head resting on John's desk. He was snoring.

John wanted them all to bugger off, so he could tidy up.

However, Barbara and her friends insisted that he go back upstairs and take a shower, clean himself up, or pop back to bed. In the meantime, they would sort it all out.

John didn't want anybody sorting out his apartment. But with ten against one, the odds were not stacked in his favour. He left them to it. Upstairs, John didn't waste any time; he showered, shaved and dressed as quickly as possible and reappeared thirty minutes later hoping to mitigate any further damage they might do.

When John ventured downstairs, afraid of what he might find, to his complete surprise he discovered that the flat was spotless. He saw Barbara in his kitchen cooking breakfast.

'Where did they all go?' John frowned. And more to the point, why was Barbara wearing his dressing gown? Although he'd woken up in his bed alone, he was having a problem recalling the events of last night. He rubbed his forehead; a headache was pulsing through his temples.

Barbara turned over a rasher of bacon in the frying pan and glanced at John. 'We should do this again. Let's throw another party.'

He looked around his spotless kitchen and shrugged. 'Yes, why not.' If this was the aftermath of the parties, he could live with that. The empty cans of lager, beer bottles, crisp packets, and other assorted debris were all gone. The kitchen looked clean and tidy. He glanced in the lounge and that was spotless too. John put his foot on the pedal bin and discovered a new bin liner inside; somebody had even taken the rubbish on their way out.

John was impressed. Unlike the aftermath of Sylvie's party, when he'd cleared up the back garden himself because her so-called friends wouldn't lift a finger to help, Barbara and her friends had cleaned, vacuumed and dusted – the works. John noticed they had even moved the furniture back into place, straightened his cushions and folded his throws.

'How about next week?' asked Barbara as she dished up the bacon, scrambled eggs and fried bread on to two plates. She brought them over to the kitchen table.

John sat down at the table. He thought about his visit to Dave's house when his brother advised him not to worry about his financial situation. All he had to do was do nothing. Sylvie would soon get the message that their financial predicament wasn't just his responsibility. John was aware he only had himself to blame for underestimating the cost of the conversion. But Dave was right: Sylvie played a part too by stubbornly refusing to move out of the garden apartment and let him finish the plan to rent it out. They were both living under the same roof; why should he be the one shouldering all the worry over the bills and the money?

John decided there and then he wasn't moving downstairs. He would take a leaf out of Sylvie's book, dig his heels in and stubbornly refuse to leave his apartment. Take one for the team? What team? They were just two individuals, living apart together, refusing to take responsibility for the situation they found themselves in. Sylvie had had her fun downstairs. Now it was her turn to worry about the money while he showed his wife how spontaneous and fun her husband could really be.

John looked across the table at Barbara. 'Okay, let's organise another party.' He glanced around his spotless apartment. 'Shall we say... same time, same place?'

Barbara nodded her head. 'That's settled then. Monday night. Your place.'

She picked up her knife and fork and smiled at John. 'Isn't it such fun reliving our youth?'

He offered a weak smile in return. John's youth comprised studying hard for his accountancy exams, saving up for his first house, and making sure he could provide for his young family. He wasn't sure he would class that as fun, although he had an idea that's not what Barbara was referring to when she talked about reliving their youth.

John's youth wasn't one long party. All that Swinging Sixties hoopla seemed to pass him by. He wasn't sorry. That was never really his thing. And these parties weren't his thing either. It was just a means to an end. A way to prove to Sylvie that he had changed and he could give her all the things she said she wanted out of a relationship, like spontaneity and surprises. He bet the party last night was a surprise. He hoped she was getting the message and feeling a little jealous into the bargain.

Barbara was busy eating her breakfast. She paused for a moment, and said, 'Last night, your wife looked a bit... upset.'

John was cutting the rind off his fried bacon when he stopped and looked up. 'Sylvie came to the party last night?' John raised an eyebrow. That was news to him.

'Well, not exactly. To be honest, she looked a bit surprised that you were having one.' Barbara studied him thoughtfully. 'You told her about the party, didn't you?'

'No, why should I?' John was rather pleased to discover he *had* surprised her. That was the whole point of the party, even though he wasn't exactly himself in the process. At least Barbara and her friends were respectful enough of his home to leave it as they found it, which was more than could be said for Julia and her hoard of miscreants. He recalled Sylvie's party and the state of her apartment the following day when nobody bothered to stay behind and clear up afterwards. Barbara and her friends were different. John had no qualms about hosting another party, especially since he found out that Sylvie paid him a visit last night. He only wished he could remember what passed between them.

Talk about *déjà vu* thought John. Barbara was in his kitchen, cooking an English breakfast, the morning after yet another party. And she was wearing his dressing gown again. John always woke up in bed alone. Despite being blind drunk the night before, he was positive that nothing of an intimate nature had taken place between them – at least he hoped not.

This morning John was nursing a hangover the like of which he'd experienced before, just last week, and the week before that – ad infinitum. It was the same day on a different week, and John had lost count of the number of parties he'd hosted in his apartment.

It had become such a regular haunt for Barbara and her friends on a Monday night that they called it Studio 67. The name didn't have quite the same ring to it as that infamous New York nightclub back in the seventies, but John got the inference. And he wasn't happy about it. Less so when he noticed a lacklustre attempt at clearing up afterwards.

The more parties he had, the less they cleared up the following morning, until Barbara's friends – including Barbara herself – made no attempt to leave his place anything like they'd found it. It was looking a lot like he remembered Sylvie's flat in the aftermath of her seventies-themed party – only worse. John had given up making any effort to clean up. It seemed pointless because before he knew it, it was Monday night again and Club 67 was in full swing.

John sat down at the table with his plate of bacon, sausages, eggs and fried bread, and had a question for Barbara, 'Why don't you or your friends ever invite me to a party at one of your homes?'

Barbara looked at John and burst out laughing.

He stared at her across the table wondering what was so funny.

'Oh John, what a silly question.'

John didn't think so.

Barbara was tucking into her breakfast when she realised he was still waiting for an answer. 'I thought it was obvious. We have neighbours…'

He looked at her askance. 'I have neighbours too, you know.'

'Yes, but most of my friends couldn't throw house parties even if they wanted to. You see, your place is different. It's a bachelor pad. Your place doesn't have—' Barbara stopped abruptly. She lowered her eyes and stared at her plate.

'I see.' John was getting the picture. His place didn't have a wife around to put a stop to the fun. John *had* a wife at home; they just lived apart. But he wasn't about to split hairs over the finer details of their unusual living arrangements. After the first party some weeks ago, from what little John could remember, Sylvie had not made another trip upstairs on Monday night.

Was she ignoring him? Or was she put out that she hadn't received an invitation? Perhaps Barbara was right: he should have at least told her about the parties. After all, Sylvie asked him to come to hers. John decided that's what he should do – invite her to the next one.

'You're not going to stop the parties, are you?'

John considered this while he polished off his English breakfast. 'No, I'm not. In fact, I think I'll invite Sylvie to the next one.'

'Oh,' Barbara peered at him, 'you don't remember.'

'Don't remember what?'

'Last night? I think you left a message on Sylvie's answerphone inviting her to Club 67 next week.'

'I did?' John didn't remember that at all. But then again, he was drinking heavily at each party. Last night was no exception. This morning, despite eating a hearty breakfast, he was still feeling the worse for wear. No wonder he couldn't remember anything.

John scratched his chin and felt a day's worth of stubble. This morning he hadn't even showered and cleaned himself up like he usually did before breakfast. On waking, he discovered that he must have fallen into bed in a drunken stupor last night because he hadn't even bothered to change into his pyjamas. He shook his head. He was still wearing the same clothes he slept in.

John finished eating some fried bread and wiped his greasy fingers down the front of his crumpled designer shirt. He looked down and wondered if the greasy finger-marks would come out in the wash. He didn't much care. John sighed. He felt like crap. He looked like crap. John wanted to crawl back into bed with his clothes on.

'I think I will lie down.' He rose from the table and staggered out of the kitchen. He made it as far as the sofa in the lounge. The hot food in his belly made him dog-tired.

'Do you want me to do some clearing up?' Barbara asked half-heartedly.

His apartment looked like a tip, but John was just too wasted to care. 'No, don't bother.' John waved that suggestion away with a flick of his hand as he lay down on the sofa. He tucked a cushion behind his head and used a throw as a make-shift blanket, pulling it up and tucking it under his chin.

John was already fast asleep in the time it took Barbara to gather her things and leave.

36

Sylvie was loading the dishwasher with her breakfast dishes when she noticed the red light blinking on her answerphone. She shut the dishwasher door and walked over to the phone on the kitchen worktop. She pressed the button to play the message. It was John. Sylvie could hear loud music playing in the background and John's voice barely audible over the din. He was drunk because he kept slurring his words. She could hardly make out what he was saying, but she got the gist; John was inviting her to another one of his parties.

Sylvie grimaced and glanced up at the ceiling in disgust. This was intolerable. She was busier than ever with work; she didn't have time for parties or another disturbed night's sleep. When Sylvie wasn't updating her blog, writing her weekly column, or researching the next topical issue to bring up at the editorial meeting, she was spending an increasing amount of time at the office answering fan mail.

Because of all the letters asking for relationship advice, Sylvie had become the magazine's new agony aunt and advice columnist. A radio show invited her to appear on their programme. However, whilst Sylvie was busy with work, taking

Julia's advice to accept every opportunity that came her way, John was doing nothing about sorting out their financial situation.

Sylvie remembered the first party upstairs when she was under the misapprehension it was just a one-off. Imagine her surprise the following Monday evening; Sylvie was tucked up in bed, looking forward to the editorial meeting the next day, when the music started. She thought it was her imagination until the doorbell rang and she heard people in the communal hall outside her apartment.

This happened the following Monday night and the Monday after that. She'd lost count of how many disturbed nights the parties caused over the last few weeks. Sylvie now dreaded Mondays. She did her utmost to ignore what was going on upstairs, hoping John would grow tired of these games. She knew what he was up to but refused to compromise so he could rent out one apartment, and now he was playing up like a spoilt child who didn't get their own way. She shook her head at the answerphone. When would he grow up and start acting his age?

Sylvie replayed the phone message, her hackles rising at the thought of yet another party. She couldn't believe John had the cheek to invite her to one after all these weeks of misery. This was the final straw. She didn't know how much longer she could put up with the loud music, the people coming and going at all hours, and the sleepless Monday nights.

She couldn't fail to see the irony of the situation. If this didn't stop, John would get what he wanted because it would force her to move out of her apartment. Only last night Sylvie lay awake listening to the thumping disco music, debating whether to pack an overnight bag and pay an extortionate sum of money to check into a London hotel for a decent night's sleep.

In the event, she didn't. But she wished she had.

Now she had another party to contend with, another sleepless night to look forward to, and another deliberation over whether to book a hotel room for the night. She wondered how long she could keep this up without being forced to move out of this house, and away from her husband, for good.

Sylvie glared at the phone as John's slurred monologue continued. He was driving her mental.

'This has got to stop!' Sylvie banged her fist down on the answerphone, cutting John off in mid-slur. After getting hardly any sleep last night, and with a full schedule at work to get through today, she couldn't stand it any longer. She finally flipped.

In his dream, somebody kept nudging his arm and calling his name. John started to rouse. Still groggy with sleep, he muttered, 'It's all right, Babs. I'll just lie here for a little while longer.'

'Who's Babs?'

His eyes shot open. That wasn't Barbara standing beside the sofa looking down at him, hands on hips.

John's first thought was that Sylvie did not look happy. His second thought was how fetching she looked in her smart grey trouser suit. Had she lost weight? He rubbed his eyes and pulled himself up to a seated position under Sylvie's watchful gaze. He offered her a tentative smile.

Sylvie did not return his smile. Instead, she just stood there watching him without saying a word.

John found it a tad unnerving. Perhaps she'd listened to his telephone message and popped up to tell him she would come to his next party? John peered up at her under his bushy eyebrows.

By the expression on her face, he didn't think that was it. What John thought was that he was in for a right telling off. He dropped his gaze and studied his fingernails.

Sylvie finally raised her finger – and her voice. 'This has got to stop!' She wagged her finger at him. 'No more parties. No more late nights. I mean it, John.' She looked him over. 'Just look at you!'

John looked down at clothes and tried to tuck his shirt back into his trousers.

'You've changed, John Baxter.'

'Have I?' He looked up at her in surprise. This was precisely what he wanted to hear.

Sylvie shook her head in disgust. 'I never thought I'd see the day...' she trailed off and gazed around his apartment before her eyes settled on John. 'You're a slob, John Baxter.'

'A what?' John's mouth dropped open. 'What did you call me?' He never thought he'd see the day when his wife called him a slob; he almost needed to hear it again just to be sure.

'Do I need to repeat myself?'

John shook his head and mouthed *no*. He stole a glance at Sylvie. He knew what he must look like with a day's worth of stubble and wearing crumpled clothes he'd slept in. His apartment looked like a disaster zone. And he knew, with all the booze he'd consumed over the last few weeks, he was putting on weight too. She was right. It was true. John realised too late he had turned into the antithesis of John Baxter. He was, without doubt, a slob.

John groaned. What had these so-called friends done to him? What had he done to himself? This wasn't the impression he was trying to make. It wasn't his intention that Sylvie saw him looking like this after all the trouble he had gone to, to make himself more attractive by buying new clothes and joining the gym. Not to mention the money he'd spent – all of it on credit.

Sylvie hadn't finished her rant. 'I know what this is all about. You're playing up because you didn't get your own way.'

'No, Sylvie, that's not it at all. I was showing you I can have fun, that I've changed.'

'Oh, you've changed all right,' Sylvie's voice was full of contempt. 'Just look at this place!'

John followed her gaze around his lounge and winced at the state of it, wondering how much longer he could keep this up. John realised he was sliding into the abyss. The parties had all too quickly become a permanent fixture at his apartment. After going all out in the pursuit of fun at Studio 67, John seemed to spend the rest of the week trying to recover from his Monday night bender. He put it down to a mixture of alcohol, getting to bed far too late which did not suit his constitution, and his age. He was no spring chicken, and these parties were taking their toll.

Most days John felt too tired to do anything constructive, even tidy up his apartment. The clean-up manoeuvre after the first party, John came to realise, was just a gesture, and that too trailed off. Now it was left to him, and he was just too weary to care. After several weeks of parties, his flat was almost unrecognisable; it now resembled student digs. John's clean and tidy bachelor pad, along with his meticulously ordered and planned life, was now a thing of the past.

Over the last few weeks, he kept reminding himself this was all for a good cause – to get Sylvie back – but John had known for some time that he'd lost his sense of purpose. The plan Dave gave him was total crap. He didn't know why he'd listened to his brother in the first place; he wasn't an expert when it came to relationships.

After paying his brother a visit at home when Dave was off work sick, John picked up on the tense atmosphere between Dave and his wife, Linda. It would never surprise him if Dave phoned to tell him that Linda had moved into their spare bedroom. There goes Plan B thought John miserably. He hoped Linda hadn't moved into the spare bedroom, as he suspected, just in case he still needed Plan B. John didn't want to move in with Dave in order to rent out his apartment, but that wasn't his decision to make. John stole a glance at Sylvie wondering if she'd take pity on him and call time on all this nonsense.

Sylvie stood there, hands on hips, staring around the room and shaking her head in disbelief.

John felt his face reddening with embarrassment. Sylvie's visit this morning was the proverbial boot up the backside. She was right: the parties, the late nights, and the booze had to stop.

She had given him a piece of her mind, voicing all the things that he already thought about himself. He'd changed all right. And neither he nor Sylvie recognised the person he had become. A person who threw parties, drank too much, fell into bed at all hours, wore expensive designer clothes, and spent a disproportionate amount of time and money at the hairdressing salon when it was not that long ago that he forked out a princely fiver down the local barbers. And then there was the dog, Alfie, who he seemed to spend an inordinate amount of time with, when it wasn't even his dog. Last time he checked, he didn't even like dogs.

That was now a regular occurrence, finding Alfie outside his apartment door with a note saying, *walk me*. Every morning, before he sat down for breakfast, John always poked his head outside his apartment door to see if Alfie was there. Tuesday mornings were the exception; Sylvie must have realised he would be hung-over. John even bought dog food so now they had breakfast together. He returned the dog each evening, leaving Alfie outside her apartment door with the lead tied to the banister and a little note saying, *feed me.*

Sylvie seemed increasingly busy these past few weeks, too busy to even walk her own dog. But not too busy to find the time to march upstairs and give him a piece of her mind. What Sylvie didn't realise was that she wasn't the only one who was sick and tired of Monday nights.

John despaired how much longer he could keep this up. Barbara was getting ever more amorous, their relationship entering serious territory. Only this morning she'd broached the idea of moving in together. John almost choked on his toast. He had no idea things had gone that far. He was mightily relieved to discover that nothing ever happened between them at Club 67. According to her friends, Barbara always got drunk and passed out in the spare bedroom. It was still a mystery how she came to be wearing his dressing gown on Tuesday mornings, but John was not bothered about that. What bothered him were the parties.

The parties had moved up a notch from amber alert, which meant they were getting on his nerves, to red alert which signalled he'd had enough. He'd had enough of Barbara. He'd had enough of her friends. And by god, he'd had enough of Club 67. And frankly he'd had enough of himself. It made him wonder if that message he'd left on Sylvie's answerphone last night was a subconscious cry for help; an SOS hoping she would come to his rescue.

John suddenly had a moment of clarity. He shook his head in disbelief at the fool he'd been. In contrast to his wife, who seemed to have got her life together without him, all John's focus of attention was on Sylvie and getting her back. Nothing worked. Perhaps there was a simple reason for that. No matter what plan he thought up. No matter what lengths he went to. It was all for nothing if she'd already moved on with her life. At no time was that more apparent than the moment he awoke to find her looking down on him as he lay depleted on the sofa.

John stared at his wife as if seeing her for the first time. It was almost as if a stranger was standing in his living room. Here was a smart professional woman, dressed in a sophisticated grey figure-hugging trouser suit, looking as though she had lost some weight, looking as though she was taking care of herself and, above all, looking as though she was going places. It had taken him all this time to figure out that, while he was so taken up with the original plan to rent out the garden apartment, she was moving on with her life and leaving him behind.

In that moment, John realised she hadn't just found a job, Sylvie had found a life. And that life didn't include the slob lying dishevelled on the sofa.

John felt his pulse quickening. Was Sylvie here to tell him it was over between them? Was this it? Had he lost her? Had he lost his Sylvie?

Sylvie was still gazing around his apartment in disbelief.

John froze on the sofa as she turned to face him. He swallowed hard wondering what was coming next.

'You've got to clean up your act, John.'

'Yes, yes – anything!' he replied, hoping he was in for a second chance.

415

'Because if you don't—' Sylvie stopped. 'God, I've been such a fool.'

'No, Sylvie, it's not you, it's me. I've been the fool.'

Sylvie wasn't listening, consumed with the thought this was what he wanted all along. This was the master plan to get her to move out of the garden apartment. She narrowed her eyes. 'If all this doesn't stop, you'll get what you want because I will have no choice but to move out.'

'You're leaving?' John sat up with a jolt. It was one thing if Sylvie moved out of her apartment and back in with him, but another thing if she moved out of the house altogether. This was not what he had in mind.

John shot up from the sofa, came over feeling woozy, and sunk to the floor on his knees in front of Sylvie. 'Please, I'm begging you, don't move out,' he pleaded. He wanted her out of the apartment downstairs, that was a given, but he never thought for one moment that these parties would drive her out of the house. That was never his intention. 'Don't do that,' repeated John still on his knees in front of her. 'I'll do anything. Please don't go.'

Sylvie's eyes went wide in surprise, trying to comprehend this complete U-turn; John was on his knees begging her to stay in her apartment. What was he up to now?

He attempted to get up from the floor and almost lost his balance.

Sylvie tutted. John was still drunk.

He held out his hand. 'I need some help to get up.'

Sylvie slapped his hand away. 'You're pathetic,' she snapped, trying hard not to feel sorry for her slob of a husband. She knew that the parties, the late-nights, and the booze couldn't have been wholly John's idea; he was never into that sort of thing. What had his so-called friends done to him?

Sylvie started for the door, casting a backward glance in his direction. She saw John struggle to his feet with the aid of the sofa and felt a twinge of guilt over her part in the whole sorry affair. Sylvie knew she was partly to blame for this mess. She'd prevented him from finishing his plan and renting out one of the apartments. It still did not excuse the fact that he should have told her about their spiralling debts.

Would she have moved out of the garden apartment if he had? She doubted it. The day the postman called was a case in point. When she found out the truth, she should have taken some responsibility and moved back in with him straight away, so he could find a tenant and get some rent money rolling in. It was that easy. It was that simple. But she didn't. She behaved like a spoilt child who refused to compromise and made both their lives miserable in the process.

Sylvie paused at the door. She watched John sit down on the sofa and stare forlornly at the floor. Little wonder he had given up. Little wonder he was getting his own back because she wasn't playing ball. Who could blame him? Sylvie thought she was getting just what she deserved. She wasn't joking when she told him that she was on the verge of packing her bags and walking out. As for John begging her not to go, Sylvie rolled her eyes. It was obvious he was still the worse for wear after the party last night. He wouldn't remember a word of their conversation this morning once he'd slept it off.

Sylvie closed the door to his apartment and made her way downstairs. Unlike John, she had a day's work ahead of her. She was already exhausted even though the working day hadn't begun yet. For Sylvie, it was a typical Tuesday morning after a sleepless party night, with the exception that this morning she would be late for work for the very first time. She sighed in exasperation when she heard the postman outside and realised it was later than she thought. She had the impulse to make it a double-first and call in sick. It was almost too much to go into work today. Almost.

Sylvie reached the bottom of the stairs. The postman whistled a tune as he stood on the doorstep putting some letters in their post boxes. Sylvie grimaced at the prospect of more red-reminder letters and more money to find. She couldn't afford to take a day off work and risk losing her job. John would not find a job anytime soon. He was in no fit state to get up in the morning let alone do a day's work.

Contrary to her earlier expectations that spending some time apart might bring them closer together, after seeing her slob of a husband this morning, she realised the gulf between them was greater than ever.

Sylvie shook her head sadly as she opened the door to her flat. She guessed neither of them had ended up where they envisaged when John started down the road of converting the house. He didn't get to finish his plan. As for Sylvie, while she enjoyed her new job, and loved living in the garden apartment, she was not pleased to be landed with an errant husband living upstairs and the sole responsibility of digging them out of a financial hole to keep the roof over their heads.

Sylvie paused at the door and glanced upstairs. From what she saw, it confirmed her suspicions that John was making no real effort to deal with their financial situation. The irony was he was justified. Although he'd misjudged the final cost of the conversion, which precipitated this financial mess, Sylvie was aware she exacerbated the situation by her refusal to move back in with him. Even after she found out the truth. They were both responsible for where they found themselves today; after all, it takes two to tango. Sylvie stepped inside her apartment and shut the door.

37

John heard Sylvie walk out of his apartment and shut the door. He lay back down on the sofa nursing a splitting headache. He pulled the throw over his head to blot out the morning sunshine streaming through the bay window and tried to figure out what he should do next to stop Sylvie moving out. If he could have another chance to speak to her and explain—

The sound of the phone ringing in the kitchen cut John off mid-thought. He ignored it. He wasn't in the mood to speak to anybody. Unless it was… John cast off the throw he was using as a makeshift blanket and hauled himself off the sofa without coming over dizzy. He rushed into the kitchen and grabbed the phone. 'Sylvie?'

John's smile faded at the sound of his daughter's voice on the end of the line. He grimaced at what Harriet said next. 'You want to come over right now?' He cast an eye around his kitchen at the empty beer cans and wine bottles littering his worktops. And the two greasy plates on the kitchen table where he and Babs left them this morning after eating a hearty English breakfast.

The thought of food made John's stomach churn. He walked

out of the kitchen with the cordless phone to get away from the cooking smells. 'Look, Harriet, now isn't a good time—'

'I want Mum there too. Will you tell her I'm popping round?'

John rolled his eyes. That was another reason he didn't want Harriet popping round now. 'Your mother and I, we're not...'

John was about to say *on speaking terms* when he glanced out the window and spotted Sylvie in the street below getting into a taxi. She was carrying a briefcase.

Did Harriet even know her mother had returned to work? John doubted it. Sylvie kept things very close to her chest lately. He didn't even know what she did for a living. What he knew was that she still looked rather fetching in that grey trouser suit.

'Dad, are you still there?'

'Harriet, you must phone her yourself because—'

'I'll do that then!' said Harriet curtly. 'Just make sure you're both in.'

John watched the taxi speed down the street. He glanced at the time and guessed Sylvie was late for work.

'I'll be round in twenty minutes.'

'Harriet, what's so important that you can't tell me over the phone? Harriet?' The line was already dead. John tossed the phone on the sofa and rubbed his temple. 'Could my day get any worse?'

The sound of a dog howling startled him.

John rolled his eyes toward the door. 'You have got to be kidding me!' Sylvie rarely left Alfie outside his door the morning after the parties; he assumed she must have realised he wouldn't be in any fit state to get up in the morning, let alone walk her dog.

Alfie kept howling, his cries piercing John's already fragile post-party head. He clamped his hands over his ears and winced.

He didn't feel in any fit state to go out, but then Sylvie knew that. He guessed she was feeling pissed off after catching her slob of a husband fast asleep on the sofa while she was up and dressed and ready to do a day's work.

He turned back to the window and glanced outside. Large black storm clouds were gathering, a downpour imminent. He sighed. 'Just great.'

John grabbed a coat and an umbrella on the way out. He glared at Alfie sitting outside the door wagging his tail. There was just enough time to walk the dog before Harriet arrived.

John left the house. He clung on to Alfie's lead as the exuberant dog pulled him down the street. He was trying to hold up an umbrella in the other hand. The umbrella kept blowing inside out until it blew right out of his hand.

John stopped and watched it do cartwheels along the pavement like tumbleweed. He didn't bother chasing after it. He stood there resigned that this was just the start of another godawful day in the Baxter household.

Alfie had had enough sitting on his rump, on the cold, wet pavement, waiting for John. He took off toward the park.

As John lurched forward, pulled down the street by Sylvie's irritating little dog, with the wind and rain lashing his face, he wondered how his life had come to this. John longed for the sofa. All he wanted to do was crawl back under the throw, close his eyes and hope, by some miracle, all this went away. He didn't want Harriet to come over with whatever problem was about to land on his doorstep, or the dog in his apartment after his morning walk leaving a trail of wet, muddy paw-prints, or Sylvie's new life downstairs, or his own stupidity for not seeing that coming.

John crossed the road and reached the entrance to Holland Park. He heaved a sigh thinking this was his life now; he'd made his bed, and now he had to wallow in it.

He let Alfie off the lead and checked the time by his wrist-watch. What was so urgent that Harriet had to speak to Mum and Dad? In person? This morning? He raised an eyebrow. Come to think of it, wasn't she at work on a Tuesday? John hoped she hadn't lost her job and wanted to borrow some money. John shook his head. He hoped that wasn't it. But if that were the case, then she'd better ask her mother for a loan because he didn't have two brass farthings to rub together.

John shoved his cold, wet hands in his empty pockets and stood watching Alfie chase a squirrel across the grass. His mind wandered back to Sylvie, wearing a smart suit, climbing into the back of a taxi off to work. This morning just proved how much they had diverged as people.

While all his energy had been focused on getting her back, he had no idea that she'd been downstairs carving out a new life for herself. He realised too late they had been dancing to a different tune. Perhaps it was time to face the fact that this dance they called their marriage was over.

John shook his head. He didn't want to face that possibility. He still wanted to believe they could salvage their relationship. If only there was something they had in common, a shared interest, something that could bring them together. But what?

John racked his brain, praying for the answer, as he trudged across the park calling Alfie. By the time he returned home and spotted Harriet sitting in her car – her face like thunder because she'd turned up and no one was home – John was still no closer to finding the answer to his conundrum.

Little did he know that Harriet's visit might just be the answer to his prayers as life in the Baxter household was about to take an unexpected turn.

The story continues in

Dear John

Paperback and Kindle eBook available to buy from Amazon

If you enjoyed It Takes 2 to Tango, I would be grateful if you'd leave a review on Amazon.

If you'd like to receive my newsletter with special offers, book recommendations, and news on forthcoming book releases please visit my website:

www.elisedarcy.com

Made in the USA
Coppell, TX
06 December 2021

67335046R00252